KT-465-187

Lose yourself
in the
magical world of

Cecelia
Ahern

Turn the page to access
a new virtual experience

Unlock an exciting
online world inspired
by Cecelia's fantastic writing

All you need is a
webcam and computer.

For full instructions visit
www.everydayismagical.co.uk

Before embarking on her writing career, Cecelia Ahern completed a degree in Journalism and Media Communications. At twenty-one years old, she wrote her first novel, *PS, I Love You* which instantly became an international bestseller and was adapted into a major motion picture starring Hilary Swank. Her successive novels, *Where Rainbows End, If You Could See Me Now, A Place Called Here, Thanks for the Memories* and *The Gift* were also bestsellers. Her books are published in forty-six countries and have collectively sold over twelve million copies. *The Book of Tomorrow* is also available as an audiobook and e-book. Cecelia lives in Dublin, Ireland.

To sign up for the exclusive Cecelia Ahern HarperCollins newsletter where you can discover all about Cecelia's books, as well as interviews, photographs and much more, log on to
www.cecelia-ahern.com

PS – don't forget to read Cecelia's other novels:

PS, I Love You
Where Rainbows End
If You Could See Me Now
A Place Called Here
Thanks for the Memories
The Gift

Acclaim for

The Book of Tomorrow

'A magical, absorbing tale'
Closer

'A mesmerising tale'
Heat

'Told with a sprinkling of magic, this is an endearing
tale of family, friendship and secrets'
Woman

'There is an almost magical quality in this book – similar
to Ahern's previous works such as *PS, I Love You*'
Irish Post

'Prepare to become totally immersed in another world …
filled with laugh-out-loud laughter, tears and morals.
Another gem of a story from Cecelia Ahern'
RTE Guide

'One of Cecelia's best'
Irish Independent

'This witty, fantastically absorbing tale shows that not
all bitchy girls are mean, not all nuns are strait-laced and that,
no matter what, you can always change your future'
Books Quarterly

'A real page-turner … original and with a colourful
cast of characters … another hit for Ahern'
News of the World

Acclaim for Cecelia's previous bestsellers

'Wild humour and heartbreak
tangled up in one great read'
Cathy Kelly

'Utterly irresistible...I devoured it in one sitting'
Marian Keyes

'The legendary Ahern will keep you guessing
what binds these stories… a classic'
Company

'The key to Ahern's success is her ability not to just tell
a good story, but sprinkle it with plenty of laughs,
tears, and a little bit of magic' *Mirror*

'The writing is ambitious, and in parts, poetic'
Telegraph

'There's more than a touch of fairytale
about Cecelia Ahern's novel'
Glamour

'Unputdownable'
Grazia

'An intriguing, heartfelt novel, which makes you
think about the value of life'
Glamour

'A sensational debut novel that proves
true love never dies'
Cosmopolitan

This novel is entirely a work of fiction. The names, characters and incidents portrayed in it are the work of the author's imagination. Any resemblance to actual persons, living or dead, events or localities is entirely coincidental.

Harper, an imprint of HarperCollinsPublishers
77–85 Fulham Palace Road, Hammersmith, London W6 8JB

www.harpercollins.co.uk

This paperback edition 2010
1

First published in Great Britain byHarperCollinsPublishers 2009

Copyright © Cecelia Ahern 2010

Cecelia Ahern asserts the moral right to be identified as the author of this work

A catalogue record for this book isavailable from the British Library

ISBN: 978 0 00 723371 7

Set in Bembo by Palimpsest Book Production Limited,
Grangemouth, Stirlingshire

Printed and bound in Great Britain by Clays Ltd, St Ives plc

All rights reserved. No part of this publication may be reproduced, stored in a retrieval system, or transmitted, in any form or by any means, electronic, mechanical, photocopying, recording or otherwise, without the prior permission of the publishers.

This book is sold subject to the condition that it shall not, by way of trade or otherwise, be lent, re-sold, hired out or otherwise circulated without the publisher's prior consent in any form of binding or cover other than that in which it is published and without a similar condition including this condition being imposed on the subsequent purchaser.

Mixed Sources
Product group from well-managed forests and other controlled sources
www.fsc.org   Cert no. SW-COC-1806
© 1996 Forest Stewardship Council

FSC is a non-profit international organization established to promote the responsible management of the world's forests. Products carrying the FSC label are independently certified to assure consumers that they come from forests that are managed to meet the social, economic and ecological needs of present and future generations.

Find out more about HarperCollins and the environment at
www.harpercollins.co.uk/green

Cecelia
Ahern

The Book of
Tomorrow

HARPER

David, Mimmie, Dad, Georgina, Nicky, Rocco and Jay, (and Star, Doggy and Sniff) – I feel like I couldn't wake up in the morning without you, never mind write a book. Thanks for holding my hand all the way along this long, exciting and intriguing path. 'Carry you . . .?!'

For the yesterdays and todays, and the tomorrows I can hardly wait for – Thank you.

The Kellys (somebody will write a book about you lot yet), Aherns, Keoghans, and my dear full-time friends and part-time therapists. Thank you.

Marianne Gunn O'Connor. Thank you.

Vicki Satlow, Pat Lynch, Liam Murphy, Anita Kissane, Gerard O'Herlihy, Doo Services. Thank you.

Lynne Drew, Claire Bord – my books wouldn't be what they are without your comments, advice and guidance. Thank you, thank you.

Amanda Ridout – there's an empty chair at the 'anything is possible' table and you'll be missed. For all your encouragement and belief in me, thank you.

The entire army at HarperCollins – for working so hard on so many fantastically new and exciting ideas. I'm extraordinarily lucky to be a part of the team. Thank you.

Fiona McIntosh, Moira Reilly and Tony Purdue – I do enjoy our road trips! Thank you.

I do want to pay tribute to Killeen Castle. While this book is certainly not about Killeen, I was looking for a setting for this story and suddenly came upon this extraordinary place. Something clicked in my head and an entire world for Tamara and her family began to form. Thank you to those at Killeen Castle for, although unknowingly, unlocking the world for *The Book of Tomorrow*.

The Booksellers – for your incredible support. In *The Book of Tomorrow* I share my belief in the magic of books, how I believe books must contain some sort of homing device, which allows them to draw the correct reader to them. Books choose their readers, not the other way around. I believe that booksellers are the matchmakers. Thank you.

For Marianne
who moves so silently but causes a right clatter.

For my readers
thank you for trusting me.

CHAPTER ONE
Field of Buds

They say a story loses something with each telling. If that is the case, this story has lost nothing, for it's the first time it's been told.

This story is one for which some people will have to suspend their disbelief. If I wasn't me and this wasn't happening to me, I would be one of those people.

Many won't struggle to believe it, though, for their minds have been opened; unlocked by whatever kind of key causes people to believe. Those people are either born that way or, as babies, when their minds are like little buds, they are nurtured until their petals slowly open and prepare for the very nature of life to feed them. As the rain falls and the sun shines, they grow, grow, grow; minds so open, they go through life aware and accepting, seeing light where there's dark, seeing possibility in dead ends, tasting victory as others spit out failure, questioning when others accept. Just a little less jaded, a little less cynical. A little less likely to throw in the towel. Some people's minds open later in life, through tragedy or triumph. Either thing acting as the key to unlatch and lift the lid on that know-it-all box, to accept the unknown, to say goodbye to pragmatism and straight lines.

But then there are those whose minds are merely a bouquet of stalks, which bud as they learn new information – a new bud for a new fact – but yet they never open, never flourish. They are the people of capital letters and full stops, but never of question marks and ellipses . . .

My parents were those kinds of people. The know-it-all kind. The 'if it's not in a book or I haven't heard it anywhere before then don't be ridiculous' kind. Straight thinkers with heads filled with the most beautifully coloured buds, so neatly manicured and so sweetly scented but which never opened, were never light or dainty enough to dance in the breeze; upright and rigid, so matter-of-fact, they were buds till the day they died.

Well, my mother isn't dead.

Not yet. Not medically, but if she is not dead, she is certainly not living. She's like a walking corpse that hums every once in a while as though testing herself to see if she's still alive. From far away you'd think she's fine. But up close and you can see that the bright pink lipstick is a touch uneven, her eyes are tired and soulless, like one of those TV show houses on studio lots – all façade, nothing of substance behind. She moves around the house, drifting from room to room in a dressing gown with loosely flapping bell sleeves, as though she's a southern belle on a mansion ranch in *Gone with the Wind*, worrying about worrying about it all tomorrow. Despite her graceful swanlike room-to-room drifts, she's kicking furiously beneath the surface, thrashing around trying to keep her head up, flashing us the occasional panicked smile to let us know she's still here, though it does nothing to convince us.

Oh, I don't blame her. What a luxury it must be to disappear as she has, leaving everyone else to sweep up the mess and salvage whatever fragments of life are left.

I haven't told you a thing yet, you must be very confused.

My name is Tamara Goodwin. Goodwin. One of those awful phrases I despise. It's either a win or it's not. Like 'bad loss', 'hot sun', or 'very dead'. Two words that come together unnecessarily to say whatever could be said solely by the second. Sometimes when telling people my name I drop a syllable: Tamara Good, which is ironic as I've never been anything of the sort, or Tamara Win, which mockingly suggests good luck that just isn't so.

I'm sixteen years old, or so they tell me. I question my age now because I feel twice it. At fourteen, I felt fourteen. I acted eleven and wanted to be eighteen. But in the past few months I've aged a few years. Is that possible? Closed buds would shake their heads *no*, opened minds would say *possibly*. Anything is possible, they would say. Well, it's not. Anything is not.

It is not possible to bring my dad back to life. I tried, when I found him lying dead on the floor of his office – very dead, in fact – blue in the face, with an empty pill container by his side and an empty bottle of whisky on the desk. I didn't know what I was doing but I pressed my lips to his regardless, and pumped up and down on his chest furiously. That didn't work.

Nor did it work when my mother dived on his coffin at the graveyard during his burial and started howling and clawing at the varnished wood as he was lowered into the ground – which, by the way, was rather patronisingly covered by fake green grass as though trying to fool us it wasn't the maggoty soil he was being lowered into for the rest of eternity. Though I admire Mum for trying, her breakdown at the grave didn't bring him back.

Nor did the endless stories about my dad that were shared at the do afterwards during the 'Who Knows George Best' storytelling competition, where friends and family had their fingers on the buzzers, ready to jump in with, 'You think that's funny, wait till you hear this . . .' 'One time George and I . . .', 'I'll never forget the time George said . . .' All were so eager, they ended up talking over one another, and spilling tears and red wine on Mum's new Persian rug. They tried their best, you could tell, and in a way he was *almost* in the room, but their stories didn't bring him back.

Nor did it work when Mum discovered Dad's personal finances were about as healthy as he. He was bankrupt; the bank had already put in place the repossession of our house and all the other properties he owned, which left Mum to sell every-thing – *everything* – that we owned to pay back the debts. He didn't come back to help us then either. So I knew then that he was gone. He was really gone. I figured if he was going to let us go through all of that on our own – let me blow air into his dead body, let Mum scratch at his coffin in front of everybody, and then watch us be stripped of everything we'd ever owned, I was pretty sure he was gone for good.

It was good thinking on his part not to stick around for it all. It was all as awful and as humil-iating as I'm sure he feared.

If my parents had flowering buds, then maybe, just maybe, they could have avoided all that. But they didn't. There was no light at the end of that tunnel, and if ever there was, it was an oncoming train. There were no other possibilities, no other ways of doing things. They were practical, and there was no practical solution. Only faith and hope and some sort of belief could have seen my father through it. But he didn't have any of that, and so when he did what he did, he effectively pulled us all into that grave with him.

It intrigues me how death, so dark and final,

can shine a light on the character of a person. The lovely stories I heard about Dad during those weeks were endless and touching. They were comforting and I liked getting lost in those tales, but to be perfectly honest, I doubted if they were true. Dad wasn't a nice man. I loved him, of course, but I know he wasn't a good man. He and I rarely spoke and when we did, it was to argue over something, or he was giving me money to get rid of me. He was prickly, snapped often, had a temper that flared easily, he forced his opinions on others and was rather arrogant. He made people feel uncomfortable, inferior, and he enjoyed that. He would send his steak back three or four times in a restaurant just to watch the waiter sweat. He would order the most expensive bottle of wine and then claim it was corked just to annoy the restaurateur. He would complain to the police about noise levels of house parties on our street that we couldn't even hear, and he'd have them shut down just because we weren't invited.

I didn't say any of this at his funeral or at the little party at our house afterwards. In fact, I didn't say anything at all. I drank a bottle of red wine all by myself and ended up vomiting on the floor by Dad's desk where he'd died. Mum found me there and slapped me across the face. She said I'd ruined it. I wasn't sure if she meant the rug or Dad's memory, but either way I was pretty sure that he'd fucked both of them up all by himself.

I'm not just heaping all the hate on my dad

here. I was a horrible person. I was the worst possible daughter. They gave me everything and I rarely said thank you. Or if I said it, I don't think I ever meant it. I don't actually think that I knew what it meant. 'Thank you' is a sign of appreciation. Mum and Dad continually told me about the starving babies in Africa, as if that was a way to make me appreciate anything. Looking back on it, I realise the best way to make me appreciate anything was probably not to have given me everything.

We lived in a seven thousand square foot, six-bedroom contemporary mansion with a swimming pool and tennis court and a private beach in Killiney, County Dublin, in Ireland. My room was on the opposite side of the house to my parents' and it had a balcony overlooking the beach that I don't think I ever looked out at. It had an en suite with a shower and Jacuzzi bath, with a plasma TV – TileVision, to be precise – in the wall above the bath. I'd a wardrobe full of designer hand-bags, a computer, a PlayStation and a four-poster bed. Lucky me.

Now another truth: I was a nightmare daughter. I was rude, I answered back, I expected everything and, even worse, I thought I deserved everything just because everybody else I knew had them. It didn't occur to me for one moment that they didn't particularly deserve them either.

I figured out a way to escape my bedroom at night and sneak outside to meet with my friends;

a climb from my bedroom balcony and down the piping, onto the roof of the swimming pool, then a few easy steps to the ground. There was an area on our private beach where my friends and I went drinking. The girls mostly drank Dolly Mixtures: the contents of our parents' drinks cabinets all in one plastic bottle. That way if we took a few inches from each bottle they wouldn't suspect anything. The guys drank whatever cider they could get their hands on. They also had whichever girl they could get their hands on. That person was mostly me. There was a boy, Fiachrá, who I stole from my best friend Zoey, whose dad was a famous actor and so – I'll be honest – just because of that I used to let him put his hand up my skirt for about a half-hour every night. I figured that one day I'd get to meet his dad. But I never did.

My parents felt it was important for me to see the world and how other people live. They kept telling me how fortunate I was living in my big house by the sea, and so to help me appreciate the world, we spent our summers in our villa in Marbella, Christmas in our Verbier chalet and Easter in the New York Ritz, on a shopping trip. There was a pink convertible Mini Cooper with my name on it waiting for me for my seventeenth birthday, and a friend of my dad's, who had a recording studio, was waiting to hear me sing and possibly sign me up. Though after I felt his hand on my arse, I never wanted to spend a moment alone in a room with him. Not even to be famous.

Mum and Dad attended charity functions throughout the year. Mum would spend more money on her dresses than the tables cost, and twice a year she'd pass on the impulse buys she never wore to her sister-in-law, Rosaleen, who lived down in the country – in case Rosaleen ever felt the need to milk cows in a Pucci sundress.

I know now – now that we're out of the world we once lived in – that we weren't very nice people. I think somewhere beneath the nonresponsive surface of my mother that she knows it too. We weren't evil people, we just weren't *nice*. We didn't offer anything to anybody in the world but we took an awful lot.

But, we didn't deserve this.

Before, I'd never think of tomorrow. I lived in the now. I wanted this now, I wanted that now. The last time I saw my father I shouted at him and told him I hated him and then I slammed the door in his face. I never took a step back, or a step outside of my little world to think about what on earth I was doing or saying, and how it was hurting anybody else. I told Dad I never wanted to see him again, and I never did. I never thought about the next day or about the possibility that they would be my final words to him and that *that* would be my final moment with him. That's a lot to have to deal with. I have a lot to forgive myself for. It's taking time.

But now, because of Dad's death and because of the thing I have yet to share with you, I have no choice but to think of tomorrow and all the people that tomorrow affects. Now, I'm glad when I wake up in the morning that there is one.

I lost my dad. He lost his tomorrows and I lost all the tomorrows with him. You could say that now, I appreciate them when they come. Now, I want to make them the best they can possibly be.

CHAPTER TWO

Two Bluebottles

In order for ants to find the safest route to food, one goes out on its own. When that lone ant has found the path, it leaves a chemical trail for the others to follow. When you stamp on a line of ants or, less psychotically, if you interfere in their chemical trail in any way, it drives them crazy. The ones that have been left behind crawl around frantically in panic, trying to regain the trail. I like watching them at first totally disoriented, running around bumping into one another while trying to figure out which way to go, then regrouping, reorganising, and eventually crossing the pathway back in their straight line as if nothing had ever happened.

Their panic reminds me of Mum and I. Somebody broke our line, took out our leader, ruined our trail and our lives descended into utter chaos. I think – *I hope* – that with time, we'll find the right way to go again. It takes one to lead the rest.

I think, seeing as Mum is sitting this one out, that it's up to me to go out front alone.

I was watching a bluebottle yesterday. In an effort to escape the living room, he kept flying against the window, hitting his head against the glass over and over. Then he stopped launching himself at it like a missile and stuck to one little windowpane, buzzing about like he was having a panic attack. It was frustrating to watch, especially because if he'd just flown up a little bit higher towards the top of the window, he'd have been free. But he just kept doing the same thing over and over again. I could imagine his frustration of being able to see the trees, the flowers, the sky, yet not being able to get to them. I tried to help him a few times, to guide him towards the open window, but he flew away from me around the room. He'd eventually come back to the same window and I could almost hear him: 'Well, this is the way I came in . . .'

I wonder if my watching him from the armchair is what it's like to be God, if there is a God. He sits back and sees the big picture, just as I could see that if the bluebottle just moved up the window to the top, then he'd be free. He wasn't really trapped at all, he was just looking in the wrong place. I wonder if God can see a way out for me and Mum. If I can see the open window for the fly, God can see the tomorrows for me and Mum. That idea brings me comfort. Well, it *did*, until I left the room and returned a few hours later to see a dead bluebottle on the windowsill. It may not have been him, but still . . . Then, to show you where my mind is right now, I started crying . . . Then I got mad at God because in my head the death of that bluebottle meant Mum and I might never find our way out of this mess. What good is it being so far back you can see everything and yet not do anything to help?

Then I realised that I was the god on this occasion. I had tried to help the bluebottle, but it wouldn't let me. And then I felt sorry for God because I understood his frustration. Sometimes when people offer a helping hand, it gets pushed away. People always want to help themselves first.

I never used to think about these things before; God, bluebottles, ants. I'd rather have been caught dead than be seen sitting in an armchair with a book in my hand and staring at a dirty fly tapping against a window on a Saturday. Maybe that's what Dad had thought in his final moments: I'd rather be caught dead here in my study than go through the humiliation of having everything taken from me.

My Saturdays used to be spent in Topshop with my friends, trying on absolutely everything and laughing nervously while Zoey stuffed as many accessories down her pants as she could manage before leaving the store. If we weren't in Topshop we'd spend the day sitting in Starbucks having a grande gingersnap latte and banana honey muffin. I'm sure that's what they're all doing now.

I haven't heard from anyone since the first week I got here, except a text from Laura before my phone was cut off, filling me on all the gossip, the biggest of all being that Zoey and Fiachrá got back together and did it in Zoey's house when her parents were away in Monte Carlo for the weekend. Her dad has a gambling problem, which Zoey and the rest of us loved because it meant when we all stayed over at her house, her parents would come home much later than everybody else's. Anyway, apparently Zoey said that sex with Fiachrá hurt worse than the time the lesbian from the Sutton hockey team hit her between the legs with the stick, which was really bad, believe me – I *saw* – and she isn't in a rush to do it again. Meanwhile Laura told me not to tell anyone but she was meeting Fiachrá at the weekend to do it. She hopes I don't mind and please don't tell Zoey. As if I could tell anyone if I wanted to, where I am.

Where I am. I haven't told you that yet, have I? I've mentioned my mum's sister-in-law, Rosaleen, already. She's the one my mum used to empty her wardrobe of all her unworn impulse buys for and send them down in black sacks with the tags still on. Rosaleen's married to my uncle Arthur, who is my mum's brother. They live in a gatehouse in the country in a place called Meath in the middle of nowhere with hardly anybody else around. We visited them only a few times in my life and I was always bored to death. It took us an hour and fifteen minutes to get there and the build-up was

14

always a let down. I thought they were hicks in the middle of the sticks. I used to call them the Deliverance Duo. That's the only time I remember Dad laughing at one of my jokes. He never came with us when we visited Rosaleen and Arthur. I don't think they ever had an argument or anything, but like penguins and polar bears, they were just too far apart ever to be able to spend any time near one another. Anyway, that's where we live now. In the gatehouse with the Deliverance Duo.

It's a sweet house, a quarter the size of our old one which is no bad thing, and it reminds me of the one in 'Hansel and Gretel'. It's built from limestone and the wood around the windows and roof is painted olive green. There are three bedrooms upstairs and a kitchen and a living room downstairs. Mum has an en suite but Rosaleen, Arthur and I all share a bathroom on the second floor. Used to having my own bathroom, I think this is gross, particularly when I have to go in there after my uncle Arthur and his newspaper-reading session. Rosaleen is a neat freak, obsessively tidy; she never ever sits down. She's always moving things, cleaning things, spraying chemicals in the air, and saying stuff about God and his will. I said to her once that I hoped God's will was better than the one Dad left behind for us. She looked at me horrified and scuttled off to dust somewhere else.

Rosaleen has the depth of a shot glass. Everything she talks about is totally irrelevant, unnecessary. The weather. The sad news about a poor person on the other side of the world. Her friend down the road who has broken her arm, or who has a father with two months to live, or somebody's daughter who married a dick who is leaving her with her second child. Everything is doom and gloom and followed by some sort of utterance about God, like, 'God love them,' or 'God is gracious,' or 'Let God be good to them.' Not that I talk about anything important, but if I ever try to discuss those things in more detail, like get to the root of the problem, Rosaleen is totally incapable of carrying on. She only wants to talk about the sad problem, she's not interested in talking about why it happened, nor in the solution. She shushes me with her God phrases, makes me feel like I'm speaking out of turn or as though I'm so young I couldn't possibly take the reality. I think it's the other way around. I think she brings things up so that she doesn't feel like she's avoiding them, and once they're out of the way, she doesn't talk about them ever again.

I think I've heard my uncle Arthur speak about five words in my life. It's as though Mum has gone through her life speaking for both of them – not that he would have shared her views on anything she said. Arthur speaks more than Mum these days. He has an entire language of his own, which I've slowly but surely learned to decipher. He speaks in grunts, nods and snot-snorts; a kind of mucous inhale, which is something he does when he disagrees with something. A mere, 'Ah,' and a throw back of the head means he's not bothered by something. For example, here is how a typical breakfast-time would go.

Arthur and I are sitting at the kitchen table and Rosaleen as usual is buzzing about the place with crockery piled with toast, and little dishes of home-made jam, honey and marmalade. The radio, as usual, is blaring so loudly I can hear every word the presenter is saying from my bedroom; some annoying miserable man talking in monotone about the terrible things happening in the world. And so Rosaleen comes to the table with the teapot.

'Tea, Arthur?'

Arthur throws back his head like a horse trying to rid his mane of a fly. He wants tea.

And the man on the radio talks about how another factory in Ireland has closed and one hundred people are losing their jobs.

Arthur inhales and a load of mucus is sucked up through his nose and then down his throat. He doesn't like this.

Rosaleen appears at the table with another plate of toast piled high. 'Oh, isn't that terrible, God love their families. And the little ones now with their daddys out of work.'

'Their mothers too, you know,' I say, taking a slice of toast.

Rosaleen watches me bite into the toast and her green eyes widen as I chew. She always watches me eat and it freaks me out. It's as though she is the witch from 'Hansel and Gretel', watching for me to become plump enough so that she can throw me into the Aga with my hands tied behind my back and an apple stuffed in my gob. I wouldn't mind an apple. It would be the fewest calories she'd ever given me.

I swallow what's in my mouth and put the rest of my toast down on my plate.

She leaves again, disappointed.

On the news they talk about some new government tax increase and Arthur inhales more mucus. If he hears any more bad news, he'll have no room for his breakfast with all that mucus. He's only in his forties but he looks and acts older. From the shoulders up he reminds me of a king prawn, always bent over something, whether it's his food or his work.

Rosaleen returns with a plate of Irish breakfast enough to feed all the children of the one hundred factory workers who have just lost their jobs.

Arthur throws his head back again. He's happy about this.

Rosaleen stands beside me and pours me tea. I'd love nothing more than a gingersnap latté but I tip the milk into the strong tea and sip it all the same. Her eyes watch me and don't look away till I swallow.

I don't know how old Rosaleen is exactly but I'm guessing somewhere in her early-to-mid-forties, and if this makes sense, I'm sure whatever age she really is, she looks ten years older. She looks like she's from the 1940s in her floral tea dresses buttoned down the middle, with a slip underneath. My mum never wore slips; she barely wore underwear. Rosaleen has mouse-brown hair, always worn down, parted sharply in the centre of her head, revealing grey roots, and it's short, to her chin. She always tucks her hair behind both ears, pink little mouse ears peeping out. She never wears earrings. Or make-up. She always wears a gold crucifix on a thin gold chain around her neck. She's the kind of woman that my friend Zoey would say looks like she's never had an orgasm in her life and I wonder, while cutting the fat off the bacon and as Rosaleen's eyes widen at me doing this, if Zoey had an orgasm when she did it with Fiachrá. Then I visualised the damage the hockey stick did to her and I instantly doubted it.

Across the road from the gatehouse is a bungalow. I have no idea who lives in it but Rosaleen pops back and forth every day with little parcels of food. Two miles down the road is a post office, which is operated from somebody's house, and across the road from that is the smallest school I've ever seen, which unlike my school at home, which has activities every hour throughout the year, is completely empty during the summer. I asked if there were any yoga classes or anything in it and Rosaleen told me she'd show me how to make yoghurt herself. She seemed so happy that I couldn't correct her. In the first week I watched her make strawberry yoghurt. In the second week, I was still eating it.

The gatehouse that is Arthur and Rosaleen's house once protected the side entrance to Kilsaney Castle in the 1700s. The castle's main entrance has a disused scary-looking gothic entrance that I imagine I see severed heads hanging out of every time we pass. The castle was built as a towered fortification of the Norman Pale – that was the area with Norman and English control in the East of Ireland, established after Strongbow invaded – sometime between 1100 and 1200, which, when you think about it, is a bit vague. It's the difference between me or my half-human, half-robot great-great-great-great-grandchildren building something. Anyway, it was built for a Norman warlord, so that's why I think of the severed heads, because they did that, didn't they?

The area it's in is called County Meath. It used to be East Meath and, along with Westmeath – surprise surprise – it made up a separate and fifth province in Ireland, which was the territory of the High King. The former seat of the High Kings, the Hill of Tara, is only a few kilometres away. It's in the news all the time now because they're building a motorway nearby. We had to debate it in school a few months ago. I was 'for' the motorway being built because I thought the King would have liked to have one in his day, as it would have made it easier for him to get to his office instead of having to go through shitty fields. Imagine the filth on his sandals. I also said it would be more accessible for tourists. They could drive right up to it or take photographs from open-top buses going one hundred and twenty kilometres on the motorway. I was only taking the piss, but our substitute teacher went crazy, thinking I actually meant it, because she was on a committee to try and prevent the motorway being built. It's so easy to give substitute teachers nervous breakdowns. Especially the ones who believe they can do some good for the students. I told you, I was nasty.

After the Norman psycho, various lords and ladies lived in the castle. They built on stables and outhouses around the place. Controversially one lord even converted to Catholicism after marrying a Catholic, and built a chapel as a treat for the family. Me and Mum got a swimming pool as our treat, but each to their own. The demesne is surrounded by a famine wall, which was a project to provide work for the starving during the potato famine. It runs right along Arthur and Rosaleen's garden and house, and creeps me out every time I see it. If Rosaleen had ever visited our house for dinner she'd probably have started building a wall around us, because none of us eats carbs. At least, we never used to eat carbs, now I'm eating so much I could fuel all the factories they're closing down.

Kilsaney descendants continued to live in the castle until the 1920s, when some arsonists didn't get the memo that the inhabitants were Catholic and they burned them out. After that they could only live in a small section of the castle because they couldn't afford to fix it up and heat it, and then they eventually moved out in the nineties. I don't know who owns it now but it's fallen into disrepair: no roof, fallen-down walls, no stairs, you get the idea. There's loads of stuff growing inside it and whatever else that scutters around. I learned all that while I was doing a project on it for school. Mum suggested I stay with Rosaleen and Arthur for the weekend and do some research. She and Dad had the biggest fight I'd ever seen or heard that day, and Dad became even more crazy when she suggested I go away. The atmosphere was so bad that I was happy to leave them. Plus, Mum trying to get me to leave the house really pissed Dad off, and so feeling it was my duty as a daughter to make his life hell, I merely obliged. But as soon as I got there, I wasn't really interested in snooping around and finding out the history of the place. I just about managed to stay with Rosaleen and Arthur for lunch, and then went to the toilet to call my Filipino nanny, Mae – who we've since had to send back home – and made her collect me and bring me home. I told Rosaleen I had stomach cramps and tried not to laugh when she asked me if I thought it was the apple pie.

I ended up taking an essay about the castle from the internet. I was called to the principal's office and she failed me for plagarism, which was ridiculous because Zoey did her project on Malahide Castle, stole everything from the internet, changed a few words and dates around, got the words and dates *wrong* to make it look like she didn't copy it, and she still got a higher score than me. Where's the justice in that?

Surrounding the castle is one hundred acres of land. Arthur is the groundskeeper here and, with one hundred acres to look after, he's out first thing in the morning and back at five thirty on the button, as dirty as a coal miner. He never complains, he never groans about the weather, he just gets up, eats his breakfast while deafening himself with the radio, and then goes out to work. Rosaleen gives him a flask of tea and a few sandwiches to keep him going and he rarely comes back, except to get something from the garage that he forgot, or to go to the toilet. He's a simple man only I don't really believe that. Nobody who says as little as he does, is as simple as you'd think. It takes a lot to not say a lot, because when you're not talking, you're thinking, and he thinks *a lot*. My mum and dad talked all the time. Talkers don't think much; their words drown out any possibility of hearing their subconscious asking, *Why did you say that? What do you really think?*

I used to stay in bed for as long as possible on school mornings and on weekends until Mae dragged me out kicking and screaming. But here, I wake up early. Surrounded by so many gigantic trees, the place is swarming with birds. They're so loud and I just wake up without feeling tired. I'm always up by seven, which is nothing short of miraculous for me. Mae would be so proud. The evenings here are long too, and so there's pressure having to keep myself busy during the daylight. That's an awful lot of hours for an awful lot of nothing to do.

Dad decided he'd had enough in May, right before my Junior Certificate exams, which was a little unfair as, up until then, I thought I was the one who was supposed to want to top myself. I did my exams anyway. I probably failed them, but I don't really care and I don't think anybody else does either. I'll find those results out in September. My entire class came to Dad's funeral, which I'm sure they loved because they got a day off school. With all that going on, can you believe I was actually embarrassed about crying in front of them. I did it anyway, which started off Zoey and then Laura. A girl in my class called Fiona, who nobody ever talked to, hugged me really tight and gave me a card from her family saying that they were all thinking of me. Fiona gave me her mobile number and her favourite book, and said she'd be there for me if I ever needed somebody to talk to. At the time I thought it was a bit lame, her trying to get in with me at my dad's funeral, but thinking about it after – which is something I do now – it was the kindest thing anybody did or said to me that day.

I started reading the book in the first week I moved to Meath. It was a kind of a ghost story about a girl who was invisible to everybody in the world, including her family and friends, even though they knew she existed. She was just born invisible. I won't give away the rest but she eventually becomes friends with someone who does see her. I liked the idea and thought Fiona was trying to say something, but when I stayed overnight in Zoey's house and told her and Laura, they thought it was the weirdest thing they'd ever heard and that Fiona was even more of a freak. You know what, I'm finding it increasingly hard to understand them.

During the first week that we moved here Arthur drove me to Dublin so that I could stay overnight in Zoey's house. The car journey was over an hour and we never spoke once. The only thing he said was, 'Radio?' and then when I nodded he turned it on to one of those channels that just talk about the problems in the country and don't play music and he snot-snorted his way through it. But at least it was better than silence. After spending the night with Zoey and Laura – and bitching about him all night – I was feeling confident. Back to my old self. We all agreed that he and Rosaleen definitely lived up to being called the Deliverance Duo and that I shouldn't allow them to pull me into their weirdo existence. That meant that I should be able to listen to whatever the hell I wanted in the car. But the next day, when he picked me up in his filthy dirty Land Rover, which Zoey and Laura so obviously couldn't stop laughing at, I felt bad for Arthur. I felt really bad.

Having to go back to a house that wasn't mine, in a car that wasn't mine, to sleep in a room that wasn't mine, to try to talk to a mother that didn't feel like mine, made me want to hold on to at least one thing that was familiar. Who I used to be. It wasn't necessarily the right thing to hold on to, but it was something. I kicked up a fuss in the car and told Arthur that I wanted to listen to something else. He put my favourite radio station on for one song and then he got so frustrated listening to the Pussycat Dolls singing about wanting boobies, he grumbled and changed it back to the talk channel. I stared out the window in a huff, hating him and hating myself both at the same time. For half an hour we listened to a woman crying down the phone to the presenter about how her husband had lost his job in a computer factory, couldn't find another and they had four children to look after. My hair was down across my face and all I could do was hope that Arthur didn't see me crying. Sad stuff really gets to me now. I heard about it before but I was kind of numb to it. It just didn't happen to me.

I don't know how long we're going to live here. Nobody will answer that question for me. Arthur simply doesn't talk, my mum isn't communicating and Rosaleen isn't able to cope with a question of that magnitude.

My life is not going as I planned. I'm sixteen and by now I should have had sex with Fiachrá, I should be in our villa in Marbella swimming every day, eating barbecued dinners, clubbing every night at Angels & Demons and finding guy number two to fancy and sleep with. If the first person I sleep with ends up being the man I marry, I think I'll die. Instead, I'm living in hicksville, in a gatehouse with three crazy people, the nearest things to us being a bungalow housing people that I've never seen, a post office that's practically in somebody's living room, an empty school, and a ruined castle. I have absolutely nothing to do with my life.

Or so I thought.

I'm choosing to start the story from when I arrived here.

CHAPTER THREE

The Beginning Began

My mum's best friend, Barbara, drove us to our new life in Meath. Mum didn't say a word the whole way. Not one word. Even when asked a question. Now that's a hard thing to do. I got so frustrated that I shouted at her in the car; this was back when I was trying to get her to respond.

It all happened because Barbara got lost. Her satellite navigation kit in her BMW X5 failed to recognise the address and so we just headed to the nearest town it could locate. When we got to the town, a place called Ratoath, Barbara had to rely on her own brain and not the equipment in her SUV. As it turns out, Barbara's not a thinker. After ten minutes spent driving down country roads with few houses and no signposts, I could tell Barbara was starting to get nervous. We were driving down roads which, according to the sat nav, didn't exist. I should have taken this as a sign. Used to going *somewhere,* and not down invisible roads, Barbara began to make mistakes, driving blindly through crossroads, veering dangerously on to the other side of the road. I'd only been there a handful of times over the years and so I was no help, but the plan was this: for me to look on the left-hand side for gatehouses and for Barbara to look on the right-hand side. She snapped at me at one stage for not concentrating, but really, I could see that there were no gates for at least a mile, so there was absolutely no point in looking. This, I shared with her. At breaking point she snapped that meant 'feck all,' seeing as we were already driving down 'fecking roads that don't exist', so she couldn't see why there couldn't be 'a fecking house without a fecking gate'. Hearing the word 'fecking' come out of Barbara's mouth was a big deal considering her usual expression of annoyance was 'fiddlesticks!'

Mum could have helped us but she just sat in the front seat smiling as she looked out the window. So, trying to help matters, I leaned forward and – okay, it wasn't right and it wasn't clever, but it was what I did, regardless – I shouted in her ear, the loudest possible scream that I could summon up. Mum jumped with fright, blocked her ears and then when her shock had died down, with two hands she swatted me across the head over and over again as though I were a swarm of bees. It really hurt me too. She pulled at my hair, scratched me, slapped me and I couldn't escape her grip. Barbara got so upset she pulled the car over and had to pry Mum's hands off me. Then she got out of the car and paced up and down the side of the road crying. I was crying too and my head was pounding from where Mum had pulled and scratched at it. It's fashionable where I'm from to have a hairstyle like a haystack but Mum just ruined it; she'd made me look like somebody from an insane asylum. We both left her in the car, sitting upright, looking straight ahead and angry.

'Come here to me, sweetheart,' Barbara said, between tears, and she reached her arms out to me.

I didn't need to be asked twice for a hug. I longed for a hug. Even when Mum was on form, she wasn't a hugger. She was bony, always dieting, had the same relationship with food as she had with Dad; loved it but didn't want it most of the time because she felt it was bad for her. I know this because I overheard a conversation she had with a friend at two a.m. on returning from a ladies' lunch. But regarding the hugging, I think she just felt awkward having somebody physically so close. She wasn't a comfortable person and so had no comfort to give anybody else. It's like words of advice; you can't give them unless you have them. I don't think it meant she didn't care. I never felt she didn't care. Well, okay, maybe I did, a few times.

Barbara and I stood on the side of the road embracing and crying while she apologised to me over and over again about how unfair this all was for me. When she'd pulled over, she'd left the car's arse sticking out on the road and so every car that came round the corner blasted us with its horn, but we ignored them.

The tension was released somewhat after that. You know the way storm clouds gather when there's going to be rain – that's what had been happening with us all the way from Killiney. It was all building, and finally it exploded. So feeling like we'd all had the chance to release at least a portion of our woes, we prepared ourselves for what lay ahead. Only we didn't have time because as soon as we rounded the next turn we were there. Home sweet home. On the right-hand side stood a gate, and just inside it on the left, was a house. Rosaleen and Arthur were standing by the little green gate of their 'Hansel and Gretel' house and God knows how long they'd been waiting there. We were almost an hour late. If they were pretending not to look worried about the whole thing, then it must have been near impossible when they saw our faces. Not knowing we were so close to the house we hadn't enough time to compose ourselves. My and Barbara's eyes were red raw from crying, Mum was in the front seat with a look of thunder on her face and my hair was high in tatters – well, more tattered than usual.

I never thought about how difficult that moment must have been for Arthur and Rosaleen. I was so busy thinking about myself and how much I didn't want to be there, I didn't once think about how they were opening their home to two people they had no relationship with. It must have been so unbelievably nerve-racking for them and I didn't thank them once.

Barbara and I got out of the car. She went to the boot to sort out the bags, and I assume give us all a moment to greet. That didn't quite happen. I stood there looking at Arthur and Rosaleen, who were still standing behind the little green swinging gate and I immediately wished I'd dropped breadcrumbs all the way from Killiney so I could find my way home.

Rosaleen looked from one of us to another like a meerkat, trying to take in the SUV, Mum, me, Barbara, all at once. She clasped her hands at her front, but kept unlocking them to smooth down her dress as though she were at a Lovely Girl competition in a country *feis*. Mum finally opened the door and got out of the car. She stepped onto the gravel and looked up at the house. Then her anger disappeared and she smiled, revealing puce lipstick on her front teeth.

'Arthur.' She held out her arms as though she had just opened the door to her home and was welcoming him to a dinner party.

He snot-snorted, inhaling the mucus – the first time I'd heard it – which made my lip curl in disgust. He stepped towards Mum and she took his hands and looked at him, her head tilted, that strange smile still pulling at her lips like a bad face-lift. In an awkward movement she leaned forward and rested her forehead against his. Arthur stayed there a millisecond longer than I thought he would, then patted the back of her neck and pulled away from her. He patted me hard on the head as if I was his faithful collie, which messed my hair even more, and then made his way to the boot to help Barbara with the bags. So that left me and Mum staring at Rosaleen, only Mum wasn't staring at her. She was inhaling the fresh air deeply, with her eyes closed, and smiling. Despite the depressing situation, I had a good feeling then that this could be good for Mum.

I wasn't as worried about her then as I am now. It had only been a month since Dad's funeral and we were both feeling numb and unable really to say much to each other or to anybody else for that matter. People were so busy talking to us, saying nice things, tactless things, whatever things popped into their heads – almost looking for us to console them and not the other way around – that Mum's behaviour wasn't noticeable so much. She was just sighing along with everybody else every now and again, and saying little words here and there. A funeral is like a little game, really. You have to just play along and say the right thing and behave the right way until it's over. Be pleasant but don't smile too much; be sad but don't overdo it or the family will feel worse than they already do. Be hopeful but don't let your optimism be taken as a lack of empathy or an inability to deal with the reality. Because if anybody was to be truly honest there would be a lot of arguments, finger-pointing, tears, snot, and screaming.

I think there should be the Real Life Oscars. And Best Actress goes to Alison Flanagan! For walking down the main aisle of the supermarket just last Monday, face in full make-up, hair freshly blow-dried, despite feeling like wanting to *die*, smiling brightly to Sarah and Deirdre from the Parents' Association and behaving as if her husband hadn't just left her and her three children. Come up here and get your award, Alison! Best Supporting Actress goes to the woman he left her for, who was just two aisles away, and who subsequently quite hastily left the supermarket, missing two items of the makings of her new boyfriend's favourite lasagne. Best Actor goes to Gregory Thomas for his performance at the funeral of his father, whom he hadn't spoken to for two years. Best Supporting Actor goes to Leo Mulcahy for playing the role of Best Man at a wedding celebrating the marriage of his best friend, Simon, to the only woman Leo has ever, and will ever, truly love. Come up and get the gong, Leo!

That's what I thought Mum was doing, just playing along, being the good widow, but then afterwards when her behaviour didn't change, when it felt like she didn't actually know what was going on and she was using those same little words and sighs in every conversation, I wondered then if she was bluffing. I'm still wondering how much of her is actually with us and how much she's pretending just so she doesn't have to deal with it. There was a crack in her, quite understandably, immediately after Dad died, but when people stopped looking at her and went back to their own lives, the crack kept growing, and it seemed like I was the only person who could see it.

It wasn't the Bank that were being exceptionally unreasonable by turfing us out on our ear. They had already given Dad the repossession date but, along with a 'Goodbye', it was just another message he'd forgotten to pass on to us. So even though they'd let us all stay for much longer than they'd threatened, we had to leave at some stage. Mum and I stayed in the back of Barbara's house, in her Filipino nanny's mews, for a week. Eventually we had to leave there too because Barbara had to go to their house in St Tropez for the summer and was obviously afraid we'd steal the silver.

Though I said I wasn't as worried about Mum as when we first arrived at the gatehouse, it doesn't mean that I wasn't concerned at all. My suggestion before we arrived here was that Mum go see a doctor, whereas now I'm thinking she should check herself into one of those places where people wear white bumless smocks all day and rock back and forth in the hallways. It was to Barbara that I suggested Mum should visit the doctor. Barbara just patronisingly sat me down in her kitchen and told me that Mum was doing what is called 'grieving'. At sixteen years old, you can imagine how delightful it was to learn that word for the first time. And then I settled down for a conversation about heavy petting. But she didn't go there. Instead, she asked if I minded sitting on her suitcase while she zipped it shut because Lulu, the glue that holds her life together, had taken the kids to their horse-riding lessons. As I sat on her bulging Louis Vuitton suitcase and she zipped in her zebra-print bikinis, gold thong sandals and ridiculous hats, I made a wish for it to burst open on the conveyer belt at the airport in St Tropez, and for her vibrator to fall out and buzz around for everybody to see.

So there we were, on the first day of the rest of my life, outside the gatehouse, Mum with her eyes closed, Rosaleen staring at me with excited wide green eyes and her little pink tongue licking her lips now and then, Arthur snot-snorting at Barbara, which meant he didn't want her to carry any bags, and Barbara watching him with bewilderment and probably trying not to gag at his snot-snorting, in her loose tracksuit, flip-flops and Oompa-Loompa orange face. She'd just had a spray tan that morning.

'Jennifer,' Rosaleen finally broke the silence over on our side.

Mum opened her eyes and smiled brightly and it seemed to me that she recognised Rosaleen and knew exactly what she was doing. If you hadn't spent every second of the last month with her as I had, you'd think she was okay. She was bluffing rather well.

'Welcome,' Rosaleen smiled.

'Yes. Thank you.' Mum chose a correct response from her little words file.

'Come in, come in, and we'll get you some tea,' Rosaleen said with urgency in her voice, as though we were all going to die unless we had some tea.

I didn't want to follow them. I didn't want to go in because then that would mean that it all had to start. Reality, that is. No more in-betweenness of funeral arrangements or Barbara's mews. This was the new arrangement and it had to begin.

Arthur, the king prawn, rushed by me and up the garden path laden down with bags. He was stronger than he looked.

The car boot slammed and I spun round. Barbara was fidgeting with her car keys and shifting from one Louis Vuitton flip-flopped foot to the other. It was only then that I noticed she had cotton wool between her toes. She looked at me, awkwardly, in a heavy silence while she figured out how to tell me she was leaving me.

'I didn't realise you had a pedicure done too,' I said to fill the silence.

'Yes.' She looked down and wriggled her toes as if to confirm it. Jewels glistened from her big toes. And then she added, 'Danielle's invited us to a drinks party on her yacht tomorrow evening.'

Most people would think those two sentences were unrelated, but I understood. You can't wear shoes on Danielle's yacht, therefore competition of the jewels and white tips would be fierce. Those women would find ways to accessorise their patellas if they were the only parts showing.

We stared at each other in silence. She was dying

to go. I wanted to go with her. I too wanted to be shoeless on the Mediteranean coast while Danielle floated around the guests holding a martini glass daintily between her squared French tips, a plunging Cavalli dress revealing tits as pert as the pimento-stuffed olive floating in her glass, and on her head a tilted sea captain's hat, making her look like Captain Birdseye in drag. I wanted to be a part of that.

'You'll be all right here, sweetheart,' she said, and I sensed sincerity. 'With family.'

I looked back uncertainly at the 'Hansel and Gretel' house and wanted to cry again.

'Oh, sweetheart,' she said, sensing this, and came at me again with her arms held out. She was really good at hugging, she obviously felt comfortable with it. That, or her implants suitably assisted in cushioning my head. I squeezed her tightly again and closed my eyes, but she let go a little sooner than I wanted and I was plunged back into reality.

'Okay,' she inched her way towards the car and placed her hand on the door handle. 'I don't want to disturb them inside so please tell them—'

'Come in, come in,' Rosaleen's voice sang out from the blackness of the hallway, stopping Barbara from climbing up into her jeep. 'Hello, there,' Rosaleen appeared at the door. 'Won't you come in for a cup of tea? I'm sorry I don't know your name, Jennifer didn't say.'

She'd have to get used to that. There was a lot Jennifer wasn't going to say.

'Barbara,' Barbara replied, and I noticed her grip tightening on the door handle.

'Barbara,' Rosaleen's green eyes glowed like a cat's. 'A cup of tea before you hit the road, Barbara? There's some fresh scones and home-made strawberry jam there too.'

Barbara's face was frozen in a smile as she thought hard for an excuse.

'She can't come in,' I responded for her. Barbara looked at me, gratefully, and then guiltily.

'Oh . . .' Rosaleen's face fell, as though I'd ruined her tea party.

'She has to go home and wash her fake tan off,' I added. I told you, I'm a horrible, horrible person, and in my eyes, even though I was none of Barbara's business and she had a life of her own, which she needed to get back to, she was still leaving me behind. 'And her toes are still wet.' I shrugged.

'Oh.' Rosaleen looked confused as though I'd spoken some odd Celtic Tiger language. 'Coffee then?'

I burst out laughing and Rosaleen looked hurt. I heard Barbara flip-flopping behind me and she passed by without looking at me. I'd made it easier for her to leave. Next to Rosaleen, Barbara – even in her velour tracksuit, flip-flops and dirty fake-tanned neck – looked like some sort of exotic goddess. And then she was sucked inside the house, like a Venus flytrap catching a butterfly.

Despite Rosaleen gazing at me hopefully, I still couldn't bring myself to go inside.

'I'm going to have a look around,' I said.

She seemed disappointed, as though I'd denied her something precious. I waited for her to go back into the house, to disappear into the blackness of the hallway, which was like another dimension, but she didn't move. She stood at the porch, watching me and I realised I'd have to move first. With her eyes searing into me, I looked around. Which way to go? To my left was the house, behind me was the open gate leading to the main road, in front of me trees and to my right a small pathway that led into the darkness of the trees. I started walking down the main road. I didn't turn round, not once, I didn't want to know if she was still there. But the further I walked it wasn't just Rosaleen that I felt was watching me. I felt revealed, as though beyond the majestic trees somebody else was watching. Just that feeling you get when you intrude on nature's world, that you're not supposed to be here, not without an invitation. The trees that lined the road all turned their heads to watch me.

If men dressed in armour had come galloping towards me on horseback and waving swords, they wouldn't have seemed out of place. The estate was steeped in history, crowded with ghosts of the past, and now here I was, just another person ready to begin my story. The trees had seen it all, yet still I held their interest, and as the light summer breeze blew, leaves swished to one another making the sounds of gossiping lips, never growing bored of another generation's journey.

I followed the main road and finally the trees, which were cleverly landscaped to conceal the castle, fell away. Even though it was me that was moving towards it, the castle felt suddenly upon me, as though it had sneaked towards me without my even noticing, a whole pile of sneaky stone and mortar on its tiptoes with a finger across its lips, as if it hadn't had a bit of fun for the past few hundred years. I stopped walking when it came in sight. Little me before big castle. It felt to me to be more domineering, more commanding as a ruin than as a castle because there it stood before me with its scars revealed, all wounded and bloody from battle. And I stood before it, feeling a shadow of who I used to be, with my scars revealed. We instantly bonded.

We studied one another and then I walked towards it, and it didn't blink once.

Though I could have walked into the castle through the gaping hole in the side wall, I felt it would be more respectful to enter through the other bite life had taken out of it, which used to be the front entrance. Respectful to whom, I don't exactly know, but I think I was trying to appeal to the softer side of the castle. I paused at the door, a respectful pause, and then went inside. There was a lot of green, a lot of rubble. It was eerily quiet within the walls, and I felt as though I was intruding on somebody's house. The weeds, the dandelions, the nettles, all stopped what they were doing to look up. I don't know why, but I started crying.

Just as I'd felt sad for the bluebottle, I felt sad for the castle, but realistically, I think I felt those things because I was mostly sad for myself. I felt like I could hear the castle moan and whine as it was left to stand here, falling apart, while the trees around it continued to grow. I moved over to one of the walls, the stones rough and so large I could imagine the strength of the hands that had carried, or which had been forced to carry, them. I hunkered down in the corner, pressed my ear against the stone and closed my eyes. I don't know what I was listening for, I don't really know what I was doing, trying to comfort a wall, but it's what I did anyway.

If I'd told Zoey and Laura what I'd done they'd have carted me off to the fashion house of bumless smocks for sure, but I felt like I'd connected to the building in some way. I don't know, maybe because I'd lost my home and I felt that I had nothing that was truly mine, coming across this building that wasn't anybody's, I wanted to make it mine. Or maybe it was just that when people are lonely they cling to anything not to feel that way any more. For me, that anything was the castle.

I don't know how long I stayed there but eventually the sun was going down behind the trees, casting a sprinkle of sparkling light on the ruin every time the trees swished from side to side. I watched it for a while and then I realised the surroundings were heading towards dusk. It must have been around ten p.m.

My legs were stiff from being in the same position for so long as I slowly rose to my feet. From the corner of my eye, I thought I saw something move. A shadow. A figure. Not an animal, yet it darted. I wasn't sure. Not wanting whatever or whoever it was to come up behind me, I kept my back to the castle entrance and moved backwards quickly. I heard another noise – an owl or something squawked and I jumped out of my skin and got ready to run. Unable to see the ground underneath the growth, I tripped over a rock and fell backwards to the ground. I smacked my head, whimpered, and I could hear the panic in my voice as I fell into the disgusting overgrowth with God knows what living in it. My vision blurred a little, black spots appearing in place of the line of the ruined roof against the indigo sky. I climbed to my feet, used my hands to push myself up, scraped against the pebbles and rocks, which cut into my skin, and I didn't look back as I ran as fast as my Uggs would take me. It felt like for ever until the house came into sight, as though the road and the trees were conspiring to keep me running on a treadmill.

Finally the house came into view. Barbara's SUV was gone from outside and I knew then that I'd been completely cut off. The drawbridge had been lifted. Almost as soon as the house came into sight the front door opened and Rosaleen stood there watching me, as though she had been standing there waiting since the moment I left.

'Come in, come in,' she said with urgency in her voice.

I finally stepped over the threshold and into my new life, and the beginning began. My once-clean pink Uggs were now filthy from the castle walk, as I stepped onto the flagstoned hallway. The house was deathly quiet.

'Let's have a look at you,' Rosaleen said, holding my wrists tightly, and took a step back to give me the once-over. But her once-over went twice, then three times . . . I tugged away from her and her grip instinctively tightened, but then as though she realised what she'd done, or she saw how my face changed, she finally let go.

Her voice was sweeter. 'I'll darn those for you. Leave them in the basket by the armchair in the sitting room.'

'Darn what?'

'Your trousers.'

'They're jeans. They're supposed to be like this.' I looked down at my ripped jeans, so torn apart that there was hardly any denim visible at all. Underneath my jeans my leopard-print tights were revealed, which was the idea. 'They're not supposed to be dirty, though.'

'Oh. Well, you can leave them in the basket in the kitchen.'

'You have a lot of baskets.'

'Just two.'

I'm not sure if what I'd said was a joke or a smart comment but she missed it either way.

'Okay. Well, I'm going to my room . . .' I waited for her to guide me but she just stared at me. 'Where is it?'

'What about a cuppa? I made an apple tart.' Her tone was almost pleading.

'Eh, no, thanks, I'm not very hungry.' I felt my stomach grumble in response and hoped she wouldn't hear it.

'Of course. Of course you're not,' she berated herself silently.

'Which way is my room?'

'Up the stairs, the second door on the left. Your mum is the last room on the right.'

'Okay I'll go see her.' I began to make my way upstairs.

'No, child,' Rosaleen said quickly. 'Leave her. She's resting.'

'I'd just like to say good night to her,' I smiled tightly.

'No, no, you must leave her,' she said firmly.

I swallowed. 'Okay.'

I slowly backed away and went upstairs, each step creaking under my foot. From the landing I could still see the hallway, Rosaleen was standing there watching me. I smiled tightly and went into my room, closed the door firmly behind me and leaned against it, my heart pounding.

I stayed in there for five minutes, barely taking in the room, knowing I had enough time ahead of me to come to terms with my new space, but first I needed to see my mother. When I opened the door again slowly, I peeped my head out and looked down from the landing balcony and into the hallway. Rosaleen was gone. I opened the door wider and stepped outside. I jumped. There she was, standing outside Mum's bedroom door, like a guard dog.

'I just checked on her,' she whispered, her green eyes glowing. 'She's sleeping. You best go and get some rest now.'

I hate being told what to do. I used to never do what I was told, but something about Rosaleen's voice, about the look in her eye, about the feel of the house and the way she was standing, told me that I wasn't in control now. I went back into my room and closed the door, without another word.

Later that night, when inside the house and outside were like woollen opaque tights – so thick with darkness I couldn't make out any shapes – I woke up thinking there was someone in the room. I heard breathing above my bed and smelled that familiar soapy lavender smell, and so I scrunched my eyes shut and pretended to be asleep. I don't know how long Rosaleen stayed there watching me but it felt like an eternity. Even after I heard her leave the room and the door gently clicked I kept my eyes tightly shut, my heart pounding so loudly I was afraid she would hear it, until I eventually fell asleep.

CHAPTER FOUR

The Elephant in the Room

I awoke the next morning at around six a.m to the sound of the birds calling to one another. Their constant whistling and chatter made me feel as though the house had been air-lifted in the middle of the night and transported to bird world. Their selfish noisy banter reminded me of the builders we'd had working on our swimming pool, who went about their business loudly and cockily, as though we weren't still living in the house. There was one guy, Steve, who kept trying to get a look at me in my bedroom while I was getting dressed. So one morning I really gave him something to look at. Don't get the wrong impression; I took three hairpieces and pinned them to my bikini – you can guess where – and I took off my bathrobe and paraded around my room like Chewbacca, pretending I didn't know he was looking. He never looked again after that, but a few of the others used to stare at me whenever I passed by, so I can only assume he told them, dirty little bugger. Well there would be no such games here, unless I wanted to send a red squirrel flying off his branch in shock.

The blue and white checked curtains did little to keep out the sunlight. The room was fully lit like a bar at closing time; all blemishes, drunkards and cheaters revealed. I lay in bed, wide awake, and stared at the room that was now *my* room. It didn't seem very *my*; I wondered if it would ever feel *my*. It was a simple room, surprisingly warm. Not just from the morning sun streaming into the room, but it was cosy warm, in an authentic Laura Ashley way and though I usually hated all that twee stuff, it worked here. Where it didn't work was in my friend Zoey's bedroom, which her mum decorated to suit a ten-year-old, in an obvious attempt to convince herself her daughter was sweet and innocent. That room was the equivalent of her sticking her daughter into a pickle jar. It was never going to work. It wasn't so much that the lid came off when her mother wasn't looking, but more that Zoey liked pickles a little too much.

The bedrooms were in the eaves of the house, the ceilings sloping towards the windows. There was a cracked white-painted wooden chair in one corner with an old blue and white checked pillow on it. The walls were a pale blue, but didn't feel cold. There was a white-painted free-standing wardrobe that was just big enough to hold my underwear. My bed had a metal frame, white linen and a blue floral duvet cover with a duck-egg-blue cashmere throw at the end. Above the door to my room hung a simple St Bridget's cross. On the windowsill was a vase of fresh wildflowers – lavender, bluebells, other things I couldn't recognise. Rosaleen had gone to a lot of trouble.

There was a noise coming from downstairs. Plates were clanging, water running, a kettle whistled, there was the sizzle of food on a pan and eventually the smell of a fry drifted upstairs and into my room. I realised that I hadn't eaten since yesterday lunchtime in Barbara's, when Lulu had made us divine sashimi. I also hadn't been to the toilet yet and so my bladder and stomach conspired to get me out of bed. Just as I thought of it, through the paper-thin walls, I heard the door next to my room close and lock. I heard the toilet lid lift and then the trickle of urine as it splashed against the bottom of the bowl. It was falling from a height, so unless Rosaleen pissed while on stilts, it was Arthur.

Judging by the sounds coming from both the kitchen and the bathroom, I guessed my mother wasn't in either room. Now would be my chance to see her. I stepped into my pink Uggs, wrapped the duck-egg-blue blanket around my shoulders and sneaked down the hall to Mum's room.

Despite my lightness of foot, the floorboards creaked with every step. Hearing the toilet flush in the bathroom, I ran down the hall and entered Mum's room without knocking. I don't know what I expected but I suppose something closer to the sight that had greeted me each morning over the previous two weeks. That sight was a dark cave-like room, and buried somewhere beneath the duvet would be Mum. But I was pleasantly surprised that morning. Her room was even brighter than mine – a kind of buttery yellow that was fresh and clean. Her vase on the windowsill was filled with buttercups and dandelions, long green grasses all tied together in yellow ribbon. Her room must have been directly above the living room as there was an open fireplace along the wall with a photograph of the Pope above it, which made me shudder. Not the Pope – I'd rather Zac Efron were on my wall – it was the fire that made me uncomfortable. I've just never liked them. The fireplace had white moulding with black inside, and it looked as though it had had plenty of use, which I thought was weird for a spare bedroom. They must have had a lot of guests, though they didn't strike me as the sociable entertaining type. Then I noticed the en suite and realised Rosaleen and Arthur must have given Mum their bedroom.

Mum was sitting in a white rocking chair, not rocking, and she was facing the window, which looked out over the back garden. Her hair was pinned back neatly, she was dressed in an apricot-coloured floaty silk robe and she was wearing the same pink lipstick she'd had on since the day of Dad's funeral. She wore a small smile, so tiny, but it was there, and she looked like she was intently studying yesterday. When I came near her, she looked up and her smile grew.

'Good morning, Mum.' I gave her a kiss on her forehead and sat down beside her on the edge of her already made bed. 'Did you sleep well?'

'Yes, thank you,' she said happily, and my heart lifted.

'I did too,' I realised as I spoke. 'It's so quiet here, isn't it?' I decided not to mention anything about Rosaleen being in my bedroom last night, in case I'd dreamed it. It would be so embarrassing to accuse somebody of that, at least until I had further evidence.

'Yes, it is,' Mum said again.

We sat together looking out into the back garden. In the middle of the one-acre garden stood an oak tree, its branches veering out in all directions, just begging to be climbed. A beautiful tree, it rose up to the sky grandly, filled with green. It was sturdy and solid and I understood why Mum kept looking at it. It was safe and secure, and if it had stood there for a few hundred years, you could trust it was going to stay there for a bit longer. Stability in our rocky lives right now. A robin hopped from one branch to the other, seeming excited to have the entire tree to itself, like a child who was playing musical chairs alone. That was something I'd never have looked at before either: a tree with a bird. And even if I'd seen it, I'd never have compared it to a child who was playing musical chairs alone. Zoey and Laura would seriously have a problem with me. I was beginning to have problems with me. Thinking of them gave me pangs for home.

'I don't like it here, Mum,' I finally said, and realised my voice shook and I was close to tears. 'Can't we stay in Dublin? With friends?'

Mum looked at me and smiled warmly. 'Oh, we'll be okay here. It will all be okay.'

I was so relieved to hear her say that, to hear the strength, the confidence, the leadership I needed.

'But how long are we going to stay here? What's our plan? Where am I going to school in September? Can I still go to St Mary's?'

Mum looked away from me then, keeping her smile but gazing out of the window. 'We'll be okay here. It will all be okay.'

'I know, Mum,' I said, getting frustrated but trying to keep my tone soft. 'You just said that, but for how long?'

She was quiet.

'Mum?' My tone hardened.

'We'll be okay here,' she repeated. 'It will all be okay.'

I'm a good person, but only when I want to be, and so I leaned up close to her ear and just as I was about to say something so truly horrible that I can't even write it, there was a light knock on the door and it was quickly opened by Rosaleen.

'*There* you both are,' she said, as though she'd been searching high and low for us.

I quickly moved my mouth away from Mum's ear and sat back down on the bed. Rosaleen stared at me as though she could read my mind. Then her face softened and she entered the room with a silver breakfast tray in her hand, wearing a new tea dress that exposed her flesh-coloured slip down by her knees.

'Now, Jennifer, I hope you had a lovely rest last night.'

'Yes, lovely.' Mum looked at her and smiled, and I felt so angry at her for fooling everybody else when she wasn't fooling me.

'That's great so. I've made you some breakfast, just a few little bites to keep you going ...' Rosaleen continued nattering like that as she moved around the room, pulling furniture, dragging chairs, plumping pillows, while I watched her.

A few bites, she'd said. A few bites for a few hundred people. The tray was loaded with food. Slices of fruit, cereal, a plate piled with toast, two boiled eggs, a little bowl of what looked like honey, another bowl of strawberry jam and another of marmalade. Also on the tray was a teapot, a jug of milk, a bowl of sugar, all sorts of cutlery and napkins. For somebody who normally just had a breakfast bar and an espresso in the morning, and only because she felt she had to, Mum had a task on her hands.

'Lovely,' Mum said, addressing the tray before her on a little wooden table and not looking at Rosaleen at all. 'Thank you.'

I wondered then if Mum knew that what had been placed in front of her was to be eaten by her, and wasn't just a work of art.

'You're very welcome. Now is there anything else you want at all?'

'Her house back, the love of her life back ...' I said, sarcastically. I didn't aim the joke at Rosaleen, her being the butt of that particular comment wasn't the intention at all. I was just letting off steam, generally. But I think Rosaleen took it personally. She looked shaken and – oh I don't know – if she was hurt, embarrassed or angry. She looked at Mum to make sure she wouldn't be broken by my words.

'Don't worry, she can't hear me,' I said, bored and examining the split ends of my dark brown hair. I pretended I wasn't bothered but really my comments were causing my heart to beat wildly in my chest.

'Of course she can hear you, child,' Rosaleen half-scolded me while continuing to move about the room fixing things, wiping things, adjusting things.

'You think?' I raised an eyebrow. 'What do you think, Mum? Will we be okay here?'

Mum looked up at me and smiled. 'Of course we'll be okay.'

I joined in on her second sentence, imitating Mum's hauntingly chirpy voice, so that we spoke in perfect unison, which I think chilled Rosaleen. It definitely chilled me as we said, 'It will all be okay.'

Rosaleen stopped dusting to watch me.

'That's right, Mum. It will all be okay.' My voice

trembled. I decided to go a step further. 'And look at the elephant in the bedroom, isn't that nice?'

Mum stared at the tree in the garden, the same small smile on her pink lips, 'Yes. That's nice.'

'I thought you'd think so.' I swallowed hard, trying not to cry as I looked to Rosaleen. I was supposed to feel satisfaction, but I didn't, I just felt more lost. Up to that point it was all in my head that Mum wasn't right. Now I'd proven it and I didn't like it.

Perhaps *now* Mum would be sent to a therapist or a counsellor and get herself fixed so that we could start moving on with our chemical trail.

'Your breakfast is on the table,' Rosaleen simply said, turned her back on me, and left the room.

And that is how the Goodwin problems were always fixed. Fix them on the surface but don't go to the root, always ignoring the elephant in the room. I think that morning was when I realised I'd grown up with an elephant in every room. It was practically our family pet.

CHAPTER FIVE

Grève

I took my time getting dressed, knowing that there was very little else I was going to be able to do that day. I stood shivering in the avocado-coloured bath as the hot water trickled down with all the power of baby drool, and I longed for my pink iridescent mosaic-tiled wet room with six power-shower jets and plasma in the wall.

By the time I had managed to wash out all of the shampoo – I couldn't be bothered battling with conditioner – dried my hair and arrived down-stairs for breakfast, Arthur was scraping the last of the food from his plate. I wondered if Rosaleen had told him about what happened in Mum's bedroom. Perhaps not because if he was in anyway a decent brother, he'd be currently doing some-thing about it. I don't think tipping the base of a tea cup with his oversized nose was going to fix much.

'Morning, Arthur,' I said.

'Morning,' he said, into the bottom of his tea cup.

Rosaleen, the busy domestic bee, immediately jumped into action and came at me with giant oven gloves on her hands.

I lightly boxed each of her hands. She didn't get the joke. Without a word, or a twitch, or a movement of any kind in Arthur's face, I sensed he got it.

'I'll just have cereal, please, Rosaleen,' I said, looking around. 'I'll get it, if you tell me where it is.' I started opening the cupboards, trying to find the cereal, then had to take a step back when I came across a double cupboard filled from top to bottom with jars of honey. There must have been over a hundred jars.

'Whoa.' I stepped back from the opened cupboards. 'Have you got, like, honey OCD?'

Rosaleen looked confused, but smiled and handed me a cup of tea. 'Sit yourself down there, I'll bring you your breakfast. Sister Ignatius gives the honey to me,' she smiled.

Unfortunately I was taking a sip of tea when she said that and I choked on it as I started laughing. Tea came spurting out my nose. Arthur handed me a napkin, and looked at me with amusement.

'You've a sister called Ignatius?' I laughed loudly. 'She's totally got a man's name. Is she a tranny?' I shook my head, still giggling.

'A tranny?' Rosaleen asked, forehead crumpled.

I burst out laughing, then stopped abruptly when her smile immediately faded, she closed the kitchen cabinets and went to the aga for my breakfast. She placed a plate piled high with bacon, sausages, eggs, beans, pudding and mushrooms in the middle of the table. I hoped her sister Ignatius was going to join me for breakfast because there was no way I was going to finish this alone. Then she disappeared, flitted about behind me, and came back with a plate piled high with toast.

'Oh, no, that's okay. I don't eat carbs,' I said as politely as I could.

'Carbs?' Rosaleen asked.

'Carbohydrates,' I explained. 'They bloat me.'

Arthur placed his cup on the saucer and looked out at me from under his bushy eyebrows.

'Arthur, you don't look anything like Mum at all.'

Rosaleen dropped a jar of honey on the floor tiles, which made me and Arthur jump and turn around. Surprisingly, it didn't smash. Rosaleen, at top speed, continued on and placed jam, honey and marmalade before me and a plate of scones.

'You're a growing girl, you need your food.'

'The only growing I want right now is here.' I gestured at my 34B chest. 'And unless I stuff my bra with black and white pudding, this breakfast isn't going to make that happen.'

It was Arthur's turn to choke on his tea. Not wanting to insult them any further, I took a slice of bacon, a sausage and a tomato.

'Go on, have more,' Rosaleen said, watching my plate.

I looked at Arthur in horror.

'Give her time to eat that,' Arthur said quietly, getting to his feet with his plates in his hands.

'Leave that down.' Rosaleen fussed around him, and I felt like grabbing a fly-swatter and attacking her. 'You get on now to work.'

'Arthur, does anybody work in the castle?'

'The ruin?' Rosaleen asked.

'The castle,' I responded, and immediately felt defensive of it. If we were going to start name-calling we may as well start with Mum. She was clearly a broken woman yet we weren't referring to her as the ruin. She was still a woman. The castle was not as it had been, but it was still a castle. I have no idea where that belief had come from but it had arrived overnight and I knew from then on, I was never going to call it a ruin.

'Why do you ask?' Arthur said, slipping his arms into a lumberjack shirt and then putting on a padded vest over it.

'I was taking a look around there yesterday and just thought I saw something. No big deal,' I said quickly, eating and hoping that wouldn't make them stop me from going there again.

'Could have been a rat,' Rosaleen said, looking at Arthur.

'Wow, I really feel better now.' I looked to Arthur for more but he was silent.

'You shouldn't go wandering about there on

your own,' Rosaleen said, pushing the plate of food closer to me.

'Why?'

Neither of them said anything.

'Right,' I said, ignoring the breakfast. 'That's settled. It was a giant, human-sized rat. So if I can't go there, what's there to do around here?' I asked.

There was silence. 'In what way?' Rosaleen finally asked, seeming afraid.

'Like, for me to do. What is there? Are there shops? Clothes shops? Coffee shops? Anything nearby?'

'Nearest town is fifteen minutes,' Rosaleen replied.

'Cool. I'll walk there after breakfast. Work this off,' I smiled, and bit into a sausage.

Rosaleen smiled happily and leaned her chin on her hand as she watched me.

'So which way is it?' I asked, swallowed the sausage and opened my mouth to show Rosaleen it was gone.

'Which way is what?' She got the hint and stopped watching.

'The town. I go out the gates and turn left or right?'

'Oh, no, you can't walk it. It's fifteen minutes in the car. Arthur will drive you. Where do you need to go?'

'Well, nowhere in particular. I just wanted to have a look round.'

'Arthur will drive you and collect you when you're ready.'

'How long will you be?' Arthur asked, zipping up his vest.

'I don't know,' I replied, looking from one to the other, feeling frustrated.

'Twenty minutes? An hour? If it's a short time he can wait there for you,' Rosaleen added.

'I don't know how long I'll be. How can I? I don't know what's in the town, or what there is for me to do.'

They looked at me blankly.

'I'll just hop on a bus or something and come back when I'm ready.'

Rosaleen looked at Arthur nervously. 'There's no buses along this way.'

'What?' my jaw dropped. 'How are you supposed to get anywhere?'

'Drive,' Arthur responded.

'But I can't drive.'

'Arthur will drive you,' Rosaleen repeated. 'Or he'll pick up whatever it is that you need. Have you anything in mind? Arthur will get it, won't you, Arthur?'

Arthur snot-snorted.

'What is it you need?' Rosaleen asked eagerly, leaning forward.

'Tampons,' I spat out, feeling so frustrated now. I just don't know why I do it.

Well, I do know. They were both annoying me. I was used to so much freedom at home, not the

64

Spanish Inquisition. I was used to coming and going whenever I pleased, at my own pace, for however long I liked. Even my own parents never asked me so many questions.

They were quiet.

I shoved another bit of sausage into my mouth.

Rosaleen fiddled with the doily underneath the scones. Arthur was hovering near the door waiting with baited breath to hear whether he was being sent out on a tampon run or not. I felt it was my duty to clear the air.

'It doesn't matter,' I said, calming down. 'I'll have a look around here today. Maybe I'll go tomorrow.' Something to look forward to.

'I'll be off then.' Arthur nodded to Rosaleen.

She jumped up out of her chair as though a finger had poked up through the straw. 'Don't forget your flask.' She hurried about the kitchen as though there was a time bomb. 'Here you go.' She handed him a flask and a lunchbox.

I couldn't help but smile, watching that. It should have been weird, her treating him like a child going off to school, but it wasn't. It was nice.

'Do you want some of this for your lunchbox?' I asked, pointing at the plate of food before me. 'There's no way in the world I'm going to eat it.'

I meant that comment to be nice. I meant that I couldn't eat it because of the quantity, not because of the taste, but it came out wrong. Or it came out right but was taken up wrong. I don't know. Anyway, I didn't want to waste the food. I wanted to share it with Arthur for his cute little lunchbox, but it was as though I'd punched Rosaleen in the stomach again.

'Ara go on, I'll have some of it so,' Arthur said, and I felt like he was saying it just to make Rosaleen happy.

Rosaleen's cheeks pinked as she fussed around in a drawer for another Tupperware box.

'It's really lovely, Rosaleen, honestly, but I just don't eat this much breakfast usually.' I couldn't believe such an issue was being made of the breakfast.

'Of course, of course,' she nodded emphatically as though she was so stupid not to have known this. She scooped it up and put it into the little plastic tub. And then Arthur was gone.

While I was still sitting at the table trying to get through the three thousand slices of toast that could easily have been used to rebuild the castle, Rosaleen collected the tray from Mum's room. The food hadn't been touched. Head down, Rosaleen brought it straight to the bin and started scraping it into a bag. After the earlier scene, I knew this would have hurt her.

'We're just not breakfast people,' I explained, as gently as I could. 'Mum usually grabs a breakfast bar and an espresso in the morning.'

Rosaleen straightened up and turned around, ears alert to food talk. 'A breakfast bar?'

'You know, one of those bars made of cereal and raisins and yoghurt and things.'

'Like this?' She showed me a bowl of cereal and raisins and a little bowl of yoghurt.

'Yes, but . . . in a bar.'

'But what's the difference?'

'Well, you bite into the bar.'

Rosaleen frowned.

'It's faster. You can eat it on the go.' I tried to explain further. 'While you're driving to work or running out the door, you know?'

'But what kind of breakfast is that at all? A bar in a car?'

I tried so hard not to laugh at that. 'It's just, you know, to . . . save time in the morning.'

She looked at me like I'd ten heads, then went quiet as she cleaned the kitchen.

'What do you think of Mum?' I asked after a long silence.

Rosaleen kept cleaning the counters with her back to me.

'Rosaleen? What do you think about the way my mum's behaving?'

'She's grieving, child,' she said quickly.

'I don't think that's the proper way to grieve, do you? Thinking an elephant is in the room?'

'Ah, she didn't hear you right,' she said lightly. 'Her head is elsewhere, is all.'

'It's in cuckoo land, is where,' I mumbled.

Because people keep throwing this 'grieving' comment at me, as if I was born yesterday and never knew that it was difficult to lose a person you spent every day of your life with for the past twenty years, I've since read up a lot on grief. What I've learned is that there's no proper way to grieve, no wrong or right way. I don't know if I agree with that. I think Mum's grief is the wrong way. The word grief comes from the old French word *grève* which means heavy burden. The idea is that grief weighs you down with sorrow and all the other emotions. I feel that way: heavier, like I have to drag myself around, everything is an effort, is dark and crap. It's as though my head is continually filled with thoughts I'd never had before, which gives me a headache. But Mum . . . ?

Mum seems lighter. Grief doesn't seem to be weighing her down at all. Instead, it feels like she's flying away, like she's halfway in the air and nobody else cares or notices, and I'm the only one standing beneath her, at her ankles, trying to pull her back down.

CHAPTER SIX
The Bus of Books

The kitchen had been cleared and cleaned; scrubbed to within an inch of its life, and the only thing left that wasn't stacked away on a shelf somewhere was me.

I had never seen a woman clean with such vigour, with such purpose, as if her life depended on it. Rosaleen rolled up her sleeves and sweated, biceps and triceps astonishingly well formed, as she scrubbed, wiping away every trace of life having ever existed in the place. So I sat watching her in fascination, and I admit with a hint of patronising pity too, at the unnecessary act of such intense polishing and cleaning.

She left the house carrying a parcel of freshly baked brown bread that smelled so good it sent my taste buds and my already full stomach into spasms. I watched her from the front living-room window power-walking across the road, not an inch of femininity about her, to the bungalow. I waited by the window, intrigued to see who would answer the door, but she went round the back and spoiled my fun.

I took the opportunity to wander around the house without Rosaleen breathing down my neck and explaining the history behind everything I laid my eyes on as she'd done all morning.

'Oh, that's the cabinet. Oak, it is. A tree came down hard one winter, thunder and lightning, we'd no electricity for days. Arthur couldn't rescue it – the tree that is, not the electricity; we got that back.' Nervous giggle. 'He made that cabinet out of it. Great for storing things in.'

'That could be a good little business for Arthur.'

'Oh no,' Rosaleen looked at me as though I'd just blasphemed. 'It's a hobby, not a money-making scheme.'

'It's not a scheme, it's a business. There's nothing wrong with that,' I explained.

Rosaleen tut-tutted at this.

Hearing myself, I sounded like my dad, and even though I had always hated this about him – his desire to turn everything into a business – it gave me a nice warm feeling. As a child if I brought home paintings from school he'd think I could suddenly be an artist, but only an artist who could demand millions for my works. If I argued a point strongly, I was suddenly a lawyer, but only a lawyer who demanded hundreds per hour. I had a good singing voice and suddenly I was going to record in his friend's studio and be the next big thing. It wasn't just me he did that with, it was everything around him. For him life was full of opportunities, and I don't think that was necessarily a bad thing, but I think he wanted to grab them for all the wrong reasons. He wasn't passionate about art, he didn't care about lawyers helping people, he didn't even care about my singing voice. It was all for more money. And so I suppose it was fitting that it was the loss of all his money that killed him in the end. The pills and the whisky were just the nails in the coffin.

'Is it that photo you've got your eye on?' Rosaleen would continue as my eyes roamed the room. 'He took that when we visited the Giant's Causeway. It rained the entire day and we got a puncture on the way up.'

And on she went.

'I see you're looking at the curtains. They need a bit of a clean. I'll take them down tomorrow and do them. I bought the fabric from a woman doing door-to-door. I never usually but she was a foreign woman, hadn't much English, or money, and had all this fabric. I like the flower in it. I think it matches the cushion there, what do you think? I've lots left in the garage down the back.'

Then I looked to the garage down the back and she'd say, 'Arthur built that himself. Wasn't here when I moved in.'

It struck me as odd phrasing. *When I moved in.* 'Who lived here before?'

Rosaleen looked at me then, with those wide

curious eyes she'd previously reserved for when I was eating. She didn't say anything. She does that a lot, at the most random times. Dropping in and out of our conversations with looks and pauses as though she loses signal on her brain connection.

She freaked me out so much that I looked away, apparently down at the rug that was given to her by somebody for something, I don't know . . . But that morning when I was alone and didn't have her nervous jabbering interfering in my thoughts, I was able to look around properly.

The living room was cosy, I suppose, if not a little old. Well, a lot old, not like my house, which is – was – modern and clean, crisp lines and everything symmetrical. This room had things all over the place. Art that didn't match the couches, funny-looking ornaments, tables and chairs with spindly legs and animal claws, two couches with totally different fabrics – one blue and ivory floral, the other as if a cat had thrown up on it – and a coffee table that doubled as a chessboard. The floor felt like it was uneven, sloping from the fireplace to the bookshelves, making me feel a little seasick. The busiest area seemed to be around the fireplace; an open fire that made me shudder with its contraptions that looked like something out of a medieval torture chamber; wrought-iron pokers with animal heads, coal shovels of different sizes, an ancient bellows, a black cast-iron fireguard with an animal of some sort emblazoned on the front. I turned my back on the fire and concentrated on the floor-to-ceiling bookcase, with a ladder, running the length of the wall. It was filled with books, photos, tins, keepsake boxes, useless trinkets, that kind of thing. Most of the books were on gardening and cooking, very specific, not at all to my taste. They were old and well-read, some ripped apart, some missing their covers, yellowing pages, and some that looked water damaged, but not a speck of dust was to be seen. There was a huge red-bound book, which looked so ancient the pages were black with the red dye running into them. It was *Lloyd's Register of Shipping 1919–1920 Volume 2*. Inside were hundreds of pages of the alphabetically arranged names of vessels, showing the dead weight and capacities of holds and permanent bunkers. I slid it back into place and wiped my hands on my clothes, not wanting the bacteria of 1919 to infest me. Another book was about faiths of the world, which had on the cover a gold emblem of a cross dug into the ground with a snake twisted around it. Then beside it was a book on Greek cooking, though I doubted very much that there'd be a place for a souvlaki next to Rosaleen's Aga. The next book was *The Complete Book of the Horse*, though it mustn't have been, for there were twelve more on the subject.

I'd read only the first chapter of the book Fiona gave me at my dad's funeral and already that was the most I'd read in a year, so the books stuffed onto the shelves didn't particularly interest me. What did interest me was a photo album filed alongside them all. It was in the large book section, beside the dictionaries, encyclopaedia, world atlas and that kind of thing. An old-fashioned album, it had the look of a printed book, or at least its spine had. It had a red velvet cover and was embossed by a frame of gold, and I took it out and ran my finger across the front, leaving a darkened trail on the velvet. I curled up in the leather-studded armchair, looking forward to getting lost in somebody else's memories. As soon as I opened the first page, the doorbell rang, long and shrill. It broke the silence and made me jump.

I waited, almost expected Rosaleen to come sprinting across the road with her teadress hitched up to her thighs, revealing hamstrings so tight Jimi Hendrix could play on them. But she didn't. Instead there was silence. There wasn't a peep upstairs from Mum. The doorbell rang again and so I placed the photo album down on the table, and made my way to the front door, the house feeling a little more like home as I did so.

Through the obscure stained glass, I could tell it was a man. When I opened the door, I saw it was a gorgeous man. Early twenties, I guessed, dark brown hair gelled straight up in the front, just like his polo-shirt collar. He could well be a rugby boy. He looked me up and down, and smiled.

'Hi,' he said, and his smile revealed perfectly straight white teeth. He had stubble all around his jaw, his eyes were bright blue. In his hand was a clipboard with a chart attached.

'Hi,' I said, arching my back as I leaned in against the door.

'Sir Ignatius?' he asked.

I smiled. 'Not I.'

'Is there a Sir Ignatius Power in this house?'

'Not at the moment. He's out fox hunting with Lord Casper.'

His eyes narrowed suspiciously. 'When will he be back?'

'After he's caught the fox, I assume.'

'Hmm . . .' he nodded slowly and looked about him. 'Are the foxes fast around here?'

'You're obviously not from around here. Everybody knows about the foxes here.'

'Hmm. Indeed I'm not.'

I bit my lip and tried not to smile.

'So he might be a long time?' he smiled, sensing I was waning.

'He might be a very long time.'

'I see.'

He leaned against the porch pillar and stared at me.

'What?' I said defensively, feeling like I was melting under his gaze.

'Seriously.'

'Seriously, what?'

'Does he live anywhere around here, at all?'

'Definitely not behind these gates.'

'What are you then?'

'I'm a Goodwin.'

'I'm sure you are, but what's your surname?'

I tried not to laugh but couldn't help it.

'Cheesy, I know, sorry,' he apologised good-heartedly, then looked confused as he consulted his chart and scratched his head, making it even more tousled.

I looked over his shoulder and saw a white bus, with 'The Travelling Library' emblazoned across the side.

He finally looked up from his clipboard. 'Okay then, I'm definitely lost. There's no Goodwin on this list.'

'Oh, it wouldn't be under my name.' Byrne was my mother's maiden name, my uncle Arthur's surname and the name this house would be under. Arthur and Rosaleen Byrne. Jennifer Byrne – it didn't sound right. It felt like my mum should always have been a Goodwin.

'So this must be the Kilsaney residence?' he said hopefully, looking up from his chart.

'Ah, the Kilsaneys,' I said, and he looked relieved. 'They're the next house on the left, just through the trees,' I smiled.

'Great, thank you. I've never been around here before. I'm an hour late. What are they like, the Kilsaneys?' He scrunched up his nose. 'Will they give me shit?'

I shrugged. 'They don't say much. But don't worry, they love books.'

'Good. Do you want me to stop here on the way back out so you can have a look at the books?'

'Sure.'

I closed the door and burst out laughing. I waited with excitement for him to return, butterflies fluttering around my heart and stomach as though I was a child playing hide-and-seek. I hadn't felt like this for at least a month. Something had been reopened inside me. Less than a minute later, I heard the bus returning. It stopped outside the house and I opened the door. He was getting out of the bus, a big smile on his face. When he looked up he caught my eye and shook his head.

'Kilsaneys not home?' I asked.

He laughed, coming towards me, thankfully not angry but amused. 'They decided they didn't want any books as it seems, along with the second floor and most of their walls, and the actual roof of their home, their bookshelf went missing.'

I giggled.

'Very funny, Miss Goodwin.'

'It's Ms, thank you very much.'

'I'm Marcus.' He held out his hand and I shook it.

'Tamara.'

'Beautiful name,' he said gently. He leaned against the wooden porch pillar. 'So seriously, do you know where this Sir Ignatius Power of the Sisters of Mercy lives?'

'Hold on, let me see that.' I grabbed the clipboard from him. 'That's not "Sir". That's "Sr". Sis-ter,' I said slowly. 'You muppet.' I tapped him on the head with it. 'He's a nun.' Not a transvestite, after all.

'Oh.' He started laughing and grabbed the end of his board. I held on tight. He pulled harder and dragged me out onto the porch. That close up he was even cuter. 'So is that you, Sister?' he asked. 'Have you received your calling?'

'The only thing I get called for is dinner.'

He laughed. 'So, who is she?'

I shrugged.

'You're intent on making me get lost, aren't you?'

'Well, I just got here yesterday so I'm as lost as you are.'

I didn't smile when I said that and he didn't smile back either. He got it.

'Well, for your sake, I really hope that's not true.' He looked up at the house. 'You live here?'

I shrugged.

'You don't even know where you *live*?'

'You're a strange man who travels in a bus filled with books. Do you think I'm going to tell you where I live? I've heard about your kind,' I said, walking away from the house and towards the bus.

'Oh, yeah?' He followed me.

'There was a guy like you who lured children into his bus tempting them with lollipops, then when they got inside, he locked them in and drove off.'

'Oh, I heard about him,' he said, his eyes lighting up. 'Long greasy black hair, big nose, pale skin, danced around in tight trousers and sang a lot. Also had a penchant for toy boxes?'

78

'That's the one. Friend of yours?'

'Here,' he rooted inside his top pocket and dug out his ID. 'You're right, I should have shown this earlier. It's a public library, licensed and everything. All official. So I promise I won't trap you inside.'

Unless I asked him to. I studied the ID card. 'Marcus Sandhurst.'

'That is I. Want to look at the books?' He held his arm out to the bus. 'Your chariot awaits.'

I looked around, not a soul nearby, including Mum. The bungalow also appeared dead. With nothing to lose, I climbed aboard, and as I did, Marcus sang, 'Children,' in the Child-Catcher's voice, and cackled. I laughed too.

Inside, both walls were lined with hundreds of books. Divided into various categories and I ran my finger along them, not really reading the titles, a little on guard at being in the bus with a strange man. I think Marcus sensed this because he took a few steps back from me, gave me plenty of space, and stood by the open door instead.

'So what's your favourite book?' I asked.

'Eh . . . *Scarface*.'

'That's a film.'

'Based on a book,' he said.

'No, it's not. What's your favourite book?'

'Coldplay,' he responded. 'Pizza . . . I don't know.'

'Okay,' I laughed, 'so you don't read.'

'Nope.' He sat up on a ledge. 'But I'm hoping that this experience will positively change me for the better and that I will be converted to a reader.' He spoke lazily, his voice so lacklustre and unconvincing it was as though he was repeating something he'd been told himself.

I studied him. 'So what happened, Daddy asked his friend to give you a job?'

His jaw line hardened and he was silent for a while, and I felt really bad, like I should take back the comment. I don't even know why I said that. I don't even know where that came from. I just had a weird feeling that I must have been close. I think maybe I recognised a part of me in him.

'Sorry, that wasn't funny,' I apologised. 'So what happens here?' I said, trying to break the tension. 'You travel around to people's houses and give them books?'

'It's the same as a library,' Marcus said, still a little cool with me. 'People join up, receive membership cards and that allows them to take out books. I go to the towns where there aren't any libraries.'

'Or life forms,' I said, and he laughed.

'You're finding it tough here, city girl?'

I ignored that comment and kept studying the books.

'You know what people around here would really appreciate instead of books?'

He smiled suggestively at me.

'Not that,' I laughed. 'You could actually make some money out of this thing if you got rid of the books.'

'Ha! Now that's not very cultured,' he said.

'Well, there's no bus service around here. Apparently there's a town fifteen minutes drive away – how is anybody supposed to get there?'

'Eh . . . the answer would be in your question.'

'Yes, but I can't drive because I'm—' I stalled, and he smiled. 'Because I'm not *able* to drive,' I finished.

'What? You mean Daddy didn't get you a Mini Cooper yet? That's totally uncool,' he imitated me.

'Touché.'

'Okay,' he jumped off the table, filled with energy. 'I have to go there now. How about we go to this wonderful magical town that no human legs can reach.'

I giggled. 'Okay.'

'Don't you need to run it by somebody? I don't want to be done for kidnapping.'

'I may not be a *driver* but I'm not a child.' I kept my eye on the bungalow. Rosaleen was gone a long time.

'You're sure?' he asked, looking around. 'Please just tell someone.'

He looked anxious and just because of that I took out my phone and called Mum's mobile, which I know she hadn't touched for a month. I left a message.

'Hi, Mum, it's me. I'm outside the house in a bus full of books and a cute guy is going to drive me to the town. I'll be back in a few hours. In case I don't come back, his name is Marcus Sandhurst, he's five foot ten, has black hair, blue eyes ... Any tattoos?' I asked.

He lifted his top. Ooh he was ribbed.

'He's got a Celtic cross on his lower abdomen, no chest hair and a silly smile. He likes *Scarface*, Coldplay and pizza, and is hoping to get into books in a big way. See you later.'

I hung up and Marcus burst out laughing. 'You know me better than most people.'

'Let's get out of here,' I said.

'Are you always so misbehaved?' he asked.

'Always,' I responded, and climbed into the passenger seat in preparation for my adventure out of Kilsaney Demesne.

CHAPTER SEVEN

I Want

There were twelve minutes of a comfortable and not-for-one-second awkward conversation with Marcus, before reaching the town. Only 'the town' wasn't at all what I was expecting. Even with my expectations lowered to an all-time low, it was so much worse. It was a one-horse town, with not even a horse in sight. A church. A graveyard. Two pubs. A chipper. A petrol station with a newsagent. A hardware store. Full stop.

I must have whimpered because Marcus looked at me, worried.

'What's wrong?'

'What's wrong?' My eyes widened as I turned to him. 'What's *wrong*? I have a Barbie Village from when I was like, *five*, bigger than this at home.'

He tried not to but he laughed. 'It's not that bad. Another twenty minutes and you're in Dunshauglin; that's a proper town.'

'Another twenty minutes? I can't even get *here*,

to this shit hole on my own.' I felt my eyes heat up with frustration, my nose started to itch, my eyes began to fill. I felt like kicking the bus down and screaming. I grunted instead. 'What the hell am I going to do around here on my own, buy a shovel in there, and dig up the dead over there? And have a bag of chips and a pint while I'm doing it?'

Marcus snorted, and had to look away to compose himself. 'Tamara, it's really not that bad.'

'Yes it is. I want a fucking skinny gingerbread latte and a cinnamon roll, now,' I said very calmly, aware that I was beginning to sound like Violet Beauregarde from *Charlie and the Chocolate Factory*. 'And while I'm there I want to use my laptop and avail myself of their Wi-Fi service, go online and check my Facebook page. I want to go to Topshop. I want to Twitter. And then I want to go to the beach with my friends and look at the sea and drink a bottle of white wine and I want to get so drunk, I fall over and vomit. You know, like normal things that normal people do. That is what I want.'

'Do you always get what you want?' Marcus looked at me.

I couldn't answer. A giant lump of oh-my-god-I'm-in-love-kind-of-feeling had gathered in my throat. And so I just nodded.

'Okay,' he said, perking up, and I swallowed, my Marcus crush sent flying down my oesophagus into my stomach. 'Let's look on the bright side.'

'There is no bright side.'

'There's always a bright side.' He looked left and then he looked right, he held his hands up and his eyes lit up. 'There's no library.'

'Oh my god . . .' I head-butted myself off the dashboard.

'Right,' he laughed and turned the engine off, 'let's go somewhere else.'

'Don't you need the engine *on* to go somewhere else?' I asked.

'We're not driving,' he said, and climbed over the top of the driver's seat and into the bus. 'So, let's see . . . where should we go?' He moved his finger along the spines of the books in the travel section and walked alongside them reading aloud, 'Paris, Chile, Rome, Argentina, Mexico . . .'

'Mexico,' I said straightaway, kneeling up on the seat to watch him.

'Mexico,' he nodded. 'Good choice.' He lifted the book from the shelf and looked at me. 'Well? Are you coming? Flight's about to leave.'

I smiled and climbed over the back of the seat. We sat on the floor, side by side, in the back of the bus and that day, we went to Mexico.

I don't know if he knows how important that moment was to me. How much he actually saved me from myself, from absolute despair. Maybe he does know and that's exactly what he was doing. But he was like an angel who came into my life with his bus of books at exactly the right time, and who whisked me away from a terrible place to a faraway land.

We didn't stay in Mexico for as long as we'd hoped. We checked into our hotel, double bed, dumped our bags, and headed straight for the beach. I bought a bikini from a man selling them on the beach, Marcus had ordered a cocktail and was going to go on a jetski alone – I was refusing to get into a wet suit – when the knock came on the bus and an elderly woman who eyed me suspiciously stepped on to find something for her to pass her time in. We got to our feet then and I browsed the shelves while Marcus played host. I came across a book about grief; about learning how to deal with personal grief or a loved one suffering from grief. I hovered by that book for a while, my heart pounding as though I'd found a magic vaccination for all worldly diseases. But I couldn't bring myself to lift it from the shelf – I don't know why. I didn't want Marcus to see, I didn't want him to ask me about it, I didn't want to have to tell him about Dad dying. Then that would mean I'd be exactly who I was. I was a girl whose dad had just killed himself. If I didn't tell him, then I didn't have to be that girl. Not to him, anyway. I would just be her on the inside. I'd let her rage inside me, bubble under my skin, but I'd go to Mexico and leave her behind in the gatehouse.

My eye fell upon a large leather-bound book in non-fiction. It was brown, thick, no author's name or title along the spine. I pulled it out. It was heavy. The pages were jagged along the edges as though they'd been ripped. 'So you're like a Robin Hood of the book world,' I said, as soon as the old woman had left with a racy romance under her arm, 'bringing books to those who have none?'

'Something like that. What have you got there?'

'Don't know, there's no title on the front.'

'Try the spine.'

'Not there, either.'

He picked up a folder from beside him and licked his finger before flicking through some pages. 'What's the author's name?'

'There's no author's name.'

He frowned and looked up. 'Not possible. Open it up and see what's on the first page.'

'I can't,' I laughed. 'It's locked.'

'Oh, come on,' he smiled, 'you're taking the piss, Goodwin.'

'I'm not,' I laughed, moving towards him. 'Honestly, look.'

I passed it to him and our fingers brushed, causing a tingle of seismic proportions to rush through every single erogenous zone that existed in my body.

The pages of the book were closed with a gold clasp and attached to that was a small gold padlock.

'What the hell . . .' he said, trying to pull at the lock, making a series of grimaces that had me smiling. 'Trust *you* to choose the only book in here that doesn't have an author or title and is padlocked.'

We both started laughing. He gave up on the padlock and our eyes locked.

This was the bit where I was supposed to say, 'I'm only sixteen.' But I couldn't. I just couldn't. I told you, I felt older. Everybody always thought I looked older. I wanted to be older. It wasn't like we were going to have sex on the floor, he wasn't going to be in prison for staring at me. But still. I should have said it then. If we were in some old *Gone with the Wind*-style southern early nineteenth-century book, back in the good old days where women were men's property and weren't protected at all, then it wouldn't have mattered, we could have rolled around in the hay in a barn somewhere and done whatever we wanted and nobody would have been accused of anything. I felt like hunting down that book from the shelves, opening it and jumping into the pages with him. But we weren't. It was the twenty-first century. I was sixteen, very nearly seventeen, and he was twenty-two. I'd seen it on his ID card. I had experience in knowing that a guy's horn didn't last until my seventeenth birthday. It was rare they felt like coming back in July.

'Don't look so sad,' he said, and reached out and lifted my chin with his finger. I hadn't realised he'd come so close to me and there he was, right before me. Toe to toe.

'It's only . . . a book.'

I realised I was hugging it close to me, both my arms wrapped around it tightly.

'But I like the book,' I smiled.

'I like the book too, very much. It's a cheeky very pretty book, but it's obvious we can't read it right now.'

My eyes narrowed, wondering if we were talking about the same thing.

'So, that means we'll both just have to sit and look at it, until we find the key.'

I smiled, and I felt my cheeks pink.

'Tamara!' I heard my name being called. A screeching, desperate call. We stopped gazing at one another and I rushed to the door of the bus. It was Rosaleen. She was running across the road toward me her face scrunched up, her eyes wild and dangerous. Arthur was standing on the pavement beside his car, looking calm. I relaxed a little then. What had Rosaleen all riled up?

'Tamara,' she said, breathless. She looked from Marcus to me, appearing like a meerkat again, on high alert. 'Come back to us, child. Come back,' she said, her voice shaky.

'I am coming back,' I frowned. 'I've only been gone an hour.'

She looked a little confused then, looked at Marcus as if he was going to explain everything.

'What's wrong Rosaleen? Is Mum okay?'

She was silent. Her mouth opened and closed as if she was trying to find words.

'Is she okay?' I asked again, panic building.

'Yes,' she said, 'of course she's fine.' She still looked confused, but beginning to calm.

'What's wrong with you?'

'I thought you'd . . .' she trailed off, looking around the village now and, as though realising where she was, she stood up straight, ran a hand across her hair to smooth it down, fixed her dress which was crumpled from the drive. She took small breaths and she visibly calmed before us. 'You're coming back to the house?'

'Yes, of course,' I frowned. 'I told Mum where I was going.'

'Yes, but your mother . . .'

'My mother what?' My voice hardened. If everything was so okay with my mother, then my telling her should have been fine.

Marcus's hand was on my back, his thumb comfortingly circling the small of my back, reminding me of Mexico, of all the other places I could be.

'You should go with her,' Marcus said quietly. 'I have to move on now, anyway. You can hold on to that.' He nodded at the book I was hugging in my arms.

'Thanks. See you again?'

He rolled his eyes. 'Of course, Goodwin. Now go.'

As I walked across the road and sat in the back of the Land Rover, I noticed the three male smokers standing outside the pub, staring. It's not unusual to be stared at but it was the way they were staring. Arthur nodded at them. Rosaleen kept her head down, her eyes to the floor. The three men's eyes followed us, and I stared back, hoping to figure out what exactly was their problem. Was it because I was new? But I knew it wasn't, because they weren't looking at me. All eyes were on Arthur and Rosaleen. In the car, nobody said a word the entire way home.

Inside the house, I went to check on Mum despite Rosaleen telling me not to. She was still sitting in the rocking chair, not rocking, and looking out at the garden. I sat with her a while and then left. I went downstairs to the living room, back to the armchair I'd been sitting in before Marcus called. I reached for the photo album but it was gone. Tidied away by Rosaleen again. I sighed and searched for it again on the bookshelf. It was gone. I went through every single book on that shelf, but it was nowhere to be found.

I heard a creak at the door and I spun round. Rosaleen was standing there.

'Rosaleen!' I said, hand flying to my heart. 'You scared me.'

'What were you doing?' she asked, her fingers creasing and then smoothing the apron over her dress.

'I was just looking for a photo album I saw earlier.'

'Photo album?' She cocked her head sideways, her forehead wrinkled, her face pinched in confusion.

'Yes, I saw it earlier, before the library came by. I hope you don't mind, I took it out to look at it but now it's . . .' I held my hands up in the air and laughed. 'It has mysteriously vanished.'

She shook her head. 'No, child.' She looked behind her and then lowered her voice to a whisper. 'Now hush about it.'

Arthur entered then, with a newspaper in his hand and she went quiet. He glanced from me to her.

She looked at Arthur nervously. 'I better see to the dinner. Rack of lamb tonight,' she said quietly.

He nodded and watched her leave the room.

The way he watched her made me not want to ask Arthur about the album. The way he watched her made me think a lot of things about Arthur.

Later that evening, I heard them in their bedroom, muffled sounds that rose and fell. I wasn't sure if it was an argument or not but it felt different from the way they usually talked. It was a conversation, instead of a series of comments thrown to one another. Whatever they were talking about, they were trying hard for me not to hear them. I had my ear up against the wall, wondering about their sudden silence, when my bedroom door opened and Arthur was there staring at me.

'Arthur,' I said, moving away from the wall, 'you should knock. I need my privacy.'

Considering he'd just caught me with my ear to the wall he did well not to say anything.

'Do you want me to bring you to Dublin in the morning?' he grumbled.

'What?'

'To stay with a friend.'

I was so delighted, I punched the air and got straight on the phone to Zoey, either forgetting to pursue or not caring as to the sudden reason for my expulsion. And so that was the time I went to stay with Zoey. It had been only two nights in the gatehouse and already I felt different returning to Dublin. We went back to our usual patch on the beach beside my house. It looked different and I hated it. It felt different and I hated that too. By the entrance gate to my house a For Sale sign had been erected. I couldn't look at it without my blood boiling, my heart rate rising and feeling an over-whelming desire to scream like a banshee, so I didn't look. Zoey and Laura were already studying me as though I had landed from another planet, gutted their best friend and zipped on her outer layer of skin like a sleeping suit, and everything I said was being picked at, analysed, misconstrued.

Seeing the For Sale sign, my two friends, with the sensitivity of a 'Geronimo' became excited. Zoey chattered incessantly about breaking into the house and spending the afternoon there, as though at that exact time in my life that was the appropriate thing to say. Laura, a little more genteel, looked uncertainly at me while Zoey's back was turned to face the gate and assess the situation, but when I didn't object, she went along with the idea, swept out into sea like a freshly flushed shit.

I don't know how I did it but I managed to kill the excitement for raiding my repossessed house in which my father had killed himself. Instead we got drunk and plotted against Arthur and Rosaleen and their evil country ways. I told them – no I didn't just tell them, I *revealed* to them – about Marcus and the bus of books and they laughed, thinking him an absolute dork, thinking of the travelling library as the most ridiculously boring thing that they had ever heard of. It was bad enough to have a room full of books but to make books even more accessible, well, that was a downright dorkfest.

That hurt me so much but I couldn't quite understand why. I tried to hide it, but the one source of excitement and escape I'd experienced in the month since Dad died was shredded in an instant. I think that's when I started building a wall up between us. They knew it too. Zoey was looking at me with those squinted dissecting eyes that she gives anybody that's in any way different, different being the worst possible offence in the world to her. They didn't know why, they never thought that the emotional impact of what I'd just gone through was going to change not just me for a few weeks, but the very core of me for ever. They just thought living in the country was having a bad effect on me. But I'd been trampled on like a plant that has been crushed underfoot but not killed, and just like the plant I'd no choice but to grow in a different direction than I had before.

When Zoey grew bored, or scared, of discussing things she knew nothing of, she called Fiachrá,

Garóid and the third musketeer, Colm, who I call Cabáiste – which means 'cabbage' in Irish. I'd never ever spoken to him properly in my life. Zoey paired off with Garóid, Fiachrá was partnered with Laura, which Zoey had seemed to have got over, and Cabáiste and I just sat and watched the sea, while the other four rolled around in the sand making sloppy noises, and Cabáiste glugged occasionally on a nagin of vodka, and I expected to be groped at any moment. He covered the bottle with his mouth and knocked back another mouthful, and I waited for that wet, sloppy, vodka-tasting kiss that slightly stung and made me want to retch at the same time.

But he didn't do that.

'Sorry about your dad,' he said quietly.

His comment took me by surprise and then suddenly I became so emotional I couldn't speak. I couldn't answer him, I couldn't even look at him. I looked the other way and allowed the breeze to blow my hair across my face, hiding and sticking to the hot tears that rolled down my cheeks.

The fact I'd been trampled on was obvious. What I called into question time and time again was which direction I was now growing in.

CHAPTER EIGHT
Secret Garden

Whenever I left home for a longer length of time than usual, say to go on a school trip abroad, or when I went on shopping trips to London with friends, I always used to bring something with me to remind me of home – just something small. One Christmas we were at a buffet in a hotel and my dad stole a little plastic penguin that was sitting on top of a pudding and he put it in my dessert. He was trying to be funny but I was having one of those days, which was much like most days, where nothing he said or did could possibly be conceived of as funny, and so somehow the penguin ended up in my pocket that day. Then months later, when I was away, I put my hand in my pocket and found the little penguin, and laughed. Dad's joke, though months way too late and not in his presence, I finally found funny. Somehow on that trip, it ended up in my washbag, and it travelled the world with me.

You know one of those things that you only have to look at and it instantly connects you to something else? I'm not a sentimental person; I never felt that attached to anything or anyone at home. Not like some people, who just have to look at something, like even a piece of fluff, and it sends tears to their eyes because it vaguely reminds them of something somebody once said once upon a time at home, when hindsight, whispering into their ear like the devil, tells them they were happy. No, bringing something with me was just a little ammunition really, to make me feel like I wasn't totally and utterly alone, that I had a little piece of home with me. Not sentimentality, just simple plain old insecurity.

I certainly wasn't attached to the gatehouse in any way. I'd only been there for a couple of days but during my great escape to Zoey's house, I brought the book I'd found in the travelling library with me. I still hadn't managed to unlock it and I certainly had no intentions of reading it while I was there, not when they were so busy telling me about their new source of entertainment – wait for it – going out without underwear on. Honestly, I had to laugh. There was a photo of Cindy Monroe, a six-and-a-half-stone, five foot tall, American reality star, getting out of a car to go to a club the day of her release from forty-eight hours spent in gaol for drink-driving, and she wasn't wearing any knickers. Zoey and Laura seemed to think this was a great new leap forward for women.

I think that when the women's lib took off their bras and burned them, this wasn't exactly what they were hoping for. I said this to Zoey and she studied me thoughtfully, her eyes squinting almost closed like she was the Queen of Hearts about to decide whether to chant 'Off with her head!' or not. But then she opened her eyes wide and said, 'No it's fine, my top was totally backless so I couldn't wear a bra either.'

Totally backless. Very dead. Another one of those phrases. It was either backless or it wasn't. I've no doubt that it was.

Anyway, when I was sent away to Zoey's house – 'sent away' being the operative words – I felt like I'd been told to go sit on the naughty step to think about what I'd done. Despite the fact I should have felt that I was heading home, that I was heading towards feeling more whole again, I didn't feel like it at all. And so, I brought a piece of the new world with me. I brought the book. I knew it was there in my bag when I was sleeping on the pull-out bed in Zoey's room, and as we stayed up all night talking about everything, I knew that it was listening to me, this foreign thing from my detested new life, gaining an insight into the life I once had. I had a witness. I felt like telling it to go home and tell what my life used to be like to all the other things there that I loathed. The book felt like my little secret from Laura and Zoey, a pointless and boring one but a secret all the same, lying beside me in my overnight bag.

And so when Arthur's Land Rover turned into the side entrance to Kilsaney Demesne, and I was gobbled up again by my new desperate non-life, I decided to take the book and go for a walk with it. I knew it would kill Rosaleen if I didn't arrive back and fill her in on the no-knickers-wearing trend, and as it was always my duty to punish, I set off. I also knew that Mum would still be in the same place, sitting in that rocking chair, not rocking, but I allowed my mind to pretend she was doing the exact opposite, like out in the garden doing naked pirouettes or something.

I'd never walked *around* the grounds before. To and from the castle, yes, but around the one hundred acres, no. All of my previous visits had been made up of tea and ham sandwiches in a quiet kitchen while Mum talked about things I didn't care about with my strange aunt and uncle. I'd do anything – eat twenty sloppy egg sandwiches and two slices of whatever cake was going – to get out of that kitchen and wander in the front garden that wrapped its way around to the back. Nowhere else interested me. I wasn't much of an explorer, anything that involved movement bored me. I was never intrigued enough by anything to take things that little bit further. On that day I still wasn't, but I was bored and so I dumped my overnight bag, which Arthur snot-snorted at and brought into the house for me, and I was gone.

I walked away from the house, away from the castle, along a narrow roadway. The route was heavily shaded by the thirty-metre-tall native oaks, ash and yew which lined it. It smelled sweet. The ground was soft, thousands of years of falling foliage and bark laid on the earth, giving me a spring in my step as if I could run from corner to corner in Lycra doing somersaults. It was a hot day, but I was cool under the elderly trees. The birds were like hyperactive monkeys, with constant chirpy calls and doing Tarzan-like swoops from one tree to another. Tired from my all-nighter with my friends, I just kept walking, my head bursting with their conversations, the things I had learned – Laura had had to take the morning-after pill – but none were as loud as the conversations I was having with myself in my head. That, I could never switch off. I don't think I'd ever thought so much, and talked so little, in my life.

Every now and then, when the trees broke their security barrier, I could see the castle in the distance, looking out over its lawn, at the lakes that dotted the grounds, at the majestic trees that stood alone punctuating the landscape. Lone tall and elegant poplars raised up like feathers to tickle the sky, wide oaks with heavy caps spread like wild mushrooms. Then the castle disappeared again, playing peekaboo with me, and the pathway began to curve to the left so that I would soon be able to turn and face the keep head on. Another twenty minutes' walk and I could see the main gateway further up ahead on my right. I immediately slowed. The darkened gothic entrance did not appeal to me, all chained up like some prisoner of war left to rot along the side of the road. Long grasses and whatever else decrepit weeds there were climbed the relatively new gate and poked out through the rusted bars, like long gangly starved arms waving at passing cars to be fed or released. The once grand roadway that led directly to the castle had been ignored, unused and unmaintained. It was overgrown and hidden by grasses, like the yellow brick road in the *Return to Oz*. I shuddered. Despite losing its glory, I didn't take to it as I had to the castle. Its scars were grotesque. Unlike the castle's which made me want to raise a hand and trace them with my finger, these scars were ugly and made me want to look the other way.

I decided to find another route to take, anything to prevent me from passing that ghastly gothic gate and so I broke through the trees and walked across the grounds instead. I felt safer then, cocooned in the bosom of the trees rather than on that well-worn path which Normans and their horses had pounded, wildly waving in the air peasants' severed heads on the tips of their swords.

The tree trunks were fascinating, aged and wrinkled like elephants' legs. They twisted around one another like lovers. Some rose from the ground arched as though in agony and reaching out, then growing on, turning and shifting to a new position. The roots snaked their way from under the surface, rising above the ground and back down again gracefully, as though they were slippery eels in the waters. I tripped often on a raised root, and was caught each time by a helpfully placed tree trunk. The trees did that – tripped me and caught me, tickled me with their leaves and webs, and smacked me in the face with their branches. I pulled back branches in order to pass by, and felt them immediately spring back like catapults to spank me cheekily on the behind.

From one city of trees I made my way to another. The air smelled sweet, bees filled the flowering trees, greedily hopping from one cluster of petals to another, wanting it all, too impatient to choose just one. Around me on the floor was fruit of some kind, there from seasons ago, some decayed and rotten, some dried out like prunes. I stopped to pick one up and tried to decipher what it once was. I smelled it. Vile. As I dropped it and wiped my hands, I realised the trunk beside me was covered in engravings. The poor tree had been carved into over and over again, like a pumpkin emptied of its flesh to bear its fangs. Clearly it hadn't been inscribed all on the same day, nor the same year, not even the same century. From seven feet up all the way down it was covered in various names etched into the bark, some framed by hearts, others in boxes, but all declaring eternal friendships and loves.

I ran my finger over the names 'Frank and Ellie', 'Fiona and Stephen', 'Siobhan and Michael', 'Laurie and Rose', 'Michelle and Tommy'. All declared eternal love. *'2gether, 4ever'*. I wondered if any of them still were. None of the other trees bore the same scars. I stepped back to examine the area and discovered why. There was more of a clearing around this tree. I could imagine blankets laid down, picnics and parties, friends gathering and lovers sneaking out to be together under the fruit tree.

I left the orchard and searched for the next tree town. A wall came into view ahead of me and suddenly my game with the trees was over.

I tried to tread carefully without making a sound, but the woods gave me away. Exaggerated sounds and echoes of twigs snapping and crunching beneath my feet and leaves rustling as I pushed through them alerted the walls to my arrival. I didn't know what building was ahead of me but it wasn't the castle, for that was too far away. I didn't know of any other buildings on the grounds apart from the dilapidated cottages at the other three gate entrances, long closed up as though there was a day, the unspoken day, when everybody upped and left. The stone of the wall wasn't the same as the castle's but to my unexperienced eye it wasn't far off. It was old and crumbling. The top of the wall was uneven, it no longer touched what it once reached for. There was no roof, just a wall. I couldn't see a door or a window for the wall's entire length, and for the most part, unlike the castle, it had survived the bites life liked to take for energy to keep going. I stepped to the edge of the woods, feeling like a hedgehog that has just left its natural habitat to be faced with a main road, revealed by headlights, and tentative. I left my tall friends behind, and under their watchful eyes I walked the length of the wall.

When the wall ended, I turned the corner and saw it continue down another way. Then suddenly I heard a woman humming, from behind the wall. I got a jolt. Apart from my uncle Arthur, I wasn't expecting to come across any other human. I hugged the book close to my chest and listened to the humming. It was soft, sweet, happy, far too liberated to be Rosaleen, too joyous to be my mother. It was passing-the-time kind of humming, a distracted sound, a tune that wasn't familiar to me, if it was a real one at all. The summer breeze blew and it brought a sweet smell and her song along with it. I closed my eyes and leaned my head against the wall, directly the other side from her and I listened.

As my head touched the brick, she stopped humming and my eyes opened quickly and I straightened up.

I looked around. She wasn't in sight, and so I couldn't have been spotted. When my heart slowed to its normal rhythm she began humming again. I moved along the wall, my fingers trailing over the grey stone, tracing the wall, cobwebs, crumbling rock, the smooth of some parts, the rough edges of others beneath my hot fingers. The sun beat down on me, the trees no longer my personal parasol. The wall came to an abrupt stop and I looked up to see a large ornamental stone archway marking the entrance.

I peeked my head inside so that I wouldn't be revealed to the mystery hummer and discovered a walled garden, immaculately kept. From my position outside the arch I could see a rose garden, large formal beds set against the backdrop of climbing roses, fully bloomed, which lined both sides of the footpath from another entrance. I dared to move a little more to see the rest of the garden. In the centre were more flowers – geraniums, chrysanthemums, carnations, others I couldn't name. Flowers tumbled out from hanging baskets and oversized ornamental stone pots that lined the central walkway through the garden. I couldn't quite believe this little oasis amidst all the green, as though somebody had taken a fizzy drink, shaken it and opened it here in the middle of these crumbling walls and this colour had burst out, spraying every inch with different shades. Bees were flying from one flower to the other, vines climbed up the walls twined around beautiful flowers. I could smell the rosemary, lavender and mint of a nearby herb garden. There was a small greenhouse in the corner of the garden, beside that a dozen or so wooden boxes on stands, and then I realised that swept away by my curiosity I had unknowingly wandered into the garden and the humming had stopped.

I wasn't sure what to expect but I definitely

wasn't expecting what I saw. At the end of the garden the source of the humming, and the person that was currently staring at me as though I had arrived from another planet, was dressed in what appeared to be a white spacesuit, her head covered in a black veil, her hands in a pair of rubber gloves and on her feet a pair of calf-length rubber boots. She looked like she'd just stepped off a spaceship and into a nuclear disaster.

I smiled nervously and waved my free hand. 'Hi. I come in peace.'

She stared at me for a little longer, frozen still like a statue. I felt a little bit nervous, a little bit awkward, and so when that happens, I did what I usually do.

'What the fuck are you staring at?'

I don't know how she took that, seeing as she had a Darth Vader helmet on. She stared at me a little longer and I waited for her to tell me that I was Luke and she was my father.

'Well, now,' she said brightly, as if snapping out of a trance, 'I knew I had a little visitor.' She took her entire head attire off, revealing herself to be far older than I expected. She must have been in her seventies.

She came towards me and I half expected her to jump from one foot to the other as though there was no gravity. She was wrinkled, very wrinkled, her skin falling downward as though time had melted her. Her blue eyes sparkled like the Aegean Sea, reminding me of a day out on Dad's yacht where when you looked down, the sea was so clear you could see the sand and hundreds of multi-coloured fish beneath. But there was nothing beneath her eyes, so translucent they practically reflected back all of the light. Then she took off her gauntlets and held her hands out.

'I'm Sister Ignatius,' she smiled, not shaking my hand, but holding it in both of hers. Despite the hot day and the heavy gloves, they were as smooth and as cool as marble.

'You're a nun,' I blurted out.

'Yes,' she laughed. 'I am a nun. I was there when it happened.'

It was my turn to smile, and I laughed, everything making sense then. The cabinet of honey jars, the dozens of boxes around the walled garden, the ridiculous spacesuit on an old woman.

'You know my aunt.'

'Ah.'

I didn't know quite how to take that response. She didn't register surprise but nor did she question me. She was still holding my hand. I didn't want to move my hand, seeing as she was a nun, but it was freaking me out. I kept talking.

'My aunt is Rosaleen, and my uncle is Arthur. He's the groundskeeper here. They live in the gatehouse. We're staying with them for ... a little while.'

'We?'

'Me and my mum.'

'Oh.' Her eyebrows lifted so high I thought they

were caterpillars about to become butterflies and flutter away.

'Didn't Rosaleen tell you?' I was a little insulted, though quite thankful for Rosaleen's respect for our privacy. At least the whole one-horse town with no horse wouldn't be talking about the new folk.

'No,' she replied. And then without a smile and with an air of finality she repeated, 'No.'

She seemed a little cross and so I jumped in to defend Rosaleen and save whatever friendship they did or didn't have. 'I'm sure she was just protecting our privacy, giving us a little time to deal with . . . it . . . before she told people.'

'Deal with . . .'

'The move here,' I said slowly. Was it bad to lie to a nun? Well I wasn't exactly lying . . . I kind of panicked then. I felt my body heat up and go clammy. Sister Ignatius was saying something, her mouth was opening and closing, but I couldn't hear a word of it. I just kept thinking about lying to her and of those Ten Commandments and hell and everything, but not just that, I thought about how nice it would be to say the words aloud to her. She was a nun, I could probably trust her.

'My dad died,' I blurted out quickly interrupting whatever nice thing she'd been saying. I heard the terrible tremble in my voice as I said that sentence and then all of a sudden, from absolutely nowhere, just as it had happened with Cabáiste, tears were gushing down my cheeks.

'Oh, child,' she said, immediately opening her arms and embracing me. The book separated us as I still clung to it, but even though she was a total stranger, she was a nun, and I rested my head on her shoulder and didn't hold back, making snotty and throaty noises and all, while she rocked me a little and rubbed my back. I was in the middle of a really embarrassing wail of, 'Why did he do it? *Whyyyyy* . . . ?' when a bee flew directly into my face and bounced off my lip. I screamed and pushed myself out of Sister Ignatius' arms.

'Bee!' I shrieked, hopping about and trying to dodge it as it followed me. 'Oh my God, get it off me.'

She watched me, her eyes lighting up.

'Oh my God, Sister, please, get it off me. Shoo, shoo!' I waved my arms around. 'They must listen to you. They're your bloody bees.'

Sister Ignatius pointed her finger and shouted in a deep voice, 'Sebastian, no!'

I stopped jerking around to stare at her, my tears gone now. 'You are not serious. You do not name your bees.'

'Ah, there's Jemima on the rose, and Benjamin on the geranium,' she said perkily, eyes bright.

'No way,' I said, wiping my face, embarrassed by my breakdown. 'I thought *I* had mental problems.'

'Of course I'm not serious,' and then she started laughing, a wonderful clear throaty childish laugh that instantly made me smile.

I think that's when I knew I loved Sister Ignatius.

'My name is Tamara.'

'Yes,' she said, looking at me and studying me as if she already knew.

I smiled again. She had a face that made me do that.

'Are you allowed to, like, talk? Shouldn't you be quiet?' I looked around. 'Don't worry I won't tell.'

'Many of the sisters would agree with you,' she chuckled, 'but yes, I'm allowed to talk. I haven't taken a vow of silence.'

'Oh. Do other nuns look down on you for that?'

She laughed again, a sweet, clear, singsong laugh.

'So have you not seen people for ages? Is this against the rules? Don't worry, I won't tell. Though Obama's the US President now,' I joked. When she didn't respond, my smile faded. 'Shit. Are you not supposed to know stuff like that? Stuff from the "outside world"? It must be a bit like being in Big Brother, being a nun.'

She snapped out of her trance and laughed again, her face seeming so childlike in a Benjamin Button way when she did that.

'Aren't you a peculiar thing?' She'd said it with a smile and so I tried hard not to be insulted.

'What's that you've got there?' she asked looking at the book that I was still hugging.

'Oh, this.' I finally stopped squeezing it. 'I found it yesterday on the . . . oh, actually, I owe you a book.'

'Don't be silly.'

'No, really I do. Marcus, I mean, the travelling library came by the day before yesterday looking for you and I didn't know who you were.'

'Then you owe me a book,' she said, a twinkle in her eye. 'Let me see, who's it by?'

'I don't know who or what it is. It's not the Bible or anything, you might not like it,' I said, reluctant to hand it over. 'There could be sex scenes in it, swear words, gay people, divorced people, things like that.'

She looked at me and pursed her lips, trying not to smile.

'I can't open it,' I said finally, giving it to her. 'It's locked.'

'Well, I'll see to that. Follow me.'

She immediately set off out the other entrance of the walled garden with the book in her hand.

'Where are you going?' I called after her.

'Where are *we* going,' she corrected me. 'Come and see the sisters. They'll be delighted to meet you. And I'll open the book while you do so.'

'Uh. No, it's okay.' I ran to catch up with her and take the book back.

'There's just the four of us. We don't bite. Particularly when eating Sister Mary's apple pie, but don't tell her I said,' she added under her breath and chuckled again.

'But, Sister, I'm not very good with holy people. I don't really know what to say.'

She laughed that laugh again and waddled in her funny-looking suit towards the orchard.

112

'What's the deal with the tree with all the engravings on it?' I asked, skipping alongside her to keep up.

'Ah, you've seen our apple orchard? You know, some people say the apple tree is the tree of love,' she said, her eyes widening, and when she smiled dimples pierced her cheeks. 'Many of the young ones around here have declared their love to one another on that tree.' She power-walked on, snapping out of her magical love story. 'Plus, it's great for the bees. And the bees are great for the trees. Oh, that rhymes,' she chuckled. 'Arthur does a wonderful job of keeping it. We get the most delicious Granny Smith apples.'

'Oh, so that's why Rosaleen makes three thousand apple tarts a day. I've eaten so many apples they're literally coming out of my . . .'

She looked at me.

'Ears.'

She laughed and it sounded like a song.

'So,' I panted, trying to keep up with her pacy strides, 'how come there's only four of you?'

'Not so many people want to be nuns these days. It's not, what you'd say, cool?'

'Well, it's not just that it's not cool, which it totally isn't by the way but, no offence to God or anything, it's probably just a sex thing. If you were allowed to have sex I'd say loads of girls would want to be nuns. Though the rate I'm going, I'll be joining you,' I rolled my eyes.

Sister Ignatius laughed. 'All in good time, my

child, all in good time. You're only seventeen. Almost eighteen, my word.'

'I'm sixteen.'

She stopped walking then and examined me, a curious expression on her face. 'Seventeen.'

'Seventeen in a few weeks.' I caught my breath.

'Eighteen in a few weeks,' she frowned.

'I wish, but seriously I'm sixteen, but people always think I'm older.'

She stared at me as though I were a foreign object then, thinking so hard I could almost smell her brain frying. Then she took off on her heel again. Five minutes' power-walk away, I was panting but Sister Ignatius had barely broken a sweat and we came across some more buildings, more like outhouses, and old stables. First, there was a church.

'There's the chapel there,' Sister Ignatius explained. 'It was built by the Kilsaneys in the late eighteenth century.'

Remembering that part from my school project I couldn't take my eyes off it, unable to believe that what I'd stolen from the internet essay wasn't just homework, it was actually real. It was a small chapel, grey stone, two pillars in the front as cracked as a desert earth that hasn't seen water for decades. On the top was a bell tower. Beside it was an old graveyard protected by three thin rusty iron railings. Whether it was to keep the buried in or the wanderers out, it wasn't clear, but it made me shudder just looking at it. I realised

I'd stopped walking and was staring at it – and Sister Ignatius was staring at me.

'Great. I live on the grounds of a graveyard. Just swell.'

'All generations of the Kilsaneys are buried there,' she said softly. 'Or as many as possible. For the bodies they couldn't find they planted headstones.'

'What do you mean, "for the bodies they couldn't find"?' I asked, horrified.

'Generations of war, Tamara. Some of the Kilsaneys were sent off to Dublin Castle to be imprisoned, others left through travel or revolution.'

There was a silence while I took in the old headstones, some green and covered in moss, others black and lopsided, the inscriptions so faded you couldn't read the letters.

'That's fucking creepy. You have to live beside that?'

'I still pray in there.'

'Pray for what? For the walls not to cave in on your head? It looks like it's about to fall apart any second.'

She laughed. 'It's still a consecrated church.'

'No way. Are there weekly masses in there?'

'No,' she smiled again. 'The last time it was used was . . .' she pinched her eyes shut and her lips moved open and closed as though she was doing decades of the rosary. Then her eyes popped open wide. 'Do you know what, Tamara, you should check the records to get the exact date. The names of everybody are included too. We have them in the house. Come in and have a look, why don't you?'

'Eh. No. You're grand, thanks.'

'You will when you're ready, I suppose,' she said and moved along again. I rushed to keep up with her.

'So how long have you lived here?' I asked, following her into an outhouse, which was used as a tool shed.

'Thirty years.'

'Thirty years here? Must have been so lonely here all that time.'

'Oh, no, it was far busier back then when I arrived, believe it or not. The three sisters were a lot more mobile then. I'm the youngest, the baby,' she said, and laughed that little-girl laugh again. 'There was the castle, and the gatehouse . . . they were indeed busier times. But I like the quiet now too. The peace. The nature. The simplicity. The time to be still.'

'But I thought the castle was burned down in the twenties.'

'Oh, it was burned out many times in its history. But it was only partly burned on that occasion. The family worked hard to refurbish it. And they did a wonderful job. It was truly beautiful.'

'You've been inside it?'

'Oh, indeed.' She looked surprised by my question. 'Lots of times.'

'So what happened to it?'

'A fire,' she said, and looked away, located her toolbox on the cluttered work table and opened it. Five drawers slid out, each filled with nuts and bolts. She was like a little DIY magpie.

'Another one?' I rolled my eyes. 'Honestly, that's ridiculous. Our smoke alarms were connected to the local fire station. Want to know how I found out? I was smoking in my room and I didn't open the window because it was absolutely freezing out and whenever I opened my doors they used to just slam shut, which was a total head wreck. So I'd turned my music up really loud and next minute my bedroom door was being bashed down by this hot fireman, pardon the pun, who thought my room was totally on fire.'

There was silence, while Sister Ignatius listened and looked through the toolbox.

'By the way, he thought I was seventeen too,' I laughed. 'He called the house afterwards looking for me but Dad answered the phone and threatened to have him put in gaol. Talk about dramatic.'

Silence.

'Anyway, was everybody okay?

'No,' she said, and when she looked at me briefly I realised that her eyes filled with tears. 'Unfortunately not.' She blinked them away furiously while she noisily rooted through the drawers, her wrinkled but sturdy-looking hands pushing through nails and screwdrivers. On her right hand was a gold ring that looked like a wedding ring, so firmly on her finger, her flesh growing around it, I doubt she could ever take it off even if she wanted to. I would have liked to ask more questions about the castle but I didn't want to upset her further and she was making such a racket as she rooted through her tool box for the correct screwdriver I wouldn't possibly be heard.

She tried and tested a few and I grew bored and shuffled lazily around the garage. Shelf upon shelf of junk filled the walls. A table spanning the three walls was also filled with knick-knacks and contraptions that I didn't know the use for. It was Aladdin's cave for the DIY obsessed.

I looked around but my head hopped with new questions about the castle. So it had been lived in after the fire in the 1920s. Sister Ignatius had said she'd been here thirty years and had been in the house after the refurbishment. That would take us back to the late seventies. I was under the impression the castle had been lying idle for so much longer than that.

'Where is everybody?'

'Inside. It's recreation hour. *Murder, She Wrote* is on now. They love that.'

'No, I mean, from the Kilsaney family. Where are they all?'

She sighed. 'The parents moved away to stay with cousins in Bath. They couldn't take looking at the castle like that. They hadn't the time nor the energy nor the money, mind you, to rebuild it.'

'Do they ever come back?'

She looked at me sadly. 'They passed away Tamara. I'm sorry.'

I shrugged. 'That's okay. I'm not bothered.' My voice was too perky, sounded too defensive. Why? I really wasn't bothered. I didn't know them from Adam – why should I care? But I did care. Maybe it was because Dad had died that I felt every sad story was my story. I don't know. Mae, my nanny, used to love watching programmes about real-life cases being solved. When Mum and Dad were out she used to take over the television in the living room and watch *The FBI Files*, which used to freak me out. Not for the gory details – I'd seen worse – but by the fact she was so fascinated by how to cover up crimes. I used to think she was going to kill us all in our sleep. But she also made the best lattes and so I didn't probe her too much in case she got insulted and would stop making them. I learned from watching one of those shows that the word 'clue' actually came from 'clew', meaning a ball or thread of yarn, because in a Greek myth, a Greek guy uses a ball of yarn to find his way out of the Minotaur's labyrinth. It's something that helps you get to the end of something, or perhaps to the beginning. It's the same as Barbara's satellite navigation kit and my line of breadcrumbs from the gatehouse to Killiney: sometimes we have absolutely no idea where we are, we need the smallest clue to show us where to begin.

Finally the lock she'd been working on gave way and unlatched.

'Sister Ignatius, you're a dark horse,' I teased her.

She laughed heartily. As she lifted open the heavy front cover my heart fluttered. The voice of Zoey and Laura told me to be embarrassed about this and I momentarily was until the Tamara of this new world beat them away with a stick. But when Sister Ignatius opened the book that embarrassment came back intensified, bringing anger with it for there was nothing in the book. Nothing at all on the pages.

'Hmm ... well, look at that,' Sister Ignatius said, flicking through the thick cream woven deckle-edged pages, which looked as though they'd come straight from another time. 'Blank pages waiting to be filled,' she continued with her voice of wonder.

'How exciting.' I rolled my eyes.

'More exciting than an already filled one. Then you definitely wouldn't be able to use it.'

'Then I could read it. Hence it being called a book,' I snapped, once again feeling this place had let me down.

'Would you prefer to be given a life already lived too, Tamara? That way you can sit back and observe it. Or would you rather live it yourself?' she asked, her eyes smiling.

'Eh, you keep it,' I said, stepping away, no longer interested in the thing I'd been hugging, feeling let down by it.

'No, dear. That's yours. You use it.'

'I don't write. I hate it. It gives me bumps on my fingers. And headaches. I'd rather email. Anyway, I can't. It's the travelling library's. Marcus will want it back. I have to meet him again to give it back.' I noticed my voice had softened on the last sentence. Quite immaturely, I fought a smile.

Sister Ignatius noticed everything and she smiled and raised her eyebrows. 'Well, you can still meet up with Marcus *to discuss the book*,' she teased. 'He'll understand, as I do, that somebody must have donated the diary to the library, mistaking it for a book.'

'If I take it don't I break a Commandment or something?'

Sister Ignatius rolled her eyes as I had been doing and, despite my bad mood, I had to grin.

'But I've nothing to write,' I said, a little softer this time.

'There's always something to write. Write some thoughts. I'm sure you've plenty of those.'

I took the book back, making a song and dance about how uninterested I was in it and ranting about how writing diaries was for dorks. But for all my talk, I was surprisingly relieved to have it back in my arms again. It felt right sitting there.

'Write what's up there,' Sister Ignatius pointed at her temple, 'and what's in there,' she pointed at her heart. 'As a great man once called it, "a secret garden." We've all got one of those.'

'Jesus?'

'No, Bruce Springsteen.'

'I found yours today,' I smiled. 'Yours isn't a secret any more, Sister.'

'Ah, there you have it. It's always good to share it with someone.' She pointed at the book. 'Or something.'

CHAPTER NINE

A Long Goodbye

The evening was closing in by the time I made my way back to the gatehouse, with my stomach grumbling, not having eaten since Zoey's Mum had made American pancakes and blueberries for lunch. As before, Rosaleen was standing at her open door looking out, her face furrowed with worry, frantically searching from left to right as though any moment I would emerge. How long had she been doing that?

She jumped to attention when she saw me coming, pushed her hands down near the crotch of her dress to smooth it out. The dress was chocolate brown with a green vine climbing from hem to collar. A humming bird flitted near her boob, and later I noticed another by her left bum cheek. I don't think that was the designer's intention, but her height dictated their ironic placement.

'Well, there you are, child.'

I felt like snapping at her that I wasn't a child

but I gritted my teeth and smiled. I needed to exercise more tolerance with Rosaleen. Tonight, Matthew, I'm Tamara Good.

'Your dinner's keeping warm in the oven. We couldn't wait any longer, I could hear himself's belly talking to me from the ruin.'

Many things annoyed me about that sentence. Firstly, that she hadn't called Arthur by his name; secondly, our discussion was once again revolving about food, and thirdly, she'd referred to the castle as a ruin. Instead of stomping my feet, Tamara Good smiled again and said sweetly, 'Thank you, Rosaleen. I look forward to it in just a few moments.'

I turned to make my way to the stairs but her sudden movement, a jerk of some sort like an athlete at a starting line anticipating the gun, kept me rooted to the spot. I didn't look at her, just waited for her comment.

'Your mother's sleeping so you'll not bother her now.' She'd lost that stammering eager-to-please tone. I couldn't figure her out but probably nor could she me. Tamara Not-So-Good ignored her and I continued to make my way upstairs. I knocked gently on Mum's door while Rosaleen's searing eyes branded me with her stare and, not expecting a response from Mum anyway, I entered.

The room was darker than before. The curtains had been drawn but it was the sun that had slipped into something more comfortable for the evening that made it cooler and dimmer. It was the first time Mum had appeared mummy-like to me for the past month, but it wasn't for her maternal instincts. The yellow blankets were pulled up to her chest, her arms were constricted down by her side under the covers as though a giant spider had rolled her into its web to kill her and eat her. I can only imagine Rosaleen had tucked her in this way; it was physically impossible for Mum to have trapped herself under the blankets so tightly. I loosened the blankets, lifted her arms out by her side and I kneeled down beside her. Her face was peaceful as though she was merely having one of her favourite crème fraiche and yoghurt wrap spa treatments. She was so still I had to move my ear to her face to make sure she was breathing.

I watched her then, her blonde hair around her on the pillow, her long eyelashes closed over her perfect blemish-free skin. Her lips were ever so slightly parted and were breathing soft, sweet, warm breaths.

Perhaps as I've been telling this story, I've been giving the wrong impression of my mother. The grieving widow mindlessly looking out of a window while sitting in a rocking chair in a bell-sleeved nightgown makes her sound so old. She's really not old at all. She's beautiful.

She's only thirty-five, much younger than all my friends' mums. Mum had me when she was eighteen. Dad was older than her, at twenty-eight. Dad loved telling me the story about how they met, though it always differed slightly each time.

I think he enjoyed it, leaving the truth as something Mum and Dad only ever knew. That was a nice thing about Dad, and I never minded if they never told me the whole truth. Perhaps hearing it wouldn't have lived up to all the other stories I'd heard and visualised. The common denominator in all of his stories is that they met at a posh banquet dinner somewhere and when their eyes met he knew he just had to have her. I started laughing and told him it was exactly what he'd said about the filly he'd seen when he came back from the Goffs sale.

He shut up then, lost the smile and the distant look, and momentarily wished he hadn't got a teenage daughter, while Mum seemed to ponder my words in a long silence. I wanted to tell them that I didn't really mean it, that it was just the way I was, awkward, and bitchy remarks dropped from my mouth without intention or preplanning. But I couldn't say that to my parents. I was too proud. I wasn't used to saying sorry. But refusing to take it back wasn't just because I was too proud, it was also because a part of me thought that it could be true. It *is* exactly what Dad had said when he came home from Goffs. It was also exactly what he said when he saw a new watch, or a new boat, or a new suit: 'You should see it, Jennifer. I have to have it.' And when Dad had to have something, he had it. I wondered if Mum was as powerless as the filly in Goffs, as the yacht in Monaco and everything else in the world that Dad had to

126

have. And if so, I don't pity her at all for her weak-mindedness.

I don't doubt that Dad loved Mum. He adored her. He was always looking at her, touching her, he opened doors for her, bought her flowers, shoes, handbags, constant surprises to show her he was thinking of her. He was always complimenting her on the most ridiculous things which annoyed me a lot. He never complimented me on any of those things. And don't go all Sigmund Freud on me, I wasn't jealous – he was my dad, not my husband, and I know the same rules do not apply, nor would I want them to. But. You can't lose a daughter, can you? A child of yours will always be your child, whether you see them or not. A wife, now that can more easily be lost. She can grow bored and wander off. She was so beautiful she could have had most men she met, and Dad knew this. His comments to Mum, meant in the most endearing way, seemed patronising to me.

'Sweetheart, tell them, tell them what you said yesterday when the waiter asked if you'd like dessert. Go on, tell them, sweetheart.'

'Oh, it's not a big deal, George, really.'

'Oh, tell them, Jennifer, sweetheart. It was so funny, really it was.'

And then Mum would tell them, 'I simply said that I'd put on the calories just looking at the dessert menu,' and people would smile and laugh lightly, while Dad's face beamed with pride at the hilarity of his wife, and Mum would smile that

127

mysterious smile that revealed nothing and I would want to stand up and shout, 'But that's fucking ridiculous! That joke is three thousand years old! And it's not even funny!'

I don't know if Mum ever saw it the way I did. She always just smiled and that smile hid a million responses. Maybe that's what made Dad nervous: how much she kept inside. Maybe he never knew how she felt. They weren't like other couples that sometimes rolled their eyes at each other, or picked each other up on comments they'd made to discuss or debate them a little further. They were just both sickeningly agreeable with each other. Mum pan-faced, Dad always complimentary. Or maybe I simply don't understand what was going on between them because I've never been in love. Maybe love is thinking that every time your partner does or says something mundane that you want to start a Mexican wave from here to Uzbekistan in utter delight. I've never had that with anyone.

I always felt Dad and I were total opposites. When he's afraid, or was afraid, of someone leaving, he complimented them on everything. For example, if Mum's friends visited, they usually annoyed him and he'd ignore them the entire time they were there, but then when they were leaving he'd make sure he gave them the warmest hugs, smile and send off possible. Dad was a 'stand at the front door and wave until you can't see the car any more' kind of person. I'd just imagine Mum's friends when they got home: 'George is such a gentleman, when I left he gave me the biggest hug and helped me into my car. I wish you'd behave like that to my friends, Walter.'

Dad was more into last impressions than first ones, which makes his death all the more symbolic. I was the opposite. Just as I'd given Barbara an easy way to leave me by making bitchy remarks to her, I'd done the same to my mum and dad all my life. I make it easier for people to leave by making them momentarily hate me. I didn't realise that other people kept and stored my spoiled behaviour, my sarcastic throw away comments. I'd been doing that since I was a child.

I used to beg Mum and Dad not to go out so much but they'd go out anyway. The only times they stayed in was to recharge their batteries, usually so exhausted and tired of being together they'd separate and spend the evening in different rooms. We never got to spend time with all of us together. I've learned now that what I desired more than some things – but not more than *any*thing – was for us to spend time together, natural and easy time around the house, not pushed together in forced moments when they'd call me into the room to proudly present me with a gift or a surprise announcement.

'Now, Tamara, you know how fortunate you are,' would begin Mum, who has the biggest problem with guilt about having all the things we had. 'There are lots of boys and girls that don't get this opportunity . . .'

And in my head I wouldn't feel the excitement they'd think I'd be feeling, though I'd be trying to show it on my face. All I'd hear was my own voice saying, yada yada yada, get to the point, what are you giving me now?

'But as you've been so good and appreciative of all the lovely things you have, and because you are such a special daughter to us . . .'

Yada yada yada. It's not a gift, I can't see it anywhere in the room. Mum's got no pockets, Dad's hands are in his, so it's not concealed on their bodies. We're going somewhere. Today's Wednesday. Dad goes to the driving range on Thursdays and Mum has her monthly colonic and without that she'd surely blow up, so we're not going anywhere till Friday. It's a weekend thing. So where's close enough to go for a weekend?

'We talked about it for a while and we feel . . .'

Yada yada yada. Perhaps, London for a weekend. But they always go to London and I've been there before, and they seem excited. So it's somewhere we don't often go. Paris. That's close enough. Stuff for them to do; Mum can shop, Dad can follow her around, secretly buying the things for her that she loves but won't get because they're too expensive, and I can do what? What can I do in Paris? Oh, I get it now. Ah. Eurodisney. Cool.

'We'll give you three guesses,' Mum almost squeals with excitement.

'Oh, gee, this is impossible, Mum. How can I

guess?' I'd say, trying to be all confused and flustered and excited, thinking hard. 'Okay,' I'd bite my lip. 'Aunt Rosaleen and Uncle Arthur's for the weekend?' I've learned that if you aim low first then it makes the parents more excited about your imminent shock and awe. I'd guess two more crappy places and watch as Mum would almost explode with excitement. Bless her.

'We're going to Eurodisney, Paris!' Mum would exclaim, hopping up and down, and Dad would dive for the brochure to show me where we're staying. Mum would search my face for the emotion; Dad head down with brochure in hand, would immediately point out the things. Things to do, things to see, things we can get, things that we'll have. Look at this, flick through the pages, look at that. Things, things, things.

No matter how clever and rewarding parents think they are, children are one step ahead.

So to get back to my point, I kicked up an awful lot of fuss one night before they went out. I hurled a lot of abuse at them, not to make them feel guilty but because, back then, I actually meant it. But they went out anyway and because they probably felt so guilty about leaving me I didn't get into any trouble for all the nasty things I'd said. I learned that they were always going to go no matter what I said, and so instead of feeling sad and embarrassed in front of Mae to be left behind at home, I pushed them away. I was in control.

Dad had been acting oddly in the weeks leading

up to his death, maybe longer but I'm not too sure. I didn't speak to anybody about this. I guess this is what diaries are for. I thought that he was going to leave us. I felt there was something peculiar, and I couldn't put my finger on it. He was unusually nice. Like I said, he was always nice to Mum, usually nice to me if I was nice back, but this kind of nice was like a long and drawn-out wave goodbye from the door. A very long and very nice last impression. Long goodbye, very dead. I felt something was coming. Either we were leaving or he was.

Even when lots of people asked about his behaviour after his death, I maintained the same innocent and confused expression as Mum: 'No, no, I didn't notice anything wrong.' Well, what was I going to tell them? For the week before Dad died I felt he was standing at the door waving us off, even long after we were out of view.

I felt something was coming and I did what I always did: I started to push him away. I was bitchier than usual, worse behaved than usual; smoked in the house, came home drunk, that kind of thing. I challenged him a lot more. Our fights were more vicious, my retorts more personal. Horrible stuff. I did what I'd done ever since I was a kid when I didn't want them to go. I basically told him to leave. I hate him that he did what he did, *when* he did it. Any other night and I could have just mourned him. Now I'm mourning him and hating me and it's almost too much for me to bear. Could he not at least have thought about how I'd feel, particularly after our last conversation? I gave him the worst goodbye and he did the worst thing in response. Maybe not because of me but I can't have helped.

I don't know if Mum felt something was wrong with him too. Maybe she did but she has never said. If she didn't sense it, then I was the only one. I should have said something. Better yet, I should have done something to stop him.

I'm sorry, Dad.

What if, what if, what if ... What if we knew what tomorrow would bring? Would we fix it? Could we?

CHAPTER TEN

Stairway to Heaven

I chose to eat breakfast with Mum in her bedroom the next morning. This seemed to concern Rosaleen, who hung around Mum's bedroom a little too long, moving furniture, setting up a table for both of us in front of the window, adjusting the curtains, opening a window, closing it a little, opening it a little more, questioning me on whether it was too breezy.

'Rosaleen, please,' I said gently.

'Yes child,' she said as she continued to make the bed, furiously thumping pillows, tucking in the blankets so tightly, I wouldn't have been surprised if she'd licked the undersheets before turning them over the blanket and sealing them like an envelope.

'You don't have to do that. I'll make it after breakfast,' I said. 'You go downstairs to Arthur. I'm sure he'll want to see you before he goes to work.'

'His lunch is on the counter all ready to go – he knows where it is.' She kept plumping, smoothing, and if it wasn't right she'd start again.

'Rosaleen,' I repeated, gently.

Even though I knew she didn't want to, she quickly glanced at me. When our eyes clicked, she knew her game was up but she just stared at me and in those eyes she dared me to say it. She didn't think I would. I swallowed.

'If you wouldn't mind, I'd just like to spend a little time with Mum. On our own, please.' There I'd said it. Tamara Grown-Up had spoken up for herself. But my request was inevitably followed by the wounded look, the slow release of the pillows falling to the bed, followed by a whispery, 'Well.'

I didn't feel bad.

Finally she left the room and I remained quiet for a while. Not hearing the creak of the landing, I knew she was still outside the door. Listening, guarding, protecting or locking us in – I wasn't sure. What was she so afraid of?

Instead of trying to drag conversation out of Mum as I'd been trying to do for the past month, I decided to stop fighting her silence and instead sit with her patiently in the silence that seemed to comfort her. Occasionally I lifted a slice of fruit to her and she took it and nibbled on it. I watched her face. She looked totally enchanted, as though she was watching a great big screen which I couldn't see, outside in the back garden. Her eyebrows rose and fell as she reacted to something somebody said, her lips smiled coyly as she remembered a secret. Her face hid a million secrets.

Having spent enough time with her, I kissed her on the forehead and left the room. The diary I had been previously hugging proudly was now hidden under my bed. I felt as if I was running off somewhere to hide a big secret. I was also kind of embarrassed, I must admit. My friends and I didn't keep diaries. We didn't even write to each other. We kept in touch through Twitter and Facebook, posting up photos of ourselves whilst on holiday, of our nights out, trying on dresses in department-store changing rooms and looking for second opinions. We texted one another continuously, we emailed gossip and forwarded generic funny emails but it was all on-the-surface stuff. We talked about things you can see, things you can touch, nothing deeper. Nothing emotional.

This diary is the kind of thing Fiona would do – the girl in our class who nobody spoke to apart from Sabrina, the other dork, but she was out of school more than in because of some kind of migraine problem. But this is what she used to do: find a quiet place to go to on her own, a corner of a classroom when the teacher wasn't in, or beneath a tree in the school grounds at lunch time and bury her nose deep in a book or furiously scribble something in a notebook. I used to laugh at her. But the joke was clearly on me. Who knew what she was writing.

There was only one place I could possibly go

to write the diary. I reached for it under my bed and ran down the stairs shouting, 'Rosaleen, I'm going out ...' My flip-flops banged down the creaky stairs, and as I leaped off the final step and landed on the ground with all the grace of an elephant, Rosaleen appeared before me.

'Jesus, Rosaleen!' My hand flew to my heart.

Her eyes moved over me quickly, registered my diary, then went to my face. I wrapped my arms around it protectively, making sure one side of my cardigan covered half the book.

'Where are you going?' she asked quietly.

'Just out ... and about.'

Her eyes flicked down to the diary again. She just couldn't help herself.

'Can I fix you some food to have with you? You'll be starving hungry.'

Starving hungry. Hot sun. Long goodbye. Very dead.

'There's some fresh brown bread and chicken, some potato salad and baby tomatoes ...'

'No, thanks, I'm still full from breakfast.' I made a move to the door again.

'Some sliced fruit maybe?' She raised her voice slightly. 'A ham and cheese sandwich? There's left-over coleslaw from—'

'Rosaleen. No. Thank you.'

'Okay.' More wounded looks. 'Well, be safe now, won't you? Don't go wandering too far. Stay within the grounds. Within eyeshot of the house.'

Within eyeshot of her, more like.

'I'm not going off to war,' I laughed. 'Just . . . around.'

In the closed space of the house, where everyone always knew where everyone else was at any time, I wanted a few hours of my place, my time.

'All right,' she said.

'Don't look so worried.'

'I'm just not sure . . .' She looked down at the floor, unclasped her hands to smooth down her tea-dress. 'Would your mother let you go?'

'Mum? Mum would let me go to the moon, if it kept me from whinging all day.'

I'm not sure if relief was what passed over Rosaleen's face. Just more worry. Suddenly a few chips fell into place for me, and I relaxed a little. Rosaleen wasn't a mother, but all of a sudden, in her quiet house, as my mum had switched to sleep mode, Rosaleen had to do the mothering of both of us.

'Oh, I understand,' I said softly. I reached out a hand and I touched her. Her body tensed so much that I quickly let go. 'You don't have to worry about me. Mum and Dad pretty much let me go wherever I wanted. I used to spend the entire day in town with my friends. I even went to London one day with my friend. We were over and back in a day. Her dad has his own jet. It was totally cool. There were only, like, six seats and it was just for me and Emily – that's the girl whose plane it was. Then for her seventeenth birthday her parents let us all fly to Paris. Her older sister

139

came with us to keep an eye on us, though. She was nineteen, in college and everything.'

She listened intently; far too eagerly, too anxiously, too quickly, far too desperately.

'Oh, isn't that lovely,' she said brightly, her green eyes hungry for all the words that came from my mouth. I could see her gobbling them up as soon as I'd said them. 'Your birthday isn't far off. Is that the kind of thing you'd get for your birthday?' She looked around the hallway of the gatehouse as if she might find a plane in there somewhere. 'Well, we wouldn't be able for the likes of that . . .'

'No, no, that's not what I meant. That's not why I told you the story. It was just . . . it doesn't matter, Rosaleen,' I said quickly. 'I'd better go.' I pushed past her to get to the door. 'Thanks, though,' I said. The last thing I saw before I closed the door was her concerned look, as though she'd said something wrong. Worrying about what their life could and couldn't offer me. Turns out my old life was offering me more than it could, anyway. Like a desperate lover it was offering me the moon and stars when it knew there was no way it could ever deliver. I stupidly believed it. I used to think that it was better to have too much than too little, but now I think if the too much was never supposed to be yours, you should just take what is yours and give the rest back. I'll take Rosaleen and Arthur's simplicity any day. That way, you never have to give back the things you love.

As I was walking down the garden path the

postman came toward me. Excited to see another person, I greeted him with a big smile.

'Hi.' I stopped and blocked him in his path.

'Hello, miss.' He tipped his hat, which I thought was very old-fashioned and kind.

'I'm Tamara.' I held out my hand.

'Nice to meet you, Tamara.' He thought I was holding my hand out for the post and he plonked some envelopes into my palm.

Behind me I heard the door open and Rosaleen came rushing out.

'Morning, Jack,' she called, power-walking down the path. 'I'll take those.' She practically tore them from my grasp. 'Thank you, Jack.' She looked at him sternly while stuffing them into her apron pouch like a mother kangaroo.

'Right so.' He bent his head as though he'd just been told off. 'And for over the road.' He handed her more envelopes, then he turned on his heel, hopped on his bike and cycled off around the corner.

'I wasn't going to eat them,' I said to Rosaleen's back, slightly stunned.

She laughed and went inside the house. Curiouser and curiouser.

There was only one place that I could go to write this diary. Feeling the heat of the road beneath my rubber flip-flops, I made my way toward the castle. I smiled when the trees gave away like a curtain parting for the main act.

'Hello again,' I said.

With great respect I wandered through its rooms. I couldn't believe that a fire had done all of this damage. There was nothing, absolutely nothing to suggest that anybody had lived here for at least a century. No fireplaces left on the walls, no tiles, no wallpaper. Absolutely nothing but bricks, weeds and a staircase that climbed to a second floor that didn't exist, leading up to the skies, as though with one giant leap you could reach a cloud. A stairway to heaven.

I took my place on the bottom steps and set the diary on my lap. I twirled in my hand the heavy pen that I'd stolen from Arthur's writing desk and stared at the closed book, trying to think of what to write. I wanted my first words to mean something, I didn't want to make a mistake. Finally I thought of a beginning and opened the book.

My jaw dropped. The first page had already been written, each line neatly filled . . . in *my* handwriting.

I stood up, alert, rigid, and the diary fell from my lap and down the concrete steps to the floor. I looked around quickly, my heart racing, trying to see if this was somebody's idea of a cruel joke. The crumbling walls stared back at me and suddenly there were movements and noises all around me that I hadn't noticed before. Shrubs and weeds rustled, rocks moved, I heard footsteps from behind and inside the walls, but nothing surfaced or showed itself. It was all my imagination. Perhaps the filled pages of the diary were too.

I took a few deep breaths and retrieved the diary from the ground. The leather, scraped by the stones and rocks, was dusty, and I wiped it against my shorts. The first page had been ripped by the fall but the writing hadn't been my mind playing tricks. It was still there – the first page, second page – and as I furiously flicked through, I could see my handwriting on the used pages.

It was impossible. I compared the date on the top to the date on my watch. It was dated tomorrow, Saturday. Today was Friday. My watch must have been wrong. I immediately thought about Rosaleen, how her eyes had run over the diary that morning. Was it she who had written it? She couldn't have. The diary had been safely stored under my bed. Feeling dizzy, I sat back down on the staircase and read the entry. My eyes jumping over the words manically, I had to go back a few times and start again.

4 July, Saturday

Dear Diary,

Is that what I'm supposed to write? I've never written one of these before, and I feel like an absolute dork, beyond words. Okay so, Dear Diary, I hate my life. Here it is in a nutshell. My dad killed himself, we lost our house and absolutely everything. I lost my life, Mum lost her mind and now we're living in hicksville with two sociopaths. A few days ago I spent the afternoon with a really cute guy called Marcus

who is Vice President of Dork Central, a
travelling library. Two days ago I met a nun who
keeps bees and breaks locks and yesterday I
spent most of the morning sitting in a ~~ruin~~

'Ruin' had been crossed out and beside it was:

castle on a stairway to heaven that looked very
tempting to climb and leap for a cloud that
would carry me away from here. Now it's
night-time and I'm back in my bedroom
writing this dorky diary that Sister Ignatius
talked me into doing. Yes, she's a nun and not
a transvestite, as I'd previously thought.

I sighed and looked up from the page. How could
this be? I searched around me for answers. I
thought about running back to the house to tell
Mum, to tell Rosaleen, to phone Zoey and Laura.
Who on earth would believe me? And even if they
did, what could they do that could help me?

The castle was so still, it seemed like the clouds,
so perfectly round and white like cherubs, were
moving at a hundred miles an hour. There was the
occasional rustle under a weed, dandelion seeds
drifted through the air, taunting me to catch them,
drifting close and then darting away suddenly as
the breeze took them. I took a deep breath, lifted
my face to the hot sun – hot sun. Very dead –
closed my eyes and exhaled slowly. I really loved
spending time in the castle. I opened my eyes and

144

continued reading, the hairs on the back of my neck standing up.

I love spending time in the castle. It should be ugly but it's not. Like Jessie Stevens with his broken nose and cauliflower ears from rugby, he should be ugly, but he's not. I should have done this sooner, this writing lark. I was denied my rant in Zoey's, when she and Laura just wouldn't shut up about the no-knickers story. Anyway.

Mum still hasn't come out of her room. Despite feeling like I wanted to curl up and die – I'm smothered with a cold after yesterday's soaking – I decided to eat breakfast in the back garden beside the tree this morning because I knew that she'd see me. I rolled out the blue cashmere blanket from my room and laid out some sliced fruit. It felt and tasted like cardboard. I wasn't hungry, all of my energy was going into trying to will Mum to come outside. I tried to look so carefree, I lay back on my elbows and crossed my ankles and looked around as though I hadn't a care in the world. It was my attempt to entice her outside but she didn't join me. I just thought that if she got some air, if she took a look around this place, came to this castle, maybe she'd see what I see, that she'd snap out of the trance she's caught in. Of course she doesn't want life to go on while she's sitting up there in that bedroom. It's only when you come outside and realise life is moving on, that you just have to go with the flow.

I don't know why Rosaleen and Arthur aren't doing more to help her. Breakfast, lunch and dinner big enough to feed an elephant aren't going to cure her. Nor is silence. I should bring it up again with Rosaleen. Maybe mention it to Arthur. He's her brother, he should be helping. As far as I can see, apart from the bizarre forehead-touching greeting they had when we arrived, he hasn't said one word to her. How weird is that?

After the rain of yesterday . . .

Okay so that's when I knew it was all ridiculous because it was the most beautiful hot day today. No rain whatsoever. I continued reading with a cocked eyebrow, armed with the knowledge that I was being punked or something, and I waited for Zoey and Ashton Kutcher to jump out from behind the crumbling pillars.

. . . I feel smothered with a cold. Rosaleen practically wrapped me up in cotton wool, stuck me in front of the fire and force-fed me chicken soup. I lost half the day sweating profusely next to that ghastly fire and trying to convince her I wasn't dying. She made me cover my head with a towel and stick my face over a bowl of boiling hot water filled with Vicks to clear my nose, and

while under there snotting myself, I was almost sure I heard the doorbell ring. She assured me it didn't. I should have taken Sister Ignatius up on her offer of drying off in her house. How scary can a house of nuns be?

Tomorrow I plan to avoid another heart attack on a plate and find a quiet place to write this. I'll probably sunbathe in my bikini. Give the pheasants something to look at. It might not be so bad. When you close your eyes you can be just about anywhere you want to be. I can lie by the lake and imagine I'm by the pool in Marbella, that the splashing of the swans as they shake out their feathers is Mum. She always used to lie, not on a sunbed like every-body else, but along the edge of the pool, near the filters. She'd allow her hand to hover over the water, slapping the water lightly. It sounded like toddler's barefeet walking about the place. It was either to keep cool or because she liked the sound. I used to like listening to it. Though for some reason I always told her to shut up. Something to say in the silence, something that would make her open her eyes and look at me.

Who could have known all of that? Only Mum.

Maybe I'll sunbathe right in the path of Arthur's lawnmower on the grass and hope he'll run me over. If it doesn't kill me, the least it could do is save me from a full body wax.

Arthur's not so bad, actually. He doesn't say much. He doesn't even make many reactions, but I get a good feeling from him. Most of the time. Rosaleen's not so bad either. I just have to try to figure her out. She reacted so unusually at dinner today – shepherd's pie, yum – when I told her I'd spent time with Sister Ignatius. She said Sister had called round to her during the morning and mentioned nothing about meeting me. That must have been when I was in the shower. Would love to have been a fly on the wall for that conversation. Then she kept interrogating me on what kinds of things Sister and I talked about. Honestly, it was constant, and even Arthur seemed uncomfortable. I mean, did she think I was lying about it? Really, it was weird. I wish I hadn't told her what I'd learned about the castle. Now I know that whatever information I need to learn, it most certainly can't be from her. I suppose Rosaleen and Arthur are just different. Or maybe it's just me that's different. I never really thought of it that way before. Perhaps it was always just me.

In case I die of dehydration and somebody finds this diary, I should mention that I cry every night. I go through the entire day, save for bluebottle and ruined-castle breakdowns, as strong as can be and then as soon as I crawl into bed and lie in the darkness and stillness, the world only then seems to me to be spinning. Then I cry. Sometimes for such long periods of time my pillow becomes soaked. Rolling down the edges of my eyes, along my ears and tickling down my neck, sometimes down to my vest, I just let the tears go wherever. I'm so used to crying, I don't notice it sometimes. Does that make sense? Before, if I cried it was because I'd fallen and hurt myself, or because I'd had a fight with Dad, or I was totally drunk and the slightest thing made me upset. But now, it's like, whatever ... I'm sad so I'll cry. Sometimes I start and then stop as I convince myself that everything will be fine. Sometimes I don't believe myself and I start again.

I have lots of dreams about Dad. Rarely is he really Dad, but instead a mixture of different people's faces. He starts off as him, then becomes a school teacher, then becomes Zac Efron and then some random person that I saw once before in my life, like the local priest or something. I've heard people say that when they dream about a loved one that has died, they feel that it's real, that the person is really there, sending them a message, giving them a hug. That somehow dreams are a blurred line between here and there, like a meeting room in a prison. You're both in the same room, yet on different sides and really, in different worlds. I used to think that people who talked like that were quacks, or fundamentalist religious freaks. But now I know that that is just one of the many things I was wrong about. It's got nothing to do with religion, it's got nothing to do with mental stability, but it has everything to do with the human mind's natural instinct, which is to hope beyond all hope, unless you're a cynical bastard. It's got to do with love, with losing somebody you love, a part of you being torn away that you'd do almost anything or believe anything to have returned to you. It's hope that someday you'll see them again, that you can still feel them near you. Hope like that, as I thought before, doesn't make you a weak person. It's hopelessness that makes you weak. Hope makes you stronger, because it brings with it a sense of reason. Not a reason for how or why they were taken from you, but a reason for you to live. Because it's a maybe. A 'maybe someday things won't always be this shit.' And that 'maybe' immediately makes the shittiness better.

I thought that we were supposed to become more cynical the older we got. Me? I was born looking warily around the hospital room, from one face to another, and just immediately knowing that this new scenario was shit and that I was better off back inside. I continued life like that. Everywhere I was, was shit, and somewhere else, in the backwards direction, was better. It's only now when the matter-of-factness of life has hit me – very dead, death – that I'm beginning to look outwards. Scientific people think they're looking outwards but they're not.

They think that emotional people only look inwards but they don't. I think the best scientists are the ones that look both ways.

Despite all that I've said, I know that Dad isn't in my dreams. There is no secret message or secret hug. I don't feel him with me here in Kilsaney. They are merely obscure dreams with no meaning or words of advice. Mirrored segments of my day broken up as though a jigsaw, and thrown in the air to hang in my head without order, meaning or sense. Last night I dreamed about Dad, who turned into my English teacher, and then the English teacher was a woman and we all had a free class and I had to sing for everybody, but I opened my mouth and nothing would come out and then the school ended up being in America but nobody spoke English and I couldn't understand anything, and then I lived on a boat. Weird. I woke up when Rosaleen dropped a pot or something downstairs in the kitchen.

Maybe Sister Ignatius was right. Maybe this diary will help me. Sister Ignatius is a funny woman. I haven't been able to stop thinking about her since I met her two days ago.

Yesterday. I'd only met her yesterday.

I like her. The first thing I like about being here – okay the second thing, after the castle – is her. It started lashing rain while I was in the

castle yesterday and I could see Rosaleen
coming down the road towards me with a coat
in her hand, so I feel bad, but I just had to run
in the opposite direction. I didn't want her
knowing that I spent time here; I didn't want
her to think that her guess was right. I didn't
want her knowing anything about me. I had no
idea where I was running to. The rain came
down really, really hard – less of a sun shower
and more of a power shower, and I was soaked
right through to the skin, but it was like I was
on autopilot, my body just switched off and I
ran, and without really concentrating I ended
up at the walled garden. Sister Ignatius was
standing in the greenhouse, waiting for the rain
to stop. She had a spare beekeeping suit for me.
She said she had a feeling I'd be back.

Because I'd interrupted her the day before she
hadn't been able to get back to checking the
hives. She'd other duties to attend to. Praying
and stuff. So she showed me the inside of the
hives yesterday. She drew on the queen bee with
a marker so that I could see which one it was,
she pointed out the drones, the worker bees too,
and then showed me how to use the smoker.
Looking at it made me feel dizzy. Something
weird happened to me. She didn't notice. I had
to put my hand out and hold on to the wall so
I wouldn't crumple to the ground. While I was
feeling like that, she invited me back next week
to help her extract the honey, which she then

*puts in jars and brings to the market. I was so
busy trying to breathe that I just said no. I just
wanted to get away. I wish I'd just told her that
I didn't feel well. She seemed so disappointed
and now I feel really bad. I also need to get to
the market so I can see more people. I'm going
insane here, seeing the same people every day.
Also I want to know if everyone will stare at
Rosaleen and Arthur like they did outside the
pub. They must have done something in the
town to be looked at like that. Organised
swinging parties or something. Gross.*

*I'm sitting with my back against the bedroom
door writing this because I don't want Rosaleen
to walk in. The less she knows about this diary,
the better. Already she is trying to climb inside
my head; I couldn't risk her knowing my
innermost thoughts are lying about my
bedroom. I'll have to hide it. There's an
interesting-looking loose floorboard over by the
corner chair that I might investigate tonight.*

*Once again, Mum zonked out straight after
eating her dinner. She's been sleeping so much
the past two days. But this time she fell asleep
in her chair. I wanted to wake her and put her
in bed but Rosaleen wouldn't let me. I'll write
this until I hear Arthur snoring and then I'll
know it's safe to check on her.*

*While I'm in the safety of the house, I just
want to say that I had a funny feeling while in
the castle yesterday morning. I felt like*

somebody was there. Like somebody was
watching me. It was such a sunny morning,
right up until that freak cloud squeezed itself
right on top of my head, and I was just sitting
on the step, with this diary on my lap, and I
couldn't think of what to write and how to
begin the first page and so I sunbathed instead.
I don't know how long I had my eyes closed
for but I wish I'd kept them open. Someone
was definitely there.

I'll write again tomorrow.

I finished reading and looked around, my heart so
loud in my ears that my breathing was rapid and
sharp. That was now. I'd been writing about me
now.

I suddenly felt a thousand eyes on me. As I stood
up and ran down the steps, tripped on the last one
and slammed into the wall. I grazed my hands and
my right shoulder, dropped the book on the floor
again. I felt around on the ground for it, and as
I grabbed it my hand brushed against something
furry and soft. I yelped and jumped away, ran into
the room next door. There were no doorways out
of there, all four walls were intact. I felt a few
raindrops on my skin and they quickly fell faster.
I went to a hole in the wall where a window used
to be and tried to climb out. Once up on the ledge,
I saw Rosaleen charging her way up the road with
what looked like a raincoat in her hands. She was
power-walking forward, a stormy look on her face,

her hand held above her head as though that alone could stop her from getting wet.

I rushed to the other window, looking out to the back of the castle and I climbed out, my knees scraping against the wall as I leaped up to catch the windowsill. I landed on concrete on the other side, feeling the sting in my feet as the lack of support in my flip-flops sent pain shooting up my legs. I spied Rosaleen coming closer to the castle. I turned away, and ran.

I had no idea where I was going. My body felt like it was on autopilot. It was only when I reached the walled garden, completely soaked to the skin, that I made the connection to the diary and a shudder went through my entire body, summoning goose pimples from head to toe.

As I stood at the garden entrance, frozen with fear and trembling, a white shadow through the frosted glass of the greenhouse caught my attention. Then the door opened and Sister Ignatius appeared with a spare bee suit in her hand.

'I knew you'd come back,' she called, and her blue eyes sparkled mischievously against her pale skin.

CHAPTER ELEVEN

Where There's Smoke

I joined Sister Ignatius in the greenhouse. I stood beside her, my body rigid and tight. My shoulders were hunched up past my ears as though I was trying to disappear into my body like a tortoise. I clung to the diary so tightly my knuckles were white.

'Oh, look at you,' she said, in her joyful, carefree voice. 'You're like a drowned rat. Let me dry you off—'

'Don't touch me,' I said quickly, taking a step away from her. I angled my body away from her but I sneaked a look at her now and then over my shoulder.

'What's happened, Tamara?'

'Don't pretend you don't already know.'

A quick look over my shoulder showed her eyes narrow momentarily, then open wide. She registered something. She knew something. She looked like someone who had been caught.

'Admit it.'

'Tamara,' she began, then paused, searching to find the right words. 'Tamara, look at me. I'm . . . let me explain . . . we should go somewhere else to talk. Not here. Not in this greenhouse. Not with you like this.'

'No. First I want to hear you admit it.'

'Tamara, I really think that we should go inside and—'

'Admit that you wrote it,' I snapped.

Her face instantly changed to utter confusion. 'Tamara, I don't understand. Admit that I wrote what?'

'The diary,' I exploded, and pushed it in her face. I flicked ferociously through the pages. 'Look, it's been written in. I hid it in my bedroom, and this morning I brought it to the castle to write it, just like you told me to, and look. How did you do it?' I shoved it under her nose and flicked through the pages, my wet hands blurring the ink. She blinked furiously to try to focus on the pages as they raced by.

'Tamara, calm down. I can't see anything, you're going too fast.'

I went faster. She reached out and with those thick hands, strangling hands, she grabbed my wrists tightly and said firmly, 'Tamara. Stop.'

It worked. She took the diary from my hands and opened the first page. Her eyes raced across the first few lines.

'This isn't for me to read. These are your private thoughts.'

'I didn't write them.' I knew by then that she hadn't either. The way her face had changed to such confusion couldn't have been faked.

'Well . . . who did?'

'I don't know. Look at the date on the first page.'

'Tomorrow.'

'Some of the things written are about what happens tomorrow.'

The rain pelted against the glass, so loud it felt like it was going to break through.

'How do you know that, if tomorrow hasn't happened yet?' Her voice had softened, as though she was trying to coax a mental patient to put down a knife. She may very well have been, only I didn't pick up the knife, somebody had put it in my hands. This was not of my own doing.

'Perhaps you got up in the middle of the night and wrote it, Tamara. Maybe you were so sleepy you don't remember doing it. I've often done funny things half asleep or half awake. I've wandered around the house looking for things when I don't know what I'm looking for, moving things, and when I wake up in the morning and go to find something, I'm in a right muddle.' She chuckled.

'This isn't the same thing,' I said quietly. 'I've written about things that have happened today that I couldn't have known about. The rain, Rosaleen and the coat, you . . .'

159

'What about me?'

'I wrote that you'd be here.'

'But I'm always here Tamara, you know that.'

Sister Ignatius kept talking then, trying to rationalise it, telling me a story about a time she'd wandered into Sister Mary's room during the night, apparently looking for gardening gloves because she'd been dreaming of planting turnips, and she frightened the life out of Sister Mary. I tuned out. How could I have written five pages and not remembered? How could I have predicted the rain, Rosaleen's arrival with the raincoat, Sister Ignatius waiting right here in the greenhouse with the spare beekeeping suit?

'Our minds do unusual things sometimes, Tamara. When we're looking for things it takes it upon itself to go down its own route. All we can do is follow.'

'But I'm not looking for anything.'

'Aren't you? Ah, now it's stopped. I told you it would. Why don't we get you to the house to dry you off and get something hot into you? I made a soup yesterday with my own grown veg. It will be just right now, I'd say, if Sister Mary hasn't sucked it up with a straw. She dropped her dentures yesterday and Sister Peter Regina accidentally stomped on them. Everything's been through a straw since.' She covered her mouth. 'Oh, forgive me for laughing.'

I was about to protest when I remembered my comments in the diary about being smothered with a cold. Perhaps I could change what was going to happen. I followed her out of the garden and through the trees to her home.

The house was just like Sister Ignatius. It lacked a deceptive brick in its making, as it was as old on the inside as it was on the outside. We entered through the back door, a small hallway filled with Wellington boots, raincoats, umbrellas and sunhats, every necessity for every kind of weather. Uneven, cracked stone flagging floored the walkway to the kitchen. The kitchen was something from the 1970s. Shaker-style cabinets, linoleum flooring, plastic counter tops, avocado and burnt orange in every possible place from an era obsessed with bringing the outside in. There was a long pine table with a bench on either side, long enough to feed the Waltons. From a room off the kitchen a radio blared. Brown swirly carpet led my eyeline to a big television set with a booty that came out thirty inches from the wall. On top, cream lace dangled over the front of the screen and a statue of Mary stood. On the wall above it was a simple wooden cross.

The house smelled old. Musty damp mixed with generations of cooked dinners and greasy cooking oil. Somewhere in there was the scent of Sister Ignatius, a clean talcum powder soapy smell, like a freshly bathed baby. Like Rosaleen and Arthur's house, this had the feel that generations of people had lived there before, families had grown up, run and shouted through the hallways, had broken things, grown things, fallen in love and pulled themselves back out of it again. Instead of the occupants owning the house, the house owned a part of each of them. We never had that feeling in our house. I loved our house but every bit of life was cleaned away by our cleaners who everyday rid the rooms of history's perfume and replaced it instead with bleach. Every three years a room was done up in a new style, old furniture thrown out, new furniture moved in, a painting to match the sofa. There was no eclectic collection of items gathered through the years. No sentimental clutter crammed together oozing secrets. It was all new and expensive, lacked anything of sentiment. Or that's how it had been.

Sister Ignatius hurried off in her beekeeping suit, walking like a toddler with a bulging nappy. I took off my cardigan, lay it across the radiator. My vest was see-through and stuck to me, my flip-flops squelched but I daren't take them off in case dirt from the previous family stuck to my sole. Too much of outside had been brought in on these floors.

Sister Ignatius returned with a towel in her hand and a T-shirt.

'I'm sorry, this is all I could find. We're not in the habit of dressing seventeen-year-olds.'

'Sixteen,' I corrected her, checking out the woman's pink marathon T-shirt.

'I ran it every year from '61 to '71,' she explained, turning to the Aga to prepare the soup. 'Not any more, I'm afraid.'

'Wow, you must have been fit.'

'What do you mean?' She struck a pose in her beekeeping suit and kissed a padded bicep. 'I haven't lost it yet.'

I laughed. I lifted my vest over my head and lay it on the radiator too, then I put the T-shirt on. It went to mid-thigh. I took off my shorts and used the belt to turn the T-shirt into a dress.

'What do you think?' I walked an imaginary runway for Sister Ignatius and posed at the end.

She laughed and wolf-whistled. 'My word, to have a pair of legs like that again,' she tutted and shook her head.

She brought two bowls of soup to the table and I devoured mine.

Outside the sun shone, the birds sang again as though the rain had never fallen, as though it had all been a figment of our imaginations.

'How's your mother?'

'She's fine, thank you.'

Silence. Never lie to a nun.

'She's not fine. She sits in her bedroom all day looking out the window, smiling.'

'She sounds happy.'

'She sounds crazy.'

'What does Rosaleen think?'

'Rosaleen thinks that a lifetime's supply of food in one day will keep anyone going.'

Sister Ignatius' lips twitched at that but she fought her smile.

'Rosaleen says it's just the grief.'

163

'Perhaps Rosaleen is right.'

'What if Mum whipped off her clothes and rolled around in mud singing Enya songs, what then? Would that be the grief?'

Sister Ignatius smiled and her skin folded over like origami. 'Has your mum done that?'

'No. But it doesn't seem far off.'

'What does Arthur think?'

'Does Arthur think?' I responded, slurping the hot soup. 'No, I take that back, Arthur thinks, all right. Arthur thinks but Arthur does not say. I mean, some brother he is. And he either loves Rosaleen so much, nothing she says bothers him, or he can't stand her so much he can't be arsed talking to her. I can't really figure them out.'

Sister Ignatius looked away, uncomfortable.

'Sorry. For the language.'

'I think you're doing Arthur an injustice. He adores Rosaleen. I think he'd do absolutely anything for her.'

'Even marry her?'

She glared at me and I felt the slap from her stare.

'Okay, okay. I'm sorry. It's just that she's so . . . I don't know . . .' I searched for the word, searched for how she made me feel. '*Possessive.*'

'Possessive.' Sister Ignatius pondered that. 'That's an interesting choice of word.'

I felt happy for some reason.

'You know what it means, don't you?'

'Of course. It's as if she owns everything.'

'Hmm.'

'I mean, she's looking after us so well and everything. She feeds us three hundred times a day, in keeping with the dietary requirements of a dinosaur, but I wish she'd just chill out, back off from me a little and let me breathe.'

'Would you like me to have a little word with her, Tamara?'

I panicked. 'No, she'll know I talked to you about her. I haven't even mentioned I've met you. You're my dirty little secret,' I joked.

'Well,' she laughed, her cheeks pinking, 'I've never been *that*.' Once she'd recovered from her embarrassment she assured me she wouldn't let Rosaleen know that I'd spoken about her. We talked more about the diary, about how and why it was happening and she assured me that I shouldn't worry, my mind was under a lot of pressure and she was sure I must have written it sleepily, and forgotten. I instantly felt better after our chat, though was more concerned about my sleeping habits by the end of it. If I could write a diary in my sleep, what else was I capable of? Sister Ignatius had the power to make me feel that everything obscure was normal, like everything was divine and wonderous, and nothing worth stressing myself about, that answers would come and the clouds would clear and the complicated would become simple and the bizarre would become ordinary. I believed her.

'My, look at that weather now.' She turned to

gaze out the window. 'The sun is back. We should go quickly and see to the bees.'

Back outside in the walled garden I was suited up and feeling like the Michelin man.

'Do you keep bees for extra time off?' I asked as we made our way with the equipment to a hive. 'I do that at school. If you sing in the choir you sometimes get classes off to take part in competitions or at church, things like when the teachers get married. If I was a teacher and I got married, I wouldn't want some snotty little bitches who give me hell all day to sing at the happiest day of my life. I'd go to St Kitts or Mauritius. Or Amsterdam. It's legal for a sixteen-year-old to drink there. But only beer. I hate beer. But if it's legal I wouldn't say no. Not that I'd be getting married at sixteen. Is that even legal? You should know, you know your man.' I jerked my head towards the sky.

'So you sing in a choir?' she asked, as though she hadn't heard a word of anything else I'd said.

'Yeah, but never outside school. I've never been there to compete. The first time we were skiing in Verbier, and the second time I had laryngitis.' I winked. 'My mum's friend's husband is a doctor so he used to give notes whenever. I think he fancied my mum. You wouldn't catch me dead at one of those competitions, though apparently our school is actually really good at the choir competitions. We won the All-Ireland under somethings, twice.'

'Oh, what kinds of things do you sing? "Nessun Dorma" was always my favourite.'

'Who's that by?'

'"Nessun Dorma?"' She looked at me, shocked. 'Well it's one of the finest tenor arias from the final act of Puccini's opera *Turandot*.' She closed her eyes, hummed a bit and swayed. 'Oh, I love it. Famously sang by Pavarotti, of course.'

'Oh, yeah, he's the big dude who sang with Bono. I always thought he was a celebrity chef, for some reason, until I saw him on the news the day of his funeral. I must have been confusing him with someone else – you know, the guy who makes pizzas with weird toppings, on The Food Channel. Chocolate and stuff? I asked Mae to make me one once but it totally made me retch. No, we didn't sing anything like his songs. We sang "Shut Up and Let Me Go" by the Ting Tings. But it sounded completely different with all the harmonies, really serious, like one of those operas.'

'The Food Channel, now I don't have that at all.'

'I know it's a part of the satellite stations. Neither do Rosaleen and Arthur. You probably wouldn't like it, but there is The God Channel. There's probably stuff on that you'd like. They just talk about God all day.'

Sister Ignatius smiled at me again, wrapped her arm around my shoulders, squeezed me close to her and we walked like that towards the garden.

'Now let's get down to bizzz-ness,' she said as

we reached the hives. 'So, very important. First question, and I probably should have asked you this earlier, are you allergic to bees?'

'I have no idea.'

'Have you ever been stung by a bee?'

'No.'

'Hmm. Okay. Well, irrespective of all the protective measures, you may receive the occasional sting. Oh, don't look at me like that, Tamara. Okay then, off you go to Rosaleen. I'm sure she's got the lovely hind legs of a cow for you to snack on while you wait for your dinner.'

I was silent.

'You will not die from this sting,' she continued. 'Unless you're allergic, of course, but that's a risk I'm willing to take. I'm brave like that.' Her eyes twinkled mischievously again. 'There'll be a slight swelling in the affected area, later followed by some itching.'

'Like a mosquito.'

'Exactly. Now this is a smoker. I'm going to blow smoke into the hive before inspecting it.'

Smoke began to exit through the nozzle. I was already feeling a little funny as everything I read from the diary early that morning was coming true, playing out before me like a script. She held the nozzle under the hive.

'If a beehive is threatened, guard bees will release a volatile pheromone substance called isopentyl acetate, known as an alarm odour. This alerts the middle-aged bees in the hive, which are the ones with the most venom, to defend the hive by attacking the intruder. However, when smoke is blown in first, the guard bees instinctively gorge themselves on honey, a survival instinct in case they must vacate the hive and recreate it elsewhere. This gorging pacifies the bees.'

I watched the smoke drift into their home. Then suddenly I thought about the panic. A wave of dizziness came over me. I reached out to hold on to the wall.

'I'm going to extract the honey next week. That suit is yours if you want to join me. It'll be nice to have a bit of company. The sisters aren't inter- ested in beekeeping. I like to be alone sometimes but, you know, it's nice to have company once in a while.'

My head swirled as I imagined the smoke in the hive, the bees gorging themselves on food, the sheer and utter panic of it all. I wanted to snap at her and tell her to stop talking, that I had no interest in extracting honey with her, but I heard the tone in her voice, the excitement, the delight over company, and I remembered the wish I'd made in my diary about wanting to take back my response. I held my tongue and nodded, feeling faint. All that smoke.

'Or at least it's nice to have somebody there who pretends they're enjoying it. I'm old. I don't care much any more. But that's great that you've volunteered. I think Wednesday will be a good day to do it. I'll have to check the weather forecast and make sure it's a good day. Don't want us getting soaked again like today . . .' On and on she went until I felt her staring at me. She couldn't see my face nor I hers underneath the netting of our headgear.

'What's wrong dear?'

'Nothing.'

'Nothing is ever nothing. It's always something. Is the diary worrying you?'

'Well, yeah, of course. That is . . . but it's not that. It's nothing.'

We were silent for a while and then as if to prove her point, I asked, 'Was there anyone in the castle when it went on fire?'

She paused before answering, 'Yes, unfortunately there was.'

'Just watching that . . . that smoke going in. I can imagine the panic and the people being so afraid.' I held on to the wall again.

Sister Ignatius looked at me with concern.

'Did anyone die?'

'Yes. Yes, indeed. Tamara, when the fire ravaged that home, it ravaged so many people's lives, you have no idea.'

That home. Home. It made it all the more mysterious that a building such as that could be called such a thing. It had meant something to people once upon a time, whoever they were.

'Where do they live now? The people who survived.'

'You know, Tamara, Rosaleen and Arthur have

been here for so much longer than I – you should really ask them that. Ask me a question and I'll never lie, you understand? But this one you should ask them. Won't you?'

I shrugged.

'Do you understand me?' She reached out and gripped my forearm. I felt her strength through my gauntlet. 'I'll never lie.'

'Yes, yes, I understand.'

'You'll ask them, won't you?'

I shrugged. 'Whatever.'

'Whatever, whatever, the language of sloths. Now, I'm going to lift this off, and I'll show you the inhabitants of the honeycomb empire.'

'Whoa. How did you get them all in there?'

'Ah that was the easy part. Like all of us, Tamara, a swarm is always actively looking for a home. Now, do you know how I'm going to show you the queen bee?'

'You're going to draw on it with a marker.'

'However did you know that?'

'Apparently I wrote it in my diary when I was sleepwalking. Lucky guess, huh?'

'Hmm.'

When I got back to the house, it was late. I'd spent the entire day out. Arthur was returning from work too, walking down the road in his lumberjack shirt. I stopped and waited for him.

'Hi Arthur.'

He threw his head back at me.

'Good day?'

'Ah.'

'Good. Arthur, could I have a word with you before we go inside, please?'

He stopped. 'Is everything all right?' Concern that I hadn't seen before crossed his face.

'Yes. Well, no. It's about Mum—'

'Well, there you are,' Rosaleen called from the front door. 'You both must be starved. I've the dinner just out of the oven, piping hot and ready to go.'

I looked at Arthur, and he looked back at Rosaleen. There was an awkward moment as Rosaleen refused to leave us. Arthur gave in and walked up the garden path and into the house. Rosaleen stepped aside for him to enter and then back to where she was to look at me, then went inside to see to the dinner. Once we were all seated at the table Rosaleen prepared Mum's food ready on a tray to bring upstairs. I took a deep breath.

'Shouldn't we try and get Mum to eat downstairs with us?'

There was a silence. Arthur looked at Rosaleen.

'No, child. She needs her peace.'

I'm not a child. I'm not a child. I'm not a child.

'She has plenty of peace all day. It would be a good idea for her to see people.'

'I'm sure she'd rather have her own space.'

'What makes you think that?'

Rosaleen ignored me and carried the tray upstairs. For one minute Arthur and I would be alone. As if reading my thoughts she came back to the kitchen. She looked at Arthur.

'Arthur, would you mind getting a bottle of water from the garage. Tamara doesn't like the tap.'

'Oh, no, I don't mind. I'd rather drink from the tap,' I said quickly, stopping Arthur from getting to his feet.

'No, it's no bother. Go on, Arthur.'

He stood again.

'I don't want it,' I said firmly.

'If she doesn't want it, Rosaleen . . .' Arthur said so quietly I could barely make out his words.

She looked from him to me and then legged it up the stairs. I had a feeling it would be her fastest trip ever.

Arthur and I sat in an initial silence. I spoke quickly.

'Arthur, we have to do something about Mum. It's not normal.'

'None of what she's been through is normal. I'm sure she'd rather eat alone.'

'What?' I threw my hands up. 'What is it with you two? Why are you so obsessed with locking her away on her own?'

'Nobody wants to lock her away.'

'Why don't you go talk to her?'

'Me?'

'Yes, you. You're her brother, I'm sure there's stuff that you can talk about that will bring her back to us.'

He covered his mouth with his hand, looked away from me.

'Arthur, you have to talk to her. She needs her family.'

'Tamara, stop it,' he hissed, and I was taken aback.

He looked hurt for a moment. A deep sadness flicked through his eyes. Then, as though he'd built up some sort of courage, he quickly looked to the door of the kitchen and then back to me. He leaned in towards me, opened his mouth, his voice was hushed. 'Tamara, listen—'

'Now, there we are. She's in great form.' Rosaleen said, out of breath, rushing back in with her little-boy walk. Arthur studied her all the way in and to her seat.

'What?' I asked Arthur, on the edge of my seat. What was he about to tell me?

Rosaleen's head turned like an antenna finding a signal.

'What's that you're talking about?'

For once it seemed Arthur's snot-snort came in handy. It was enough of a response for Rosaleen.

'Dig in,' she said perkily, fussing about with serving spoons and bowls of vegetables.

It took Arthur a while to begin. He didn't eat much.

That night I sat staring at the diary for hours. I kept it open on my lap, waiting for the moment the words would arrive. I couldn't even last until midnight because when I woke up at one a.m., the diary was still open on my lap, every single line filled in my handwriting. Gone was yesterday's

174

forecast and instead was another entry, a different entry for tomorrow.

Sunday, 5 July
   I shouldn't have told Weseley about Dad.

I read that sentence a few more times. Who on earth was Weseley?

CHAPTER TWELVE

The Writing on the Wall

I suppose it was inevitable I would dream the dream I dreamed that night.

As I lay in bed caught in the irony of forcing myself to drift away, my mind went over and over the diary entry I had read in the castle before it had cleared and made way for the next one. Thankfully, I had read it so many times before the words disappeared and were replaced by a new entry that I knew almost every line off by heart. Everything that I'd read had come true that day. I wondered if tomorrow would yield the same supernatural results, if it would all somehow be revealed as somebody's cruel idea of a joke, or if Sister Ignatius was right and the late-night scribbles of a sleep-walker would reveal themselves to be mere inconsequential babble.

I had heard about things people did when they were asleep. Sleep epilepsy, carrying out weird sexual acts, cleaning or even homicidal somnambulism, which is sleepwalking murder. There were a few famous cases where people committed murders and claimed to be sleepwalking. Two of the murderers were acquitted and ordered to sleep alone with their doors locked. I don't know if that was one of the documentaries Mae watched or if it was an episode of *Perry Mason* called 'The Case of the Sleepwalker's Niece' that educated me on that. Anyway, if all of those things were possible, then I supposed it was also possible that I could have written my diary in my sleep and, while I was writing it, predicted the future.

I believed more in the homicidal somnambulism defence.

Knowing the dream that I was going to have – well, according to the Tamara of Tomorrow – my mind tried to think of ways to change the dream, of ways to stop Dad from becoming my English teacher and keep him around so that we could actually talk. I tried to think of a special code that only he would understand, which I could say to him and somehow summon him from the dead to communicate with me. I obsessed about it all so much, I inevitably dreamed about exactly what I'd written: about my dad, whose face morphed into that of my English teacher, and then my school moved to America but I couldn't speak the language, then we lived on a boat. The only difference was that I was being repeatedly asked to sing by the students, some of whom were the cast of *High School Musical*, and when I tried to open my mouth no sound would come out because of the laryngitis. Nobody would believe me because I'd lied about it before.

The other difference, which felt far more disturbing, was that the boat that I lived on, the wooden Noah's Ark style boat, was crammed full of people like millions of bees in a hive. Smoke kept drifting through the halls but nobody noticed except for me, and they kept on eating, stuffing their mouths over and over with food while seated at long banquet tables, which then felt like a *Harry Potter* film, and all the while the smoke filled the rooms. I was the only one who could see it, but nobody could hear me because the laryngitis had taken away my voice. Boy and Wolf come to mind.

You could say that the diary was right, or a more cynical mind would suggest that because I'd allowed my mind to obsess over the details of the already documented dream, I inevitably forced myself to dream the dream. But I did, as forecast, wake to the sound of Rosaleen dropping a pot on the floor with a yelp.

I threw the covers off and fell to the floor on my knees. Last night I had taken my own fore-casting voice's advice by hiding the diary under the floorboard. If Tamara of Tomorrow felt it was important then I was going to follow her advice. Who knew why she – or I – was going to such great lengths to hide silly hormonal thoughts? Maybe Rosaleen had gone snooping and she, or I, hadn't written about it. The last few nights I'd taken to blocking the bedroom door with the wooden chair. It wouldn't keep Rosaleen out but it would at least alert me to her presence. She hadn't watched me sleep since the first night. As far as I knew.

I was sitting on the floor beside the bedroom door rereading last night's entry again when I heard steps on the stairs. I looked through the keyhole and saw Rosaleen leading Mum back up the stairs. I almost jumped up and did a song and a dance when, after Mum's door closed, Rosaleen knocked at mine.

'Morning, Tamara. Is everything all right?' she called from outside.

'Eh, yes, thank you, Rosaleen. Did something happen downstairs?'

'No, nothing. I just dropped a pot.'

The doorknob began to turn.

'Em, don't come in! I'm naked!' I dived and pushed it closed.

'Oh, okay . . .' Talk of bodies, particularly naked ones, embarrassed her. 'Breakfast will be ready in ten minutes.'

'Fine,' I said quietly, wondering why on earth she had lied. Mum going downstairs was *huge*. Not to any normal family but to mine at present it was right up there.

That's when it struck me how important each line in the diary was. Each was that trail of bread-crumbs I longed to drop from my old home to here. Each word was a clue, a revelation, of something that was happening right under my nose. When I'd written that I'd woken to Rosaleen dropping a pot and yelping I should have read into it more. I should have realised that she would never normally do such a thing, that something must have happened to make her drop the pot. Why would she have lied about Mum going downstairs? To protect me? To protect herself?

I settled back down on the floor, my back to the door, and read the entry I'd discovered last night.

Sunday, 5 July
I shouldn't have told Weseley about Dad. I hate the way he looked at me, with such pity. If he didn't like me, he didn't like me. A dad who'd committed suicide wasn't going to make me any nicer – though seemingly that was the case – but how was he to know that? It's probably really hypocritical for all this to come from me but I don't want people's opinions of me to change just because of what Dad did. I always thought I'd want the opposite, to really milk the sympathy, you know. I'd have everybody's attention, I could be all I wanted to be.

I thought I'd love it. Aside from the first month, immediately after Dad's death – I found him, so there were a lot of questions, cups of tea and nice pats on the back, all while I blubbered over my statements to the gardaí; and, of course, at Barbara's mews where Lulu was assigned to tend to our every whim, which for me was mostly hot chocolate with extra marshmallows on an hourly basis – I haven't been getting any special attention. Unless this is special attention from Arthur and Rosaleen, and next month I become the cinder girl.

I really couldn't stand this new girl, Susie, in my class but then I found out her brother played rugby for Leinster and all of a sudden I was next to her in every maths class and I stayed in her house every weekend for a month, until her brother was suspended from the team after being arrested for jumping on and crushing someone's car, after one too many vodka and Red Bulls. The tabloids tore him to shreds and he lost his sponsorship for the contact lense company. Nobody wanted anything to do with him for about a week. And then I was gone.

I can't believe I wrote that. Cringe.

Anyway, Weseley totally changed when I told him Dad killed himself. I should have said something else, like he died in war or – I don't know – just something else like a more common kind of death. Would it be too weird if I said, 'By the way, about the suicide thing? I was just joking. He really died of a heart attack. Ha ha ha.'

No. Maybe not.

Who the hell was Weseley? I looked at the date. Tomorrow, again. So between now and tomorrow evening I'd meet a Weseley. Absolutely impossible. Was he going to climb up the wall of Fort Rosaleen to say hello to me?

After having the weirdest dreams last night, I woke up feeling more tired than before I went to bed. After zilch sleep all I wanted to do was lie in bed all morning – actually, all day. This wasn't going to happen. The talking clock rapped on my door once before entering.

'Tamara, it's nine thirty. We're off to ten o'clock mass and then the market for a short while.'

It took me a while to figure out what she was saying but eventually I mumbled something about not being a mass person and waited for a bucket of holy water to come pouring down on me. But there was no reaction of the sort. She gave my room a quick look to make sure I hadn't spread feces all over the walls overnight and then said it was fine if I stayed home and kept an eye on Mum.

Hallelujah.

I heard the car leave the drive, imagined her in a twinset with a brooch and a hat with flowers, even though I'd seen she wasn't wearing one. I imagined Arthur in a top hat driving a convertible Cadillac and the whole world sepia-coloured outside as they went off to

Sunday mass. I was so happy they'd allowed me to stay, I didn't think that perhaps she didn't want to be seen with me at mass or at the market, until later on when the hurt, though minute, set in. I drifted off again but awoke I don't know how much later to the sound of a car horn. I ignored it and tried to sleep again but it honked louder and longer. I scrambled out of bed, and pushed open the window, ready to shout abuse but instead started laughing when I saw Sister Ignatius squashed into a yellow Fiat Cinquecento with three other nuns. She was in the back seat, the window was rolled down and half her body was through the gap as though she'd suddenly spurted towards the sun.

'Romeo,' I called, pushing open the window.

'You look like you've been dragged through a hedge backwards.' And then she tried to make me go to mass with her. Her efforts were in vain. Then one of the other sisters tried to pull her back into the car. She folded herself back into the car and immediately it took off, not slowing or indicating as they rounded the corner. I saw a hand wave as they roared away and heard, 'Thanks for the boooook!' as they flew round the corner.

I dozed for another few hours, enjoying the space and the freedom to be lazy without clanging pots hinting at me from the kitchen or a vacuum cleaner hitting against my bedroom door as Rosaleen hoovered the landing carpet. For the moments I was awake I pondered what Rosaleen had said the night before. About calling Mum a liar. Had they fought? Had Arthur and Mum fought? She seemed perfectly happy to greet him when we arrived, though. What had changed, if anything had at all? I needed to find time alone with Arthur to really talk to him.

I checked on Mum, who at eleven a.m. was still sleeping, which was unusual for her, but a hand under her nose proved to me she was still alive and there was a picked-at breakfast tray beside the bed, which Rosaleen had left for her. I nibbled at some fruit from the kitchen, wandered around the house, picking up things, studying the few photographs dotted around the living room. Arthur with a giant fish, Rosaleen wearing pastels and holding on to her hat, while laughing, on a windy day. Then Rosaleen and Arthur together, always side by side, never touching, like they were both children forced to stand beside one another and pose for a photograph on their communion day; hands by their sides, or clasped on their fronts, like butter wouldn't melt.

I sat in the living room and continued to read the book Fiona had given me. At one o'clock on the button, when Arthur and Rosaleen's car returned to the house, a sense of heaviness came over me. My space was gone,

*rooms would be shared again, games would be
played, mysteries would continue.*

What on earth had I been thinking?

*I should have explored. I should have
broken into the shed and seen how much space
they really had. I think Rosaleen is lying about
that. I should have called a doctor and had
Mum looked at. I should have investigated
across the road, or at least peeked in the back
garden. I should have done lots of things, but
instead I had sat in the house and moped. And
it would be another week until I'd have that
time again.*

What a wasted day.

*Note to self: don't be an idiot in future, and
leave the window open.*

I'll write again tomorrow.

I put the diary back into the floor and replaced
the board. I took a fresh towel from the cupboard
and my good shampoo which was almost empty
and irreplaceable due both to convenience and,
for the first time in my life, cost. I was about to
get into the shower when I remembered the
mention of Sister Ignatius' visit this morning. It
would be the perfect opportunity to test the diary.
I kept the shower running and waited on the
landing.

The doorbell rang and that simple thing spooked
me.

Rosaleen opened the door and before she even

spoke I could tell from the atmosphere it was Sister Ignatius at the door.

'Sister, morning to you.'

I peeked round the corner and saw Rosaleen's back and backside only. Today's tea dress was sponsored by Fyffes. Clumps of bananas decorated her dress. The rest of her was squeezed out of the small slit she'd made in the opened door, almost as if she didn't want Sister Ignatius to see past her. And had it not started to rain at that very moment I don't think Sister would have found herself any closer to me than on the porch. They both stood in the hallway then and Sister Ignatius looked around. We caught eyes, I smiled and then hid again.

'Come in, come in to the kitchen,' Rosaleen said with urgency as though the hallway ceiling was about to cave in.

'No, I'm fine here. I won't stay too long.' Sister Ignatius stayed where she was. 'I just wanted to come over and see how you are. I haven't seen sight nor heard from you for the past few weeks.'

'Oh, yes, well, I'm sorry about that. Arthur's been terribly busy working on the lake and I've been . . . keeping things together here. You'll come to the kitchen won't you?' She kept her voice down as though a baby was sleeping.

You've been hiding a mother and her child, Rosaleen, cough it up now.

From Mum's bedroom, I heard her chair drag across the floor.

Sister Ignatius looked up. 'What's that?'

'Nothing. You must be getting ready for honey season now, I suppose. Come to the kitchen, come, come.'

She tried to take Sister Ignatius by the arm and lead her away from the hallway.

'I'll be extracting the honey on Wednesday if the weather holds up.'

'Please God, it does.'

'How many jars would you like me to drop by?'

Something dropped in Mum's room.

Sister Ignatius stopped walking. Rosaleen pulled her along and kept talking, boring small talk. Natter natter natter. So and so died. So and so was taken ill. Mavis from down the town was hit by a car in Dublin after being out to buy a top for her nephew John's thirtieth. She died. She bought the top and all. Very sad as her brother had died the previous year of bowel cancer, now there's no one left in the family. Her father is alone and had to move to a nursing home. He's taken ill over the past few weeks. Eyesight is in great decline and didn't he used to be an excellent darts player. And the thirtieth party was a very sad one as they were all devastated about Mavis. Blather blather blather about crap. Not once were Mum and I discussed. The elephant in the room again.

After Sister Ignatius had left, Rosaleen momentarily leaned her forehead against the door and sighed. Then she straightened up and twirled around to look up on the landing. I moved quickly.

When I ducked my head round the corner I saw that Rosaleen's bedroom was ajar. A shadow flickered by.

I couldn't stand to sit with Rosaleen and Arthur for breakfast. I'd have rather been anywhere but in that kitchen with the smell of a fry making me feel sick. But of course I knew what I'd do next. I went to Mum's room.

'Mum, come outside with me, please.' I picked up her hand and gently tugged her.

She was still as a rock.

'Mum, please. Come out to the fresh air. We can walk around the trees and the lakes, we can see the swans. I bet you've never even walked around these grounds before. Come on. There's a beautiful castle and lots of lovely walks. There's even a walled garden.'

She looked right at me then. I could see her pupils dilate as she focused on me. She said, 'Secret garden,' and she smiled.

'Yes, Mum. Have you been there?'

'Roses.'

'Yes, there's lots of roses.'

'Mmm. Pretty,' she said softly, then as though she'd suddenly become from the North of England and dropped a few words, she said, 'Prettier than rose.' She said this looking out the window and then she looked at me and used her forefinger to trace the outline of my face. 'Prettier than rose.'

I smiled. 'Thanks, Mum.'

'She's walked around here before, hasn't she?'

I exploded into the kitchen, full of energy, which startled Rosaleen.

She raised her finger to her lips. Arthur was on the phone, an old-fashioned thing that was stuck to the wall.

'Rosaleen,' I whispered, 'she talked.'

She stopped rolling out dough and turned to me. 'What did she say?'

'She said that the walled garden was a secret garden and that I was as pretty as a rose,' I beamed. 'Or prettier, actually.'

Rosaleen's face hardened. 'That's nice, dear.'

'That's nice? That's fucking nice?' I exploded.

Rosaleen and Arthur both shushed me.

'Yes. That's Tamara,' Arthur said.

'Who's on the phone?'

'Barbara,' Rosaleen said, strands coming loose around the front of her pinned-back hair and really starting to sweat as she now put some elbow grease into rolling the dough.

'Can I talk to her?' I asked.

He nodded. 'All right. All right. We'll come to some sort of arrangement. Yes. All right. Indeed. All right. Bye.'

He hung up.

'I said I wanted to talk to her.'

'Oh, well, she said she had to go.'

'She's probably sleeping with the pool boy. Busy, busy,' I said cattily. I've no idea where that came from. 'So what did she call about?'

Arthur looked at Rosaleen. 'Well, unfortunately

they're having to sell the place where all your things were being stored and so they can't keep them any more.'

'Well, there's no space here,' Rosaleen said immediately, turning back to the counter and tossing flour on the worktop.

This was familiar to me.

'What about the garage?' I asked, the diary now making sense.

'There's no space.'

'We'll find space,' Arthur said to me, pleasantly.

'We won't because there is none.' Rosaleen picked up the next dough ball and threw it down on the counter, and started pushing her hands into it, squeezing it, punching it, making some sort of shape.

'There's room in the garage,' Arthur said.

Rosaleen stalled but didn't turn around. 'There's not.'

I looked from one to the other, initially intrigued by this, for once, public disagreement.

'Why, what's in there?' I asked.

Rosaleen kept rolling.

'We'll have to make room, Rosaleen,' Arthur was saying, really firmly now, and just as she was about to interject he raised his voice: 'There's nowhere else.'

That was final.

I had a horrible feeling then that the conversation about me and Mum moving in with them wouldn't have gone too differently.

They didn't object when I brought the blanket outside to the garden with a plate of fruit and sat under the tree. The sun shower had left the grass wet but I wasn't planning on moving. The air was fresh and the sun was fighting its way back out again. From my place on the grass I could see Mum sitting at the window gazing outside. I willed her to come out, for the sake of my own sanity as well as hers. Not surprisingly, she didn't join me.

Rosaleen busied herself about the kitchen. Arthur was sitting at the table listening to the radio at full blast and flicking through the paper. I watched Rosaleen leave the kitchen with the tray and a minute later she appeared in Mum's bedroom. I watched her do her usual fussing about. Window, table, linen, cutlery.

After Rosaleen had placed the tray down on the table she stood straight and looked at Mum. I sat up. It was unusual, whatever she was doing. Then her mouth opened and closed, as she said something.

Mum looked up at her, said something, then looked away.

I stood up automatically, watching them both.

I ran inside, almost knocking Arthur over, and charged up the stairs. I pushed open Mum's door and I heard a yelp and a smash as it smacked against Rosaleen and her tray. Everything dropped to the floor.

'Oh, my!' Rosaleen hunkered down and grabbed everything in a panic. Her dress lifted up her thigh and she had surprisingly youthful legs. Mum had twisted around in her chair to see, looked at me, smiled and then faced the window again. I tried to help Rosaleen but she wouldn't let me, swatting me away and racing to pick up every item I reached for time and time again. I followed her down the stairs, like a puppy, almost nipping at her heels.

'What did she say?' I tried to keep my voice down so Mum wouldn't hear us talking about her.

Rosaleen, still in shock from my attack was trembling and a little pale. She wobbled her way into the kitchen with the big tray.

'Well?' I asked, following her.

'Well, what?'

'What was that noise?' Arthur asked.

'What did she say?' I asked.

Rosaleen looked from Arthur to me, her eyes wide and bright green, her pupils so tiny her green eyes glowed.

'The tray dropped,' she said to Arthur and then to me, 'Nothing.'

'Why are you lying?'

Her face transformed. Morphed into something so angry, I wanted to take it all back straightaway: it was my imagination, I had made it up, I was looking for attention . . . I don't know. I was confused.

'I'm sorry,' I stuttered. 'I didn't mean to accuse you of lying. It just looked like she said something. That's all.'

'She said, thank you. I said she was welcome.'

I forced myself to remember Mum's lips. 'She said sorry,' I blurted out.

Rosaleen froze. Arthur lifted his head from the newspaper.

'She said sorry, didn't she?' I asked, looking from one to the other. 'Why did she say that?'

'I don't know,' she said quietly.

'You must know, Arthur.' I looked at him. 'Does that mean anything to you? Why would she say sorry?'

'I suppose she just feels she's being a nuisance,' Rosaleen jumped in and spoke for him. 'But she's not. I don't mind cooking for her. It's no bother.'

'Oh.'

Arthur clearly couldn't wait to leave and as soon as he'd gone, the day returned to what it always was.

I wanted to have a look around the garage when Rosaleen was gone and I learned the best thing to do was to pretend you didn't want her to go. That way, she was never suspicious.

'Can I bring something over with you to the bungalow?'

'No,' she said, agitated, still annoyed with me.

'Oh, okay, but thank you very much for offering, Tamara.' I rolled my eyes.

She took out the freshly baked brown bread, the fresh apple pie. A casserole dish of something else and a few Tupperware boxes. Enough for a week's dinner.

'Well, who lives there?'

No answer.

'Come on, Rosaleen. I don't know what happened to you in your last life but I'm not the Gestapo. I'm sixteen years old and I only want to know because there's absolutely nothing for me to do. Perhaps there's somebody over there who I could talk to that's not nearing death.'

'My mother,' she said finally.

I waited for the rest of the sentence. My mother told me to mind my own business. My mother told me to always wear tea dresses. My mother told me never to reveal her apple pie recipe. My mother told me to never enjoy sex. But nothing else came. Her mother. Her mother lived across the road.

'Why have you never mentioned it?'

She looked a little embarrassed. 'Oh, you know . . .'

'No. Is she embarrassing? Sometimes my parents were embarrassing.'

'No, she's . . . she's old.'

'Old people are cute. Can I meet her?'

'No, Tamara. Not yet, anyway,' she softened. 'Her health isn't the best. She can't move around. She's not good with new people. It makes her anxious.'

'So that's why you're always back and forth. Poor you always having to look after everybody else.'

She seemed touched by that.

'I'm all she has. I have to take care of her.'

195

'Are you sure I can't help you? I won't talk to her or anything.'

'No, thank you, Tamara. Thank you for asking.'

'So did she move closer to you so you could take care of her?'

'No.' She spooned chicken and tomato sauce into a casserole dish.

'Did you move closer to her so that you could take care of her?'

'No.' She put two boil-in-the-bag rice sachets into another Tupperware box. 'She's always lived there.'

I thought about that for a minute while watching her.

'Hold on, so that's where you grew up?'

'Yes,' she said simply, placing everything on a tray. 'That's the house I grew up in.'

'Well, you didn't move far away, did you? So did you and Arthur move in here after you were married?'

'Yes, Tamara. Now that's enough questions. You know curiosity killed the cat.' She smiled briefly before leaving the kitchen.

'Boredom killed the fucking cat,' I shouted at the closed door.

I sloped into the living room as I had done every morning and watched her scurry across the road, like a little paranoid hamster anxious for a hawk to swoop down and grab her.

She dropped a dishtowel and I waited for her to stop and pick it up. But she didn't. She didn't appear to notice. I quickly went outside and down the garden path, stalling at the gate like an obedient child as I waited for her to come running back out.

I bravely stepped beyond the gate. And then once I'd done that, I walked to the entrance of the grounds, expecting by now for her to have noticed her missing dishtowel. Red alert; there was an apple pie somewhere emitting heat. The bungalow was a red-brick boring-looking thing, two windows covered in white netting, like two eyes with glaucoma, and separated by a snot-green door. The windows seemed dark and even though they weren't, the glass seemed tinted and only reflected the light from outside, showing no signs of life inside. I picked up the blue chequered dishtowel from the middle of the road, which was mostly always – mostly always, very dead – empty of traffic. The gate to the front garden was so low I could lift my leg over it. I thought it would be the safest way, or fifty years of rusted gate would give me away. I slowly walked up the path and looked through the window on the right of the building. I pressed my face up against the glass and tried to see through the horrific netting. After all the mystery I don't quite know what I was expecting to see. Some great secret, a crazy sect, dead bodies, a hippy commune, some weird sex thing with a lot of keys in an ashtray . . . I don't know. Anything, anything, but an electric heater in place of a real fire, surrounded by dodgy brown tiles and tiled mantel, green carpet and jaded chairs with wooden handles and green crushed-velvet cushions. It was all a bit sad, really. It was all a bit like a dentist's waiting room, and I felt a little bad. Rosaleen hadn't been hiding anything at all. Well, not quite: she'd been hiding the biggest home design disaster of the century.

Instead of ringing the doorbell I walked round the side of the house. Immediately as I turned the corner I could see that there was a small garden with a large garage, just like the one at the back of the gatehouse, at the bottom of the land. From the window of the workshed something sparkled. At first I thought it was a camera flash, but then I realised that whatever had dazzled my eyes and momentarily blinded me only did so each time it caught the sunlight. As I neared the end of the side passage I yearned to see what was around the corner.

Rosaleen stepped in front of me and I jumped, my scream echoing down the narrow alleyway. Then I laughed.

Rosaleen instantly shushed me, seeming jittery.

'Sorry,' I smiled. 'I hope I didn't scare your mum. You dropped this on the road. Just came to give it to you. What is that light?'

'What light?' She stepped a little to her right and my eyes were protected but my view blocked.

'Thanks.' I rubbed my eyes.

'You best go back to the house,' she whispered.

'Oh, come on, can I not at least say hello? It's

all a bit too Scooby-Doo for me. You know, mysterious.'

'There's no mystery. My mother isn't good in the company of strangers. Perhaps we'll have her over for dinner some day if she's up to it.'

'Cool.' Another over-fifty to add to my list of acquaintances.

I was going to try again one last time, seeing as she'd softened so much but I heard a vehicle coming down the road and hoping it was Marcus, I saluted Rosaleen, turned around and ran.

If it hadn't been Marcus, then that five seconds of hope would have been the most exciting thing that had happened that day. But it turned out it was him. He was standing at the porch of the gatehouse by the time I ran across the road, running his hand through his hair and glancing at his reflection in the glass.

'There's a hair out of place just over your ear,' I called from the gate.

He spun round with a smile. 'Goodwin. Good to see you.'

'Have you come for the book?'

He smiled. 'Eh, yeah, the book, of course. Couldn't stop thinking about ... that damn book.'

'Actually, there's a problem with the book.'

'What's wrong with you?'

'No, I mean the actual book, the real book.'

'You lost it.'

'No I didn't lose it ...'

'Don't believe you. Do you know what the punishment for losing library books is?'

'Spend a day with you?'

'No, Goodwin. If you do the crime you have to do the time. I am revoking your travelling library card.'

'Nooo, anything but my travelling library card.'

'Yes. Come on, give it to me.' He came close and started poking and prodding my body. 'Where is it? Is it in here?' His hands were everywhere, in my jeans pockets, padding down my stomach.

'I refuse to give it up,' I laughed. 'Seriously, Marcus, I haven't lost it but you can't have it back.'

'I don't think you understand the rules of the travelling library. You see, you borrow a book, you read it, or dance around with it if that makes you happy, and then you return it to the handsome librarian.'

'No, you see, what happened, was that somebody broke the lock and discovered that it wasn't a book, but in fact a diary. All the pages were totally blank.'

Totally blank. Very dead.

'So then, somebody wrote in it.'

'Ah ... *somebody*. That wouldn't happen to be you?'

'Actually, no. I don't know who wrote in it.' I smiled but of course I was being serious. 'It's just the first few pages. I could rip them out and give you back the book but ...'

'You could just say you lost it. It would be easier.'

'Stay there a minute.'

I ran into the house and upstairs, lifted the floor-board and took the diary out. I brought it outside, hugged it close to my chest.

'You can't read it but here's proof that I haven't lost it. I'll pay or do whatever . . . I just can't give it back.'

He realised I was serious.

'No, that's fine. One book isn't going to make a difference. Can I read it? Is there anything in there about me?'

I laughed and lifted it out of his reach. But he was too good for me, much taller, and he grabbed it. I panicked. He opened the first page and I waited for him to read the embarrassing admittance that Dad had killed himself.

'I shouldn't have told Weseley about dad,' he read. 'Who's Weseley?' he asked, looking at me.

'I have no idea.' I tried to grab it from him, no longer laughing. 'Give it back, Marcus.'

He handed it back. 'Sorry I shouldn't have read it but you got the date wrong. The fifth is tomorrow.'

I just shook my head. At least it wasn't just me imagining it. This diary thing was really happening.

'I'm sorry for reading it.'

'No, it's really okay. I didn't write this.'

'Maybe it was one of the Kilsaneys.'

I shuddered and closed the book. I wanted so much to read it again.

'Oh, by the way, I found Sister Ignatius!'

'Alive, I hope.'

'She lives on the other side of the grounds. I'll direct you.'

'No, Goodwin, I don't trust you. The last residence you led me to was a dilapidated castle.'

'I'll bring you to her myself. Come on, Bookman, to the Bookmobile!' I ran down the path and hopped on the bus.

He laughed and followed me.

We pulled up outside the sisters' house and I pressed down on the horn.

'Tamara, you can't do that. It's a convent.'

'Honestly, this isn't a regular convent.' I sounded the horn again.

A woman dressed in a black skirt, black jumper, white shirt with a gold cross and a black and white veil opened the door, looking very cross. She was older than Sister Ignatius. I jumped out of the car.

'What's all this racket?'

'We're looking for Sister Ignatius. She wanted to borrow a book.'

'It's prayer time, she can't be disrupted.'

'Oh. Well, hold on a minute.' I rummaged around in the back of the bus. 'Could you please give her this and tell her it's from Tamara. It's a special delivery. She ordered it last week.'

'I will indeed.' The nun took the book and closed the door immediately.

'Tamara,' Marcus said sternly. 'What book did you give her.'

'*Bedded by the Turkish Billionaire*. One of Mills and Boon's greats.'

'Tamara! You'll get me fired.'

'Like you care! Drive, Bookman! Take me away from here!'

We drove to the town and pulled over for the public. But really we went to Morocco. He even kissed me by the Giza Pyramids.

'So what have you been doing the last few days?' Rosaleen asked happily, spooning three thousand calories onto my plate. The diary had been correct, shepherd's pie.

She'd grabbed me almost as soon as I'd got home. I'd had just enough time to hide the diary upstairs and come back down. I didn't want to mention I'd spent the day with Marcus in case she tried to stop me. But she couldn't complain about my hanging around with a nun, now could she?

'I've been spending most of my time with Sister Ignatius.'

She dropped the serving spoons into the bowl and then with awkward fidgeting fingers, she scooped them out.

'Sister Ignatius?' she asked.

'Yes.'

'But . . . when did you meet her?'

'A few days ago. So how was your mum today? Is she coming over for dinner sometime?'

'You never mentioned meeting Sister Ignatius a few days ago.'

I just looked at her. Her reaction was identical to the one I'd written about in the diary. Was I supposed to say sorry? Was I supposed to have tried to prevent this? I didn't know what to do, how to manage the information I was being given. What was the point of it?

Instead I said, 'I never mentioned I got my period on Tuesday either but I did.'

Arthur sighed. Rosaleen's face hardened.

'A few days ago you met her, you say? Are you sure?'

'Of course I'm sure.'

'Maybe you just met her today.'

'No.'

'And does she know where you live?'

'Yes of course. She knows I'm here.'

'I see,' she said breathlessly. 'But . . . but she was here this morning. She never said anything about you.'

'Really? And what did you say to her about me?'

Sometimes your tone can change things, I know that. Sometimes in text messages, people don't pick up tones, or they pick up tones that aren't there and completely misinterpret innocent messages. I've had countless arguments with Zoey over what she thought I meant by a five-word text. But this statement I made, it came with a tone, a deliberate one. And Rosaleen picked up on that. And being clever, she then knew that I must have heard their conversation. She knew that while she'd been talking to Sister Ignatius, she'd heard the shower running, and she'd known I'd earwigged on her conversation.

'Is there a problem with my friendship with her? Do you think she's a bad influence? Am I going to join some weird religious sect and dress in black everyday. Oh, no, hold on, maybe I will! She's a nun!' I laughed and looked at Arthur, who was glaring at Rosaleen.

'What do you talk about?'

I detected panic.

'Does it matter what we talk about?'

'I mean, you're a young girl. What would you have to talk about with a nun?' She smiled, to hide her panic.

That was the point where I was going to talk about the castle, about the fire and the fact it had been lived in far more recently than I'd thought. I was going to ask Rosaleen the question about who died and where everybody was when I remembered the diary entry. *I wish I hadn't told her about what I'd learned about the castle.* Was this what I shouldn't have mentioned? Rosaleen was staring at me in the long time it took me to think of an answer. I took a forkful of minced meat, to give myself some more thinking time.

'You know . . . we talked about a lot of different kinds of stuff . . .'

'*What* kinds of things?'

'Rosaleen,' Arthur said quietly.

Her head snapped round to face him like a

deer who'd heard a trigger pulled back in the distance.

'Your dinner will get cold.' He looked at her plate, which remained untouched.

'Oh. Yes.' She picked up her fork and stabbed a carrot, but didn't lift it to her mouth. 'Carry on, child. You were saying.'

'Rosaleen,' I sighed.

'Let her eat her dinner,' Arthur said quietly.

I looked to Arthur to thank him but he didn't look up, just continued shovelling food in his mouth. There was an awkward silence as we ate, and the sounds of munching and cutlery scraping dishes took over the room.

'Excuse me, please. I'm just going to the bathroom,' I finally said, unable to bear it any more.

Only I stayed outside the door to listen.

'What was that all about?' Arthur barked.

'Ssh, keep your voice down.'

'I'll not keep my voice down,' he hissed back, but his voice was lowered.

'Sister Ignatius called here this morning and said nothing of Tamara,' she hissed back.

'So?'

'So she acted as if she knew nothing about her. If Tamara had met her, surely she'd have said. Sister Ignatius isn't the kind to not say so. Why wouldn't she?'

'So what are you suggesting? That Tamara's lying?'

My mouth dropped and I almost barged in there,

except the next sentence from Rosaleen's lips, spoken with such bitterness, stopped me.

'Of course she's lying. She's just like her mother.'

There was a long silence. Arthur said nothing.

CHAPTER THIRTEEN

Bouncing Castle

I lay in bed trying to block out Rosaleen's words which were being repeated over and over in my mind. There was a history I knew nothing of, that was certain, but there was nothing I could do now to try and find out what that was and what she could have meant. Yesterday was a closed book, tomorrow, however, was another story. I reread the entry for tomorrow over and over again, feeling fired up. There was much to plan for. As I lay in bed running through all the things I should do in my limited time tomorrow, knowing that Rosaleen and Arthur wouldn't be returning until one o'clock on the button, it did little to help me relax. It was a humid July night. It was either going to be a stormy night or tomorrow would be a scorcher. I opened my bedroom window, hoping for some air, and kicked off my covers. I lay in the blue light of the moon, watching the oily sky glisten with stars.

As I listened to the silence, I suddenly heard owls hoot, the occasional sheep and cow call for attention; the sounds of the country night that I'd grown used to drifted into my room. Now and then there was a welcome light breeze and each time I heard the leaves on the trees gently rustle, they too thankful for the cool air. Eventually I became a little chilly and reached to close the window when I realised the sounds that I'd thought were birds chirping were actually voices in the distance. In the country who knew how far such sounds could carry, but as I listened out for them again, I heard the distinct rise and fall of conversation and sudden laughter, perhaps music and then silence again as the breeze stopped carrying their noise. It was coming from the direction of the castle.

It was 11.30 p.m. I threw on a tracksuit and trainers, the floor creaking beneath my feet as I moved around as daintily as possible in my room. With each creak I froze, expecting the sleeping giant to awaken at any moment. I moved the chair away from the bedroom door and gently opened it. It would be a feat to get downstairs and out the front door without alerting the mistress of the house. I heard Rosaleen cough and I stalled, then immediately closed my door again. I'd never heard her cough at night before, I took it as a warning.

I climbed on the bed to avoid walking on the creaky floorboards and crawled along the mattress to reach the window. It was an old springy mattress and it made a noise but at least it sounded legitimately as though I was turning over. I took the torch from the bedside locker and pushed the window open further. Sizewise, I could fit through it without a problem. My bedroom was directly over the front porch. Though the roof was pointed, I could, with great concentration, land on it. From there it would be a relatively easy climb down the wooden fencing on the porch and straight to the ground. Easy.

Suddenly Rosaleen and Arthur's bedroom door opened and there were quick footsteps down the corridor. I dived back into the bed and covered myself from head to toe with the duvet, making sure my tracksuit and trainers, and the torch, weren't visible. I scrunched my eyes shut just as my bedroom door opened. The window was wide open and to my trained ear the voices from afar seemed so loud I was sure my intentions would be obvious.

My heart thudded loudly in my chest as the person was suddenly in my room. The floorboards creaked, one by one as the figure came closer to me. It was Rosaleen. I knew by the way she held her breath, by the scent. The creaking stopped, which meant she was standing still. Watching. Watching *me*.

I fought hard not to open my eyes. I tried to relax my lids, not allow my eyeballs to roll around too much. I tried to breathe normally, a little louder than usual to show my deep slumber. I felt a body hover over me and I almost jumped up to attack, but I heard the window close and realised she was leaning over me to reach it. I contemplated opening my eyes, catching her out, making a drama. But what could I gain from this?

'Rosaleen.' I heard a hiss from my bedroom door. 'What are you doing?'

'I'm just making sure she's all right.'

'Of course she's okay. She's not a baby any more. Come back to bed.'

I felt a hand on my cheek, then fingers gently pushed my hair back to behind my ear just like my mother used to do. Then I waited for the duvet to be pulled off me and for my midnight prowl costume to be revealed, but instead I felt her breath on my face, felt her lips brush against my fore-head in a gentle kiss, and then she was gone. The door closed.

She's not a baby any more.

After she left I waited until Arthur's snores began again. Then I got out of bed, pushed the window open and didn't think twice before climbing out and landing gently on the slate archway of the porch. It was only when I landed on the grass and looked up at the house, at my bedroom, at the closed-over window, that I understood the meaning behind my message to myself not to close the window.

Using the torch I made my way towards the castle, following the voices. I could see only a few feet ahead of me, the rest of the world had been swallowed up by the black hole of night. The trees seemed to hold even more secrets at night-time, and in the darkness their 'sssh' sound to one another led me to believe there was more they weren't telling me. As I got closer to the castle, I heard voices, I smelled smoke, heard music, heard the clink of glasses or bottles. I could see light coming from the entrance hall and the room with the intact windows to the right. The rest of the rooms to the left and to the back were black. I turned off the torch and made my way around the back of the castle, passing two rooms that I'm sure had a grand view of the lake behind and the hundreds of steps that led down to it. I reached the window room I'd climbed out of before, and I listened.

A night light made up of stars circled the old wall. Yellow stars moved around and, thinking the room was empty, I leaned in to watch, though the real ones which were visible through the opposite window were far more impressive. I thought I was alone watching them until I heard the slurping sound of kissing. And that was quickly followed by a scream.

There was lots of running, lots of shushing, lots of cans and bottles being knocked over. Lots of whispering. Then I felt a hand pull at my hair and grab me by the scruff of my neck and I was literally dragged all the way to the castle.

'Hey, let go.' I kicked. 'Get your fucking hands off me.'

I swatted at the hands around my waist, which were definitely male hands as I was half lifted and half dragged. I thanked Rosaleen for her carbo-hydrate-rich diet then and the extra few pounds I'd put on since arriving, or else I'd have been easily thrown over his shoulder. Once inside and placed fully on the ground, he kept his arm round my waist and remained behind me. I turned round a few times to see an ugly-looking thing with fluff on his chin. Six people stared at me. Some were sitting on the stairs, others on crates on the floor. I felt like shouting at them to get out of my house.

'She was watching us,' the screamer said, arriving at the doorway, panting as though about to faint from the ordeal.

'I wasn't watching,' I rolled my eyes. 'That's totally gross.'

'She's an American,' one guy said.

'I'm not American.'

'You sound American,' another one said.

'Hey it's Hannah Montana.'

Lots of laughs.

'I'm from Dublin.'

'No she's not.'

'Yes I am.'

'You're a long way from Dublin.'

'I'm just here for the summer.'

'On vacation,' someone said, and they all laughed again.

A guy appeared at the doorway behind the squealer. He listened for a while as I tried to defend myself with a screechy embarrassing voice that I just couldn't seem to control, and I wondered how on earth I had ended up being the uncool person in this room of hicksville inhabitants.

'Gary, let go of her,' the latest arrival finally said.

Gary fluffy chin let go immediately. I'd identified the leader.

Once released, I gathered myself.

'Can I take any more questions from the room? Perhaps you sir, in the fleece jacket and Doc Martens, would you like to ask a question to me about the days when Guns n'Roses were cool?'

Someone smirked, was elbowed, then cried out in pain. Gary fluffy chin, still behind me, dug me in the back, which really hurt.

'I just heard you all from my room. I was in bed.' I realised I sounded like the greatest annoyance on the planet, like a child who'd interrupted on her parents' dinner party.

'You live nearby?'

'She's lying.'

'Well, where the hell do you think I live? I just flew over from LA for a midnight stroll?'

'Are you staying in the gatehouse?'

'The *royal* gatehouse,' somebody else said and they all started laughing.

Okay, so it was far from being Buckingham Palace, but it was better than a lot of the other shithole barn houses I saw as we drove here. I looked from one face to the other, trying to decide my answer. How stupid would it be of me to tell them where I was staying?

'Oh, no, I just live in a cowshed and sleep with pigs just like the rest of you,' I snapped back. 'I don't know what your big problem is. It's not as if he looks like he's from around here, either.'

I was referring to the dark-skinned leader of the gang who was standing at the doorway just staring at me. Go for the leader in hostage situations, take them out. It wasn't the cleverest idea really.

They all looked at each other with wide eyes and I could hear 'racist' being said over and over.

'That's not racist.' I rolled my eyes. 'He's wearing Dsquared. Last time I checked hicksville, population nil, it didn't stock Dsquared.'

Really, I wasn't being very clever. I've seen *Deliverance*; I know what they can make you do and I'd already accused them of sleeping with pigs, which wasn't a great beginning to what probably should have been an apology. I saw their leader's teeth flash as he smiled briefly and then he covered his mouth with his hand as the rest of the gang went into overdrive, squaring up to me with pointed fingers and calling me a racist over and over again, even though I'd clearly explained my thoughts on why he stood out. The guy at the doorway called them all to stop, tried to reason with the squealer and a few drunken others, and then eventually grabbed me and pulled me outside and round the back of the castle, back to the scene of the crime; the window where I'd supposedly spied.

'Is this where you pretend to kill me but really let me loose?' I asked, a little nervously. A lot nervously. Okay, I thought he was going to beat me up.

He smiled. 'You're Tamara, aren't you?'

My mouth dropped. 'How did you . . .' And then the penny dropped. 'You're Weseley.'

It was his turn to look surprised. 'Arthur told you about me?'

'Arthur? Eh, yeah, of course he did. He talks about you all the time.'

He looked confused. 'He told me about you too.'

'He did?'

I didn't think Arthur would speak of me at all. I couldn't even imagine what he'd say.

'Smoke?'

I took one and he struck up a match. When he lit it I could see his face properly. His skin was a milky chocolate, not ebony, but beautifully dark. His eyes were big and brown, his eyelashes so long, I was momentarily jealous as in my previous life I spent a lot of my pocket money on false ones with glitter. His lips were big and juicy, his teeth perfectly straight and white, with a nice jaw, perfect cheekbones. He was so good-looking I was kind of jealous. He was taller than me, a head taller. The match burned down to his finger and he dropped it. I realised then he must have been looking at me too. He lit it again and I inhaled. It had been too long.

'Thanks.'

'No problem.'

'What the hell are you doing, Wes? Oh, now you're having a smoke with her? She's related to that freak family, I hope you know.' The squealer appeared round the corner, another girl in her wake, and wobbled her way unevenly to us, filling the air with the scent of a Body Shop gift basket.

'Calm down, Kate,' he said.

'No, I will not fucking calm down . . .' She went on a tirade of drunken nonsense and then started to hit him over and over again with her purse. Her friend pulled her away.

'Fine.' She shook her friend off, then grabbed her again before she fell, almost bringing her down with her. 'I'm going home anyway.'

'Ouch.' I looked at him.

'It didn't hurt.'

'A fake Louis Vuitton – are you joking? I felt the pain just looking at it.'

'You're a snob,' he smiled.

'You're a bad boyfriend.'

'She's not my girlfriend.'

'Whatever.'

'You want a drink?'

I nodded way too enthusiastically. He laughed, then disappeared headfirst through the window, back into the castle. I followed him in.

'Hey Weseley, you're not giving Hannah Montana our cans, are you?'

Weseley ignored Gary and handed me a can.

'What is this?'

'Diamond White.'

'Never heard of it.'

'How can I explain this so that you'd understand?' He thought hard. 'Think of it as champagne, but made with apples.'

I rolled my eyes. 'If you think I drink champagne then you don't know me at all.'

'Well, I don't, do I? It's cider. Americans call it hard cider.'

'I'm not American.'

'You don't sound Irish.'

'And you don't look Irish. Maybe Irish as the world knows it has changed.' I gasped sarcastically. 'Oh my God, who should we tell?'

'My mam has red hair and freckles.'

'So she must be Swedish.'

He laughed, then pointed at a crate behind me and I sat down. He sat opposite me.

'Where's your dad from?'

'Madagascar.'

'Cool, like in the movie?'

'Yep, *exactly* like the Disney animation,' he said heavily.

'You ever go there?'

'No.'

'How come he moved here?'

'Because.'

'Ah.' I nodded understandingly. 'Always a good reason.'

We both laughed.

Someone in the next room said something about me being a racist again.

'I only meant your clothes,' I said quietly. 'You're dressed better than John Boy in there, and Mary Ellen, who walked off in her fake Uggs in a puff of Dewberry.'

He laughed and exhaled at the same time, his eyes steady on mine. 'She's not my girlfriend.'

'So you said. But that's not what my super spy glasses told me.'

'Yeah well that was just . . .' He stomped out his cigarette and then put the butt in a jar. I was thankful for that. I felt like I was a parent and had returned home to find the kids had trashed my house. 'There are buses, you know,' he said. 'Things with wheels that carry people to the big smoke.'

'From where?' I think my reaction would have been the same if he'd revealed a cure for cancer. A way out of here . . .

'Dunshaughlin. It's less than thirty minutes in the car.'

'And how do you get there?'

'My dad drives me.'

Well, mine is dead.

'By the way, is this yours?' He rooted around in a bag and handed me a pen. It was the one I'd stolen from Arthur's writing desk and had dropped yesterday.

I had a feeling someone was there. Someone was watching me.

'Were you here yesterday?'

'Em . . .' he thought hard.

'You shouldn't have to think about it,' I snapped.

'I don't know. No. Yes. No, I don't know if I was. I found the pen tonight, if that's what you mean.'

'You weren't here yesterday when I was here?'

'I'm here most days with Arthur.' He still didn't answer the question.

'You are?'

'Well, I have to be, don't I?'

'You do?'

'I work with the man.'

'Oh.'

'I thought you said Arthur told you.'

'Oh . . . yeah. So does Rosaleen know you work with Arthur?'

He nodded. 'I don't think she likes me being around, but since Arthur put his back out he needs a hand around here.'

'How long have you worked with him?'

He thought hard and stared into the distance, 'Ooh let's see. Me and Arthur go back about . . . three weeks now.'

I started laughing.

'We only moved here last month,' he explained.

'Really?' I felt my heart lift. He was one of my kind. 'From where?'

'Dublin.'

'Me too!' My excitement was way too *Famous Five*. 'Sorry,' I felt my face flush. 'Just a little overexcited to meet a member of the same species. So how did you rise to be leader so quickly? Did you cast a spell? Show them how to make fire?'

'I find that politeness goes a long way. Spying, party crashing and insults is a bit of a no-no when you're trying to fit in.'

'I don't want to fit in,' I said sulkily. 'I want to get out of here.'

We were silent then.

'Do you know anything about what happened here? In this castle?' I asked.

'You mean with the Normans and everything?'

'No, not that. What happened to the family who lived here, more recently.'

'There was a fire or something, then they moved out.'

'Wow, you should write history books.'

'We've just moved here,' he smiled. 'Why do you want to know?'

'I'm just wondering.'

He studied me for a while. 'We could ask them if you want.' He meant the group next door.

There was an eruption of laughter from the next room. I think they were playing Spin the Bottle.

'No, it's okay.'

'Sister Ignatius would know. You know her, don't you?'

'How do you know that?'

'I told you, I work around here. I'm not blind.'

'But I've never seen you.'

He shrugged.

'She told me to ask Rosaleen and Arthur,' I explained.

'You should. You know Rosaleen lived in the bungalow across the road from the entrance all her life? If anyone knows, she would. She could probably tell you everything that's happened around here for the past two hundred years.'

I couldn't tell him that the diary stated I should not ask her anything. 'I don't know . . . I don't think they want to talk about it. She's so secretive. They must have known the people and if somebody died, well then, I don't just want to blurt it out. I mean, they probably still know them. Arthur can't be working for free. Actually,' I clicked my fingers, 'who pays you?'

'Arthur does. Cash.'

'Oh.'

'So how come you're here?'

'I told you, I heard you from my bedroom.'

'No, I mean, here in Kilsaney.'

'Oh.'

Silence. I thought fast. Anything but the truth. I didn't want his sympathy.

'I thought you said Arthur told you about me.'

'I'd deserve an award if I got anything more out of him. He just said that you and your mam are staying with them.'

'We just, you know, we just had to move. Just for a little while. Probably only for the summer. We sold our house. And we're waiting to buy a new one.'

'Your dad's not around?'

'No, no, he, em . . . he left Mum, for someone else.'

'Oh, man, sorry to hear it.'

'Yeah, well . . . she's a twenty-year-old model. She's famous. She's always in magazines. She brings me out clubbing with her.'

He frowned at me and I felt like an idiot. 'Do you still see him?'

'No. Not any more.'

I was following the rules of my diary. *I wish I hadn't told Weseley about Dad.* But I didn't feel better for it. I was lying to Marcus as it was, and that was kind of justifiable because everything with Marcus was one big fat lie, but I didn't feel like lying to Weseley. Besides, he'd only find out from Arthur, in about ten years.

'Weseley, sorry, that's a lie.' I rubbed my face. 'My dad . . . he died.'

He sat up. 'What? How?'

I should have said something else, like he died in war or – I don't know – just something else like a more common kind of death.

'Eh. Cancer.' I wanted us to stop talking about it now. I couldn't go there. I couldn't do it. I wanted him to stop asking me. 'In his testicles.'

'Oh.'

That did it.

I'd left after that. I thanked him and climbed back out the window. Halfway towards the house I stopped walking and turned round and ran back.

'Weseley,' I whispered, slightly out of breath, standing at the window. He was tidying away all the cans and butts from the window room.

'Did you forget something?'

'Eh, yeah . . .' I whispered.

'Why are we whispering?' he whispered, smiling, and came towards the window and leaned on his elbows.

'Because em . . . I don't really like saying this out loud.'

'Okay . . .' His smile faded.

'You'll think I'm weird—'

'I already think you're weird.'

'Oh. Okay. Em. My dad didn't die of cancer.'

'No?'

'No. I just said that because it was easier. Though the testicle part wasn't very easy. That was just weird.'

He smiled gently. 'How did he die?'

'He killed himself. He swallowed a bottle of pills and whisky at the same time. On purpose. And I found him.' I swallowed.

There it was. The face change that I wrote about. The pure look of sympathy. The nice look you'd give any horrible person. He was silent.

'I just didn't want to lie,' I started to move away.

'All right. Thanks for telling me.'

'I've never told anyone.'

'I won't tell anyone.'

'Okay thanks. I'm really going now.'

Cringe.

'Good night.'

He leaned further out the window and raised his voice. 'I'll see you around, Tamara.'

'Yep. Sure.'

I just wanted to get out of there.

The gang in the entrance hall all whistled and laughed and I disappeared back to the darkness.

I learned something important that night. You shouldn't try to stop everything from happening. Sometimes you're supposed to feel awkward. Sometimes you're supposed to be vulnerable in front of people. Sometimes it's necessary because it's all part of you getting to the next part of yourself, the next day. The diary wasn't always right.

CHAPTER FOURTEEN
One o'Clock

The diary told me I had until one o'clock that day.

It was quite unusual really, the morning playing out exactly as I'd read the night before. Rosaleen waking me, telling me to stay home, and it seemed so obvious then – the second time round – that she just didn't want me visible to the rest of her little world. Imagine the horror and shame of having to tell people that Mum and I existed; that a man had taken his life, the worst sin of all. I'd felt angry about that and had to fight my desire to demand I go to mass too but I stayed under the covers, and as I listened to their car drive away in the sepia-coloured day, here's where my day differed to the diary. It was unusual, having things happening that I felt had technically already happened, but I was sort of getting used to it.

Instead of falling back asleep after Rosaleen and Arthur had driven off, I got dressed and ran downstairs. I was sitting on the garden wall when the yellow Cinquecento came flying down the road, with the window rolled down.

'Ah!' Sister Ignatius' eyes lit up. 'Just the girl I wanted to see. Are you coming to mass?'

I looked in the car at the four nuns squashed together.

'Oh, you can sit on Sister Peter Regina's knee,' she teased, and I heard a 'pah' from inside. 'We sing at all the morning masses. You're part of a choir, you should join us if the laryngitis isn't still at you.'

Can't, I mimed, grabbing my throat and opening and closing my mouth.

'Gargle some salt and you'll be as right as rain,' she glared at me, then brightened. 'Thanks for the book, by the way.'

'You're welcome,' I broke my silence. 'I picked it especially for you.'

'I thought so,' she chuckled. 'You know at the beginning, I didn't like her, Marilyn Mountrothman. She was stuck up and expected far too much, but by the end I grew to love her. Just like Tariq. It didn't seem an obvious pairing but the way he knew just what she was thinking all the time, particularly when she was crying about the message from her father but wouldn't tell him. Oh, that got me, I must admit. But he figured it out. He knew that she loved him. Smart man! I suppose that's how he made his millions and became the oil tycoon. I like it when they put the photos of them on the front covers. It helps me visualise them all the way through. Him with his hair slicked back and all those muscles . . .'

'You actually read it?'

'Oh, yes, of course I did. Sister Conceptua has started it now.'

The woman in the front passenger seat twisted around. 'Don't tell me what happens. He's just chartered the private plane to Istanbul.'

'Oh, you've the best bits to get to yet,' Sister Ignatius clapped her hands. 'Two words – Turkish delight,' she said.

'I said sshh,' Sister Conceptua snapped. 'You'll give it away.'

'We have to go,' Sister Mary barked from behind the wheel. 'We'll be late.'

'Think of coming next week, okay?' Sister Ignatius said to me then, seriously.

'Okay,' I nodded. 'I'm thinking of going back to bed for the morning. If you see Rosaleen, you might just let her know that?'

Her eyes narrowed. 'Are you?'

'Yes, I'm really thinking about it.'

'I see. What are you getting up to?'

'We really have to go,' Sister Mary started up the engine.

'Wait,' I panicked slightly. 'I just need something from you. A name.'

Moments later I was watching them fly around the corner, no indication or brake lights visible, but Sister Ignatius' arm high in the air in a salute.

It was ten o'clock.

I had my priorities in order and Mum was top of my list. I flicked through the phone book and searched for the name Sister Ignatius had given me. The phone rang once, twice, three times, then just as it went to answering machine a man answered.

'Hello?' he croaked, then cleared his throat. 'Hold on.' I could hear he was out of breath and he fought with trying to turn the answering machine off.

I cleared my throat. Tamara Big-Girl had work to do.

'Hello, I'm calling to make an appointment with Dr Gedad.'

'Uh, he's not here.' He sounded half-asleep. 'Can I take a message?'

'Em ... no ... will he be back before one o'clock?'

'His surgery isn't open on Sundays.'

I paused. There was something familiar.

'It's actually a house call.'

'Is it an emergency?'

I held my breath. Then: 'Weseley, is that you?'

'Yeah. Who's this?'

Lie, Tamara, lie, make up a name.

'It's Tamara. Sorry for waking you.'

'Tamara.' He sounded a little more awake now. 'Are you okay? You need a doctor? He's my dad.'

'Oh ... it's not for me, it's for my mum. But it's not an emergency or anything. Do you think he'll be back by one?'

'I don't know. They go to mass and then the market. Usually they're back at around one.'

'What is it with the bloody mass and market here?'

'I know, they all love it.' He yawned. 'I think my dad goes just to hand out business cards to anyone that coughs.'

I laughed. 'Did you stay out much later last night?'

'About another hour. Didn't you hear us?'

'It took me about a half-hour to climb back into my bedroom. I closed the window by mistake and broke all my nails prying it back open.'

He laughed. 'You should have come back, I'd have helped you get in. I know where Arthur's secret stash of tools are. Do you want me to get my dad to call around at one?'

'No, it's okay. Before one suits me best.'

'What about tomorrow?'

I would have to wait another week for Rosaleen and Arthur to leave. Unless ... I had one small window of opportunity when Rosaleen called to her mother.

'Between ten and eleven tomorrow?'

'I'll run it by him. I'll get him to call you.'

'No,' I said quickly. 'He can't call here.'

'Well, do you have a *cell*?' he teased.

'No.'

'Okay,' he sighed. 'It's far too early in the morning for me to have to think. Give me a second.'

I waited.

'Right, I take it you don't want Rosaleen and Arthur to know, so when my dad gets back I'll find out if he's available and then I'll meet you at the castle at two to let you know.'

I smiled. He could have phoned; he wanted to see me again.

I rang off, feeling fired up. One thing almost crossed off my list.

Mission two was to explore the bungalow. Or at least to have a look in the back garden; I didn't want to scare the life out of the old lady. With my alibi prepared, I emptied a few berries into a bowl, I boiled the kettle, toasted a few slices of bread, scrambled a few eggs . . . very badly, managing to burn the bottom of the pan. I soaked it in the sink and dreaded the look on Rosaleen's face when she saw it. I put everything on a tray and covered it with a tea towel just as Rosaleen did each morning. Feeling proud of my first attempt of breakfast, probably ever, I left the house and made my way, very slowly, so as not to spill the cup of tea I'd prepared. With two hands holding the tray, climbing over the gate without being able to lean on the pillar was difficult. The towel became soaked with tea but I pressed on. I passed the net-curtained living room and walked down the side passage. Again, my vision was taken from me as a bright light shone directly at my face. I closed my eyes tightly, then tried to balance the tray against the wall on one side so that I could rub them. I almost dropped the tray, making a racket as cups and plates collided. When the light had left my eyes and my vision returned, I continued on, choosing to look at the ground as I walked. As soon as I reached the end of the passageway, I stepped into the back garden and prepared to be blown away, prepared to see a little old lady tending her garden, giant mushrooms and fairies and unicorns and an entire magical world that Rosaleen was hiding. But I saw nothing. Nothing but a long grassy field, with trees on either side. Rosaleen's mother didn't have green fingers, that was for sure.

The back of the bungalow was as deserted-looking as the front. Again, each window was covered by lace net curtains. There were two windows and a back door. I knew one was the kitchen, as I could just about make out the tap on the sink. The doorway seemed like the newest addition to the house. It was brown with yellow-tinted obscured glass. The second window gave nothing away.

I turned my attention to the workshed, where the object in the window continued to glisten and beckon me forward. I ignored the bungalow and began to make my way towards it. Halfway down I realised I should have left the tray, but I continued. On closer inspection, what glistened so much appeared to be a twisted piece of glass, hanging from a piece of twine. It spiralled elegantly and smoothly to a sharp point, the same shape as a bunch of grapes and was about sixty inches in length. As the draughty window blew it, it spun in circles, twirling and giving the illusion that it was spiralling down, catching the light at different points over and over again. It was hypnotising.

As I was staring at the glass, something else caught my eye. A movement. Thinking it was a reflection in the grass, I turned to see who was behind me but there was nothing but the trees moving in the breeze. I thought I'd imagined it but on further inspection, there it was again. A figure inside the shed. I moved slowly closer to the work-shed, trying not to make much noise with my tray and really wishing I hadn't bothered with it now, as the eggs and tea would surely be cold and the buttered toast would be soft. The workshed windowledge was shoulder height. I stood at the corner on my tiptoes to see inside. I didn't dare look round the rest of the room, but kept my eyes on Rosaleen's mother in case she saw me and came at me with a sharp piece of glass.

I could see only her back. Her figure, in a long brown cardigan was hunched over a workbench. She had long scraggy hair, more brown than grey, which looked like she hadn't brushed it for a month. I watched her for a while, trying to decide whether to knock or not. I didn't even know her name. I didn't even know Rosaleen's maiden name to be able to address her. Eventually I built up the courage. I knocked gently.

The figure jumped and I hoped I hadn't given her a heart attack. She halfturned, slowly and stiffly. The side of her face that was towards me was covered mostly by her long tatty hair. Over her eyes were a pair of oversized goggles, protective glasses that covered half her forehead and pinched her cheeks. She was all hair and goggles, like a nutty professor.

I balanced the tray on one knee and while the cups and plates clinked and slid, wobbled and spilled, I quickly waved, giving the biggest smile I'd ever given a person just so she'd know I wasn't here to kill her. She just stared at me, no expression, no registering of any kind. I lifted the tray as high as I could, then balanced it on my knee again to quickly make an eating motion. There was still no response. I knew then that I was going to be in big trouble; it had not gone to plan. Rosaleen was right: her mother was not ready for perfect strangers and even if she was, I should have waited for Rosaleen to introduce us. I took a few steps back.

'I'm leaving this here for you,' I said loudly, hoping she'd hear me. I placed the tray down on the grass and backed away. As I was moving backward, I glanced down past the workshed at the rest of the garden. My mouth dropped and I sidestepped to take a closer look. Rows of washing lines filled the lawn. There must have been between ten and twenty lines. On each line were dozens of glass mobiles, all different shapes, glass twisted and turned to make unique shapes, some ridged, some smooth, dangling in the breeze, catching the light, sparkling and silently swaying. A field of glass.

I passed by the workshed and went into the back lawn to further investigate. They were all far apart enough not to hit against one another. If they had been even a centimetre closer I'm sure they would surely have smashed. The lines were pulled tight, attached to a wall at the bottom of the garden and run tightly all the way to a pole at the other end. They stood taller than me so I was constantly looking up, seeing the light of the sky through the glass. They were the most beautiful things I had ever seen. Some appeared to drip, full and fluid, from the twine like giant tear drops but instead of falling, they'd frozen mid-air. Others had fewer swirls and curves, and were rigid spikes, more angry and sharp, hanging like icicles, like weapons. Each time the wind blew they swayed from side to side, I walked down the middle of one row, stopping occasionally to examine them. I'd never seen anything like them, so clear and pure. Some had bubbles trapped inside, others were completely clear. I held my hand up and looked at it through the glass, seeming obscured in some, perfectly as it was in others. Fascinating and beautiful, some distorted and disturbing others pretty and so fragile, as though touching them would shatter them.

I was going to go further and investigate the other lines when I turned round to make sure I was still alone and I saw Rosaleen's mother had all of a sudden moved to a window that over-looked this second half of the garden. She was looking at me, her hand pressed up against the glass. I stopped walking and stood in one row, feeling like a Cabbage Patch girl in a field of glass, and smiled back, wondering how long she'd been watching me. I tried to make out her face, to see her features, but it was impossible. She was yet again showing only her silhouette, her long hair falling to her shoulders, not grey as I had thought earlier, but a mouse-brown with white streaks. She seemed to be ageless, faceless, even more mysterious to me now than she was before I'd seen her.

I left the field of glass mobiles, taking them all in as though I'd never see them again as punishment for trespassing. Once I'd passed into the other garden, I could see her watching me still, not at the window but further away, deeper in the room.

I waved again, pointed to the tray on the grass, made eating gestures, as though it was feeding time in the zoo. She continued to stare at me making no reaction. Completely uncomfortable – hot sun, good win, very dead – I turned round and quickly walked away from the garden, not looking back once but feeling as I used to feel as a little girl, running from my friend's house to my own house in the dark, and thinking there was a witch behind me.

It was twelve o'clock.

I paced the living room, back and forth, up and

down, left and right. Sat down, stood up. Made my way to Mum's room, then stopped and went back to the room again. I wrung my hands and looked out the window now and then, expecting to see Rosaleen's mother come racing across the road on her wheelchair, doing wheelies and cracking a whip. I also expected Rosaleen and Arthur to round the corner at top speed too. Rosaleen had lain traps around the bungalow: I'd tripped a wire, a blade of grass was out of place, I'd walked through a beam and triggered an alarm in her handbag. She was going to tie me to a bed, break my legs with a sledgehammer and force me to write her a novel. I couldn't do that. I could barely keep a diary. I don't know – I felt something, anything could happen. I broke the rules at home all the time, here it was different. Here it was all so strict and ancient, like living on an excavation site and everybody was tiptoeing around, not walking here, but only walking there, speaking quietly so as not to crumble the foundations, using little brushes and tools to scratch at the surface and blow away dust, but never going any deeper and I'd arrived stomping through the place with a shovel and spade and I'd ruined everything.

And now I'd have to go back and get the tray or else Rosaleen would know what I'd done. I hoped I hadn't poisoned her mother – oh God, what if I had? Eggs could be dangerous things and I'd forgotten to wash the berries. Was salmonella lethal? I almost picked up the phone and called

Weseley again but I resisted. After spending far too long frantically worrying, I realised nothing was going to happen – not immediately, anyway – and I really hadn't done anything wrong either. I'd tried to be nice to an old woman. So shoot me. I hoped she was enjoying my eggs.

I calmed down then. Next on my list was the garage at the bottom of the garden. I opened the back door which led from the kitchen to the garden, and ran down the lawn, then through Rosaleen's vegetable patch, which ran along the bottom. I looked up at Mum's bedroom window, which was empty as she continued to sleep on.

As garages go, it was a fine one. It was clad in the same limestone as the house, or near enough to it, and looked better built than any of my dad's developments. I say that with the greatest respect to my dad who was proud of what he built, I just don't think he cared much for architecture. It was more about space and how to give the least possible amount of it to everybody. The garage almost filled the full width of the garden, twenty-five metres long. To the right of the house, on the other side of the neatly manicured hedge was a tractor trail, yet another path that meandered around the grounds. But before it left the house's vicinity there was a turn-off which led to the garage's double doors. I'd never seen Arthur park the tractor inside. Perhaps Rosaleen was correct, perhaps there wasn't room inside for our possessions. I favoured this way into the garage because I wouldn't be visible from the house, but there was a bigger door to open, a bigger lock to pick. I looked in all of the windows but I couldn't see anything. They'd been covered on the inside by black sacks. I tried the single door, which was locked and then I went round to the double doors again. I pulled and pushed, I kicked and banged. I used a rock to continuously hammer at the lock, but that did nothing but dent the metal.

It was twelve-thirty by the time I returned to the house, none the wiser on the garage. I washed my hands and changed my clothes, which were filthy from my breaking-and-entering attempt. I checked on Mum, who was finally awake and taking a shower. I took my time getting dressed, knowing exactly how long I had until Rosaleen and Arthur returned. I sat on my bed and looked across to the bungalow. Something caught my eye.

On the pillar by the front gate was the tray. I stood up, examined the garden, the house. Nobody was in the garden, nobody watched from the window. I checked to see if Rosaleen had returned but the car was still gone.

It was 12.50 p.m.

I ran downstairs and outside, across the road. The tray was covered by the tea-cloth as I had laid it down. Underneath, the food was gone, the tea cup was empty. They gleamed as though they had just been cleaned. On the plate sat the tiniest version of one of the glass mobiles that I had been studying. Like a small tear drop, it was soft and smooth and fit perfectly into the palm of my hand. There was nothing else. No card, nobody to tell me it was for me. I waited, but nobody came. It was dangerously close to one o'clock and I couldn't wait any longer. I couldn't risk Rosaleen returning to find me on the wall with a tray and a glass tear drop. I put the piece of glass in my pocket. I ran across the road as quickly as I could without shattering the contents of the tray. Just as I closed the front door behind me, I heard Rosaleen and Arthur's car return. Shaking, I placed the cleaned cups and saucers, and plate back in the kitchen cupboards. I put the tray back where it belonged. I grabbed my book from the living room, ran upstairs into my Mum's room and dived on the bed. Mum, who was coming out of the bathroom, looked at me in shock. Seconds later the door opened and Rosaleen looked in.

'Oh, sorry,' she said, as Mum tightened her towel around her.

She stepped back further from the door so that she could only see me.

'Tamara, is everything okay?'

'Yes thanks.'

'What did you do all morning?' It wasn't an interested enquiry, it was a concerned one, and not concern for my boredom either.

'I was just here with Mum all morning, reading my book.'

'Oh, very good.' She stalled a bit, always afraid to leave a room, 'I'll be downstairs if you need me.'

She closed the door and when I looked at Mum, I realised she was looking at me and smiling. She laughed then and shook her head and I almost felt like cancelling Dr Gedad.

The door opened again. Rosaleen looked at Mum's breakfast tray.

'Jennifer you didn't eat again.'

'Oh,' Mum said looking up while putting on another of her cashmere lounge robes. 'Tamara will eat it for me.' Then she smiled sweetly at Rosaleen.

'No, no,' Rosaleen said hastily coming inside and taking the tray. 'I'll take that away.'

Mum kept watching her, blue eyes shining.

'Tamara, your lunch will be ready soon,' Rosaleen told me nervously, and backed out of the room.

I looked at Mum in confusion, for an explanation, but she had disappeared again, back into her shell. Turtles either disappear into their shells because they're scared or because danger lurks and they're protecting themselves. Either way, as soon as those shells grow, they never lose them because they're physically a part of them.

During that summer if ever people tried to convince me that Mum was never returning to the way I remember her before Dad died – and some people hinted at it – I kept thinking of those turtles. She would keep the new shell she'd grown over the past few months, and she would carry it around with her for the rest of her life but that didn't mean she would disappear into it. I saw proof that day that Mum hadn't disappeared for good, I saw it in her eyes. I remember the exact moment when I saw her again. It was at one o'clock.

CHAPTER FIFTEEN

Things You Find in a Pantry

Rosaleen looked different today, having made an effort for Sunday mass and market. Her Sunday clothes were a knee-length beige-coloured skirt with a small slit up the middle at the back. She wore a cream slightly see-through blouse with puffy shoulders, which was tied in a bow at the neck and underneath I could see a lacy bra, though I doubted she knew about its transparency. It was actually quite sophisticated. She'd worn a matching beige jacket with a peacock feather brooch on the lapel, and on her feet were nude patent slingback peep-toes. Only an inch or two high but she looked good. I said so and her face brightened and her cheeks pinked.

'Thank you.'

'Where did you buy it?'

'Oh,' she was embarrassed about talking about herself. 'In Dunshauglin. About a half-hour away there's a place that I like. Mary's very good, God bless her soul . . .'

I awaited Mary's tragic news with bated breath. It involved a dead husband and lots of God blessing her.

I tried again with another conversation.

'Do you have any brothers or sisters?'

'A sister in Cork. Helen. She's a teacher. And I've a brother, Brian, in Boston.'

'Do they ever visit?'

'Now and then. It's been a while. Usually Mammy would visit them, Helen in Cork at least, to give her a change of scenery, but now she can't. She has MS.' She looked at me then, opening up. 'Multiple Sclerosis – do you know what that is?'

'Kind of. Something about your muscles no longer working.'

'Close enough. It's got worse over the years. It gives her awful trouble. That's why I'm back and forth. I can't travel, I don't like to leave her, you know. She needs me.'

It seemed like a lot of people needed Rosaleen. But it struck me that with so many people needing one person, maybe it was more that she needed them to need her. I never wanted to need Rosaleen.

Her mother never arrived to point the accusing finger at me, but two o'clock did. I snuck out of the house unnoticed while Rosaleen was getting the makings of her tarts ready. I'd learned that the three thousand various pies she'd made during the week not only fed us and her mother, but she'd brought them to the Sunday farmers' market where she sold them along with her home-made jam, and organic home-grown vegetables. She'd carried a pouch stuffed with notes and coins to the table, turned her back to take something out of it and then squeezed twenty euro into my hand. I was honestly so touched, I refused to take it but she wasn't having any of it.

When I reached the castle, Weseley was sitting on the stairs – my stairs. He was wearing blue jeans, a black T-shirt with a blue skull on it and blue trainers. Even in the daylight he was cool.

He looked up and pulled his earphones out. 'He can come tomorrow at ten.'

There was no hello or anything. I was a little put out.

'Oh. Great, thanks.' I waited for him to stand up and flutter away, like a little pigeon who'd delivered its message, but he stayed. 'Actually, could he come at ten fifteen, just in case Rosaleen is delayed leaving?'

'Yeah, sure, I'll tell him.'

'Okay, great, thanks,' I repeated.

He still didn't leave and so I stepped in further and leaned against the wall directly opposite him.

'Do you know the woman who lives in the bungalow?'

'Rosaleen's mother? I saw her the first week we moved but not since then. She doesn't really go out much. She's old. I think she's got Alzheimer's or something.'

'Have you ever been to her house?'

247

'I've dropped a few things over for Arthur. Firewood, coal, some furniture, that kind of thing. But Rosaleen always escorts me on and off the premises.' He smiled. 'It's not as if there's anything over there to steal, if that's what she's worried about.'

'Well she's worried about something. So Arthur never goes over to the bungalow himself . . .' I thought aloud. 'They mustn't get along. I wonder why.'

'Check you out, Nancy Drew. Or how about, I'm now Arthur's dogsbody so he couldn't be arsed carrying over dodgy rocking chairs to his mother-in-law when he's paying me next to nothing to do it for him.'

'But he never even visits her.'

'You're really looking for something, aren't you?'

It reminded me of what Sister Ignatius had said about my mind doing unusual things when it searches. She had known before I did that I was looking for something.

'It's just that . . .' I thought about it, 'to be perfectly honest, I'm so bored here.' I laughed. 'If I had some sort of life, or friends, or someone to talk to then I wouldn't be making something out of nothing. I wouldn't care about Rosaleen and her secrets.'

'What secrets?' he laughed. 'Rosaleen doesn't have secrets. She just doesn't understand the art of conversation. She's so used to spending time on her own, I don't think she knows to offer information about herself.'

'I know that, and I had thought of that, but . . .'

'But what?'

I don't know how or why but I suddenly started telling him about everything about the past few days. All the odd conversations, the missing photo album, Arthur's unusual comment about thinking Mum didn't want to see him, the way Rosaleen couldn't stand for me to be in the room with anyone on my own without her there, Rosaleen failing to mention me in her conversation with Sister Ignatius, Sister Ignatius wanting me to ask Rosaleen questions, the comment about Mum lying, Rosaleen wanting to keep Mum up in the room all the time, the secretive way she disappears to the bungalow and not wanting me to cross over, what I'd seen in the back garden, the tray being left on the wall, the argument about not wanting to put our belongings in the garage.

He listened patiently, making enough reactions to encourage me to keep going and not to hold back.

'Okay . . .' he said as soon as I'd finished. 'That all does sound a little odd, and I get how you can be really suspicious but it could probably all be explained too. Just by the fact that Rosaleen is a bit of a weirdo – no offence,' he said quickly. 'I know she's your aunt.'

'No offence taken.'

'I'm not really here long enough to know

anybody properly but Rosaleen doesn't really speak to anybody in the town. Whenever my mam passes her, she always puts her head down and walks on. I don't know if she's just shy or what it is. And about how she is with you, what does she know about being a mother? But that's not to say that you're not right Tamara. There could be something they're keeping from you. I don't know what the hell that could be, but if anything else weird happens, tell me.'

'Something else hugely weird *is* happening,' I said.

My heart drummed. I couldn't believe I was going to tell him about the diary. I just wanted him to believe me so much.

'Tell me.'

'You'll think I'm psychotic.'

'I won't.'

'Just please believe me that I'm not lying.'

'Okay. Tell me,' he said, getting impatient.

I told him about the diary.

He quite understandably leaned back from me, folded his arms, all body language the equivalent to a computer shutting down. Oh God. He looked at me differently. Never mind the face change when I'd told him dad had died, this was on a whole new level. The guy thought I was a nut.

'Weseley,' I began, but I didn't know what else to say.

'Yoo-hoo,' a voice called suddenly and Weseley snapped out of it and looked towards the doorway.

A beautiful blonde entered. She looked directly at him, not noticing me along the wall.

'Ashley,' he said, surprised, 'you're early.'

'I know, sorry, blame the excitement of wanting to see you. I brought a blanket.' She shimmied the basket in her hand. She rushed towards him and dropped the basket by their feet, threw her arms around his neck and kissed him, and not in a sisterly way. I felt a surprising twinge of envy, which I shrugged off. As though she'd sensed herself being shrugged off, she opened her eyes and saw me standing there, arms folded, bored with their display.

'Cute PDA but I'm bored now. Can I go?'

Weseley broke their embrace and turned to me with a smile.

'Who are you?' She looked at me like I was a bad smell. 'Who is she?' she asked him.

'I'm his secret lover. We love to do it in old castles fully clothed while I'm leaning against the wall and he's sitting on the stairs on the other side of the room. It's tough but we love a challenge. Kinky. Later, lover,' I winked at him while walking to the door.

'That's Tamara,' I heard him say as I left the castle. 'She's just a friend.'

She's just a friend. Four words that could possibly kill any woman, but, they made me smile. Not only had my freakish rendition of the weirdest story you could ever be told in your life failed to send him charging at me with a torch, wanting to

251

burn me at the stake, but also here in this place, I had made a friend.

And the castle was my witness.

'Tamara,' I heard him calling just as the house was coming into view. I took a few steps back, moved closer to the trees so that a peeping Rosaleen wouldn't see us talking.

He was out of breath by the time he got to me.

'About the diary thing . . .'

'Yeah, I'm sorry, forget it—'

'I want to believe you, but I don't.'

I was both complimented and insulted at the same time.

'But if you tell me what's going to happen tomorrow, and then it happens, then I'll believe you. That makes sense, doesn't it?'

I nodded.

'If you're right, then I'll help you do whatever it is you're supposed to be doing.'

I smiled.

'But if you're making this up,' he shook his head and he looked at me oddly again, 'then you know . . .'

'I know. Then you'd like to be my boyfriend. I understand.'

He laughed. 'So what's going to happen?'

'I haven't read it yet.'

I'd left the house last night before the entry had arrived in the diary and I'd been so busy all morning with my missions that I hadn't had time to read the diary.

He looked doubtful. I mean, even I barely believed myself and I knew I wasn't lying.

'I'll read it when I get back to the house and then I'll call you later. Or will you be home? I don't want to disturb you and *Yoo-hoo.*'

He laughed. 'All right, call me later.' He started to leave, 'But by the way, she's not my girlfriend.'

'Sure she's not,' I called back.

Once in the house I made a point of sitting with Arthur and Rosaleen in the lounge, pretending to read the book Fiona had given me. Then I could wait no longer. I yawned, stretched and excused myself from the room and went upstairs. I removed the diary from underneath the floorboard, moved the chair up against the door again and sat down. I opened the book in hope more than expectation, hoping the new entry had arrived in the early hours of the morning.

As soon as I opened the cover, I saw the words of the previous day disappear as though the new day had drained the ink away, and in their place the neatest writing – *my* neatest writing – began to appear in loops and lines, word after word, so quickly I could barely keep up. The first line made me nervous.

Monday, 6 July
What a disaster! This morning Dr Gedad showed up just like planned. Rosaleen left at ten o'clock for feeding time at the zoo just as I predicted. I watched to make sure nothing fell

that would cause her to come running back early. Dr Gedad showed up at ten fifteen on the button. I prayed she wouldn't look out the window and see his parked car but there was nothing I could do about that. I just needed to get him in and out of the house as quickly as possible. I was waiting for him at the door and he seemed such a warm and lovely man. I shouldn't have been surprised really, with Weseley as his son. We were in the entrance hall when the front door opened and Rosaleen stepped in. Honestly, the look on her face when she saw him, it was like she'd been caught by the police. Dr Gedad didn't seem to notice. He was as friendly as anything and introduced himself because they'd never met. Rosaleen just stared at him as though an unearthly thing had been beamed into her precious house. She went on a rather nervous rant about an apple pie; she'd tasted the apple pie and she'd added salt instead of sugar, which was the first time she'd ever done that. She seemed really upset, as though it was the worst thing in the world that anybody could ever do. She'd come home to get the other pie that she'd made for dinner. She was sure me and Arthur would understand if we allowed her to bring it to her mother to eat instead. I mean, it was only an apple pie, but she was practically shaking. I don't know if it was because she'd made a mistake or because I'd arranged a doctor for Mum behind her

back. Dr Gedad asked after her mother, whom
he'd heard was unwell, and in the most bizarre
twist ever, he ended up talking to Rosaleen in
the kitchen, without my being allowed to sit
with them, and when they'd finished, Dr Gedad
said to me that he was sure that his presence
wasn't needed at all. He was very sorry for my
loss, gave me a pamphlet about some
counselling and then left.

Now things are worse than they were before
I started this. I can't stand this any more. I
can't stand being here any more. Next time
Marcus comes along in his bus, I'm hijacking it
and I'm forcing him to take me home.
Wherever that is, it's not here.

Don't count on my writing tomorrow.

With shaking hands I returned the book to under
the floorboard and knew that I had to fix this. I
went downstairs and in the kitchen Rosaleen was
making her pies for the next day.

I sat and watched her, nervously biting my nails
and trying to decide what to do. If I stopped her
from using the salt in the pie then that would mean
that I could stop her from returning to the gatehouse too early. But if I changed everything then
Weseley would never believe me. Which did I need
more, a doctor for Mum or an ally here to help me?

'Tamara, would you mind fetching me the sugar
from the pantry, please?' she broke into my
thoughts.

255

I froze.

She turned round. 'Tamara?'

'Yes,' I snapped out of it. 'I'll get it now.'

'Can you just fill this up to there, that'll make it easier,' she smiled pleasantly, enjoying the bonding.

I took the measuring jug from her and I felt like I was outside of myself as I walked to the pantry. In the small room off the kitchen I looked at the floor-to-ceiling shelves stocked with everything a person could possibly need for ten years. Condiments separated into Mason jars with screw-on lids, labelled in perfect penmanship with contents and expiry dates. A shelf of root vegetables: onions, potatoes, yams, carrots. A shelf of canned goods: soups and broths, beans, tinned tomatoes. Below that the grains, all in their glass jars: rice, pasta of all kinds of shapes and colours, beans, oatmeal, lentils, cereals and dried fruits – sultanas, raisins, apricots. Then there was the baking supplies: flour, sugar, salt and yeast, and so many jars of oils, olive oil, sesame oil, balsamic vinegar, oyster sauce, rails and racks of spices. There were even more jars of honey and jam: strawberry, raspberry, blackberry and even plum. It was endless. The sugar and salt had both been emptied from their packets and poured into jars. The jars were labelled, in that perfect handwriting. My hand shook as I reached for the salt jar. I remembered my lesson from last night: I could change the diary. I didn't need to follow its story. If I hadn't found it, life would be going on without any of my knowledge.

But then I thought of Weseley. If I gave Rosaleen the sugar, then she wouldn't return home tomorrow, she wouldn't catch the doctor before he went upstairs, she wouldn't convince him not to see Mum. If I changed the diary, then I would have absolutely no idea what would happen, so I wouldn't be able to tell Weseley and he wouldn't believe me about the diary. I'd have lost a new friend and looked like the biggest weirdo on the planet.

But if I told him what was to happen tomorrow, then Mum wouldn't see a doctor. How much longer could I wait here while she sat upstairs sleeping and waking as though there was no difference between either?

I made my decision and reached for a jar.

CHAPTER SIXTEEN

Total Abstraction

I got very little sleep that night. I tossed and turned, felt too hot and kicked off the covers, then felt too cold and covered up again, one leg out, one arm out, nothing was comfortable. I could find no happy medium. I daringly went downstairs to the kitchen to phone Weseley about the diary entry. I didn't use the stairs, instead I did my gymnastics teacher proud by climbing over the banister and landing gently on the stone floor. Anyway, I did pretty well not to make a sound going down the stairs and yet *still,* just as I reached for the phone in the kitchen, Rosaleen appeared at the door in a nightdress from the 1800s, which went to the floor and hid her feet making her appear as though she was floating like a ghost.

'Rosaleen!' I jumped.

'What are you doing?' she whispered.

'I'm getting a glass of water. I'm thirsty.'

'Let me get that for you.'

'No,' I snapped. 'I can do it. Thank you. You go back to bed.'

'I'll sit with you while you—'

'No, Rosaleen,' I raised my voice. 'You need to give me space, please. I just want a glass of water, then I'm going back to bed.'

'Okay, okay.' She raised her hands in surrender. 'Good night.'

I waited to hear the creaks on the steps. Then I heard her bedroom door close, her feet moving across her bedroom and then the springs in her bed. I rushed to the phone and dialled Weseley's number. He picked up after half a ring.

'Hi, Nancy Drew.'

'Hi,' I whispered, then froze, suddenly so uncertain about what I was doing.

'So, did you read the diary?'

I searched for any sign that I shouldn't tell him. I listened out for tones – was he jesting me? Was he setting me up? Was I on speaker phone in a room full of his hillbilly friends – you know, the kind of thing I would have done if some dork that had moved to my area gatecrashed my party and started spurting crap about a prophesying diary.

'Tamara?' he asked, and I could hear no tone, nothing to make me change my mind.

'Yes, I'm here,' I whispered.

'Did you read the diary?'

'Yes.' I thought hard. I could tell him I was joking, that it had been a *hilarious* joke, just like the one about my dad dying. Oh, how we'd laugh.

'And? Come on, you've made me wait until eleven o'clock,' he laughed. 'I've been trying to guess all kinds of things. Will there be any earth-quakes? Any lotto numbers? Anything we can make money out of?'

'No,' I smiled, 'just boring old thoughts and emotions.'

'Ah,' he said, but I could hear his smile. 'Right then, out with it. The prophecy please . . .'

That night, I woke up every half hour, the outcome of the day to come keeping me on edge. At three-thirty a.m. I couldn't take it any longer and I reached for the diary to see how the day had been affected and what the events of tomorrow would hold.

I reached for the torch beside the bed and with a pounding heart opened the pages. I had to rub my eyes to make sure what I was seeing was correct. Words were appearing, then disappearing, sentences half-formed, which didn't make sense, would appear then vanish again as quickly as they'd arrived. The letters seemed to jump off the page as everything was jumbled, without order. It was as though the diary was as confused as my mind, unable to formulate thoughts. I closed the book and counted to ten, and full of hope, I opened it again. The words continued to jump around the page, finding no meaning or sense.

Whatever plans I had put in place with Weseley, tomorrow had certainly been affected. However, exactly in what way was still unclear, as it obviously depended on how I lived the day when I awoke. The future hadn't been written yet. It was still in my hands.

In the moments that I did manage to sleep, I dreamed of glass shattering, of me running through the field of glass but it was a windy day and the pieces were blowing, scraping my face, my arms and my body, piercing my skin. But I couldn't get to the end of the garden, I kept getting lost among the rows and a figure stood at the window watching me, with hair in front of her face, and every time the lightning flashed I could see her face, and she looked like Rosaleen. I woke up in a sweat each time, my heart thudding in my chest, afraid to open my eyes. Then I'd eventually go back to sleep only to walk myself straight back into the same dream. At six-fifteen I couldn't force myself back to sleep again, and I was up. And though my entire plan was to help Mum get back to being herself again, I checked on her with the faintest hope that she still wasn't okay. I don't know why – of course I wanted her to get better with all of my heart – but there's always the part of you, the part that hides in the shadows protecting the self-destruct button, that doesn't ever want to leave the dark behind.

I was the first person downstairs at six forty-five for the first time since I'd moved here. I sat in the living room with a cup of tea and tried to force myself to concentrate on the book about the invisible girl that Fiona had given me. I was averaging about a paragraph a day but I must have got lost in the story without noticing because I didn't see or hear the postman approach the house, but I heard the envelopes land on the mat in the front hall. Always happy to do something different in the house where everything went like clockwork, I went to the hall to retrieve them. They were literally just beyond my grasp when a hand came in and stole them away from me, like a vulture had flown down and scooped up its prey.

'No need for you to do that, Tamara,' Rosaleen said brightly, shoving the envelopes into the front pocket of her apron.

'I don't mind. I was only picking them up, Rosaleen. I wasn't going to read them.'

'Of course you weren't,' she said as though the thought had never crossed her mind. 'You just relax and enjoy yourself,' she smiled, and rubbed my shoulder.

'Thanks,' I smiled. 'You know, you should let somebody do something for you for once.' I followed her to the kitchen.

'I like doing it,' she said, getting to work on the breakfast. 'Besides, Arthur is good at a lot of things but he'd be boiling an egg till September if you let him at it,' she chuckled.

'Speaking of September, what's going to happen?' I asked finally. 'The plan was for us to stay for the summer. It's July now, and well, nobody's talked about September.'

263

'Yes, and it's almost your birthday.' Her eyes lit up. 'And we need to talk about what you'd like to do for that. Have a party? Go to stay with some friends in Dublin?'

'Actually, I might like a few friends to come stay with me here,' I said. 'I'd like them to see where I live now, see what I do everyday.'

Rosaleen looked a little shell-shocked by that. 'Here? Oh . . .'

'It was only a thought,' I back-tracked quickly. 'It's so far for Laura and Zoey to come, and it would probably be too much hassle for you . . .'

I waited for her to jump in and reassure me, but she didn't.

'Anyway, I'd rather talk about my future than about my birthday.' I changed the subject. 'If we're still here in September, which is looking like what's going to happen, how am I going to get to St Mary's from here? There aren't any buses, or at least none that pass by here. I doubt Arthur would want to drive me to and from school every day . . .' I waited for her to tell me that's exactly what was going to happen. But again, she didn't. She started getting breakfast ready, taking out the pots and pans that usually served as my wake-up call.

'Well, that's something you'll have to discuss with your mother, I suppose. I can't tell you the answers.'

'But, Rosaleen, how am I supposed to discuss anything with Mum?'

'What do you mean?' Clatter, clatter, bang, crash. All systems go in the kitchen.

'You know what I mean.' I jumped up and stood beside her, but she still wouldn't look at me. 'She doesn't talk. She's completely catatonic. I don't get why you refuse to admit this.'

'She's not catatonic, Tamara.' She finally stopped and looked at me. 'She's just . . . *sad*. We need to give her space and time and let her figure it all out herself. Now, will you be a good girl and fetch me the eggs from the fridge and I'll show you how to do a nice big omelette this morning,' she smiled. 'How about I put a few peppers in it for you?'

'Peppers,' I said perkily and her face lit up. 'Lovely juicy problem-solving *peppers*,' I said happily, then dragged my feet to the fridge to fetch them, as her face fell. I took out a green and a red one. 'Oh, look, hello, Mr Green Pepper. How's about you solve the problem for me? Where am I going to go to school in September?' I held it to my ear and listened. 'Oh, no, it mustn't be working.' I shook it. 'Maybe I'll try the red one. Hello, Mr Red Pepper. Rosaleen seems to think you can solve the problem about my life. What do you think is going to happen? Shall we send Mum to a madhouse or should we leave her upstairs for ever?' I listened again. 'No. Nothing.' I tossed the peppers down on the counter. 'Looks like the peppers can't help us out today. Maybe we should try some onions,' I said, faking excitement. 'Or grated cheese!'

'Tamara,' I heard Arthur say, warning in his tone, and I stopped. I trudged out and sulked in the living room. Even though we're not allowed to eat in the living room, Rosaleen brought the omelette in to me. A decent kind person would have apologised, instead, I asked for salt.

At ten o'clock I watched Rosaleen scurry out of the house with the tray loaded with enough food to feed an entire family, and among all of my worries about the day, one of them was that her mother would reveal my visit to her. Just because I hadn't written about it, it didn't mean it couldn't happen. At ten fifteen, Dr Gedad's car pulled up outside the house. I took a deep breath and opened the door.

'You must be Tamara,' he beamed, while walking up the path. He immediately made me smile. He was tall, slender, fit-looking. His hair was greying and was tight on his head. He had high cheekbones and soft eyes, which gave him a slightly feminine look, but yet he was masculine and handsome. I welcomed him in and shook his hand.

'Well good morning to you. Isn't it a great summer we're having.' He spoke from the back of his throat, as though he'd a piece of bread stuck there, slightly muffled, but in a lovely singsong way. His Madagascan accent was mixed with some words that were spoken with a pure Irish *blás*. It was a lovely, peculiar sound. I liked that I felt somebody from outside of here was going to freshen things up, shake things up, fix them.

'Can I take your briefcase?' I was nervous, jittery, unsure what to do. I looked anxiously at the door.

'No, thank you, Tamara. I'll need this with me,' he smiled.

'Oh yes. Of course.'

'I believe I'm here to see your mother?'

'Yes, she's upstairs. I'll show you the way.'

'Thank you. Tamara. I'm very sorry to hear about your father. Weseley shared the sad news with me. It must be a very difficult time for you both.'

'Yes, thank you,' I smiled, and tried to swallow that lump that always arrived whenever anybody mentioned Dad.

I made to lead Dr Gedad upstairs and I was almost beginning to believe that I was going to get away with it, was hopeful about getting Mum back, but was devastated about losing Weseley, when the front door opened. Rosaleen stepped into the hall with a tin-foil-covered plate in her hands. She looked at Dr Gedad as though he was the grim reaper. Her face went white.

'Good morning,' Dr Gedad said pleasantly.

'Who . . . ?' She looked from the strange man in her hall to me, then back to the man again. Her eyes narrowed. 'You're the new doctor.'

'I am indeed,' he said cheerfully, going back down the stairs.

No! I shouted at him in my head.

'It's very nice to meet you, Mrs—'

'Rosaleen,' she said quickly, glancing at me then

back to him. 'Rosaleen will do fine. Well, welcome to the town.'

They shook hands.

'Thank you very much. And I must thank you and your husband for giving young Weseley a job here.'

Rosaleen glanced at me, the discomfort all over face. 'Well, yes, he's a great help,' she brushed him off. 'Doctor,' she said looking confused, 'what's . . . why . . . Tamara, are you sick?'

'No, I'm fine, thank you, Rosaleen. If you'll just follow me, Dr Gedad,' I said quickly, going upstairs.

'Where are you going?'

'To my mum's room,' I said as politely as possible.

'Oh, you won't want to disturb her, Tamara,' she said with a smile to me and a little frown to Dr Gedad, hinting to him as though I was some kind of weirdo. 'You know how important her sleep is to her.' She looked at the doctor. 'She hasn't been sleeping much, which is understandable, of course, under the circumstances.'

'Of course,' he nodded gravely. He looked at me then. 'Well, perhaps I should let her have her rest. I can come back another time.'

'No!' I interjected. 'Rosaleen she's been sleeping non-stop most days for the past week.' I couldn't control my voice, shrieking like a squeaky violin.

'Because of her restless nights, of course,' Rosaleen said firmly. 'Won't you have a cup of tea, Doctor? You wouldn't believe it but it seems I used salt in the baking rather than sugar. My mother almost fell over,' she laughed. 'Though she shouldn't have been having pie for breakfast, I know that,' she said apologetically.

'How is your mother?' he asked. 'I hear that she's unwell.'

'I'll tell you over a cup of tea,' she said chirpily, and he laughed and made his way back down the stairs again. 'You're a difficult woman to say no to Rosaleen.'

I stood on the stairs, my mouth agape at what was occurring. I had read it but didn't believe that the doctor would so easily obey her when an apparently sick patient was upstairs.

'I'll just give your mother a little more rest, Tamara,' Dr Gedad said, 'and then I'll see to her.'

'Okay,' I whispered, trying to hold back my tears, because I knew that whatever Rosaleen was going to say to Dr Gedad, he wouldn't make it up those stairs. Despite knowing the outcome, I tried to join them in the kitchen but Rosaleen stopped me at the door.

'If you don't mind, Tamara, I'm going to have a few private words with the doctor about my mother. Just to make sure everything's okay. She's been slightly off for the last few days.'

I gulped, initially guilty that my visit to her had made her worse but as soon as the guilt arrived, it disappeared and the anger returned. I really didn't care about her mother, I was so angry about her taking the doctor from Mum.

'Yes, of course I understand, Rosaleen. I was just trying to do exactly the same thing for my own mother,' I replied bitchily. I turned my back on her before she had a chance to respond and I stormed upstairs. I heard the door close and I went into Mum's room. She was still asleep, curled in a ball as though still in the womb.

'Mum,' I whispered gently, falling to my knees and pushing back her hair.

She groaned.

'Mum, wake up.'

Her eyes fluttered open.

'Mum, I need you to get up. I called a doctor for you. He's downstairs but I need you to go down to him, or else call him. Please, do that for me?'

She groaned and closed her eyes again.

'Mum, listen, this is important. He'll help you get better.'

She opened her eyes again. 'No,' she croaked.

'I know, Mum, I know you miss Dad more than anything else in the world. I know you loved him so much, and you probably think that nothing in the whole world can ever make you feel better, but it can get better and it will get better.'

She closed her eyes again.

'Mum, please,' I whispered, tears welling. 'I need you to do this for me.'

Mum's breathing was slow and deep again as she fell back asleep. I kneeled beside her, crying.

Below the bedroom, I heard Dr Gedad and

Rosaleen's muffled conversation. Then the kitchen door opened and I wiped my tears away and shook Mum again to wake her.

'Okay Mum, he's coming. All you have to do is go as far as your door. That's all, no further.'

She looked alarmed, seeing as I'd just woken her.

'Please, Mum.'

She seemed confused. I swore and left her side to run downstairs just as Rosaleen was opening the front door.

'Ah, Tamara, I had a few words with Rosaleen and I think it's best that I leave your mum for the time being and return again if she needs me. If you feel any need to call, here's my card.'

'But I called so you'd see her today.'

'I know, but after speaking with Rosaleen I realise that it is not necessary. There's really nothing to worry about. Your mother is indeed going through a difficult time but there is little cause for you to worry so much for her health. I'm sure she'd just want you to relax and have a clear mind,' he said in a fatherly tone.

'But you haven't even seen her,' I said, angrily.

'Tamara . . .' Rosaleen had a warning in her voice.

Dr Gedad looked uncomfortable, then uncertain about his decision. What reason had he not to trust Rosaleen, I could see him asking himself. Rosaleen could too, and she moved quickly.

'Thank you so much for calling around, Doctor,'

she said gently. 'Please pass on my regards to Maureen and your boy . . .'

'Weseley,' he said. 'Thank you. And thank you for the tea and buns. I did not taste a bit of salt in it.'

'Oh, no, that was in the apple tart.' She laughed like a child.

And he was gone. She closed the door and turned to face me but I marched past her to the front door, opened it and slammed it loudly behind me. I charged up the road. Outside the air was warm and smelled sweet with cut grass and cow manure. I could hear Arthur's lawnmower in the distance, the noise of the engine blocking the reality for Arthur as he concentrated on remedial tasks. I spotted Sister Ignatius to my left in the far distance on the other side of the grounds; a navy and white thing in the middle of green. I ran to her, the anger rushing through my blood like a Soda-Stream. She had set up an easel and stool in the middle of the grasslands in front of the castle, which was a quarter of a mile away, and she stood directly in front of one of the swan lakes, in the shade of a giant oak tree. The morning was already hot, the sky perfectly indigo without a cloud visible. She must have been concentrating intently, her head close to the page, her tongue moving around her lips as she moved the brush around.

'I hate her,' I shouted, breaking the silence and sending a flock of birds up from a nearby tree into the sky where they tried to regroup and relocate.

I stomped across the scorched grass in my flip-flops.

Sister Ignatius didn't look up as I neared. 'Good morning, Tamara,' she said brightly. 'Another lovely morning.'

'I hate her,' I said louder, coming close, my voice still raised.

She looked at me then, eyes wide in panic. She shook her head quickly, and waved her arms about as if she was in the middle of a railway track trying to stop an oncoming train.

'Yes, that's right, *hate* her,' I kept shouting.

She put her finger in front of her lip, jiggling around like she needed to go to the toilet.

'She is Satan's spawn,' I spat.

'Oh Tamara!' she finally exploded, and threw her hands up in the air, looking distraught.

'What? I don't care what *he* thinks. I *want* him to strike me down. Get me out of here, God, I'm fed up and I want to go *home*,' I whinged in frustration, then fell back onto the grass. I lay on my back and looked up at the sky. 'That cloud looks like a penis.'

'Oh, Tamara, would you stop it,' she snapped.

'Why, do I offend you?' I asked sarcastically, just wanting to hurt absolutely everybody I came into contact with, no matter how good and gentle they were.

'No! You chased off the squirrel,' she said, the most frustrated I'd ever seen her. I sat up, shocked, and listened to her long vehement speech. 'I've

273

been trying to get him all week. I laid out some treats on a plate and finally got him – he didn't want nuts so all those stories about a squirrel and its nuts need to be changed. He wouldn't touch the cheese, but he loves the Toffee Pops, would you believe. But now look, he's gone and he'll never come back and Sister Conceptua will eat me alive for taking her Toffee Pops. I think you and your dramatics gave him a heart attack,' she sighed, calmed, then turned to me. 'You hate who? Rosaleen, I suppose.'

I looked at her painting. 'That's supposed to be a squirrel? It looks like an elephant with a bushy tail.'

Sister Ignatius looked angry first. Then, as she examined it further, she began to laugh. 'Oh, Tamara, you really are the perfect dose, you know that.'

'No,' I huffed, getting to my feet. 'Apparently I'm not. Otherwise I wouldn't have to call a doctor for Mum. I could just fix her all by myself.' I paced up and down before her.

She turned serious then. 'You called Dr Gedad?'

'Yes, and he came this morning. I planned it for when Rosaleen was over at her mum's stuffing her with food – and by the way, I've seen her mum and there's no way in the world she's putting away all that food everyday unless she's got worms. But Rosaleen came home early before Dr Gedad even got up the stairs because – stop the press – she put salt in her apple tart instead of sugar and yes,

274

you're right to look at me like that because I did it and I don't care and I'd do it again tomorrow and I'll know soon enough whether I do or not actually.' I took a breath. 'Anyway, she came back to get the apple pie that was supposed to be for me and Arthur, not that I care because all her food makes me fart fifty times a day, and she managed to talk the doctor out of seeing Mum. So he's gone now and Mum is still in the bedroom, probably drooling right now and drawing on the walls.'

'How did she send him away?'

'I don't know. I don't know what she said to him. He just said that right now Mum just needed to rest and if I needed him again for an emergency or whatever, I should call.'

'Well the doctor would know,' she said uncertainly.

'Sister, he didn't even *see* her. He just listened to whatever Rosaleen said.'

'So why shouldn't he trust Rosaleen?' she asked.

'Well, why *should* he? I'm the one that called him, not her. What if I'd seen her try to kill herself and I never told Rosaleen?'

'Did she try?'

'No! But that's not the point.'

'Hmm.' Sister Ignatius went silent as she dabbed her brush in a mucky brown colour and applied it to the paper.

'Now it looks like an inbred animal who's just eaten a bad nut,' I said.

She snorted and laughed again.

'Do you ever, like, pray? All I see you do is make honey, or garden or paint.'

'I enjoy creating new things, Tamara. I've always believed the creative process is a spiritual experience where I cocreate with the Divine Creative Spirit.'

I looked around, wide-eyed. 'And is the divine creative spirit on his lunch break?'

Sister Ignatius was lost in thought. 'I could go see her, if you like?' she asked quietly.

'Thank you, but she needs more than just a nun. No offence.'

'Tamara, do you know what it is that I actually do?'

'Uh, you pray.'

'Yes, I pray. But I don't only pray. I have taken vows of poverty, chastity and obedience like all Catholic sisters, but on top of that, I vow to help service the poor, sick and uneducated. I can talk to your mother, Tamara. I can help.'

'Oh. Well I suppose she's two out of the three.'

'And besides I'm not "just a nun", as you say. I'm also trained in midwifery,' she said, dabbing at the paper again.

'But that's ridiculous, she's not pregnant.' Then I registered what she'd said. 'Hold on, you're a what? Since when?'

'Oh, I'm not just a pretty face,' she chuckled. 'That was my first job. But I always felt that God was calling me to a life of spirituality and service and so I joined the sisters, and with them I travelled the world with the great gift of being able to be both nun and midwife. I spent most of my thirties in Africa. All around. Saw some harsh things but also wonderful things. I met the most special and extraordinary people.' She smiled at the memory.

'Did you meet somebody there who gave you that?' I smiled and nodded at her gold ring with the tiny green emerald. 'So much for your vow of poverty. If you sold that you could build a well somewhere in Africa. I've seen it on the ads.'

'Tamara,' she said, shocked. 'I was given that almost thirty years ago for twenty-five years as a nun.'

'But it looks like you're married – why would they give you that?'

'I am married to God,' she smiled.

I screwed up my face in disgust. 'Gross. Well, if you'd married a real man that exists, I mean one that you could actually see and who doesn't put his socks in the wash basket, then you'd have got a diamond for twenty-five years' service.'

'I'm perfectly happy with what I have, thank you very much,' she smiled. 'Did your parents never bring you to mass?'

I shook my head and imitated my father. '"There's no money in religion." Even though Dad's totally wrong. We were in Rome and saw the Vatican. Those guys are loaded.'

'That sounds like him all right,' she chuckled.

'You met my dad?'

'Oh, yes.'

'When? Where?'

'When he was here.'

'But I don't remember him ever being here.'

'Well, he was. So there you go, Miss Know-It-All.'

I smiled. 'Did you hate him?'

Sister Ignatius shook her head.

'Go on, you're allowed to say that you hate him. Most people did. I did too sometimes. We used to row a lot. I was nothing like him and I think he hated me for that.'

'Tamara.' She took my hands in hers and I was mildly embarrassed. She was so sweet and so soft, it was like a bit of reality would blow her over, but with all her travels and her daily work, she'd probably seen more of it than I. 'Your father loved you very much, with all of his heart. He was good to you, blessed you with a wonderful life, was always there for you. You were an extraordinarily lucky girl. Don't speak of him like that. He was a great man.'

I immediately felt guilty, and with old habits dying hard, I did what I always did. 'You should have married him then,' I snapped. 'You'd have had a gold ring on every finger.'

After a long silence in which I was supposed to apologise, but didn't, Sister Ignatius went back to her crap painting. She dabbed her brush in the green paint and flattened the bristles on the paper where she embarked on a journey of unusual jerking motions with her wrist, like a music conductor with a paint brush, to make the green blob look like leaves, or something.

'There's no tree in front of you.'

'There's no squirrel either. I'm using my imagination. Anyway, it's not a tree, it's the ambience my poor little squirrel inhabits that I'm trying to depict. Think of it as abstract art; a departure from reality in depiction of imagery,' she taught. 'Well, it's partially abstract, as artwork that takes liberties, for instance altering colour and form in ways that are conspicuous is considered so.'

'Like your brown elephant having a huge tail instead of a trunk.'

She ignored me. 'Total abstraction, on the other hand,' she continued, 'bears no trace of any reference to anything recognisable.'

I studied her work a little more closely. 'Yeah, I'd say yours is a little more like total abstraction. Like my life.'

She chuckled. 'Oh, the drama of being seventeen.'

'Sixteen,' I corrected her. 'Hey, I went over to Rosaleen's mum yesterday.'

'You did? And how is she?'

'Well, she gave me this.' I took the glass tear drop out of my pocket and moved it around in my hand. It was cold and smooth, calming. 'She has loads of them over there. It's so weird. In her back garden there's a shed, that's like her factory, and behind the shed there's an entire field of these glass things. Some are totally freaky and pointy but most of them are beautiful. They're hanging from clothes lines, about ten of them, all tied on with wiry cords, and they catch the light. I think she makes them. She certainly doesn't grow them. But it's like a glass farm,' I laughed.

Sister Ignatius stopped painting and I dropped the tear drop into her hand. 'She gave this to you?'

'No, well, she didn't exactly hand it to me. I saw her in the shed. She was working on something, all bent over, wearing goggles, doing something with glass, and I think I gave her a fright. So I left the tray down in the garden for her. I'd made her some food.'

'That was nice of you.'

'Not really. You should have seen the state of it. And Rosaleen didn't know I was there so I had to go back to collect the tray, which I was totally expecting to be full. But it was on the wall outside of the house, and all the dishes were clean and all the food was eaten and everything. And this was sitting on the plate.' I took it back from her and examined it again. 'Sweet of her, wasn't it?'

'Tamara . . .' Sister Ignatius reached her arm out and held on to the easel, which was so light it offered her no support.

'Are you okay? You look a little . . .' I didn't get to finish as Sister Ignatius looked so weak, I immediately wrapped my arms around her and remembered that despite her youthful aura and her childish giggles, she was in her seventies.

'I'm fine, I'm fine,' she said, attempting to laugh. 'Stop fussing. Tamara, I need you to slow down when you speak, and go back over what you said. You found that on the tray when you went to collect it?'

'Yes, on the front garden wall,' I said slowly.

'But that's impossible. Did you see her put it there?'

'No, I just saw the tray from my bedroom window. She must have done it when I was elsewhere in the house. Why are you asking so many questions? Are you mad at me for going over? I know I probably shouldn't have, but Rosaleen was being so secretive.'

'Tamara,' Sister Ignatius closed her eyes and she looked more tired when she opened them, 'Rosaleen's mother, Helen, has multiple sclerosis, which has unfortunately been getting worse with the years. She's wheelchair-bound, which is why Rosaleen has become her full-time carer. So you see, she couldn't have wheeled herself out to the front garden with this tray.' She shook her head. 'Impossible.'

'She could have,' I replied. 'If she just put the tray on her lap, then she'd have her hands free to wheel herself—'

'No, Tamara, there are steps in the front garden.'

I looked in the direction of the bungalow and even though I couldn't see it from where we were, I visualised the steps. 'Oh, yeah. That's odd. So who else lives in the bungalow?' I asked.

Sister Ignatius was quiet, her eyes moving around as she thought hard. 'No one, Tamara,' she whispered. 'No one.'

'But I saw someone. Think, Sister,' I barked, panicking. 'Who did I see in the workshed? A woman all hunched over with goggles, work goggles, and long hair. There were these glass things all over the place. Who could she be?'

Sister Ignatius shook her head over and over.

'Rosaleen has a sister – she told me about her. She lives in Cork. She's a teacher. Maybe she came to visit. What do you think?'

Sister Ignatius continued to shake her head. 'No. No. It couldn't be.'

Shivers ran down my spine and my body was covered in goose bumps. The look on Sister Ignatius' usually calm face didn't do much to calm me either. She looked as though she'd seen a ghost.

CHAPTER SEVENTEEN
Possessed

I stopped interrogating Sister Ignatius. She had become grey in the face and had lost all of her colour.

'Sit down, Sister. Come on, sit here on the stool. You're okay, it's just hot out today.' I tried to remain calm as I helped her to the wooden stool. I moved it nearer to the tree trunk so that she was completely shaded. 'Let's just rest here for a minute and then we'll go back to the house.'

She didn't respond, she just let me guide her, one hand around her waist, the other holding her hand. Once seated, I pushed back some loose strands of hair from her face. She didn't feel hot.

I heard my name being called in the distance and saw Weseley running. I waved my hands wildly to let him know I could see him. By the time he reached me he was breathless and had to hunch over, hands on his knees, to catch his breath.

'Hi, Sister,' he finally said, giving her a goofy

wave even though he was right beside her. 'Tamara,' he turned to me, alert, 'I heard it all.'

'Heard what?' I asked impatiently, while he tried to catch his breath.

'Rosaleen.' Pant. 'In the kitchen.' Pant. 'With my dad.' Pant. 'You were right. About it all. About the sugar and the salt and,' pant, 'her coming home early. How did you know?'

'I told you,' I quickly looked at Sister Ignatius but she was staring distantly into space, looking as though she was going to faint at any moment. 'It was written in the diary.'

He shook his head disbelievingly and I became angry. 'Look, I don't care if you don't believe me, just tell me what—'

'I believe *you*, Tamara, I just don't believe *it*. You know?'

'Yeah, I know. I'm the same.'

'Okay, I broke away from Arthur at ten o'clock this morning. We separated so that I'd take care of the walnut trees on the south of the grounds. We're having a problem with walnut blight,' he looked to Sister Ignatius, 'so we've to try to maintain the soil pH above 6.0, cut out all the affected shoots—'

'Weseley, shut up,' I interrupted.

'Right, sorry. I couldn't stop thinking about what you'd said and so I went to the gatehouse and I hid outside the kitchen window in the back garden. I heard it all. Rosaleen started talking about her mum first of all, saying her health had deteriorated. She has MS. She asked him a few questions about her, some advice that kind of thing. I think she was just delaying him.'

I nodded. This matched Sister Ignatius' story so at least I knew Rosaleen hadn't lied to me about her mother.

'My dad really annoyed me. I felt like yelling at him and telling him to go upstairs. But just as he said he was going up to your mam, Rosaleen started talking about her. My dad was keen to get upstairs to see her, but Rosaleen was insistent. She said that . . .' He paused.

'Come on, Weseley tell me.'

'Just promise to be calm when I tell you, till we work something out.'

'Okay, okay,' I hurried him.

'Right.' He spoke slower now, studying me as he spoke. 'She said that this had happened before. That your mum was prone to depression and that she regularly goes into states like this where she withdraws from everybody—'

'That's bullshit!'

'Tamara, listen. And she said that your dad and your mum kept it from you all of your life and so you weren't to know about it. She said your mum was on antidepressants and that the best thing to do was to leave her alone in her room until the depression passed. She said that's what they always did.'

'Bullshit!' I interrupted again. 'That's a lie! That's a fucking lie! My mother has never been like this

285

before. She's, she's – uughh, she's a lying bitch! How dare she say that Dad never told me? I would know. I was home with them every day. She was never like this. Never!'

I was pacing, I was shouting, my blood was boiling. I felt so angry I wanted to tear the sky down. I felt so out of control, like there was nothing I could do to make everything okay again. I questioned myself. Was there some way that I could have missed Mum's behaviour? Had she been like this before and I couldn't remember? Was I such a terrible daughter that I could so easily be put off? I thought about the weekends away – were they somewhere else? I thought about her faint smiles to Dad, the fact that she was never over-enthusiastic like other mums, the fact she never gave anything away. No, that meant nothing. She just wasn't emotional, she never cried, she wasn't sentimental, but it didn't make her *depressed*. No, no, no, how dare Rosaleen say that my father had lied when he could do nothing to defend himself. It was wrong. It was all wrong.

Weseley tried to take hold of me and calm me down but I was screaming, that much I can remember. And then I remember Sister Ignatius finally coming to, standing and coming towards me with open arms and that sweet, sad, but older, so much older face than a few minutes ago, that was now so sad and pitying that I could hardly look at her.

'Tamara, you have to listen to me now . . .' she

was saying, but I didn't want to hear. I thrashed and squirmed away from them. And then I remember running, running so fast while I heard them shouting my name. I fell a few times, felt Weseley behind me, then grabbing me. I screamed and kept running, faster and faster thinking he was on my heel. I don't know when he stopped running, when he decided to let me go, but I kept on going despite feeling an ache in my chest and finding it hard to breathe. Hot tears ran from the corner of my eyes and straight back to my ears, my speed not giving them opportunity to fall down properly. I ran out of the woods and straight onto the road, and the roar of an engine and a screech of tyres and a long car horn sounded in my ear and I froze. I absolutely froze. I waited to be hit, for the bumper to crash into my side and for me to go flying up over the windscreen, but it didn't happen. Instead I felt the heat of the grid beside my leg, so close, too close, and the dark part of me in the shadows felt it wasn't close enough. Then the vehicle door opened and there was shouting. A man. My hands were over my ears, I was crying over and over, unable to catch my breath and I could hear my name being yelled over and over. Angry, aggressive, accusing. Like it was my fault.

Finally it got softer and arms were around me and then I was being rocked gently, the noises died down, and I realised I was in Marcus's arms, the travelling library was beside us and I was sobbing uncontrollably onto his shirt.

I finally looked up at him. His face was concerned, afraid.

'So where should we go now? Paris? Australia?' he asked softly, smiling.

'No,' I sobbed. 'I want to go home. I just want to go home.'

I was silent in the bus on the way to Killiney. Marcus had tried to ask questions but gave up after a while. I finally stopped crying, my body stopped shaking and now only trembled a little. I felt weak from the emotion, tired from it all. I finally wiped my eyes with my snotty tissue one last time, and took a deep breath and exhaled.

'That sounds better,' Marcus said, looking at me as we stopped at red lights. 'So, are you going to talk to me now?'

I cleared my throat and smiled at him. 'Hello, Marcus. I want to get really drunk.'

'You know what, that's exactly what I was thinking.' He smiled mischievously and pulled the bus over outside the off-licence as soon as the lights were green. 'You're a woman after my own heart,' he said before closing the door and running into the shop.

I should have told him then. Again. My age that is. I could have saved a lot of heartache. Less than three weeks to go till my seventeenth birthday and that was probably still too young for him. I'm not quite sure what I was thinking, if I was really able to think at all. I felt numb, and wanted to be more numb. I didn't want to feel, I didn't want to have to think. My life felt so out of control that I wanted to lose control of me too. Just for a little while, at least.

We were only an hour away from Killiney. An hour was nothing, but it was a world away for me. I'd been ripped away from my home, my place; I felt like my identity had been taken away with it. I don't think some people know what it's like to be taken away from their home. Sure, you can be homesick, or you can move away and miss an area. But we were forced to move. Some bank, some place that had nothing to do with warmth, with memories, with families, had chased my father, had tormented him so much he'd taken his own life. Then, after they'd done that, they'd taken our building of memories, our sense of place, the foundations of our family. And while we were cast out, forced to live with family members we barely knew, it just sat here, huge and empty, with a For Sale sign nailed to the boundary wall like two fingers being held up to us, while we had to sit outside and watch it like strangers, without being able to return.

'Do you still have the keys to this place?' Marcus asked as we weaved through the windy roads that led through the area.

I nodded. Another lie.

'Hey, slow down there, Tamara.' He looked at me knocking back my third can of beer. 'Leave some for me,' he laughed.

I finished it and burped loudly.

'Sexy,' he laughed, keeping an eye on the road.

If you ask me now, I'll honestly say that's the first moment that I consciously decided what I wanted to do. Of course I can blame him for putting it in my head, but really it was me. Perhaps I'd known from the second I ran out onto the road and he put his arms around me that we'd end up at the house and I'd end up on the floor with him in my bedroom. Maybe I'd decided it the first day I met him. Maybe I did have it all planned. Maybe I was more in control than I thought. Or maybe, the third beer had played havoc with me in my emotional state. I pointed out places to Marcus as we drove, telling him stories, telling him the names of people who lived there. I didn't wait for responses. It wasn't really relevant if he answered or not. I was saying them for me. My voice felt like it was coming from elsewhere. I didn't feel like me. I didn't really care who I was any more. I had given up pretending to be the person I'd kept trying to be, the same as Zoey and Laura, the same as everybody else around us, as though by being that way we'd get along in life so much better. Well, it wasn't working. It wasn't working for Laura, it hadn't worked for Zoey and it most certainly hadn't worked for me.

We pulled up outside the house. I told Marcus to park the bus down a nearby laneway so that it wouldn't be seen from the road. The last thing we wanted was for the neighbours to come looking for books. The house wasn't visible from the road.

The large black gates, with cameras, locked between the tenfoot walls were enough to dissuade any burglar. Dad had put so much time and effort into those gates: drawn plans up over and over again, asked me and Mum what we thought, so proudly walked me to the entrance to ask my opinion and I had never answered; told him I never cared. I hurt him all the time.

I think I was telling Marcus this as we walked along, but I wasn't sure.

'I don't have the zapper for the gate on my keys,' I heard myself say. 'I'll have to climb over and open the gates from the house.'

I'd a system. I'd done this so many times. Mum and Dad had taken my keys most evenings after school so that I wouldn't escape, but despite its height I'd navigated the gate safely on many an occasion. I could hear Marcus warning me, pointing out which way to go, but I didn't follow him. On autopilot I just scaled the gate and landed safely on the other side. I heard him applauding as I walked the long driveway to our house. He may have thought he was there with me, but I was nowhere near him.

Our house – glass, stone, wood, bright, light, modern, airy. It was like something from a catalogue. Stone to camouflage parts of the house to match the rock it was built into, wood to blend into the woodlands surrounding it, glass to give us views of the sea that stretched on for ever. Dad had tried to create the most perfect place that neither of us would ever want to leave. He did that right. I knew the front door would be locked, and still on autopilot I made my way round the back of the house.

I saw the tennis ball in the back garden that was always there, lying soggy and wet. It had flown over from our nearby tennis court into the garden and I'd been too lazy to collect it. I'd been playing with Dad that day. Spring had arrived, we'd started using the outdoor court again, but I was playing horrendously. After a winter of having not picked up a racket, I was rusty. I kept missing the ball, kept hitting it over the fence and had grown tired of the times I'd had to search for the ball in the garden. Dad had been patient, he hadn't yelled, he hadn't said anything. He'd even gone searching for the ball when it wasn't his fault. He even purposely fluffed a few shots, and that had angered me even more. I remember him in his little white tennis shorts, his white collared T-shirt, his sport socks that he pulled up too high, which embarrassed me even though I was the only one who could see. My lovely Dad . . .

In the back there were the same garden statues – an old chubby couple with gardening tools in their hands, the man revealing the crack of his behind – that my granddad, my dad's dad, always used to talk to before he died. He called the woman Mildred and the man Tristan, for no particular reason, but it had made me laugh since I was a child and Mildred and Tristan had become part of the family. But Mum obviously hadn't arranged for them to be moved and so Mildred and Tristan remained the only inhabitants of the house. Near the washing line there was a red plastic peg in the grass, dropped there from the last wash.

I climbed up onto the swimming pool roof, where the old weather-beaten wooden ladder was still lying. I'd stored it there for my midnight escapes. In the newest addition to the house, the pool was covered over by a blue canvas, our six pool loungers lay diagonally by the window, still with their pink cushions waiting for me and my morning swim. A deflated swimming ring sat on one of the sun loungers. I'd brought it back from Marbella. It was a pink flamingo. Manuel, a boy I'd kissed last year, had given it to me and I was intent on bringing it home. It lay there now with nobody to use it. A discarded kiss.

Once on the roof, I climbed the ladder to my bedroom balcony. Nobody ever locked my bedroom balcony door. It was supposedly too high up, too inaccessible for any burglar to reach. My head was spinning as I finally pulled myself up onto the balcony. The weather had cooled now as we had driven towards the coast. The sea air was cold, the wind took away the July heat and brought the scent of seaweed and salt. I looked out to the beach and took in the view, remembered sixteen years of summers with Mum and Dad, and nights out with friends. I don't know how long I'd been standing there watching the imaginary family writing their names in the sand and the little girl burying her daddy in the sand, when I remembered Marcus at the gates.

As soon as I opened the balcony door, the alarm went off. I ran inside, immediately, hoping they hadn't changed the code. They hadn't, of course. What owners in their right minds would ever want to break back in to their repossessed house?

After failing on the first attempt, due to shaky fingers, I remembered what to do and the alarm finally stopped. I took a few breaths, waited till the ringing died down in my ears. I pressed the button for the gate, then went downstairs and opened the front door. While I waited for Marcus to make his way up the road, I wandered around the house. I ran my fingers over all the surfaces. Some were slightly dusty. I heard Marcus behind me, his voice echoing in the entrance hall. I heard him whistle, impressed.

I went into the kitchen, saw family dinners at the table, rushed breakfasts at the breakfast counter, Christmas dinners in the nearby dining area, noisy parties, birthday parties, New Year's Eve. I remembered fights, Mum and Dad, Me and Dad. I remembered dancing. Dancing with my dad for everyone at one party. I remember Dad's party trick, a long story that I never really understood but loved to hear him tell. He would come alive, he would love the limelight in the company of those he trusted. His cheeks would be flushed with alcohol, his blue eyes glazed but he would recant the tale perfectly and confidently, just dying to get to that final line to see everybody erupting in laughter. I could see Mum's area where she'd prop herself with her lady friends for the night, all huddled together, elegant women with expensive shoes, thin ankles, tanned skin and highlighted hair.

As I turned away, I saw Dad wander through the halls, wink at me, cigar in hand as he went to the only room Mum would let him smoke in. I followed him in there. I watched him enter and greet his friends. They all cheered as he opened the best brandy, as they settled down for a chat or to play snooker. I looked around the walls and remembered the photographs. His achievements, his degrees, his sports trophies, his family photographs. Me teary-eyed on my first day of school, me on his shoulders in Disney World, wearing a Mickey Mouse T-shirt with my hair in pigtails, a silly smile with missing front teeth. I moved into the next room. Dad and his friends on the top of a ski slope in Aspen. A photo of Dad playing golf with Padraig Harrington at a celebrity charity event.

I moved into the television room and saw him sitting in his favourite armchair watching television. Mum in the other corner, legs curled up underneath her, her arms wrapped around her legs protectively, the two of them laughing at some comedy show. Then he looked at me and he winked again. He stood up and I followed him.

We walked through the entrance hall, past Marcus, who was watching me, then he walked through the closed office door. He disappeared. I couldn't go in there.

The fight. The horrible fight we'd had. I'd slammed that door in his face and run upstairs. I should have told him I loved him. I should have said sorry and hugged him.

'I never want to see you again. I hate you!'

'Tamara, come back!' His voice. His lovely voice that I want to hear again. Oh, Daddy, I'm here, I'm back. Please come out of the office.

Then the next morning, seeing him, my beautiful dad. My handsome dad on the floor. Not the way he was supposed to be. He was supposed to live forever. He was supposed to mind me forever. He was supposed to interrogate my boyfriends and walk me down the aisle. He was supposed to gently persuade Mum when I couldn't get my way, he was supposed to wink at me when he caught my eye. He was supposed to look at me proudly for the rest of my life. And then when he got old I was supposed to protect him, I was supposed to be there for him, paying it all back.

It had been my fault. It had all been my fault. I'd tried to save him but I didn't even know how to do that properly. If I'd learned how, if I'd paid attention at school, if I'd tried to be an interested, better person than the selfish one I'd been, then maybe I could have helped. They'd said I got to him too late, that there was nothing I could possibly have done, but still you never know. I'm his daughter – maybe that would have helped.

That room, his room, that smelled of him. His aftershave, of cigars, of wine or brandy, of books and wood. The room he'd taken his life in, with the vomit-stained rug from where I'd thrown up the red wine on the night after his funeral. I couldn't go in there.

I heard the clink of cans and the rustle of a plastic bag, and I turned around. Marcus was watching me.

'Nice house.'

'Thanks.'

'You okay?'

I nodded.

'Must be weird being back here.'

I nodded again.

'You're not very chatty today.'

'I didn't really bring you here to talk.'

He looked at me then. I could see it in his face, he wanted it too.

Tell him. Tell him.

'So come on, let me show you the best room in the house,' I smiled. I took him by the hand and I led him upstairs.

Back in my bedroom, I lay down on my bedroom floor, on the soft plush cream carpet where my king-sized bed used to be with the white leather headboard. My head spun from the alcohol and from all that had been going on. I wanted to forget everything that had happened that day – Sister

Ignatius, Weseley, Rosaleen, Dr Gedad, the mystery woman in Rosaleen's mother's house. I wanted to forget my mother as I'd tried to drag her limp frail body out of bed. I wanted to forget Kilsaney and all the people in it. I wanted to forget we'd ever left this house and that Dad had ever done what he'd done. I wanted to go back to the night I'd crept out and then had the fight with him. I wanted everything to change.

And then everything changed.

Everything.

And if I'd managed at any stage to upstand the dominoes, they all started to fall again.

CHAPTER EIGHTEEN

RIP

Though two years ago our house in Killiney could have fetched a whopping eight million euro, it stood for sale for half of that now. I know how much it had been worth because Dad regularly had it valued. Each time the new valuations would come through, he'd surface from the cellar of his eight-million-euro home with a €600 bottle of Chateau Latour to share with his perfect model wife and his perfectly hormonally imbalanced teenage daughter.

I don't begrudge Dad his success. I'm not one of those people and not just because his success was inevitably our success – ironically, his failures became ours too – but because he worked hard, early mornings, late nights, weekends. He cared about what he did, he donated regularly to charities. Whether he did it in a tuxedo, in front of a flashing camera, or with his hand raised high at a charity ball auction was entirely irrelevant.

He gave and that's what mattered. There was nothing wrong with having an expensive home, nothing wrong at all. There's a pride in building something up, working hard to achieve something. But it shouldn't have been his manhood that increased with each new success, it should have been his heart. His success was like the witch in the 'Hansel and Gretel' fairy tale: it fed him for all the wrong reasons, fattening him in all the wrong places. Dad deserved his success, he just needed a masterclass in humility. I could have done with one too. How special I thought I was in the silver Aston Martin in which he drove me to school some mornings. How special am I now, now that somebody bought it from a depot of repossessed cars, for a fraction of the price. How special indeed.

The reason I mentioned the price of the house is because though the sale price had been halved, and judging by the dust that had settled inside it would be reduced even further, the house was still asking a high price and so was still a priority sale for the estate agents. Little did I know that when I opened the balcony door to my bedroom and set off the alarm, it sent an automated response phone call to the estate agent, who in her worryingly quiet offices, immediately jumped into her car and came to check the premises. While I was three flights upstairs, facing the wrong direction, of course I didn't hear the electric gates open half a mile down the driveway. While I was in the throes of it all, I also didn't hear her open the front door and step into the entrance hall.

But she heard us.

And so the next people that paid us a visit were the gardaí. Three flights of heavy pounding on the stairs allowed us at least not to be doing what we'd been previously doing on the floor of my bedroom, but it didn't give us enough time to clothe ourselves and so I huddled behind Marcus, with my clothes scattered around me, I met Garda Fitzgibbon, an overweight man from Connemara, with a redder face than mine, who I'd regularly been acquainted with on the beach with my friends. This was not the time for reunions.

'I'll give you a minute to get dressed, Miss Goodwin,' he said, immediately looking away.

Twenty-two-year-old Marcus, who'd been invited to an eighteen-year-old girl's house which hadn't yet been sold, found the entire thing mildly embarrassing, but mostly amusing. He didn't know that the girl he'd just slept with was a few weeks away from her seventeenth birthday, and so not only were the bottles of beer highly illegal, so was half of what they'd done on the carpet. He kept looking at me and snorting while we quickly got dressed. I was panicked, my heart thudding so loudly I could barely think, feeling so queasy I was afraid I'd vomit right there in front of them all.

'Tamara, relax,' he said cockily. 'They can't do anything. It's your house.'

301

I looked at him then, and I hated myself more than he was ever going to.

'It's not my house, Marcus,' I whispered, my voice refusing to work.

'Well your parents', whatever . . .' he smiled, and pulled his jeans up one leg.

'The bank took it,' I said, sitting there, dressed, feeling completely out of it. 'It's not ours any more.'

'What?' A giant domino fell. I felt the floor vibrate as it thudded to the floor, like a great big skyscraper crashing down.

'I'm sorry,' I said, then started crying. Then the words I wanted to say to him for so long, finally came out, but all in the wrong way and totally at the wrong time. 'I'm sixteen,' I panicked.

Thankfully Garda Fitzgibbon, who'd been standing at the door, was on alert after the first raised voice and heard the rest of the conversation. He at least would believe Marcus didn't know, but it was up to Marcus to prove that in court. He also had to step in as Marcus came flying at me in anger, not to hit me, but shouting at me with such ferocity I wanted him to throw more at me, call me everything under the sun, but he just yelled and I knew that I'd ruined everything for him. Whatever arrangement he'd made with his dad in that travelling library, it'd probably been his last chance. We'd never spoken about it but I recognise somebody on their last chance. I used to see it in the mirror every day.

We were brought to the station. Went through the humiliation of giving statements of the entire account. I was hoping the first time I finally had sex I could write all the juicy and embarrassing details in a diary, not at a police station. Tamara Goodwin. Tamara Fuckup, ripping things apart as usual.

Rosaleen and Arthur had to drive to Dublin to collect me from the station. As soon as Marcus's dad found out, he sent a car for him. I tried to apologise over and over again, desperately between tears and trying to cling to him so he'd stop and listen, but he wouldn't listen to me. He wouldn't even look at me.

Arthur stayed in the car while Rosaleen met with the garda, the next most embarrassing thing that happened to me that day. Rosaleen seemed more concerned about Marcus, what would happen to him. They told her the maximum sentence for sleeping with a "child" under seventeen was two years. I broke down crying at that. Rosaleen seemed as distraught as I was. I don't know if it was because I'd soiled their name, even more so than my father's suicide had, or if she was genuinely fond of Marcus. She asked question after question about Marcus until Garda Fitzgibbon seemed to calm her with the news that he seemed to genuinely not know what age I was and that if he could argue this in court then he'd be okay. It seemed to be enough for Rosaleen but it wasn't enough for me. How long would this take him?

How many sessions in court? How much humiliation? I'd ruined his life.

Rosaleen didn't even try to talk to me, she barely even looked at me. She curtly told me Arthur was waiting and then she left the station. I eventually followed her. There was the most horrific tension in the car when I sat inside, as though they'd had a fight. I suppose what had happened to me was enough cause for there to be tension. I was mortified, absolutely mortified. I couldn't look at Arthur. He said nothing when I sat in the car and then we pulled away and headed back to Kilsaney. I was actually relieved to be going so far away, to be so disconnected from what had happened. It had finally ripped through the umbilical cord that tied me to this place. Maybe that had been my intention.

I cried the entire way home, so embarrassed, so disappointed, so angry. All of those emotions were directed at myself. My head thumped as the male voice on the radio entered my ears and got closer and closer to my brain, and as the alcohol left its calling card. About thirty minutes in, Arthur pulled the car over outside a shop.

'What are you doing?' Rosaleen asked.

'Could you get some bottles of water and some headache tablets?' he asked quietly.

'What? Me?'

There was a long silence.

'Are you all right?' she asked him.

'Rose,' he merely said.

I'd never heard him call her that. It struck with me as familiar – I'd seen it somewhere, heard it somewhere – but I couldn't think. Rosaleen looked back at me and then at Arthur, her worst fear having to leave us two alone. I thought fast. Eventually she got out of the car and practically ran into the shop.

'Are you okay?' Arthur asked, looking at me in the mirror.

'Yes, thanks.' My tears welled again. 'I'm so sorry, Arthur. I'm so embarrassed.'

'Don't be embarrassed, child,' he said softly. 'We all do things when we're young. It will pass.' He gave me a small smile. 'Just as long as you're okay?' He gave me a look then, a worried look of a paternal concern over what I'd done.

'Yes, I'm fine, thank you.' I rooted for my tissues again. 'It wasn't . . . he didn't . . . I knew what I was doing.' I cleared my throat awkwardly. I could see Rosaleen at the end of a long queue, anxiously looking out to us in the car.

'Arthur, this depression that Mum has, does it run in the family?'

'What depression?' he asked, turning round in his seat.

'You know, the depression that Rosaleen told Dr Gedad that Mum has, this morning.'

'Tamara.' He looked at me and knew what I was at. He checked Rosaleen in the shop. There were three people in front of her. 'Tell me straight.'

'I made an appointment with Dr Gedad to see

Mum this morning. She needs help, Arthur. There's something *wrong*.'

He seemed extremely worried by this. 'But she has her daily walks, at least. She gets some fresh air.'

'What?' I shook my head. 'Arthur, she hasn't left the house since we arrived.'

His jaw hardened and he gave a quick glimpse – good win, very dead – at Rosaleen in the shop. 'What did Dr Gedad say when he saw her?'

'He didn't even get up the stairs. Rosaleen told him that Mum has suffered from depression for years and that Dad knew about it but he decided never to tell me and . . .' I started crying, unable to finish. 'It's all lies. He's not even here to defend himself, or to be able to tell me . . . it's all lies. Though I know I'm not one to talk,' I sniffed.

'Here, Tamara, hush now. Rosaleen is just trying to care for her the best that she can,' he said quietly, almost whispering, in case she'd hear him from the shop. There was only one person in front of her in the queue now.

'I know, Arthur, but what if it's the wrong way? That's all I'm saying. I don't know what happened between them years ago but if there's anything – anything – that Mum did to Rosaleen to hurt her or annoy her, do you think that this could be . . .'

'Could be what?'

'Could be a way of maybe, getting her back? If Mum did something to her, lied in anyway . . .'

The door opened and we both jumped.

'Gosh you'd think I was the bogey-man,' Rosaleen said, offended and worried as she sat in. 'Here.' She dumped a bag in Arthur's lap.

He looked at her then, a cold long stare that chilled me, made me want to look away. He passed the bag back to me. Rosaleen seemed surprised.

'Here, this might help,' he said, then started up the engine.

None of us spoke for the next hour.

When we arrived back at the gatehouse the sky had clouded over and darkened the bright day. There was a chill in the air and the clouds promised rain. The breeze was welcoming to my muffled head. I took a few deep breaths before going into the house and making my way upstairs.

'You'll know you won't be going anywhere for a time to come,' Rosaleen said.

I nodded.

'There'll be a few tasks for you to do around here,' she added.

'Of course,' I said quietly.

Arthur stood by and listened.

'Stay within the grounds when you're out,' he added, and it seemed to take him a lot to say it.

Rosaleen looked at him, surprised and then annoyed that he'd stepped in. He didn't meet her eye. Obviously her plan had been to keep me inside the house where I couldn't cause any trouble. Arthur wasn't being so strict.

'Thank you,' I said, then went upstairs to Mum. She was asleep in bed. I crawled in beside her and wrapped my arms around her, squeezing her tight to me. I breathed in the scent of her freshly washed hair.

Downstairs a storm brewed as I heard Rosaleen and Arthur's voices in the living room. First they were just talking, then it grew louder and louder. Rosaleen tried to hush him a few times but he shouted over her and she gave up. I couldn't hear what they were saying, I didn't even try to. I'd given up poking my nose in where it didn't belong. All I wanted was for Mum to get better and if Arthur's raised voice was going to get me that, then fine. I scrunched my eyes shut and wished that today had never happened. Why hadn't the diary warned me?

The argument between Rosaleen and Arthur became worse. Unable to listen any more, I decided to leave, to give them and me the space we needed. I hated that I'd brought this upon them too. Before we'd arrived, they'd been so happy with their life, their little routines, just the two of them. My arrival had caused a rip in their relationship and it was slowly tearing more and more with each day. As soon as there was a break in their argument, I knocked and Arthur called out to me to enter.

'Sorry to disturb you,' I said quietly. 'I'm just going out for a walk to clear my head. Around the grounds. Is that okay?'

Arthur nodded. Rosaleen had her back to me and I could see her fists clenched by her side. I quickly closed the door and left. It would be light for another hour or so, which gave me enough time for a brief walk and the opportunity to clear my head. I wanted to go to the castle but I could hear Weseley and his friends gathered. I wasn't in the mood for them, I just wanted to be alone. I turned in the opposite direction and headed towards Sister Ignatius, despite knowing I wouldn't call in to her. At this hour I didn't want to cut through the woodlands. I stayed on the path and kept my head down as I strode by the dark gothic entrance, still chained up and left to rot.

As soon as I had the chapel in sight I realised I'd been holding my breath. I could see Sister Ignatius' house from here, and so felt safe enough to go inside. It was only big enough to hold ten people at most. Half the roof had caved in but above it the oak trees bent their branches to protect it. It was quaint. No wonder Sister Ignatius was so fond of it. There were no pews. I assumed it had been dressed for the more recent ceremonies. Above the altar, a simple but large wooden cross had been secured to the stone wall. I guessed Sister Ignatius had something to do with hanging it there. The only other thing that stood in the chapel was a large oversized – good win, very dead – marble bowl, chipped and cracked in places around the rim, yet it was still solid, firmly fixed to the concrete floor. Spiders and dust lived in it now, but I imagined generations upon generations of Kilsaneys all gathering here to baptise their children. There was a wooden door that led to the small graveyard beside. I chose not to go through that but instead returned through the main door where I'd entered. From behind the gate that protected the graveyard, I strained my eyes to read the headstones, though many were covered in moss, ravaged by time. In an oversized crypt rested an entire family: Edward Kilsaney, his wife Victoria, their sons Peter, William and Arthur and their daughter, something beginning with B. The rest had eroded with time for the unfortunate soul whose name began with B. Maybe Beatrice, or Beryl, Bianca or Barbara. I tried to give her a name. For Florie Kilsaney 'Farewell thy mother, we mourn thy loss'. Robert Kilsaney, who died at one year old, 26 September 1832, then his mother Rosemary, followed him ten days after. For Helen Fitzpatrick in 1882, 'Husband and children bear her in tender regard'. Some were just names and dates, and were all the more mysterious for it: Grace and Charles Kilsaney 1850–1862. Only twelve years old, both born and died on the same day. So many questions.

Each gravestone that was clear enough to make out had various symbols on it. Some had arches, some doves, arrows, birds, others had spooky-looking animals, the symbolism of which I had no understanding of but wished to know. I planned to ask Sister Ignatius whenever I felt I could face her. I scanned the headstones again, not feeling as scared as I had been the first time I'd passed by.

Maybe I'd grown up a little bit at least. A large cross climbed high up to the sky, with various names added as families joined one another, their names and inscriptions more legible as the years went by. The newest and freshest inscription was at the bottom and as soon as my eye rested upon it, I couldn't believe I hadn't noticed it earlier. On the bottom of the cross was a large block of stone with the most recent names upon it. On the ground before it was a bunch of flowers – fresh flowers – tied together with long grass. I climbed up on the fence to see the engraving. 'Laurence Kilsaney 1967 – 1992 RIP'.

Only seventeen years ago. He must have died in the fire in the castle. Which made him only twenty-five. How sad. Even though I didn't know Laurence, or any of his family, I started to cry. I picked a few wild flowers, tied them together with my hair bobbin and, against my better judgement, jumped over the fence. I laid the flowers on the grave and reached out to touch the gravestone, but just as my fingers touched the cold stone, I heard a noise behind me: a click. The hairs rose on the back of my neck. I spun round, expecting to come face to face with a stranger, so close I felt their breath on the back of my neck. I looked in every direction, almost dizzy with the effort of trying to focus. Just trees, trees and more trees as far as my eye could see. I tried to tell myself I was spooked because I was standing in an ancient graveyard surrounded by generations of a family who'd been lost to plague, war, suffering, fire and, more humanely, to old age. I tried to tell myself that, but somebody was there all right, I was sure of it. I heard a twig snap and my head darted around to follow the sound.

'Sister Ignatius, is that you?' I called. The response was merely my trembling voice echoing back to me. Then I saw the trees move, heard the rustle moving further away, as somebody pushed their way through the trees in the opposite direction.

'Weseley?' I called, the tremble in my voice echoing back.

Whoever it was had left in a hurry. I swallowed hard and rushed from the grave, climbed over the fence and moved quickly away, shaking myself out as though I'd walked through a giant spider web.

I hurried back to the gatehouse, turning around over and over again to make sure I wasn't being followed. It was dusk by the time I got back to the house. Rosaleen was in the living room knitting, with the television on quietly in the background. Her face looked haggard, weary from fighting. Arthur was in the garage in the back garden, making an angry racket. My curiosity had been killed. I no longer cared what they had in there. I felt I was chasing a secret and now the secret was chasing me. I was afraid. I just wanted the time to pass so that Mum would stop her grieving, get better and we could move on from here and this place that felt so haunted by the ghosts of the past, a past that, despite my having nothing to do with it, was dragging me further and further into it.

CHAPTER NINETEEN

Purgatory

I was grounded for the next two weeks, going up and down the stairs for breakfast, lunch and tea, and doing whichever chores Rosaleen decided would be appropriate punishment, such as vacuuming the living room, polishing the brass, removing all the books from the shelves and dusting, watching her tend to her vegetable and herb garden while explaining to me what she was doing. I think she enjoyed the entire thing, babbling away to me chirpily as though I was a toddler and everything she said was the first time I'd ever heard it. I think it gave her a lease of life to have so many drained souls living around her, like a vampire. The more exhausted we got, the stronger she grew. I couldn't even bring myself to read the diary. It was as if I had given up on everything. Every day that went by I felt there was more life coming from Mum's room than from mine. The more energy I lost, the more she gained.

I would hear her pacing the room like a caged lioness.

I was rebelling against the diary. I held it responsible for getting me in this position in the first place. I felt that every decision I had made up until this point had been because of what the diary said and I didn't want that life any more. I wanted control over my days. I wanted to lie in bed and let the world pass by under my nose, just like it had before.

Every day I waited for Marcus to call. He didn't.

Every day Sister Ignatius called by. I was so mortified, I refused to see her. I'm sure she knew what had happened; I'm sure the whole town knew. So much for my new start. I didn't want a lecture. I didn't want a stern stare. I missed the honey extraction, which I'd promised to do with her, I missed going to the market. Yet every day she called round. I should have helped her, but instead I lay in my bedroom, hiding under my bedclothes, mortified at the very thought of what had happened. Arthur made a few attempts to see Mum. He'd wait until Rosaleen was out in the back garden and he'd knock lightly on her bedroom door. If he thought she was going to call out to him to enter, then it was clear he really didn't get it. After a minute or two he'd just walk away.

One night, Rosaleen and Arthur had another fight. I heard Arthur say, 'I can't do this any more.' Then he stormed up to Mum's bedroom, where he stayed for fifteen minutes. Rosaleen listened outside the door the entire time. I couldn't hear him talking.

On Sundays I stayed in bed all day. I heard the sisters honking the horn to get me out of bed, but I didn't move. I didn't even look out the window. I just want to hide away from them all. I wondered if maybe I should contact Marcus, maybe I should write to him. But I did know what on earth I should say. All I could think of was sorry and that wasn't enough.

One day the removal van arrived with all of our stuff from Barbara's husband's warehouse. I watched them back the van down the trail that leads to the garage and didn't feel an ounce of excitement. Those things didn't belong to me any more. They belonged to that girl who used to live in that house. It was not who I was any more. I didn't know who I was any more. I fell back asleep again. I woke up when I heard the doorbell ring. It was Sister Ignatius again. She was being very persistent. At first I just thought she was friendly, then concerned, but that day she was a little frantic. I listened to her from my bedroom. It was all mumbling, but then Sister Ignatius raised her voice.

'Are you just going to *muffle muffle* lie up there and let her think she's done something wrong, let that poor boy *muffle muffle* all that?'

Muffled words.

'Tell her that she must come to see me.'

Muffle, muffle.

Then the door closed. I looked out the window,

317

just peered above the windowsill, and I saw Sister Ignatius, wearing a floral shirt and skirt, head down and walking away. My heart broke for her but also, in a weird way, it lifted. She was telling Rosaleen to make sure I didn't feel guilty. Maybe she'd forgiven me after all. Even thinking that that was possible lifted my spirits. It gave me hope, made me think I was overreacting and that I should just learn from everything and get over it.

That night I couldn't settle, I couldn't sleep at all. I took the diary from the floorboards and waited and waited for the words to appear, hoping that by ignoring it I hadn't made it all disappear. When it finally arrived it made me sit up and take notice.

Wednesday, July 22
I called Marcus today. I found his name in the phone book. There aren't many Sandhursts in Meath. Turns out his dad is a big legal eagle and has a famous firm in Dublin. How much more embarrassment could I have caused Marcus? I was terrified I was going to have to speak to his parents first but some woman answered, sounded all official and then put me straight through to him. As soon as he heard my voice I had to plead with him not to hang up. Then when I'd convinced him, I had no idea what to say. I apologised so much, going on and on and on, that he eventually stopped me. He said that all the charges had been dropped. Hadn't I been told?

318

No.

I asked him if his dad had arranged that. He couldn't believe I'd asked him that. He said I'd far more problems than he'd thought if I didn't know. He wished me well and hung up.

What on earth was he talking about? If I didn't know what?

I called Marcus the next day, feeling less nervous knowing his dad wouldn't answer. It all went exactly as I'd written except instead of my asking if his dad had arranged for the charges to be dropped, I asked, how they had been dropped. An entire night to think about it and that's the best I could come up with. I still didn't get any answers. In fact, he may have hung up sooner.

Thursday 23 July
I spent time with Mum in her bedroom before I went to bed. She was humming a tune to herself. I don't know what it was but it made her smile. I told her I'd something for her and I took the glass tear out of my pocket and laid it down beside the bedside table. She stopped humming as soon as she saw it. She lay on the bed, her eyes turned enough for her to see it. She just kept staring at it.

'It's pretty, isn't it?' I said.

She looked at me, a sharp look that took me aback a little, then she stared at the glass tear again. It seemed like its very presence offended her and so I reached for it, to take it back. Her hand came up quick and landed on mine. It didn't hurt but I got a shock and so I just left it with her.

Later that night I was fast asleep dreaming of visiting Marcus in prison when I felt a hand on my shoulder. In the dream it was a prison guard but I quickly woke up and Mum's face was close, her nose almost touching mine. I swallowed my scream. She whispered into my ear, 'Where did you get it?'

I was still half-asleep, I didn't know what she was talking about. I didn't know if she meant the diary, or if it was the packet of cigarettes I'd hidden in my wardrobe.

'The tear,' she whispered again with urgency in her voice.

I panicked, to be honest. I thought I was going to be in trouble for going over to Rosaleen's mother's house when I wasn't supposed to. I was half-asleep, like I said, and in shock that she was here in my room – talking – in the middle of the night. Now and then I could hear the springs in Arthur and Rosaleen's bed move and I just felt frozen in some kind of strange fear. And so, well, I lied. I told her that I found it around the house, that I thought it was nice so I kept it.

As soon as I'd said it to her, I immediately knew what was different in her, apart from the fact that she was talking. It was the light that

had suddenly arrived in her eyes, making them
alive again. I had missed that. But the only
reason I noticed the light was because as soon
as I said those words, as soon as I lied, the
light faded again. Her eyes were dull, empty,
lifeless. I'd killed whatever excitement was
rushing through her, I'd thrown water on the
fire. She left the room silently then and returned
to her bedroom.

Rosaleen's door opened. Footsteps down the
corridor. My bedroom door opened. The long
white nightie was illuminated in the moonlight.
She interrogated me for a few minutes about
hearing a door close but I denied it. She stared
at me in a long silence, as if trying to decide
whether I was telling the truth or not, nodded,
then closed the door. I heard her bedsprings and
after that, silence.

I couldn't sleep after that. I just kept thinking
about whether my lie to Mum was right or
wrong. By the time morning light had flooded
my room, I realised I had made a mistake. I
should have just told her the truth.

I'll write again tomorrow.

After reading that entry, I had the day to plan
what I was going to say to Mum. I felt anxious
throughout the day, watching Mum's silent living
and knowing that soon enough that spell would
be broken. I tried to remember the diary entry
word for word. I didn't want to get it all wrong.

I wanted to do and say exactly the same things as I'd written so as to summon the same response. I wanted her to come to my room in the middle of the night. Then I wanted to tell her the truth about the glass tear drop. I waited all day.

Finally after dinner I went upstairs to her bedroom. She was lying in bed, examining the ceiling, humming softly.

'I have something for you,' I said, my voice so croaky that the words were barely audible. I started again. 'I have something for you.'

She kept humming as I reached into my pocket and felt around for the glass, which was warm from my body. I placed it down on the bedside table. The gentle tapping sound made her eyes turn, but not the rest of her head. When her eyes landed on the glass tear drop, she instantly stopped humming and her finger stopped twirling her hair.

'It's pretty, isn't it?' I asked.

She looked at me then, and I recognised the moment that spark entered her eyes. She returned her stare to the tear drop. Not wanting to but knowing I should follow protocol, I reached for it and just as I'd written, out came her hand and it landed on mine to prevent me from taking it.

'No,' she said firmly.

'Okay,' I said, smiling. 'Okay.'

I sat up in bed, unable to sleep, knowing she would awaken me. I read the diary entry for the next day, unsure whether it would be accurate as events that were about to unfold would probably alter the day that Tamara of Tomorrow had.

Friday 24 July
Happy Birthday to me. Seventeen. I decided to get out of bed this morning and Rosaleen was surprised to see me. I think I almost gave her a heart attack in the pantry when I entered the kitchen. I thought she was up to something, because she looked as guilty as sin and shoved something in the pocket of her apron. It could have been something for the cake but I don't know ...

She gave me an awkward hug and kiss, and then danced off with Mum's tray to give her her breakfast and then to get my gift from her bedroom. She returned with a perfectly wrapped gift, pink paper with white and pink ribbon. It was a basket of Strawberry bubble bath, soaps and shampoo. She was practically hyper-ventilating while I opened it, leering over me with a nervous smile to see if I liked it or not. I told her I did. I told her it was perfect and I genuinely did like it. It was different for me. Last year for my sixteenth birthday, I'd received a Louis Vuitton handbag and a pair of Gina shoes, this year, a bubble bath and shampoo set, but weirdly I was more grateful for this because I actually needed it. I was running out of shampoo and the red squirrels weren't easily impressed by the Louis Vuitton bags.

Then she said an extraordinary thing – 'I saw it last month, would you believe, and I thought to myself and I even said it to Arthur, "That's got Tamara's name written all over it." I've been hiding it in the garage since then and I was so terrified you'd find it,' she giggled nervously.

That comment chilled me. Rosaleen was cleverer than I gave her credit for. There was no way that she would have avoided my going to the garage, or tried to stop us storing our belongings in there because she was hiding a little soap basket. She was either cleverer or she thought I was stupid. My hunger to get inside that garage has been stirred even more.

Mum slept all day again. Zoey and Laura both phoned the house. I told Rosaleen to tell them I was out.

Sister Ignatius called by with a present for me. Rosaleen offered to pass it on but Sister wouldn't give it to her. The longer I ignore her, the worse I'm making it. Now I've so much more to apologise for. I think she's been the best friend I've ever had but I just feel like hiding from the world. I can't bear being seen.

After dinner, Rosaleen emerged from the pantry with a chocolate cake with candles singing 'Happy Birthday'. That must have been what I almost caught her doing in the pantry this morning. It's probably too late to check that apron pocket now.

I'll write again tomorrow.

I must admit I hadn't thought much about my birthday during the past couple of weeks and the times I had thought about it, it was with a heavy feeling for poor Marcus. If only we'd just waited. If only I'd just told him. I hadn't thought about what kind of celebrations I could have or would have had in my previous life or what kind of presents I would have been adorned with from the moment I woke up to the moment I fell asleep. But after reading today and yesterday's entry, I was fired up. I was excited.

It was as though I'd spent the past days wandering through a misty glen and I couldn't see past my own nose. But now the fog had lifted. My mind had just been so busy mulling over something in all that time that it couldn't concentrate on anything else. It seemed to have come to the end of its wander because I was sitting up in bed, fully alert, my heart racing, feeling breathless as though I'd run for miles. I was intent on figuring out what on earth Rosaleen had been doing, or was about to do in the pantry tomorrow morning.

As I was working out a plan, I heard Mum's door open. I quickly lay down and closed my eyes. She closed the door behind her ever so quietly, aware that she needed to be silent. She sat on the edge of my bed and I waited for her hand on my shoulder. There it was. The urgent squeeze.

I opened my eyes, not feeling the panic I'd written about, but instead feeling totally prepared.

'Where did you get it?' she whispered, her face close to mine.

I sat up.

'Across the road. In the bungalow,' I whispered back.

'Rosaleen's house,' she whispered, and immediately looked out the window. 'The light,' she said, and I noticed a kind of a light flashing on my bedroom wall opposite the window. It had the same effect of trees swishing from side to side across the moonlight causing the light to appear and disappear in the room. Only it wasn't the trees because it seemed to sparkle more, like glass, releasing prisms of colour. It reflected against Mum's pale face and she seemed caught in its field, entranced. I immediately looked out my window and across to the bungalow. Hanging in the front window a glass mobile caught the light, sending beams flashing outward, almost like a lighthouse.

'There are hundreds more of them over there,' I whispered. 'I wasn't supposed to be there, it's just that, she . . .' we both looked to the wall as we heard the springs in Rosaleen and Arthur's bed, 'she was being so secretive. I just wanted to say hello to her mother, that's all. I brought her over some breakfast a couple of weeks ago and I saw someone in the shed in the back garden. It wasn't her mother.'

'Who?'

'I don't know. A woman. An old woman, with long hair. She was working in there. Making them. She must blow the glass herself. Do you think she's allowed to do that? Legally?' I looked at the tear drop in her hand. 'There were hundreds of them. All hanging on lines. I'll show you them. When I went back to collect the tray, it was sitting on the wall outside. This was in it.'

We both looked at the tear drop.

'What does it mean?' I broke the silence.

'Does she know?' Mum asked, not answering my question.

I took the 'she' to mean Rosaleen. 'No. What's going on?'

She squeezed her eyes shut and covered them with her hands. She rubbed her eyes fiercely, then ran her hands through her hair as though trying to wake herself up.

'I'm sorry. I feel so fuzzy. I just can't seem to . . . wake up,' she said, rubbing her eyes again. Then she looked at me directly, her eyes shining. She leaned in and kissed me on the forehead. 'I love you, sweetie. I'm sorry.'

'Sorry for what?'

But I was asking her back view as she rose and quietly left my bedroom. I looked outside again at the light, the jagged glass twirling around as though being blown from inside. Then, as I was concentrating on that, the curtain moved and I realised someone had been watching me. Or had been watching us.

Then I heard Rosaleen's door open, footsteps down the hall and my door opened. There she stood in her vision of white.

'What's wrong?' she asked.

'Nothing,' I said, following the diary.

'I heard a door close.'

'Nothing's wrong.'

After a long stare, she left me alone to ponder what I had achieved by telling Mum the truth. Something good had to come of it surely, and I was sure I was about to find out. I opened the diary again to see if the entry had changed. I held my breath.

As I opened the front page, the pages started to slowly curl inward at the edges, becoming browned and charcoaled, as though they were burning before my very eyes. Eventually they stopped retreating and the burned stained pages stared back, hiding tomorrow's world from me.

CHAPTER TWENTY

The Housewife in the Pantry with the Cocoa Powder

I hardly slept after the incident in the early hours of the morning. I lay with my covers up to my chin, rigid with a cold fear that had me hopping in my bed every time I heard the slightest noise. I was pretty sure that the woman in the bungalow was the person who'd followed me to the graveyard the week before last, and as the morning moved on and the sun shed light on the shadows, I became less frightened of her. Perhaps she wasn't dangerous, perhaps just a little odd. By the look of her hair and clothing at the studio, she wasn't somebody that saw people regularly. Besides, she'd given me a gift of the small tear-shaped glass. She was obviously reaching out.

But the burned diary gave me a sense of impending doom.

When I did sleep I dreamed of fire: of castles on fire, and books on fire. I dreamed of glass being made, blobs of molten hot glass being shaped and dripping. After waking up to a dark room, with my heart beating wildly in my chest, I tried hard to stay awake. I watched the pages of the diary for the rest of the morning, waiting for the burned pages to uncurl themselves, for the writing to magically appear in its neat loops and crosses. But they remained the same.

I was up early the next morning determined to catch Rosaleen do whatever she was doing. Catching the Housewife in the Pantry with the Cocoa Powder wasn't exactly the most exciting thing in the world, but I had realised that the diary was leading me somewhere, was trying to show me something, pointing to the way out just as I had been trying to show the bluebottle. I would be a fool to ignore the miracle of what was occurring. Every word was a clue, every sentence an arrow, a signpost for me to get out of here.

The radio was blaring in the kitchen, Arthur was having a shower and Rosaleen thought she had the morning entirely to herself. She turned and headed to the pantry, and I ducked out of sight behind the hall door just in time. I could see her in the pantry through the crack in the door.

She had Mum's breakfast tray on the counter and she reached into a box, hidden behind another box and took out a container of pills. My heart hammered. I had to block my mouth to make sure

I didn't scream. I watched her tip two capsules into the palm of her hand, open them and sprinkle the powder into the porridge and mix it around. I fought with whether to jump out then and confront her. I had her. I'd known she was up to something but now I had to stop myself. They could merely be headache pills and my pouncing on her would backfire, *again*, or else they were something more serious, which were making Mum sicker. I leaned in closer to the crack in the door but as I did so, the floorboard under my foot creaked. Rosaleen immediately dropped the container into her apron, picked up the tray and swivelled around as though nothing had happened. I quickly stepped out from behind the door.

'Oh, good morning,' she said, a bright smile. 'How is the birthday girl today?' I might have been paranoid but I was convinced her eyes were searching my face to see if I'd witnessed her actions.

'Old.' I returned the smile, doing my best to regain my composure.

'Oh you're not old, child,' she laughed. 'I remember when I was your age.' She threw her eyes to heaven. 'It's all ahead of you yet. Now I'll bring this up to your mother and I'll be back down to give you a special birthday breakfast.'

'Thanks, Rosaleen,' I said sweetly, and watched her race up the stairs.

As she disappeared into Mum's bedroom and the door closed behind her, the mail landed on the mat by the front door. I stalled, waiting for

Rosaleen to come flying down on her broomstick to snatch it, but she didn't. She didn't hear it. I reached for the post – only two white envelopes, probably bills – and rushed into the kitchen with them. I didn't know what to do. I looked around quickly for somewhere to hide them. I wouldn't have time to read them now. I heard Rosaleen's feet on the stairs again and my heart slammed in my chest. Last minute, I decided to tuck the envelopes into the back of my tracksuit bottoms and covered them over with my baggy boyfriend cardigan. I stood in the centre of the kitchen with my hands behind my back looking as guilty as sin.

She slowed when she saw me. The muscles in her neck protruded.

'What are you doing?' she asked.

'Nothing.'

'You're not doing nothing. What's in your hands, Tamara?' she said forcefully.

'Fucking thongs,' I said, pulling at the back of my trousers.

'Show me your hands.' She raised her voice.

I took my hands out from behind my back; waved them at her cockily.

'Turn around.' Her voice quivered.

'No,' I said defiantly.

The doorbell rang. Rosaleen didn't move. Neither did I.

'Turn around,' she repeated.

'No,' I repeated, stronger, firmer.

The doorbell rang again.

'Rose!' Arthur shouted down the stairs. Rosaleen didn't answer and we heard boots on the stairs as he made his way down. 'I'll get it so,' he said, glancing at us with frustration. He opened the door.

'Weseley.'

'I couldn't back the van up any more, is that okay? Is it in far enough? Oh, hi, Tamara,' he said, looking in past Arthur.

Rosaleen's eyes narrowed even more.

I smiled. Yes I had a friend that she didn't know about.

I looked at Weseley with wide eyes, willing him to pick up that something was wrong. I didn't want him and Arthur to leave.

'We'll see you later so,' Arthur said.

The door closed behind them and we were left facing one another in the kitchen.

'Tamara,' Rosaleen said gently. 'Whatever you are hiding, and I think I know what it is, just give it back.'

'I'm not hiding anything, Rosaleen. Are you?'

She twitched.

On that note we heard a bang from upstairs, a crash of plates and then feet on the floorboards. We both snapped out of our staring match and immediately looked up.

'Where is he?' I heard my mother screech.

I looked at Rosaleen and ran past her.

'No, child.' She pulled me back.

'Rosaleen, let go, she's my mother.'

'She's not well,' she said nervously.

'Yes, and I wonder why that is!' I yelled in her face, and ran upstairs.

I didn't make it that far. Mum had flung the door open and with wide eyes, terrified eyes, was searching the corridor.

'Where is she?' she said, unable to focus on me.

'Who? Rosaleen?' I started, but she pushed by me when she saw her at the bottom of the stairs.

'Where is he?' she demanded, standing at the top of the stairs in her dressing gown.

Rosaleen, wide-eyed, was wringing her hands in her apron. I could still see the outline of the container of pills in the pocket. I looked from one to the other, not understanding what was going on.

'Mum, he's not here,' I said, trying to hold her hand. She shook it away.

'He is. I know it. I can feel him.'

'Mum, he's not here.' I felt tears welling. 'He's gone.'

Her head twisted round to me immediately then and her voice lowered to a whisper. 'He's not gone, Tamara. They only said he was but he's not. I can *feel* him.'

I was crying now. 'Mum, stop, please. That's just . . . that's just . . . his spirit that you feel around you. He's always going to be with you. But he's gone . . . he's really gone. Please . . .'

'I want to see him,' she demanded of Rosaleen.

'Jennifer,' she said, her hands reaching out even

though she was too far away to touch her, 'Jennifer, just relax, go back and lie down.'

'No!' Mum shouted, her voice trembling now. 'I want to see him! I know he's here. You're hiding him!'

'Mum,' I cried, 'she's not. Dad's dead, he's really dead.'

Mum looked at me then, and for a moment she seemed so sad. Then she was angry and ran down the stairs. Rosaleen ran for the door.

'Arthur!' she yelled outside.

Arthur, who was only in the driveway with Weseley, loading equipment into the Land Rover, jumped to attention.

Mum ran out to the garden, shouting, 'Where is he?' over and over.

'Jen, stop it now. Relax, it's okay,' Arthur called to her calmly over and over.

'Arthur,' Mum cried, running for him and throwing her arms around him. 'Where is he? He's here, isn't he?'

In shock, Arthur looked to Rosaleen.

'Mum!' I cried. 'Arthur help her. Do something to help her, please. She thinks Dad is still alive.'

Arthur looked at her with what seemed to me to be a broken heart. He took her in his arms and as Mum's skinny body shook with tears and she asked over and over again, where he was and why, he rubbed her back soothingly.

'I know, Jen, I know, Jen, it's okay. It's okay . . .'

'Please help her,' I cried, standing in the middle

of the garden, looking from Rosaleen to Arthur, who was keeping Mum up. 'Send her somewhere. Get somebody to help.'

'My dad's at home now,' Weseley offered quietly. 'I can call him and tell him to come round.'

Something twisted inside me. A cold fear. An instinct of some sort. I thought of the burned diary, of the fire in my dreams. I had to get Mum out of the house.

'Take her to him,' I said to Arthur.

Arthur looked at me in confusion.

'To Dr Gedad,' I said so that Mum couldn't hear.

In Arthur's arms, Mum twisted and slid downwards, grief overtaking her.

Arthur nodded at me then, solemnly. Then he looked at Rosaleen.

'I'll be back soon.'

'But you—'

'I'm going,' he said firmly.

'I'm coming too,' she said hurriedly, swiftly taking off her apron and rushing into the house. 'I'll get her coat.'

'Weseley, stay with Tamara,' Arthur instructed.

Weseley nodded and took a few steps closer to me.

Moments later they were all in the Land Rover, Mum in the back crying and looking so lost.

Weseley put his arm round my shoulders protectively.

'It's going to be all right,' he said gently.

When we arrived here I felt like me and Mum were all washed up, two people who'd landed on the beach coughing and spluttering after our boat had gone down. We were a mess, we had nothing, belonged to nothing, felt aimless, as though we were trapped in a waiting room with no doors.

I've realised that when things are washed up, they haven't just been torn apart – they're the survivors. I didn't think it until I was forced to watch some nature documentary such as Arthur loves. It was about the South Pacific islands, how they're so far apart it was difficult to explain how life spread from one to another at all, apart from the birds. Then these coconuts came bobbing along. All washed up, the narrator said. Two lost things that had survived the seas and arrived on a coastline. What did they do? They implanted themselves in the sand and grew into trees and lined the beaches. Sometimes a lot can come of being all washed up. You can really grow.

Even though Mum had a hissy fit, thought that Dad was still alive, and appeared to be falling apart, I felt like it was the start of something new, something better. And as we watched them drive away, Rosaleen looking back at us with concern, not wanting to leave us but not wanting to leave Arthur and Mum alone, I really couldn't help it. But I smiled and I waved.

CHAPTER TWENTY-ONE

K is for ... Kangaroo

As soon as they were gone, I raced into the house. On the coat stand, Rosaleen's apron had been messily strewn across the top in her effort to hurry outside. I grabbed it and dug my hand into the pocket.

'Tamara, what are you doing?' Weseley was close behind me. 'Maybe I should make you a cup of tea or something, to calm you dow— What the hell is that?'

He was referring to the container of pills I held up in my hand.

'I was hoping you could tell me that.' I gave him the pills. 'I caught Rosaleen putting them in Mum's breakfast.'

'What? Whoa, Tamara,' Weseley said. 'She was putting *pills* in her food?'

'I saw her opening them and emptying the powder stuff into the cereal and then mixing it around. She doesn't know I saw her.'

339

'Well maybe they're prescription pills.'

'You think? Let's see, shall we? Despite the fact Rosaleen likes to pretend that I know nothing of my own mother's medical history, I do know that her name isn't . . .' I read the label of the container, 'Helen Reilly.'

'That's Rosaleen's mother. Let me see them.' He took them from me. 'They're sleeping pills.'

'How do you know?'

'It says it on the label. Oxazepam. That's a sleeping pill. She's putting these in your mum's food?'

I swallowed, tears sprung in my eyes.

'Are you sure you saw her do this?'

'Yes I'm sure. And Mum hasn't stopped sleeping since we arrived. Non-stop.'

'Does your mum usually take them? Is Rosaleen just trying to help her, maybe?'

'Weseley, Mum is so drugged she can barely remember her own name. This is not *helping* her. It's almost like Rosaleen's trying to make her worse. This *is* making her worse.'

'We have to tell somebody.'

The relief at hearing 'we' came like a tidal wave.

'I have to tell my dad. He'll have to tell somebody, okay?'

'Okay.'

I felt relieved then that I was no longer alone. I sat on the stairs while he phoned his dad to tell him.

'Well?' I jumped up as soon as he'd hung up.

'They were in the room with him so he couldn't comment on it. He just said he'd take care of it. We'll just have to keep these safe in the meantime.'

'Right.' I took a deep breath. What will be, will be. 'So will you help me get Arthur's toolbox, please?'

'What do you need that for?' he asked, completely baffled now.

'To break open the lock on the garage.'

'What?'

'Just . . .' I searched for the words, 'help me, please. We don't have much time and I'll explain everything later. But for now can you please, please help me? They're rarely out of the house. This is my only opportunity.'

He thought about it in a long silence, turned the container of pills around in his hand while thinking. 'Okay.'

While Weseley ran into the workshed beside the house, I paced the garden, hoping they wouldn't return before I'd had a chance to have a good look round. I stopped pacing to peer at the bungalow, wanting to see if the glass that shone directly into my bedroom was still there. It was gone. But something on the garden wall caught my attention. A box. I moved closer.

'Weseley.'

He immediately heard the warning in my voice and turned round, following where my finger was pointing.

'What's that?' he asked.

I crossed the road and examined it. Weseley followed me. The package was covered in brown paper and my name was written on the front along with 'Happy Birthday'.

I picked it up and looked around. There was nobody at the windows, behind the net curtains. I opened the brown paper to reveal a brown shoe box. I lifted the lid. Inside was the most beautiful glass mobile, a series of different-sized tears mixed with hearts, joined together with wires through tiny holes. I lifted it up and raised it to the light. It sparkled against the sun and spun around in the breeze. I smiled and looked to the house to wave, to smile, to thank somebody.

Nothing.

'What the hell . . .' Weseley said, examining it.

'It's a gift. For me.'

'I didn't know it was your birthday.' He took it and examined it.

'Well, she did.'

'Who? Rosaleen's mother?'

'No.' I stared at the bungalow again. 'The woman.'

He shook his head. 'And I thought my life was weird. Who is she? My mam and dad didn't think anybody other than Mrs Reilly lived there.'

'I have no idea.'

'Let's go in and meet her. To say thanks.'

'You think I should?'

He rolled his eyes. 'You were given a present – it's the perfect opportunity to go in there.'

I chewed on my lip and looked at the house.

'Unless, of course, you're afraid.'

That's exactly what I was.

'No, we've got more important things to do right now,' I said. I crossed the road and hurried to the back garden, to the garage.

'You know, Sister Ignatius has been going crazy trying to see you. You just ran off that day and you gave her a fright. You gave us both a fright.'

I glared at Weseley while he poked around in the toolbox for the correct tool to break the lock.

'I heard about what happened. You okay?'

'Yes, I'm fine. I don't want to talk about it,' I snapped. 'Thank you,' I added more gently.

'Heard your boyfriend is in a bit of trouble.'

'I said I don't want to talk about it,' I snapped. 'And he's not my boyfriend.'

He started laughing at that. 'So you know just how I feel.'

Despite all that had gone on that morning, I smiled.

It didn't take Weseley long to pick the lock. We were in and I was immediately faced with my old life, all of it piled up, out of order, the kitchen with the living room, my bedroom piled on top of the games room, the spare bedroom with the bathroom towels. It fit together as perfectly as the thoughts in my head. Leather couches, plasma TVs, ridiculous-shaped furniture that seemed cheap and soulless now.

I was more interested in seeing what Rosaleen

and Arthur had hiding in here. As Weseley threw the dustsheets off the far end of the garage I was highly unimpressed. Just more old furniture, destroyed by time, eaten away at by dust mites and smelling of mothballs. I don't know what I'd been expecting – a dead body or two, a money printer, boxes of guns and weaponry, a secret entrance to Rosaleen's batcave. Anything else other than this mothball-laden stinky furniture.

I made my way back to my belongings. Weseley soon followed, oohing and aahing at a few items as he rooted around in the boxes. Taking a break from his investigations of Arthur and Rosaleen's hidden life, we sat on my once-upon-a-time living-room couch, looking through my photo album while Weseley laughed at the various stages of my adolescence.

'Is that your dad?'

'Yeah,' I smiled, looking at his happy animated face, on the dancefloor at a friend's wedding. He loved dancing. He was crap at it.

'He's so young.'

'Yeah.'

'What happened?'

I sighed.

'You don't have to talk about it if you don't want to.'

'I don't mind.' I swallowed. 'He just ... borrowed so much money, he couldn't pay it back. He was a developer, very successful. He had properties all over the world. We didn't know but he was in big trouble. He'd started selling up every-thing to pay back the debts.'

'He didn't tell you there was a problem?'

I shook my head. 'He was too proud. He would have felt he'd failed us.' My eyes filled. 'But I wouldn't have cared, I really wouldn't have.' I was protesting too much. I could have imagined Dad trying to tell me he was selling off everything. Of course I would have cared – I would have moaned and whinged. I wouldn't have understood, I would just have been embarrassed about what everyone thought of us. I would have missed Marbella in the summer, Verbier for New Year. I would have shouted at him, called him everything under the sun and I would have stormed off to my bedroom and slammed the door. Greedy little pig that I was. But I wish he'd have given me the opportunity to understand. I wish he'd have sat me down and talked about it, and we could all have worked it out together. I'd live anywhere – in one room, in the castle ruin right now – if it meant we could all just be together.

'I don't care about losing anything now. I'd rather have him anyday,' I sniffed. 'We've lost everything now, including him. I mean, what was the point? When they repossessed the house, I think that was it for him.' I studied him golfing with Mum, his face serious as he looked into the distance for his ball. 'They could take everything but not that.'

I turned the page and we both laughed. Me,

two front teeth missing as I hugged Mickey Mouse in Disney World.

'Aren't you . . . I don't know . . . angry at him? If my dad did that, I'd . . .' Weseley shook his head, unable to imagine it.

'I was,' I replied. 'I was so angry at him for so long. But over the last few weeks I've been thinking about what he must have been going through. Even in my lowest days I never could do what he did. He must have felt so much pressure, he must have been so miserable. He must have felt so trapped, must just not have wanted to be here so much. And . . . well, when he died they couldn't take anything else. Mum and I were protected.'

'You think he did it for you?'

'I think he did it for a lot of reasons. For all the wrong reasons, but for him they were all right.'

'Well, I think you're very brave,' Weseley said and I looked up at him and tried not to cry.

'I don't feel brave.'

'You are,' he said. Our eyes locked.

'I've made the most stupid embarrassing mistakes,' I whispered.

'That's okay. We all make mistakes,' he smiled wryly.

'Well, I don't think I make as many as you,' I added, trying to lighten the atmosphere. 'You seem to make different mistakes with different people almost every night.'

He laughed. 'Okay let's see what Rosaleen's hiding under here.'

Unable to take my eyes off the photo albums, I began another and found my baby photos. I got lost in another world and lost time. In the background I could hear Weseley commenting on things he was finding, but I ignored him. Instead I stared at my beautiful dad, happy and handsome, with Mum. Then there was a photo of my christening day. Just me and Mum. Me so tiny in her arms all that was visible beneath the white blanket was a little pink head.

'Holy shit, Tamara, take a look at this.'

I ignored him, lost in the photo of me and Mum in the church. She was holding me in her arms, a big smile on her face. Whoever had taken the picture – Dad, I assume – had left their finger over the corner of the lens, blocking the priest's face. Knowing Dad, it was probably on purpose. I rubbed his big white finger bright from the flash, and I laughed.

'Tamara, look at all this stuff.'

The photograph captured half of the priest, Mum, me in her arms at the baptism bowl, another person cut off on the right-hand side, thanks to the dodgy photo skills, but somebody's hand was resting on the top of my head. A woman's hand, I could tell from the ring on her finger. Probably Rosaleen, my godmother who never seemed to do what my friends' godmothers did, which was just send cards at every occasion with money inside. No, my godmother wanted to spend time with me. Puke.

'Tamara.' Weseley grabbed me and I jumped. 'Look at this.' His eyes were wide. He took me by the hand and a tingle shot up my arm.

I shoved the christening photograph in my pocket and followed him.

Any funny feelings for him quickly evaporated. I looked around the section that Weseley had unveiled of its sheets.

'What's the big deal?' I asked unimpressed. It was hardly as exciting as he was making it out to be. Old furniture as dated as anything I'd ever seen. Books, pokers, crockery, paintings all covered up, fabrics, rugs, fireplaces leaning up against the wall, all kinds of bric-a-brac.

'What's the big deal?' His eyes were wide as he jumped about the place, picking things up, unveiling more oil paintings of evil-looking children with collars up past their ear lobes, and fat unattractive ladies with big boobs, wide wrists and thin lips. 'Look at all this, Tamara. Look, don't you notice anything?'

He knocked down a rug and kicked it with his foot. It unrolled onto the dusty floor.

'Weseley, don't make a mess,' I snapped. 'We don't have long before they get back.'

'Tamara, open your eyes. Look at the initials.'

I studied the rug, a dusty-looking thing that might belong on the wall as a tapestry instead of on the floor. It had Ks all over it.

'And look at this.' Weseley uncovered a box of

348

china. It too had Ks stamped all over the plates, the teacups, the knives and forks. A dragon draped around a sword, climbing up from flames. Then I remembered the same emblem on the fireguard in the living room of the gatehouse.

'K,' I said dumbly. 'I don't get it. I don't . . .' I shook my head, looking around the garage, which at first had felt like rubbish and now seemed like a treasure chest.

'K is for . . .' Weseley said slowly as though I was a child, and looked at me, holding his breath.

'Kangaroo,' I said. 'I don't know, Weseley. I'm confused, I don't—'

'Kilsaney,' he said, and chills rushed through me.

'What? But it can't be,' I looked around. 'How could they have all this stuff?'

'Well, they either stole it . . .'

'That's it!' It all made sense to me. They were thieves – not Arthur, but Rosaleen. I could believe that.

'Or they're storing it for the Kilsaneys,' Weseley interrupted my thoughts. 'Or . . .' he grinned at me, eyebrows going up and down.

'Or what.'

'Or they *are* the Kilsaneys.'

I snorted, dismissing it immediately, then became distracted by a flash of red beneath a roll of carpet that Marcus had knocked over. 'The photo album!' I said, seeing the red album I'd found the week

I'd arrived. 'I knew I wasn't imagining it.'

We sat down and looked through it, though probably getting dangerously close to the moment when Arthur and Rosaleen would return. There were black and white photographs of children, some sepia-coloured.

'Recognise any of them?' Weseley asked.

I shook my head and he speeded up as he flicked through.

'Hold on.' One photo caught my eye. 'Go back.'

There was a photograph of two children surrounded by trees. One little girl, and a little boy a few years older. They stood facing one another, holding hands, their foreheads touching. An image of Arthur and Mum's bizarre greeting on our first day here flashed through my mind.

'That's Mum and Arthur,' I said, smiling. 'She must be only around five years old there.'

'Look at Arthur. He wasn't even handsome as a child,' Weseley teased, squinting and studying it closer.

'Ah, don't be mean,' I laughed. 'Look at them. I've never seen Mum as a child.'

The next page there was a photograph of Mum, Arthur, Rosaleen and another boy.

I gasped.

'Your Mum and Rosaleen knew each other as kids,' Weseley said. 'Did you know that?'

'No.' I was breathless, dizzy. 'No way. Nobody ever mentioned it.'

'Who's the guy at the end?'

'I don't know.'

'Does your mum have another brother? He looks the oldest.'

'No, she doesn't. Not that she ever mentioned...'

Weseley slipped his hand underneath the plastic covering and pulled the photo from the paper.

'Weseley!'

'We've gone this far – you want to know all this or not?'

I swallowed and nodded.

Weseley turned the photograph over.

It read: 'Artie, Jen, Rose, Laurie. 1979'.

'Laurie, apparently,' Weseley said. 'Ring any bells? Tamara, you look like you've seen a ghost.'

'Laurence Kilsaney RIP' on the gravestone.

Arthur had called Rosaleen 'Rose' in the car on the way back from Dublin.

'Laurie and Rose' engraved on the apple tree.

'He's the man who died in the fire in the castle. Laurence Kilsaney. His name is on a grave in the Kilsaney graveyard.'

'Oh.'

I stared at the photograph of the four of them, all smiling, the innocence on their face, everything ahead of them, a future of possiblities. Mum and Arthur were holding hands tightly, Laurence had his arm draped coolly around Rosaleen's neck; it dangled limply across her chest. He stood on one leg, the other crossed it in a pose. He seemed confident, cocky even. His chin was lifted and he smiled at the camera with a grin as if he'd

351

just shouted something at the photographer.

'So, Mum, Arthur and Rosaleen hung around with a Kilsaney,' I thought aloud. 'I didn't even know she lived here.'

'Maybe she didn't. Maybe she came here on holidays.' Weseley continued flicking. All of the photographs were of the same four people, all at different ages, all huddled close together. Some pictures were of them on their own, some in couples, but most of them together. Mum was the youngest, Rosaleen and Arthur closer in age and Laurence the oldest, always with a great smile, a mischievous look in his eye. Even as a young girl Rosaleen had an older look, a hardness in her eye, a smile that never grew as large as the others'.

'Look, there they all are in front of the gate-house,' Weseley pointed at the four of them sitting on the garden wall. Nothing much had changed apart from some of the garden trees, which were now big and full, but then had just been planted or were merely shrubs. But the gate, the wall, the house, everything was exactly the same.

'There's Mum in the living room. That's the same fireplace.' I studied the photo intently. 'The bookcase is exactly the same. Look at the bedroom,' I gasped. 'That's the one I'm in now. But I don't understand. She lived here, she grew up here.'

'You really didn't know any of this?'

'No.' I shook my head, feeling a headache coming on. My brain was overloaded with so much information and not enough answers. 'I mean, I knew she lived in the country but . . . I remember when we visited Arthur and Rosaleen when I was young, my granddad was always here. My grandma died when my mum was young. I thought he was just visiting Arthur and Rosaleen too but . . . my God, what's going on? Why did they all lie?'

'They didn't really lie though, did they?' Weseley tried to soften the blow. 'They just didn't tell you they lived here. That's not exactly the most exciting secret in the world.'

'And they didn't tell me that they'd known Rosaleen practically all their lives, that they lived in the gatehouse and they once knew the Kilsaneys. It's not a big deal, but it is if you keep it a secret. But why did they hide it? What else are they keeping from me?'

Weseley looked away from me then, continued flicking through the photo album as if to find my answers. 'Hey, if your granddad lived in the gate-house, that made him the groundskeeper here. He had Arthur's job.'

A startling image flashed through my mind, I was young, my granddad was down on his knees with his hands deep in muck. I remember the black beneath his fingernails, a worm in the soil wrig-gling around, Granddad grabbing it and dangling it near my face, me crying, and him laughing, and wrapping his arms around me. He always smelled of soil and grass. His fingernails were always black.

'I wonder if there's a photo of the woman.' I flicked through the pages further.

'What woman?'

'The woman in the bungalow who makes the glass.'

We studied the following pages, my heart thudding so loudly in my chest, I thought I was going to keel over. I came across another photograph of Rosaleen and Laurence together. 'Rose and Laurie, 1987'.

'I think Rosaleen was in love with Laurence,' I said, tracing their faces with my finger.

'Uh-oh,' Weseley said, turning over a page. 'But Laurence didn't love Rosaleen.'

I looked at the next photograph, eyes wide. On the next page was a picture of Mum, as a teenager, beautiful, long blonde hair, big smile, perfect teeth. Laurence had his arms thrown around her, was kissing her cheek by the tree with the engraving.

I looked at the back of the photograph. 'Jen and Laurie, 1989'.

'They could have been just friends . . .' Weseley said slowly.

'Weseley, look at them.'

That's all I had to say. The rest was plain to see. It was right there in front of us. They were in love.

I thought about what Mum had said to me when I'd returned from the rose garden the first day I'd met Sister Ignatius. I'd thought she hadn't been speaking properly, I thought she was telling me that I was prettier than a rose. But what if she'd meant exactly what she'd said: 'You're prettier than Rose'?

And away from them, at the other edge of the photograph, Rosaleen sat on a tartan rug with a picnic basket beside her, staring coldly at the camera.

CHAPTER TWENTY-TWO

Dark Room

I didn't know how long we had until Rosaleen and Arthur returned with Mum, if they were returning with her at all, but I had given up caring about being caught. I was done with their secrets, tired of tiptoeing around and trying to peek underneath things when nobody was looking. Weseley, in full support of my next move led me to the bungalow across the road. We were both looking for answers and I had never in my life met anybody like Weseley who was going out on a limb to help me so much. I thought of Sister Ignatius and my heart tugged. I had abandoned her. I needed to see her too. I remembered how during one of our first meetings she had grabbed my arm and told me she'd never lie to me. That she would always tell me the truth. She knew something. She had practically told me then that she knew something, now that I look back, had quite obviously asked me to question her, and I hadn't realised it until now.

Weseley led me down the side passage. My knees trembled as I walked and I expected them at any time to give way and send me to the ground like a house of cards. The morning was darkening and the wind was picking up. It was only noon and already the sky had clouded over, great big grey clouds gathering as though the sky's eyes were covered by bushy eyebrows, its forehead furrowed in concern as it watched me.

'What's that noise?' Weseley asked as we neared the end of the passageway.

We stopped and listened. It was a tinkling sound.

'The glass,' I whispered. 'It's blowing in the wind.'

It was a slightly disturbing sound. Unlike the tinkling of a chime, it sounded as though the glass was smashing, as the little pieces, the round and the jagged, hit against each other in the wind. Multiplied by hundreds, it was an eerie sound.

'I'm going to go down and check it out,' Weseley said once we'd stepped into the back garden. 'You'll be fine, Tamara. Just tell the woman you came over to thank her and take it from there. She might tell you more after that.'

I nervously watched him walk across the lawn, past the workshed and he disappeared into the field of glass.

I turned to the house and looked in at the windows. The kitchen was empty. I lightly rapped on the back door and waited. There was no answer. With a shaky hand, which I admonished myself about being so dramatic, I reached out and pulled down the handle. The door was unlocked. I pulled it open a crack and peered inside. It was a narrow hallway, which turned sharply to the right. There were three doorways off the hallway, all closed, one on the right, two to the left. The first on the left led to the kitchen – I already knew there was nobody in there. I stepped inside, trying to keep the door open so that I wouldn't feel so trapped and so it wouldn't feel like I was totally breaking and entering, but the wind was so strong it blew shut. I jumped and once again told myself how stupid I was being. An old woman and the woman who'd given me a gift were hardly going to hurt me. I rapped lightly on the door to my right. There was no answer and so I gently turned the handle and slowly opened the door. It was a bedroom, definitely the bedroom of an old lady. It smelled damp and of talcum powder and TCP. There was an old dark wood bed with floral duvet cover, slippers by the bed and a duck-egg-blue carpet that had seen more than a few Shake 'n' Vacs. There was a free-standing wardrobe probably containing all of her worldly outfits. A small dresser with a tarnished mirror sat against the door wall, a hairbrush, medication, the rosary and the Bible all neatly laid out on its surface. Facing the bed was the window overlooking the back garden. There was nothing else, nobody inside.

I closed the door gently and continued down the hall. The carpet was covered by an unusual kind of plastic mat, as if to keep the tiles clean. It made a scraping noise beneath my feet and I was surprised nobody had heard me coming. Unless the woman was in the workshed again, which meant that she'd see Weseley. I froze and almost went back outside but I'd come this far and there was no going back. I reached the end of the hall, where it turned to the right. There was another door at the end of the hall, which led to the television room, which I had already seen through the window. With the television up loud so that I could hear the *Countdown* clock ticking, I assumed that was where Rosaleen's mother was, but after all my wondering about her now wasn't the time for me to introduce myself. It wasn't her I was looking for. There was a small entrance hall at the front door and to the left of me there was another door, behind which I guessed was the second bedroom.

I knocked so gently the first time I barely even heard it myself. My knuckles brushed against the dark wood as though they were a feather. The second time round I knocked harder and I waited longer, but there was no sound.

I turned the handle. The door was unlocked and it opened.

With my overactive imagination, I had envisaged much about Rosaleen's secrets over the past few weeks, possibly years, but in reality they had all disappointed me. The findings in the garage, while intriguing and hurtful for me not to have known that Arthur and Mum were friends of

Rosaleen since childhood, didn't live up to the scenarios I had created in my mind. The initial mystery behind the house turned out to be Rosaleen's ailing mother; the dead bodies in the garage had actually been everything the castle had been stripped of. While intriguing, it was slightly disappointing because it didn't match up to the level of tension I felt around Rosaleen. It didn't match up to the level of secrecy she was shrouded in.

But this time I wasn't disappointed.

This time I wished for seventies carpets and dark wood, for the smell of damp and a badly designed bedroom. Because what I saw shocked me to the core so that I just stood there, frozen, my mouth agape, unable to breathe properly.

On each of three walls, covered from floor to ceiling were photographs of me. Me as a baby, me at my Communion, me on a visit to the gatehouse when I was three years old, four years old, six years old. Me at my school plays, me at my birthday parties and other parties, a flower girl at my mum's friend's wedding, dressed as a witch at Halloween, a scribbled drawing I'd done during my first year at school. There was a photograph of me at the entrance to the gatehouse from only last week, sitting on the wall, swinging my legs, my face up to the sun. There was a photograph of me and Marcus, him first calling to the house, of another day when we climbed into the bus and went on a journey. There was a photograph of the morning Mum, Barbara and I arrived at the gatehouse for the first time. Then me at the age of around eight years old, standing in the middle of the road to the castle by the house, bored as my mother talked with Arthur and Rosaleen over egg sandwiches and strong tea. There was a photo of me only a fortnight ago at the graveside, placing flowers by Laurence Kilsaney's grave. There was a photograph of me walking towards the castle. Photographs of me with Sister Ignatius, walking, talking, lazing on the grass, and one of me in the castle, sitting on the steps the morning I first discovered the diary entry, with my eyes closed face up to the sun. I had known somebody was watching. I had written it. The photos were endless like a history of my whole entire life, scenes that I'd long forgotten and some which I never knew had been captured on celluloid.

In the corner of the room there was a single bed, unkempt, untidy. There was a small locker beside that, its surface filled with pills. Before I turned around to leave, my eye caught sight of a familiar picture. I walked to the far wall and took the now crumpled photograph out of my pocket. I held it up to the wall, they were almost a perfect match, though the one on the wall was much clearer. Gone was the finger before the lens and so the priest's face was visible, Mum beside him with me in her arms. On my pink head was a hand with the ring. This photograph on the wall was much bigger than the one I had found. It had been blown up and zoomed in on and so the ring was very clear, very much in focus and the person who belonged to it was obvious.

Sister Ignatius.

Beneath the christening photograph was my mother holding me over the basin, and the priest trickling water on my head. I recognised that basin. It was filled with spiders and dust now in the chapel in the grounds. Beside that was a flushed face of my mother lying in bed, hair sticking to her damp forehead, me wrapped up in her arms, just born. Another photograph of Sister Ignatius holding me. Just born.

I'm not just a nun. I'm also trained in midwifery. She'd said that only days ago.

'Oh my God,' I trembled, my knees buckling from under me. I reached out to the wall but there was nothing for me to cling to apart from photographs of myself. My fingers caught on them and pulled them down as I fell to the floor. I didn't pass out but I couldn't stand. I wanted to get out of here. I put my head between my legs and slowly breathed in and out.

'You're lucky today,' I heard a voice say behind me and I snapped to attention. 'Usually this door is locked. Even I have never seen in here. He's been busy.'

Rosaleen was standing at the door, leaning against the doorway, her arms behind her back. So calm.

'Rosaleen,' I croaked, 'what's going on?'

She chuckled. 'Oh, child, you know what's going

on. Don't pretend to me you haven't been snooping.' She looked at me coldly.

I shrugged nervously, knowing straightaway that I appeared guilty.

She threw something at me and it landed on the floor.

The envelopes I'd taken that morning and left in the kitchen when I'd found the pills in Rosaleen's apron pocket. Then she threw something else, heavier, which thudded when it hit the carpet. I knew what it was straightaway. I reached out to grab the diary. I fumbled with the lock in an effort to open it and see if the burned pages were gone. Perhaps I'd changed the course already. But my questions were answered before I'd time to find out for myself.

'You spoiled my fun, burning those pages.' She smiled a crooked smile. 'Arthur and your mother are at the house. I probably shouldn't have left them . . .' She looked off towards the house while chewing on the inside of her mouth. She appeared so vulnerable then, the sweet aunt who was trying to carry the world on her shoulders, that I almost reached out to her but when she turned to me the coldness was back in her eyes. 'But I had to leave them. I knew you'd be here. I've an appointment to meet with Garda Murphy later today. You don't know what that's about, I suppose?'

I swallowed hard and shook my head.

'A bad liar,' she said quietly, 'just like your mother.'

'Don't you dare talk about my mother like that.'
My voice trembled.

'I was only trying to help her, Tamara,' she said.
'She wasn't sleeping. She was tormenting herself.
Going over and over the past all the time, starting
to ask questions every time I brought a meal ...'
She was speaking to herself now, almost as though
she was trying to convince herself. 'I did it for her.
Not for me. And she was barely eating, so it's not
as though she took much of it. I did it for her.'

I frowned, not knowing whether to interrupt or
let her talk it out with herself. While she was deep
in thought, I reached for the envelopes. Looked at
the name on the outside.

Arthur Kilsaney,
The Gatehouse,
Kilsaney Demesne
Kilsaney,
Meath

The next envelope had the same address printed
on it but it was addressed to both Arthur and
Rosaleen.

'But ...' I looked from one envelope to another.
'But ... I don't—'

'But, but, but,' Rosaleen mimicked me and it
sent shivers running down my spine.

'Arthur's surname is Byrne. Just like Mum's,' I
said in a shrill voice.

Rosaleen's eyes widened and she smiled. 'Well,

well, well. The cat wasn't quite as curious as I thought.'

I tried to gather the energy to stand. When I did, Rosaleen seemed to ready herself, to do something with one arm still behind her back.

I looked at the envelopes again, trying to figure out what was going on.

'Mum isn't a Kilsaney. She's Byrne.'

'That's right. She isn't a Kilsaney, was never a Kilsaney, but she always wanted to be.' Her eyes were cold. 'She only wanted the name. She always wanted what wasn't hers, thieving little bitch,' she spat. 'She was a bit like you, always showing up when she wasn't wanted.'

My mouth dropped, 'Rosaleen,' I breathed. 'What's . . . what's wrong with you?'

'What's wrong with me? Nothing's wrong with me. I've only spent the past weeks cooking and cleaning, doing everything, looking after everybody, holding everything together, as usual, for two ungrateful little . . .' her eyes widened then and her mouth opened wide and she shouted out with such anger I had to block my ears, '. . . LIARS!'

'Rosaleen!' I shouted. 'Stop! What's going on?' I was crying now. 'I don't know what's going on!'

'Yes, you do, child,' she hissed.

'I'm not a child, I'm not a child, I'm not a child!' I finally shouted, the words that I'd been saying over and over in my head finally coming out now louder with each breath.

'Yes, you are. You should have been MY CHILD!' she shouted. 'She took you from me! You should have been mine. Just like him. He was mine. She took him from me!' Then, as if that took all the energy out of her, she seemed to collapse in on herself.

I was silent while I searched hard. She couldn't have been talking about Laurence Kilsaney any more – that was years ago, before I was born, she must have been talking about . . .

'My dad,' I whispered. 'You were in love with my dad.'

She looked up at me then, such hurt in her face I almost felt for her.

'That's why Dad never came back here with Mum. That's why he always stayed in Dublin. Something happened between all of you all those years ago.'

Then Rosaleen's face softened and she started laughing. Quiet chuckles at first, but then she threw her head back and laughed loudly.

'George Goodwin? Are you serious? George Goodwin was always a loser, ever since he came here in his pretentious little car with his equally pretentious father, offering to buy the place. "It'll make a great hotel, it'll make a great spa,"' she mimicked, and I could see him saying it, could imagine him arriving in his pinstripe suit with Granddad Timothy. Only short of pressing the red button to call in a bulldozer to knock the castle down, he must have been the devil to these people who wanted to protect their castle and their land. 'He had to have everything, including your mother, even if she did have a child. Best thing he did was take your mother and you away from here. No! In fact, the best thing he ever did was end his life so those *suits* couldn't take this land away too. That's the best thing and only thing George Goodwin ever did. And he knew it too. I bet he knew it right up until he took that first sip of whisk—'

'STOP IT!' I shrieked. 'STOP IT!' I ran at her to hit her, slap her, anything I could do to stop her from saying all these lies, these horrible nasty dirty evil lies, but she got to me before I got to her. Those strong arms, toned from punching dough, rolling apple pies all day, toiling her organic vegetable patch, carrying trays up and down those stairs every morning, were strong. With one arm held out she pushed me so hard I instantly felt winded, as though my chest had been crushed. I went flying backward and hit my head against the corner of the locker. I lay on the floor gasping. Then I started to cry. My vision was blurred, I tasted blood in my mouth but didn't know how as I'd hit my head. I was disoriented, couldn't stand up, couldn't find the door.

After a time, I don't know how long, I finally saw Rosaleen at the doorway, her image blurred. Feeling woozy I sat up, I touched my head and blood was on my trembling fingers.

'Now, now,' Rosaleen said gently, 'why did you

do that, child? Why did you make me do that? We'll have to work out what we're going to say,' she said. 'We can't have you going back like this, after seeing all of this. No. No, I must think. I must think now.'

I mumbled something so incoherent I have no idea what exactly I was trying to say. All that I could think of was that she'd said my dad had taken me and my mum away from here, that Mum already had me. It was impossible. Nothing made sense. They'd met at a banquet dinner, a posh meal with lots of people, and as soon as he'd lain eyes on her he had to have her. He said it himself, he said it all of the time. They fell in love straight-away. They had me. That was the story, that's what Dad had told me. Maybe I'd heard it wrong, maybe Rosaleen was making it up. But I had such a headache and now I was so tired, my eyelids so heavy, I just needed to close them. I realised then that Rosaleen was talking, but not to me. I opened my eyes again. She was looking down the hall, looking a little fearful.

'Oh,' she had her small voice on again, 'I didn't hear you come in. I thought you were in the work-shed.'

The woman who made the glass. If I shouted out I could get some help but I heard a man's voice and that made me nervous. It wasn't Arthur's voice. It wasn't Weseley – oh, where was he? Had he been hurt? He'd gone to the field of glass, all that glass. I'd had nightmares about that glass almost every night. Blowing in the wind, it would scrape and scratch, pierce and stab as I ran up and down the field, trying to get out, and the woman would be watching me. Where was the woman now?

'Why don't you go into the kitchen and I'll make you a cup of tea? Wouldn't that be nice? What do you mean? How long have you been standing there? But she ran at me. I was only trying to defend myself. I'm going to bring her back to the house now as soon as I sort her out.'

He said something else and I could hear the sound of the plastic floor. A footstep, followed by a dragging sound, a step again, then a dragging.

I pulled myself up to a sitting position and then I held on to the bed to try to stand up. Rosaleen was so busy talking to the man that she didn't notice me stand. I couldn't hear what the man was saying but her voice got harder then. It lost its nervous sweet edge and was back to the Rosaleen from moments ago. Possessed.

'Possessive,' Sister Ignatius had pondered my surmise of Rosaleen weeks ago. 'That's an interesting choice of word.'

'Is this why you never let me into the room? Is this how you intended me to find out? This isn't right, you know.'

His voice again, followed by a stamping sound, then a dragging.

'And what's this?'

Finally her arm came out from behind her back and she whipped out the glass mobile that had been given to me. I wanted to shout out that it was mine but there was so much commotion in the hallway.

'This wasn't part of the deal, you know, Laurie. I was happy to let you play around with the glass because you wanted it so much, I thought the fire and the glass would be healing for you after ... well after everything, but you've taken it too far. You've ruined everything, you've ruined absolutely everything. Things have to change now. Things most certainly have to change.'

Laurie. Laurence Kilsaney RIP.

I was chilled. She was imagining him. Or she was seeing a ghost. No, that wasn't right. I could hear him too.

There were some angry words and then Rosaleen swung her arm back and flung the glass mobile down the hall. I heard a scream. Then she dived at him and I saw a walking stick being swung and it knocked her away, and she fell back against the wall with a thud. She looked at him fearfully and I backed into the corner, huddled my head into my legs tightly just wanting to get out of there, wanting to be anywhere else but there but not able to move.

'Rose?' I could hear a voice call.

'Yes, Mammy,' she said, scrambling to get to her feet, her voice trembling. 'I'm coming, Mammy.' She gave the man one last look, then ran down the hall to the television-room door.

The man stepped into the doorway and I

prepared myself but when I saw him, I screamed. Beneath long scrawny hair, a face which was so distorted stared back at me. One side of the face looked as though it had melted and had been pulled at and the skin had been put back in the wrong place. He quickly lifted a hand to his hair and tried to cover his face. He was wearing a long sleeve but as he lifted his hand to his face it revealed a stump. His left side was completely burned, his shoulder drooped downward as though it were candlewax sliding down the side of the left-hand side of his body. His eyes were big and blue, one was perfectly framed against soft smooth skin, the other was pulled down so much that it appeared to leap from its socket, revealing the white of the eye and all that was beneath. He started to come towards me and I began to cry.

I heard the back door open and the wind whooshed in. I heard steps on the plastic covering and the man Rosaleen had called Laurie turned in fright.

'Leave her alone!' I heard Weseley shout, and Laurie raised his hands in the air, looking shocked, sad, shaken. Then Weseley came in and saw me. I must have looked a mess because his face changed, anger took over, and he pushed Laurie up against the wall, his hand around his neck.

'What did you do to her?' he growled in his face.

'Leave him,' I heard myself say, but I couldn't get sounds out.

'Tamara, get out of there,' Weseley said, his face red, the veins throbbing in his neck from the effort it was taking to hold him off.

I don't know how but I finally stood up, grabbing the diary, and pushed myself forward. I managed to lay a hand on Weseley to stop him. He let go of Laurie, grabbed me and pulled me from the room, pushed Laurie inside, slammed the door and locked it. He took the key and put it in his pocket, while I heard the man shouting to let him out.

CHAPTER TWENTY-THREE

Breadcrumbs

Just as I reached the end of the passageway, Rosaleen swung herself round the corner to block me. She'd obviously left through the front door. She reached out and grabbed my arm, but I moved just within her grasp and her nails dug into my skin as she pinched me and tried to hold on. I screamed.

'Follow me,' Weseley said, and turned and ran.

I was running but was abruptly jerked backward, feeling a pain in my neck as Rosaleen grabbed my hair and tried to pull me back. I elbowed her hard in the stomach and she released me. Despite her behaviour to me over the past hour I still felt bad and stopped to see if she was okay. She was doubled over, winded.

'Tamara, come on!' Weseley shouted.

But I couldn't. This was ridiculous. I didn't understand why we were fighting, why she had turned on me. I had to see if she was all right. As

I came near her, she looked up, pulled back her right arm and slapped me hard across the face. I felt the sting long after her hand left my face. Weseley tugged on me and I had no choice but to run.

We ran down the back garden and past the work-shed which separated domestic life from the secret field of glass. Once in the field I realised how much the wind had picked up. It was blustery now and my hair was billowing around my face wildly, sometimes blinding me, sometimes stuffing my mouth with a lock of hair. Weseley was squeezing one of my hands so tightly I needed the other to balance myself as we ran across the lumpy grass, so I couldn't move the hair from my face. The glass was swinging violently in the wind, back and forth but with no rhythm so it was hard to judge whether it was going to come flying at our faces as we darted past. It was difficult to dodge and an effort to avoid being scraped by its jagged points.

I held on tightly to Weseley's hand and I just remember thinking, don't let go, don't ever let go. Every now and then he turned round to make sure I was still there, although his hand was wrapped so tightly around mine it was crushing my fingers. I saw the worry in his face, the panic in his eyes. We were in this together and I had never been so grateful to have such a friend. We ducked under lines of glass mobiles and made our way to the edge of the garden. Weseley began to figure out a way we could get over the wall. I stood there keeping watch, feeling my arms stinging as the scrapes on my arms and possibly on my face started to bleed and the cold air blew on them. I kept watch for Rosaleen who quickly appeared at the workshed and was scanning the garden for us. Our eyes met. She surged forward.

Weseley moved quickly, gathering crates and concrete blocks, layering them up, building them up so that we could get over the wall. He stepped up and finally he could reach the top of the wall.

'Right Tamara. I'll lift you up.'

I put the diary down and he lifted me from the waist. I scrambled to pull myself to the top, my bare elbows scraping the concrete, my knees banging against the wall, but finally I was there. Weseley handed me the diary and I jumped in to the field on the other side. Pain shot though my ankles and up my legs as I landed. Weseley wasn't far behind. He grabbed my hand again and we ran.

Across the road and straight into the gatehouse, I screamed for Arthur and Mum between heaving breaths. There was no answer, the house stared back silently at us, with its empty rooms, the ticking of the grandfather clock in the hall the only response. We both ran up and downstairs, flinging open doors, shouting into every eave. I had been worried before that, then I started to panic. I sat on my bed, the diary in my arms, not knowing what to do. Then, as I hugged it tightly and started to cry, it became clear.

I opened the diary. Slowly but surely the burned pages began to uncurl right before my eyes, unfolding and lengthening, and words no longer neatly looped and lined appeared in jagged and messy scrawls as though written in blind panic.

'Weseley,' I called.

'Yes!' he shouted up the stairs.

'We have to go,' I shouted.

'Where?' he yelled. 'We should call the gardaí. What do you think? Who was that guy? My God, did you see his face?' I could hear the adrenaline pumping through his words.

I stood up quickly. Too quickly. All the blood rushed to my head and I felt dizzy. Black spots formed before my eyes and I tried to keep walking, hoping they'd eventually disappear. I made my way out to the hall, holding on to the wall, trying to take deep breaths. The pulse in my forehead beat an insane rhythm, my skin felt hot and clammy.

'Tamara, what's wrong?' was all I heard.

I felt the book fall from my hand and hit the ground with a thud. After that – nothing.

I woke up to find myself staring at a painting of Mary, smiling down upon me in a baby-blue-coloured veil. Her thin lips smiling and telling me it was all going to be okay, her hands held out and open as though giving me some invisible gift. Then I remembered what had happened in the bungalow and I sat up with a start. My head felt like it was being crushed, as though the atmosphere was pushing down on me.

'Ow,' I groaned.

'Hush, Tamara, you must lie down. Slow down now,' Sister Ignatius said calmly, taking my hand in hers and placing another on my shoulder to coax me gently back down.

'My head,' I croaked, lying back down and taking in her face.

'That's a nasty bang you got,' she said, taking a cloth, dipping it in a dish and carefully dabbing at my skin above my eye.

It stung and I tensed.

'Weseley,' I panicked, looking around, and pushing her hand away from me. 'Where is he?'

'He's with Sister Conceptua. He's fine. He carried you all the way here,' she smiled.

'Tamara.' I heard another voice, and Mum came rushing over to me and fell to her knees. She looked different. She was dressed, for one thing. Her hair was scraped back into a ponytail and her face was thinner, but it was her eyes . . . despite being bloodshot and swollen as if she'd been crying, her eyes had life back in them again. 'Are you okay?'

I couldn't believe she was out of bed. I just kept staring at her, studying her, waiting for her to go into a trance again. She leaned forward and kissed me hard on the forehead, so much it almost hurt. She ran her hands through my hair, kissing me again and telling me she was sorry.

'Ouch,' I winced as she grabbed my wound.

'Oh, love, I'm sorry.' She let go immediately and moved back to examine me. She looked concerned.

'Weseley said he found you in a bedroom. There was a man, with scarring . . .'

'He didn't hit me.' I jumped to his defence immediately though I didn't really know why. 'Rosaleen showed up. She was so angry. She kept spouting all of these lies about you and about Dad. I ran at her to tell her to stop and she pushed me . . .' I placed my hand on my cut. 'Is it bad?'

'It won't scar. Tell me about the man.' Mum's voice trembled.

'They were having a fight. She called him Laurie,' I suddenly remembered.

Sister Ignatius held on to the couch tightly as though the floor were swirling beneath her. Mum looked at her, her jaw tightened, and then she looked back at me. 'So it's true. Arthur was telling the truth.'

'But it's not possible,' Sister Ignatius whispered. 'We buried him, Jennifer. He died in the fire.'

'He didn't die, Sister. I saw him. I saw his bedroom. He had photographs. Hundreds and hundreds of photographs all over the walls.'

'He loved taking photographs,' she said, quietly as though thinking aloud.

'They were all of me.' I said, looking from one to the other. 'Tell me about him. Who is he?'

'Photographs? Weseley didn't mention that,' Sister Ignatius said, shaking, her face pale.

'He didn't see, but I saw everything. My whole life was on the walls.' The words caught in my throat but I kept going. 'The day I was born, the christening,' I looked at her then and an anger came flooding through me. 'I saw you.'

'Oh.' Her wrinkled bony fingers went flying to her mouth. 'Oh, Tamara.'

'Why didn't you tell me? Why did you both lie?'

'I so wanted to tell you,' Sister Ignatius jumped in. 'I told you I'd never lie, that you could ask me anything, but you never asked. I waited and waited. I didn't think it was my place, but I should have. I realise that now.'

'We shouldn't have let you find out this way,' Mum said, her voice trembling.

'Well, neither of you had the guts to do what Rosaleen did. *She* told me.' I pushed Mum's hand away and turned my face away from her. 'She told me some ridiculous story about Dad arriving here with Granddad, wanting to buy the place to develop it into a spa. She said he met Mum, *and* he met me.' I looked at Mum then, waiting for her to tell me it was all lies.

She was silent.

'Tell me it's not true.' My eyes filled up and my voice trembled. I was trying to be strong but I couldn't. It was all too much. Sister Ignatius blessed herself. I could tell she was shaken.

'Tell me he's my dad.'

Mum started to cry and then stopped again, took a deep breath and found strength from somewhere. When she spoke her voice was firm and deeper. 'Okay listen to me, Tamara. You have to believe that we didn't tell you this because we believed it was the right thing to do all those years ago, and George . . .' she wavered, 'George loved you so much, with all of his heart, just like you were his own . . .'

I yelped at that, couldn't believe what I was hearing.

'He didn't want me to tell you. We fought about it all the time. But it's my fault. It's all my fault. I'm so sorry.' Tears gushed down her cheeks and though I wanted to feel nothing, to stare her down and show her how she'd hurt me, I couldn't. I couldn't feel nothing. My world had shifted so viciously, I was spinning out of orbit.

Sister Ignatius stood up and placed a hand on Mum's head as she ferociously tried to stop her tears, wipe her cheeks and comfort me instead. I couldn't look at Mum so my eyes followed Sister Ignatius as she then crossed to the other side of the room. She opened a cupboard and brought something back over to me.

'Here. I've been trying to give this to you for some time now,' she said, her eyes filled. It was a wrapped present.

'Sister, I'm really not in the mood for birthday presents right now, what with my Mum telling me she's lied to me my whole entire life,' I spoke with venom and Mum pursed her lips and her forehead creased. She nodded slowly, accepting whatever it was I threw at her. I wanted to shout at her more then. I wanted to use that opportunity to say all the bad things in the world that I've ever felt about her, just like I used to do when fighting with Dad but I stopped myself. Consequences. Repercussions. The diary had taught me that.

'Open it,' Sister Ignatius said sternly.

I ripped off the paper. It was a box. Inside the box was a rolled-up scroll. I looked to her for answers but she was kneeled beside me, her hands clasped and her head dipped as though in prayer.

I unrolled the scroll. It was a certificate of baptism.

This Certificate of Baptism is to certify that
Tamara Kilsaney
was born on the 24th day of July, 1991,
in Kilsaney Castle, County Meath
and was Presented to the World
with Love
by
Her mother, Jennifer Byrne, and her father,
Laurence Kilsaney
On this day
1st January 1992

I stared at the page, reading it over and over, hoping my eyes had deceived me. I didn't know where to begin.

'Well, first things first. They got the date wrong.' I tried to sound confident but I sounded pathetic and I knew it. This was something I couldn't beat with sarcasm.

'I'm sorry, Tamara,' Sister Ignatius said again.

383

'So that's why you kept saying I was seventeen.'
I thought back over all our conversations. 'But if
this was right, then I'm eighteen today . . . Marcus.'
I looked up at her. 'You were going to let him go
to gaol?'

'What?' Mum looked from one to the other.
'Who's Marcus?'

'None of your business,' I snapped. 'I might tell
you in twenty years.'

'Tamara, please,' she pleaded.

'He could have gone to gaol,' I said angrily to
Sister Ignatius.

Sister Ignatius shook her head wildly. 'No. I
asked Rosaleen over and over to tell you. If not
tell you, to tell the gardaí. She kept insisting he'd
be fine. But I stepped forward. I told the garda,
Tamara. I went to Dublin to Garda Fitzgibbon and
gave him this certificate myself. There was a
breaking-and-entering charge too, but bearing in
mind the circumstances, it's all been dropped.'

'What's been dropped? What happened?' my
Mum asked, looking at Sister Ignatius with
concern.

'God, Tamara, if you don't know that by now,
then you've far more problems than I thought.
Listen, I wish you good luck with everything but
. . . don't call me again.'

That had been our last conversation. He'd
known then why the charges had been dropped.
How messed up was I that I didn't even know my
own age? I had been so relieved for Marcus that

my anger subsided momentarily. Then that faded and I was fuming again. My head pounding, I held my hand to my wound. They had been feeding me lies, dropping a trail of breadcrumbs in their path which I had been forced to follow in order to learn the truth for myself.

'So let me get this straight. Rosaleen wasn't lying. Laurie *is* my father. The freak . . . with the photographs?' I shouted then. 'Why didn't anybody tell me? Why did everybody lie? Why did you all let me think I lost my dad?'

'Oh, Tamara, George *was* your father. He loved you more than anything in the world. He raised you as his own. He—'

'IS DEAD,' I shouted. 'And everybody let me think I'd lost my dad. He lied to me. You lied to me. I can't believe this.' I was up then, my head spinning.

'Your mother thought Laurie had died, Tamara. You were only one year old. She had a chance to start a new life. George loved her, he loved you. She wanted to start again. She didn't think you needed this hurt.'

'And that makes it okay?' I addressed Mum, even though Sister Ignatius had defended her.

'No, no, I didn't agree with it. But she deserved to be happy. She was so broken when Laurie died.'

'But he's not dead,' I shouted then. 'He's living in the bungalow, eating sandwiches and apple pie every bloody day. Rosaleen knew he was alive.'

Mum broke down at that and Sister Ignatius held her tightly in her arms, her face revealing her heartbreak. I stopped then, realising that it wasn't just me that was lied to. Mum had just found out the man she loved hadn't died after all. What kind of a sick joke had they all been playing?

'Mum, I'm sorry,' I said softly.

'Oh, darling,' she sniffed, 'maybe I deserve it. For doing this to you.'

'No. No, you don't deserve this. But he doesn't deserve you either. What kind of sicko must he be to pretend to be dead?'

'He was trying to protect her, I suppose,' Sister Ignatius said. 'He was trying to give the both of you a better life, one that he couldn't give you.'

'Arthur said he was badly disfigured?' Mum looked at me then. 'What . . . what does he look like? Was he kind to you?'

'Arthur?' I snapped to attention again. 'Arthur Kilsaney? He's Laurie's brother?'

Mum nodded and another tear fell.

'It's just one thing after another with you all,' I said, but not as angrily this time. I hadn't the energy.

'He didn't want to go along with it,' she said, drained now too. 'Now it makes sense to me why he was so against it. He said he wanted to always be your uncle. We never said he was my brother. Not until you just assumed it and then . . .' she waved her hand, sensing the ridiculousness of it all.

Weseley arrived in the room then. 'Okay the gardaí are on their way. Are you all right?' He looked at me. 'Did he hurt you?'

'No, no, he didn't.' I rubbed my eyes. 'He saved me from Rosaleen.'

'But I thought he . . .'

'No.' I shook my head.

'I locked him in his bedroom,' Weseley said guiltily, producing the room key from his pocket. 'I thought he was trying to hurt you.'

'Oh, no.' My main anger passed then. I felt sorry for him. He had been defending me. He had been reaching out to me giving me gifts. He'd remembered my birthday. My eighteenth birthday. Of course he had. And how had I thanked him? I'd locked him away.

'Where's Arthur?' Sister Ignatius asked.

'He's gone to the bungalow, to Rosaleen.'

And then I remembered. The diary. 'No!' I scrambled to get up again.

'Honey you should relax,' Mum said trying to coax me back down again, but I jumped up.

'He needs to get away from there,' I panicked. 'What have I been doing here all this time? Weseley, call the fire brigade, quick.'

'Why?'

'Honey, just relax now,' Mum said, worried. 'Lie down and—'

'No, listen to me. Weseley, it's in the diary. I have to stop it. Call the fire brigade.'

'Tamara, it's just a book, it's only—'

'Been right every single day until now,' I responded.

He nodded.

'What's that?' Mum suddenly asked, walking to the window.

Over the tree tops in the distance, plumes of smoke were drifting up into the sky.

'Rosaleen,' Sister said then with such venom, that it chilled me. 'Call the fire brigade,' she said to Weseley.

'Give me the key,' I said, grabbing it from Weseley and running from the room. 'I have to get him. I'm not losing him again.'

I heard them all calling to me as I ran, but I didn't stop, I didn't listen. I ran through the trees and followed the smell, ran straight towards the bungalow. I had just lost the father who'd raised me. I wasn't about to lose another.

CHAPTER TWENTY-FOUR
Dreams About Dead People

When I reached the bungalow there was a squad car parked outside. I could see Rosaleen standing on the grass alongside her mother. Talking to her was a rather impatient garda, who kept asking her over and over if anybody was inside. Rosaleen was wailing, hands covering her face, and looking back at the house as though she couldn't decide. Beside the garda was Arthur, who was barking at Rosaleen, shaking her by the shoulders and trying to get her to answer.

'He's in the workshed!' she finally shrieked.

'He's not, I looked!' Arthur yelled.

'He has to be!' she shrieked. 'He has to be. He always locked his bedroom door when he went to the workshed.'

'Who?' the garda was saying over and over again. 'Who's in the house?'

'He's not there.' Arthur's voice was hoarse. 'My God, woman, what have you done?'

'Oh my God,' Rosaleen was shrieking over and over again. Her mother was softly crying.

Sirens were wailing in the distance.

I ignored them all. I ran past them unnoticed, down the side passage and in through the back door of the bungalow. Smoke was everywhere, filling the halls, so black and thick that as soon as I inhaled it I was choked. It sent me to my knees, retching and gasping, stinging my eyes so badly I rubbed them over and over but it only made them worse. I placed my cardigan across my face. I had soaked it in cold water from the outside tap and put it across my mouth and nose to help me breathe. Peering out from one eye, I felt my way along the wall. The plastic beneath my feet was dangerously hot and sticky, so that the rubber in my trainers was sticking to it. I kept to the sides of the hallway, where it was tiled. I felt my way along the wall to his bedroom door. When I placed my hand on the metal door handle it burned me so badly I let go and cowered over, cradling my hand, coughing, eyes stinging, retching, hand burning. The open door at the end of the hall relieved the hallway at least of some smoke and I knew it wasn't far. I could always run out the door.

I shoved the key in the door, hoping the whole thing hadn't melted, and I turned it. Stepping back, I used my foot to push down the handle and the door swung open. More smoke followed me in and I pushed the door closed. The corners of the photographs were curling with the heat. I couldn't see any fire, just smoke, thick black heavy smoke that hurt my lungs. I tried to call out but couldn't, just kept coughing over and over, hoping he'd hear me, that he'd know I was there.

I felt my way along the bed, felt his body, felt his face. His beautifully scarred face, ruined just like the castle, which carried such a story I was drawn to it and not repelled. His eyes were closed; I could feel his eyelids. I shook him, moved my hands all over his body to try to wake him. Nothing. He was unconscious. Behind me I felt intense heat, felt fire. It would quickly close in on me, in this room of photographs. I pulled at the net curtains, bringing a little light into the grey smoky room. I felt around to try to open the windows. They were locked. There weren't any keys. I picked up a chair, threw it at the window over and over to smash it, but I couldn't. I tried to pull at him, but he was too heavy. I tried to get him to his feet. I was getting tired, running out of energy, feeling dizzy. I lay down beside him, trying to wake him. I held his hand, the two of us huddled together on the bed. I wasn't going to leave him.

Suddenly I dreamed of the castle, of a banquet with a long table filled with pheasant and pig, everything dripping with grease and sauces, wine and champagne, the most delicious duck and vegetables. Then I was with Sister Ignatius and she was shouting at me to push, but I didn't know what to push. I couldn't see her but I could hear her. Then the darkness faded and the room was filled with such wonderful light, and I was in Sister Ignatius' arms. Then I was in the field of glass, running, running, with Rosaleen hot on my heels. I was holding Weseley's hand just like before only it wasn't Weseley, it was Laurie. Not as I knew him from today but as I first saw him in the photographs, handsome, young, mischievous. He was turning round and smiling at me, his perfect white teeth opening and closing as he laughed, and I realised then how alike we were, how I'd always wondered why I didn't look like Mum or Dad, and now it all made perfect sense. His nose, his lips, his cheeks and eyes – all were like mine. He was holding my hand and telling me we were going to be okay. We were running together, laughing and smiling, not worried at all about Rosaleen because she couldn't catch us. Together we could outrun the world. Then I saw my father, at the end of the field, clapping and cheering us on as though I was a child again, at the community races in the rugby club. Laurie was gone and it was me and Mum for a moment, legs tied together in the three-legged race, just like we used to do when I was young. She was anxious-looking, not laughing but worried, and then she left and Laurie was back. We were running, tripping up, and there my dad was, laughing and cheering, beckoning us forth, arms open and ready to catch us when we fell across the line.

Then the glass mobiles in the field exploded all around us, shattered into millions of pieces and I lost Laurie's hand. I heard Dad scream my name and I opened my eyes. The room was filled with glass, it was all over our bodies, all over the ground and the smoke was pluming out through the window. I saw a claw, a giant yellow claw, disappear through the glass and the smoke drifted out. But it didn't stop the fire. It ravaged the photographs, racing through them with such speed and ferocity it was eating away at everything around us and leaving us until last. We would be next. Then I saw Arthur. I saw Sister Ignatius. I saw my mother's face, alive, present, terrified. She was outside, moving, talking and, despite her alarm, I was relieved. Then there were arms around me and I was outside, coughing, spluttering. I couldn't breathe, I was on the grass. Before I closed my eyes I saw my mother, felt her kissing my head, then saw her embracing Laurie, crying and crying, her tears falling onto his head as if they alone could put out the fire between them.

For the first time since I'd found my father on the floor of his office, I exhaled.

CHAPTER TWENTY-FIVE
Little Girl

Once upon a time there was a little girl who lived in a bungalow. She was the youngest child, with an intelligent older sister, and cute older brother so handsome that he turned heads in the street, invited conversations with strangers. The little girl was what some people would call a surprise baby. To her parents, who had long finished having children, she was not just unplanned but unwanted and that she knew well. At forty-seven years old and twenty-two years since she'd had her last baby, her mother was not prepared for the arrival of another child. Her children had grown up and moved away, her daughter Helen to Cork to be a primary school teacher and her son Brian to Boston, where he was a computer analyst. They rarely came home. It was too expensive for Brian, and her mother preferred to go to Cork for holidays. The little girl didn't know these two strangers she rarely met and who called themselves her brother and sister. They had children older than she; they knew little of who she was or what she wanted. She'd arrived too late, she'd missed the bonding that they had all had together.

Her father was the gillie at Kilsaney Castle grounds, which was across the road from her home. Her mother was the cook. The little girl loved the position her family were in, so close to such grandeur that the children at school considered her to be a part of it too. She loved that they were privy to bits of gossip that nobody else was. They were always the benefactors of great Christmas bonuses, leftover food, fabrics or wallpapers from recent refurbishings or clear-outs. The grounds were strictly private but the little girl was allowed to play inside its walls. It was an absolute honour for her and there was nothing she wouldn't do to please the family, such as odd jobs around the house, running from her father Joe to the groundsman, Paddy, with messages from her mother on what to catch that day, what vegetables to choose for dinner.

She loved the days she was allowed to enter the castle. If she was off sick from school her mother couldn't very well leave her at home. They were good like that, Mr and Mrs Kilsaney. They allowed her mother to bring her child to work, knowing there was nowhere else she could possibly leave her child and there was nobody else who could take care of their three meals a day so well, feeding them so well with money that was lessening by the year. The little girl would remain quiet in the corner of the great big kitchen where she'd watch her mother sweat all day over steaming pots and a roaring Aga. She would be quiet, never giving any trouble, but she'd take it all in. She'd take in her mother's cooking but also she absorbed the goings-on in the house.

She noticed how, whenever Mr Kilsaney had a decision to make, he'd disappear into the oak room and stand in the middle with his hands behind his back while he stared at the portraits of his forefathers, who grandly watched over him from their great big oil paintings with elaborate gold framing. He would exit the oak room, chin high, fired into action as though he was a soldier who'd just received a good talking-to from his sergeant-major.

She also saw how Mrs Kilsaney, who was so besotted with her nine dogs and ran around the house in a frenzy, trying to catch them, failed to notice much of what went on around her. She paid more attention to her dogs, in particular the mischievous King Charles spaniel named Messy, who remained the only dog who couldn't be tamed and who took up most of her thoughts and most of her conversation. She didn't notice her two young boys play-acting around the halls for her attention, or her husband's fondness for the none-too-attractive chambermaid Magdelene, who revealed a black tooth when she smiled and who spent much time dusting the Kilsaneys' master bedroom when Mrs Kilsaney was outdoors with the dogs.

The little girl noticed that what made Mrs Kilsaney mad was dead flowers. She would inspect every vase as she passed, almost as though it were an obsession. She would smile with delight when the nun would arrive every third morning with fresh bouquets from her walled garden. Then, as soon as the door closed, she would pick at them, while grumbling, pulling out anything that was less than perfect. The little girl loved Mrs Kilsaney, loved her tweed suits and brown riding boots, which she wore even on days when she wasn't riding. However, the little girl decided she would never allow so much to go on in her own home without her knowing. She adored the mistress, but she thought her a fool.

She didn't think much of the husband frolicking in plain sight with the ugly chambermaid, tickling her behind with a feather duster and acting younger than the little girl herself. He thought she was too young to notice him, too young to understand. She didn't much like him, but he thought her a fool.

She watched everything. She made a pact with herself always to know everything going on in her home.

She loved watching the two boys. They were always up to mischief, always racing around the halls knocking things over, breaking things, making the chambermaid scream, causing a ruckus. It was the older one she watched all of the time. It was always he who initiated the plan. The younger one who was more sensible and went along with it only because he wanted to look out for his older brother. Laurence was the elder, or Laurie, as they called him. He never noticed the little girl, but she was always there on the outskirts, feeling involved without being invited, playing along in her imagination.

The younger boy, Arthur, or Artie, as they called him, noticed her. He didn't invite her to play, he didn't do anything of his own accord, he merely followed his brother's ideas, but if Laurie did something silly he'd look to the little girl and roll his eyes or make a joke for her benefit. She'd rather he didn't. It was Laurie she wanted to notice her and the more he didn't see her, the greater her longing grew. Sometimes when he was alone and running, she would deliberately stand in his way. She'd want him at least to look at her or stop, or shout at her, but he never did. He ran around her. If he was searching for Artie in a game of hide-and-seek, she'd help him by pointing out his hiding place. He wouldn't acknowledge her, he'd search somewhere else, then shout to Artie that he was giving up. He wanted nothing from her.

The little girl stayed home from school a lot, just so she could spend time in the castle. Summer holidays were the best, having every day free to herself around the grounds without having to pretend to cough or to have a sore tummy. It was during one of these summers, when the little girl was seven, Artie was eight and Laurie was nine that she was outside in the grounds playing alone as always when her mother called her to the castle. The Kilsaneys were gone out for the day, fox-hunting with their cousins in Balbriggan. Mrs Kilsaney had called her up to her room to help her pick out her dress, a floor-length silk olive-coloured dress, to be worn with pearls and a fur coat. The little girl's mother was in charge for the day and when she reached the front of the castle she could tell from the look on the boys' faces that they were in trouble.

'It's a beautiful day so play outside and get some fresh air and don't be getting under my feet,' her mother said. 'Rosaleen will play with you too.'

'I don't want to play with her,' Laurie sulked, still not looking at her, but at least she knew that she wasn't invisible to him, that he could see her after all.

'Be nice to her, boys. Say hello, Rosaleen.'

The boys were tight-lipped, but the little girl's mother barked at them then.

'Hello, Rosaleen,' they both mumbled, Laurie looking at the ground, Artie smiling at her shyly.

The little girl had no name before that. When she heard her name pass his lips, it was as though she had been christened.

'Now off with you,' her mother said and the boys ran off. Rosaleen followed.

Once they were deep in the woods, they stopped running as Laurie went to study an ant hole.

'I'm Artie,' the younger one said.

'Don't talk to her,' Laurie huffed, picking up a stick from the ground and waving it around as though he were in combat.

Laurie ignored them and concentrated on poking the stick in the hole of a tree trunk. Suddenly they heard voices and Laurie, ears pricked, followed the sound. He held his hand up and they stalled and they all spied through the trees and saw the groundsman, Paddy, on his knees, sorting through some brambles while beside him, in the wheelbarrow, lay a little girl aged about two, with white-blonde hair.

'Who's that?' Laurie said, and his voice sent warning signals straight to Rosaleen's heart but, excited for their first conversation, she replied, with a pounding in her chest, conscious of her voice, wanting it all to be so perfect for him.

'That's Jennifer Byrne,' she said, ever so prim and proper as Mrs Kilsaney spoke. 'Paddy is her dad.'

'Let's ask her to play,' Laurie said.

'She's only a baby,' Rosaleen protested.

'She's funny,' Laurie asked, watching her lazing about in the wheelbarrow.

From that day on it was the four of them. Laurie,

Artie, Rosaleen and Jennifer played together every day. Jennifer because she'd been invited, Rosaleen because they'd been forced. Rosaleen always remembered that. Even when Laurie kissed her in the bushes or when they were boyfriend and girlfriend for a few weeks, she always knew that little Jennifer was his favourite. She always had been. She captivated him. Whatever it was about the things she said and the way that she moved, Laurie was entranced by her, always wanted to be around her.

Jennifer grew even more beautiful year by year though she was completely unaware of her beauty. Her big boobs, her tiny waist, her hips that all of a sudden appeared during one summer. Without a mother in her life since she was three years old, she was quite the tomboy, hanging out of trees, racing both Artie and Laurie, stripping off and diving into the lakes without a care in the world. She always tried to get Rosaleen to join in but never understood why she wouldn't. Rosaleen on the other hand was biding her time. She knew that the tomboy act would wear off with the boys. They'd lose interest. They'd want to find a real woman some day and she was going to be that woman. She could be like Mrs Kilsaney, she could keep the castle, cook the food, train the dogs, make sure the nun brought her nothing less than perfect flowers. She dreamed of Laurie someday being hers, that they could live together in the castle, looking after the dogs and the flowers while Laurie received inspiration in the oak room from his forefathers on the walls.

When the boys went off to boarding school, Laurie wrote only to Jennifer. Artie wrote to both of them. Rosaleen never let Jennifer know this. She would pretend that she had received a letter too but that it was too personal to read aloud. Jennifer never seemed to mind, having so much confidence in her friendships it made Rosaleen even more jealous. Then when the boys went off to college, Rosaleen's mother's MS was deteriorating, her ageing father was ill, they needed money, and Rosaleen's brother and sister were too far away to help, so Rosaleen's parents relied on the child they never wanted to look after them. Rosaleen was forced to leave school and take over her mother's job at the castle, while Jennifer continued to prosper, taking trips to Dublin to visit the boys.

Those were the worst days for Rosaleen. The weeks were long and boring without them. She lived for Laurie to return; she lived in her head, dreaming of all that was past and creating all that could be in the future, while they were off in the city doing exciting things – Laurie at art college, sending home his glass work, Artie studying horticulture – Jennifer being offered modelling jobs every time she stepped outside of the door. When they returned home during the breaks, Rosaleen's life couldn't be happier except that she yearned for Laurie to look at her as he did Jennifer.

She didn't know how long their romance had been going on. She could only assume it started in Dublin while she was at home plucking pheasants and gutting fish. She wondered if they were ever going to tell her, if it hadn't been for that embarrassing day when she brought him to the apple tree to finally tell him how she felt, showed the carving in the tree, 'Rose Loves Laurie'. She was so sure he would be blown away, that he would see her for who she really was, how she had been keeping the castle going without him, how capable she was. She'd imagined the day for months, for years.

But it hadn't worked that way. It hadn't gone exactly as she'd imagined for all those years and for all those months alone in the kitchen in the castle. Life became dark and cold then. Her father passed away, the boys returned from college to attend the funeral, her older sister tried to take her mother away with her to Cork but without her mother, Rosaleen had nothing. She promised to look after her. Jennifer offered her a firm friendship and Rosaleen accepted it while all the time hating her. Hating everything she said, everything she did, hating that Laurie had fallen for her.

The autumn of 1990 Jennifer fell pregnant. Rosaleen's life fell apart. Jennifer was welcomed in the Kilsaney household with open arms. A delighted Mrs Kilsaney showed her her wardrobes, the wedding dress, the everything that should have been Rosaleen's. Jennifer and her father were invited to dinner weekly. Rosaleen cooked for them. The humiliation was beyond repair.

The child was born, two weeks early and with not enough time to get to the hospital. Rosaleen had run through the dark night to fetch the old nun. They had a little girl. They called her Tamara, after Jennifer's mother, who'd passed away when she was a child. The couple weren't yet married but living in the castle. Rosaleen and Arthur were godparents. The christening was in the castle chapel.

But life in the castle was not easy. The Kilsaneys were finding it difficult to keep the castle going, money wasn't coming in, they were becoming desperate. All those rooms to keep, to heat, to maintain – it was all too much. They would meet at dinner to talk about it. Rosaleen, as though hiding in the walls would hear it all.

Perhaps they would open the castle to the public. Every Saturday allow the public to trample through their home, taking photographs of their eighteenth-century writing desks and the oak room filled with portraits, at their chapel, at their age-old letters from generations ago between lords and ladies, politicians and rebels, during times of great unrest.

'No,' Mrs Kilsaney would cry, 'I can't let them visit us as though we're a zoo. And still how will we afford the place? A few pounds admission fee per adult won't fix the roof, it won't pay Paddy's wages, it won't pay the heating bills.'

They found a solution, though. Developers Timothy and George Goodwin arrived in Kilsaney in their Bentley on the most beautiful day of the year and they couldn't believe their eyes when they saw the grounds, the view, the lakes, the deer, the pheasants. It was like a theme park. They saw money everywhere they looked. Timothy Goodwin, a dapper but rude old gentleman in a three-piece suit, and with a cheque-book in his inside pocket, fell in love with the property. George Goodwin fell in love with Jennifer Byrne. This was the happiest day of Rosaleen's life. While serving them during their banquet meal in the great dining room, she couldn't help but observe how George Goodwin had eyes only for Jennifer, how he had little to say to Laurie and a lot of time to play with the child. Everybody at the table saw this, certainly Laurie. Jennifer was kind to him but she adored Laurie.

The Goodwins returned over and over, to measure, to bring builders, architects, engineers, surveyors. George returned far more often than his father, taking over the project. Rosaleen saw her opportunity to get Laurie back. One night she over-heard George offering Jennifer the sun, the moon, and the stars. Everybody fell for Jennifer. It was her fault – she sent out vibes, caught people in her web, had no idea how many lives she ruined in the process. But while she found George Goodwin a pleasant and kind man, she rejected his advances.

Not so in Rosaleen's eyes.

Laurie caught her in the scullery crying her eyes out. She wouldn't tell him at first, she didn't want to hurt him. It was none of her business, Jennifer was her friend. But he gently coaxed her into telling him what she'd seen. She'd felt bad for causing the hurt that went through his eyes. So bad that she almost took it back right there and then, but then he'd taken her hand and squeezed it, given her a hug and told her what a great friend she'd always been, how he hadn't always acknowledged that. Well, how could she take it back then?

It was a long night, a long argument. Rosaleen allowed them to fight it out between themselves, their own words then doing more damage than hers ever could. Laurie didn't tell Jennifer that it was Rosaleen that had told him. She was glad of that. Instead she let Jennifer cry on her shoulder, while she gave half-hearted advice. Jennifer was sleeping in the gatehouse that night, Laurie didn't want her anywhere near him. Jennifer came to Rosaleen as she was happily clearing up the kitchen, contented with the latest argument she'd started. She came to Rosaleen with a letter. A letter that Rosaleen read and, though she rarely cried, it made her do so. Jennifer's wish was for her to pass it on to Laurie. Rosaleen burned it. But the child wandered in, the toddler who looked so like her father that she got a shock. Rosaleen shook out the letter and the fire subsided and she threw it in the bin. She picked up the child and returned her to her bed. Rosaleen went home then.

That was the night of the fire. She can't be sure if it was the burned letter that caused it, though they say it came from the kitchen, but nobody ever blamed her. The child was saved by Laurie. Then he went back in to fetch some valuables. As far as Jennifer knew, he died in that fire. Laurie didn't want Jennifer to take him back just because she felt she had to. As far as he was concerned, George Goodwin had her heart and could offer her more. Though it was his own decision, a little probing from Rosaleen helped Laurie to decide that was the best thing. He could offer them nothing. No castle, land that was sold, he'd lost the use of an arm and a leg. He was badly burned, beyond recognition. Ugly as though he'd rotted away. Artie didn't agree, but he couldn't talk his brother out of the decision to deceive Jennifer. The brothers never spoke again, not even when living across the road from one another.

For months Jennifer mourned, refusing to leave her house, refusing to live. But there's only so much of that you can take, particularly when there was a handsome successful gentleman knocking on her door and wanting to rescue her and take her away. Rosaleen once again was at the helm of that decision. She engineered it all so wonderfully. She hadn't meant to start the fire, hadn't meant to hurt poor Laurie like that but it had happened and it worked in her favour. Artie moved in with Paddy and they worked the grounds together. Laurie moved into the bungalow where Rosaleen could care both for him and for her mother. He thanked her everyday but still he couldn't give her what she wanted. He didn't love her. He relied on her to keep him alive. She realised then that she'd never have him exactly the way she wanted. She'd never become a Kilsaney.

When Paddy died and Artie was living in the gatehouse alone that she turned her attention to him or, returned the attention he had been giving her ever since she'd been a little girl. Rosaleen finally became a Kilsaney, though they never used their titles, and Laurie was still in her life, needing her. Rosaleen had never liked going to town anyway, had hated hearing the locals gossip about things they knew nothing of. The only times she surfaced were for mass and to sell her vegetables. Any shopping would be done in the further town where nobody could question her.

That was seventeen years ago and it was all going well, not perfectly, but it was going well until George Goodwin, valiant until the end, had protected Kilsaney and refused to let it be taken and messed up her plans and that awful little child who looked so like her father, and who should have been hers, had come back into their lives to throw it into turmoil again. It would all have been all right if Jennifer had stopped asking questions, if she had just been able to heal so that she and Tamara could both move on with their lives in Dublin. But she had reverted back to her time when she grieved for Laurie, had taken on the same behaviour. She was confused, she was grieving for the wrong person. Rosaleen just wanted them to get their finances sorted out so that they could leave as soon as possible, but it hadn't worked that way.

Rosaleen couldn't cope with losing anything else. She loved Laurie more than anyone in her life, but the lie he had forced her to keep had led to so much unhappiness for so many people. She could see that now. And she was tired. Tired of fighting for her marriage to the wonderful, lovely Arthur who had never agreed with Laurie's decision and Rosaleen's agreement to go along with it. Her beautiful kind and soft husband who was torn apart every day by the lie to Jennifer and Tamara, who deserved more. She was tired of keeping the secret, tired of running back and forth, tired of being unable to look anybody in the eye in the village for fear of them knowing what she had done, guessing what was going on in the bungalow and in the workshed, where smoke funnelled out night and day. She wanted everything to go away. She wanted this bungalow, which had always felt like a prison to her, which had become one for Laurie and her mother, to be gone. She was going to release them all. She made sure her mother was safe before she struck the match.

Why, Rosaleen, why? They asked her over and over outside the burning bungalow. *Why?* They still didn't know, they still had to ask her. All that she had been through, her silent torture. But that was why. That was always the reason why. From a little girl to a grown woman, she had loved Laurie too much.

CHAPTER TWENTY-SIX
What We Have Learned Today

Friday 7 August
*I heard Mum and Laurie talking until the sun
came up. I don't know what they were saying,
but the tone was a lot more improved than it
has been over the past couple of weeks. Sister
Ignatius has been helping them talk through
everything. It's like anything bad or scary that
happens, when you finish it or get through it
you're so relieved you forget how terrifying it
was or how miserable you were and you want
to do it again, or you just remember the good
parts, or you tell yourself it's helped you get to
the new part of yourself.*

*All is not well in this household. All is not
perfect. But then it never has been. Gone is the
elephant from the room, though. He was
released, is running riot down the roads, while
we all try to tame him. It's just like when a
card dealer shuffles the pack – he messes them*

all up, ruins the order just so he can deal and the pack will eventually find its way to order again. That's what had happened to us. A long time ago things were shuffled, we were all dealt our cards. Now, we're tidying them up, trying to make sense out of them all.

I don't think Mum or I will ever forgive Laurie, Rosaleen and Arthur for keeping such a secret from us, for propelling such a lie for so long. All that we can do is try to understand that Laurie did it because he wanted the best for us, no matter how misguided it was. He tells us that he did it because he loved us and he thought it would give us a better life. It's not forgivable, and it's not enough to hear all that Rosaleen had told him, how she'd swayed his opinion, how she'd fed him and Mum with so many lies that they didn't know what they were doing. It's not forgivable, but we have to try to understand. Maybe when I understand it properly I can forgive it. Maybe when I can understand why both Mum and Dad lied to me about my real father, I'll be able to forgive it. I think that's all a little too far off for me to imagine. But I can thank Laurie for giving me such a wonderful dad. George Goodwin was a good man, an amazing father, thinking of us, again no matter how misguided, until the end. He fought his father all the way to the end of his father's life about developing Kilsaney. He knew it was the one thing that my biological

*father could have left behind for me, had things
gone the way they should have, had he not
perished in the fire. It was also Mum's home.
Where she grew up, where she carried all of her
memories, and when the banks came knocking,
he couldn't let it go. I would rather have my
father than Kilsaney, but I know how much he
loved us, what he was attempting to do. Both
of my fathers gave up so much for us. I can
only thank them and feel fortunate to be loved
so much by two people. That may be
completely incomprehensible to anybody else,
but it's my life, it's how I've learned to cope.*

*Arthur is back and forth to Rosaleen in the
hospital every day. She's been the luckiest
person in the world to have him and she never
knew it. She'll know it now, when everybody
else has turned their backs on her. And Arthur
is still there, despite discovering all that she'd
done, trying to bring back the woman he loves.
I find his loyalty to her unfathomable but then
again, I've never been in love. It seems to do
crazy things to people. He just wants her to get
better but, between you and me, I don't think
she'll ever get out of that place. Whatever is
wrong with Rosaleen is so deep-rooted that it
has reached from her past life and is growing
far into her next life, already uprooting
whatever is sprouting there.*

*Arthur and Laurence have been reunited.
Arthur will never forgive Laurence for what he*

did, for making him promise to be a part of this entire thing. But I think he'll forgive him quicker than he'll ever forgive himself. He tormented himself every single day about not having stepped forward, for not stopping the plan from going ahead, for allowing the lie to grow, watching me growing up while my father was across the road in a room, watching my mother grieve while her love was right across the road. He says lots of things stopped him, but seeing how much my mum loved George and how much of a great father he was was the greatest reason of all. I suppose it's easier to see the way out of anything when you've found your way out of that maze. When you're stuck in the middle, in a series of dead-ends making circles, it's difficult to make any sense of anything. I know that feeling.

Me? I'm a little wobbly but oddly, I feel stronger. I've said goodbye to Zoey and Laura completely after they asked for photographs of my burned hand for their Facebook pages. I'm planning on inviting Fiona, the girl who gave me the book at the funeral, to this house very soon. When things have calmed down at least a little.

So that's the story. The whole story. As I said at the beginning, I don't expect you to believe it but it's the truth, every single word of it. All families have their secrets, most people would never know them, but they know there are

416

spaces, there are gaps where the answers should be, where someone should have sat, where someone used to be. A name that is never uttered, or uttered once and never again. We all have our secrets. At least ours are unearthed now, or at least, are beginning to be. I constantly wonder how much of my life I would have learned if it hadn't been for the diary. Sometimes I think I would have found out sooner or later, most of the time I think that's what the diary's purpose was, because it most certainly had a purpose. It led me to here. It helped me discover the secrets but it also made me a better person. That sounds really slushy, I know, but it helped me to realise that there are tomorrows. Before, I concentrated on just now. I would say and do things in order to get what I wanted in that instant. I never gave a second thought to how the rest of the dominoes would fall. The diary helped me to see how one thing affects another. How I can actually make a difference in my life and in other people's lives. I always think back to how I was drawn to that book in Marcus's travelling library, almost like it was there just for me that day. I think that most people go into bookshops and have no idea what they want to buy. Somehow, the books sit there, almost magically willing people to pick them up. The right person for the right book. It's as though they already know whose life they need to be a part

417

of, how they can make a difference, how they can teach a lesson, put a smile on a face at just the right time. I think about books a lot differently now.

When I was in primary school the teacher used to tell us to write a paragraph at the end of every day titled 'What I Learned Today'. I feel in this circumstance it would take far less to say 'What I Haven't Learned', for what haven't I learned? Nothing. Absolutely nothing. I've learned so much, I've grown so much and it's never ending.

I thought this whole thing – finding out who I am – was the purpose for the diary. I thought after the fire the diary would become a notepad again and I would have returned it to the travelling library and replaced it on the non-fiction shelf and allowed somebody else to benefit from it. But I can't do it. I can't let it go. It continues to tell me about tomorrow and I continue to live it and sometimes I try to live it better.

I closed the diary, left the castle and made my way toward the orchard where I'd arranged to meet Weseley by the apple tree with the engravings.

'Uh-oh,' he said eyeing the diary under my arm. 'What now?'

'Nothing bad.' I sat down beside him on a blanket.

'I don't believe you. What is it?'

'It's actually about you and me,' I laughed.

'What about us?'

I raised my eyebrows suggestively at him.

'Oh, no!' He threw his arms up dramatically. 'So now, as well as saving you from burning houses, I have to kiss you?'

I shrugged. 'Whatever.'

'Where does it happen? Here?'

I nodded.

'Okay. So.' He looked at me seriously.

'So,' I replied. I cleared my throat. Readied myself.

'Does it say that I kiss you or that you kiss me?'

'You definitely kiss me.'

'Okay.'

He was silent for a moment and then he leaned in and kissed me tenderly on the lips. In the middle of the most luscious nicest kiss I'd ever had, he opened his eyes and pulled away.

'You just made that up, didn't you?' he asked, eyes wide.

'What do you mean?' I laughed.

'Tamara Goodwin, you just made that up!' he grinned. 'Give me that book.' He swiped it from my hands and pretended to hit me over the head with it.

'We have to make our own tomorrows Weseley,' I teased. I fell back on the blanket and looked up at the apple tree that had seen so much.

Weseley leaned over me, our faces close together, our noses almost touching.

'What did it really say?' he asked softly.

'That I think it'll all be okay. And that I'll write again tomorrow.'

'You always say that.'

'And I always do.'

'Are you ready?' he asked, studying me closely.

'I think so,' I whispered.

'Right.' He sat up and pulled me up with him. 'I brought this.'

He took a clear plastic bag from beside him and held it open. I dropped the diary in. Reluctantly at first, then as soon as it was in, I knew it was the right decision.

He wrapped the diary up in the plastic bag and handed it back to me.

'You do it.'

I looked up at the apple tree, at the engravings of the names of my Mum, Laurie, Arthur, Rosaleen and the dozens of others who had so many hopes for tomorrow under this tree, and then I kneeled down and placed the diary in the hole that Weseley had dug and we filled it again with soil.

I didn't lie when I said I couldn't let it go. I can't let it go. Not completely. Maybe some day when I'm in trouble again I'll dig it up and see what it has to say. But in the meantime, I'll have to find my own way.

Thanks for reading my story. I'll write again tomorrow.

THE END

Cecelia
Ahern

Making the
everyday magical

Inside:

• Q&A with Cecelia on her inspiration
behind the book and why it's as good
to cry as it is to laugh

• Keep up-to-date with Cecelia's
latest news on her website

• Don't miss Cecelia's other bestsellers

Q&A for *The Book of Tomorrow*

What inspired your latest book, *The Book of Tomorrow*?

It's about my love for books. I believe they're magical and
sometimes they choose you rather than the other way round.
Books can come into your life at a time when you're going
through a rough patch, with the power to rescue you, and this is
what happens in this one. I came up with the concept first – a
diary that writes itself, leading me to ask who would find it and
why they would need it – and then the characters developed from
there.

Do you keep a journal?

I've been writing one since I was eight. Two years ago, I lost the
latest book after hiding it in such a safe place, even I couldn't
find it. I didn't want to start a new one because I wanted to keep
the continuity of my story. I had such a busy year last year – two
books published in one year, the TV show, the Mrs Whippy play
– that the last thing I wanted to do after putting the pen down at
work was to pick the pen up again and document my feelings.
Recently I found it so I've begun writing it again. I had a lot to
fill in! As you get older, you analyse everything and examine how
you felt at the time, or how you think you thought you felt, but a
journal allows you to write exactly what you're feeling at the
time before you rationalise it, which is always different. In the
moment, emotions are more raw and real.

I've always had a head full of thoughts and whenever I've felt
angry, upset or excited, it's really helped putting pen to paper. I
don't document events as a story, it's more about chronicling my
feelings, which has helped me through the usual ups and downs
of growing up. When I write my diaries, I write as if I'm
addressing a person. Writing helps my head feel less full – and
calmer. Perhaps that's why I write fiction in longhand – putting
pen to paper is cathartic, like you're really getting issues out as it
flows onto the paper.

Will future generations lose out not having access to journals as we have stopped writing them?

It depends on the person – I find it really helpful. All these social networking sites like Facebook and MySpace – the modern version of journals – lack soul to me. They just don't go very deep, it's all on the surface stuff and they don't impress me. They offer no scope for reflection. But as a mechanism to reach broader audience I think they're a great idea but for that reason I think people should be careful about what kind of information they share with the world.

What are the main themes in *The Book of Tomorrow*?

My central themes are about loss – both grieving the loss of oneself and of a loved one – going back to basics and taking responsibility for your actions. When I got my initial concept of the diary that writes itself, recording the events of tomorrow, I came up with the character of Tamara as someone who doesn't think far ahead at all. The central character, Tamara, lives in the moment, and lives to satisfy herself without thinking about the consequences of her actions and how her decisions can affect other people. Now as her life is turned upside down, she's forced to face the reality of what tomorrow can bring. She is so busy living in the now that she gives very little thought to why or how.

Another big theme is the importance of going back to basics and not having too much – and you should never feel a sense of entitlement. I have that Irish guilt where the more you have, the more you feel you should give it away. I felt Tamara was too materialistic and had too much. There's nothing wrong with having things but it's about the attitude you have towards owning them. You should appreciate them. You shouldn't define yourself by the things that you have – your possessions do not make you who you are, as having things is not an identity. Tamara defines herself by the things that she has, and as soon as they are all taken away from her she feels her identity has been peeled away from her. However the opposite is true, once all of those defences are taken away she gets to the core of who she really is.

Relying on intuition is another theme running through your books. Do you think it's important?

Yes, and more so as I've got older. Writing professionally has allowed me to be creative which brings it out instinctively even more in me. If I had to sit in an office 9am - 5pm I wouldn't have the opportunity to go with how I feel all the time, I'd have to do what I was told!

I use intuition in everyday life. If I meet someone and it doesn't feel right, I'll go with that. I'm careful. I have to feel right in my heart about each decision I make in my life. I never leap before thinking ahead, which doesn't mean I don't take chances. I take lots of risks and chances but only if they feel right!

What's the most important lesson life has taught you?

It's what I put into my books – that incredible human spirit. I always write about people who have endured something difficult but found the strength to get through it. When tragedy strikes, you may be at your lowest but it can change you for the better, or make you look at things from a different perspective. The world can seem wider and more open. I agree that hard times can make you stronger. Initially, you think: Why, why, why? It's not until later that you realise it has been the making of you. I love that about the human spirit. We're stronger than we think. I'm fascinated with how the mind finds a way to cope.

Most of your books carry a moral message, in that the central character is improved in some way. What guides your morality?

I believe in karma. Believing in it makes me feel better even if it's not true. It's important to me to know who I am. I know what I believe in, I know what's important to me in life and I can't be easily swayed by others. You can't go wrong if you're the best person you can possibly be. Be decent and good and life will be too, hopefully, and if it's not, you work through it. If you're doing something for selfish reasons, if you're taking advantage of anything or anyone or being disloyal in any way, you can prepare yourself for the negative effects in your life. It will always come back to get you. I do have faith, I do believe in something. I don't feel alone. Those scary times when the plane drops, or those good times when a whole series of things come together so perfectly for something wonderful to happen, you either ask for help or you say thank you. To whom do we have this other conversation with? I pray every night. I believe that something is overseeing it all.

I'm very open-minded and I don't think I follow any one particular religion. What I believe in is being a good person and doing good to others.

A theme running through most of your books is that the central character is lost, lonely, and at their most vulnerable, someone, somewhere keeps an eye out for them. Do you feel 'protected' by a guardian angel?

There's no one in particular who I feel has saved me but I do have that sense that I'm not completely alone in a situation. It's a nice feeling. I don't know if we do that to make ourselves feel less alone, or because there is something in us that connects us to something else – this great big universe that's helping things happen. Books like *The Secret* are about sending positive messages out there and I believe in the power of positivity making things more possible. If someone walks around with a dark cloud hovering over their head always thinking how terrible things are, how unlucky they are, how they are always the victims, then that's how life will be. But if you're more hopeful and positive then there's an attachment to something that helps makes things happen.

How would you explain the magical element to your books?

If it allows people the opportunity to escape from their daily grind then that's fantastic, but I don't include "magic" for that reason. I love my readers, but quite selfishly I don't write for them at all! I find that too much of a distraction and quite contrived because then I'm trying to appeal to somebody else, and always wondering what other people will think, and then it takes the honesty out of my work. It's important to me to keep balance in all aspects in my books whether that's darkness and light, comedy and sadness and also with the magical element. I can only make the magic work if what the character is going through and their emotions are utterly real and raw. I think you can take the readers anywhere in fiction if they believe in the character's journey and most importantly if they can identify with their emotions.

I also believe that when people are going through difficult situations in life it causes them to search a lot more. They search life and search their soul. When you're searching, you are suddenly a lot more open to the world around you, to the possibilities, to things you never thought about before. That is why these characters have found themselves in new worlds open to believing in new things. When you're happy, you don't question the world so much. When you're lost, you question everything.

Do you believe in a parallel world?

I have a very over-active imagination and believe it's possible, but I've never experienced anything first-hand. I believe others who have. To think that we know it all just because we haven't experienced it ourselves is wrong. I think writing is the closest I've come to a spiritual experience – it's the most connected I've ever felt to anything. Writing is about being in the flow of doing something you absolutely love. You're in that heightened moment when you feel you're at your happiest, completely absorbed – and you feel connected to something. I know it sounds weird but that's the creative process, feeling connected to something else, where your mind is completely open and time is absolutely not of the essence. That's the power of the mind. So we don't often have to look very far to feel connected to something else, when I'm writing, it's almost as if I am in a parallel world.

What is the future of reading for kids of today?

My adorable nephews are two and a half and their parents encourage reading and I can see the difference between children who read books and children who don't. It's important to get their little minds working but not all parents agree. I feel sad when I see all the Christmas gifts and it's plastic toy after plastic toy. During family holidays as a little girl, I used to play games endlessly on my own. I had a lot of different characters, one of my favourites was Detective Casey and I ran around on missions solving crimes, creating all these different characters and scenarios. As kids we all used to play out on the road, and I don't see them any more. They're playing computer games or doing more organised activities like an hour of basketball or tennis.

I think it's so important to keep reading and writing alive. Let children sit in a room with no toys and use their imagination. Einstein said imagination is more important than knowledge and I agree with that.

Have readers come to your writing because we have lost our innocence and want to reconnect with the magic that has been stamped out by the influence of 21st Century technology?

I write about ordinary people's lives – ordinary people who find themselves in extraordinary situations. The drama and tragedies that strike them aren't innocent or unrealistic. People tell me what happens to my characters happened to them or a friend, or they could imagine it happening to them. I learned the importance of identification for readers from *PS I Love You*, because I took that idea from thin air. It wasn't from personal experience or from anybody around me.
I knew I had to do justice to the experience of grief but never really thought about how intensely meaningful it could be to those that had lost someone. But I still receive letters now from readers saying how much it helped them. So when I write my novels, I think that however bizarre the idea, someone could have experienced it. No matter what our culture or what

country we live in, we're the same people – with the same fears and hopes. It really opened my eyes.

I find it uniting and comforting to think that no matter what's going on in different countries, we're essentially all made of the same stuff.

Why do women love to have a good cry when they read a book?

It's not just women that cry when they read a book. Crying is a release of emotion. When you've had a good cry, you feel like you've cleared your head. Also some people reading books imagine themselves in that situation and go on the whole journey, usually comforted by the thought, 'God if it happened to me, I could face it'. It's a relief.

I always remember books and films that I've cried over – because they've touched me in some way. People like to feel connected to something and if you experience that intensity of emotion, you feel that connection. I cry – whether I'm happy or sad – almost every day. I can't watch the news or Oprah or even some rubbish makeover on TV without crying. I cry when I'm frustrated, which is really annoying when you're having an argument. I cry for everything – and generally feel better afterwards. Some people feel ashamed or afraid to but I treat it the same way as laughing – it's just a reaction to something. It doesn't make you weak, in fact it can make you stronger because it helps you get something out your system.

What's the best feedback you've had from a fan?

One woman who had lost her husband wrote to say that *PS, I Love You* had been recommended to her by her counsellor. It meant a lot to me at the time because critics were saying: 'What does she know about grief?' She told me how she identified with the journey Holly was going on, and that it made her feel as though she wasn't alone just by knowing other people experienced the same emotions.

When in San Fransisco on a book tour a man told me that his

sister's husband had passed away the previous summer. At Christmas time she went up to the attic to remove the decorations as they always did and found a box of presents, all wrapped and addressed to each member of the family, from her husband. He had arranged this months in advance. Others told me about letters and gifts that were left behind, in a similar way to *PS, I Love You*. I think writing letters is such a personal way of communicating, each word has poured from someone's heart and mind and you can keep them and treasure them forever.

I received a letter about *If You Could See Me Now* from a social worker and she told me that she had recently cared for someone who after losing somebody close in their life began to see a new friend who couldn't be seen by others. It could be a coping mechanism that the mind creates to help them survive the tragedy but this woman told me she believed that people really do have guides – that we may not see - who help them through their tough times and she had seen it a few times. However light and fun some people may have viewed that story idea, I was happy to know that I was writing accurately about people who were lonely or suffering in some way.

After *Where Rainbows End* had been published, I received a letter from someone saying she had loved her best friend all her life, but had never told him. My book gave her the confidence to tell him. By the time of writing, she said they were engaged and she was pregnant with their first baby. Incredible!

Keep up to date
with Cecelia!

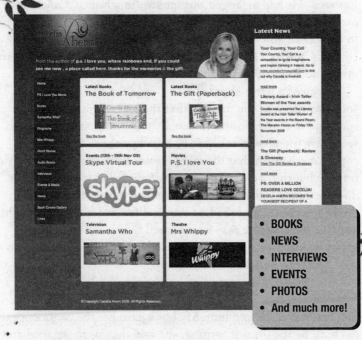

- **BOOKS**
- **NEWS**
- **INTERVIEWS**
- **EVENTS**
- **PHOTOS**
- **And much more!**

Log on to www.cecelia-ahern.com
for the latest Cecelia news,
photographs and interviews.

You'll also find details on all Cecelia's books and short stories, as well as the film adaptation of *PS I Love You* and hit US comedy *Samantha Who?*, co-created by Cecelia.

There are details of forthcoming events, plus links to other Cecelia websites.

And why not sign up for the exclusive HarperCollins Cecelia Ahern newsletter while you're there?

NOW A MAJOR FILM

P.S I LOVE YOU

**Some people wait their whole lives to find their soul mates.
But not Holly and Gerry.**

Childhood sweethearts, they could finish each other's sentences
and even when they fought, they laughed.
No one could imagine Holly and Gerry without each other.

Until the unthinkable happens. Gerry's death devastates Holly.
But as her 30th birthday looms, Gerry comes back to her.
He's left her a bundle of notes, gently guiding Holly into her new life
without him, each signed 'PS, I Love You.'

As the notes are gradually opened, and as the year unfolds, Holly
is both cheered up and challenged. The man who knows her better
than anyone sets out to teach her that life goes on. With some help
from her friends, and her noisy and loving family, Holly finds herself
laughing, crying, singing, dancing – and being braver than ever before.

Life is for living, she realises – but it always helps if there's
an angel watching over you.

'A bitter-sweet storyline guaranteed to tug on your heartstrings' *Glamour*

'A wonderfully life-affirming witty debut' *Company*

www.cecelia-ahern.com

978-0-00-725892-5 · £6.99

Save 10%

when you buy direct
from HarperCollins
– call 08707 871724.

Free postage and packing
in the UK only.

978-0-00-726308-0 · £6.99

WHERE RAINBOWS END

Rosie and Alex – best friends or soulmates?

Since childhood, Rosie and Alex have stuck by each other through thick
and thin. But they're suddenly separated when Alex and his family move
from Dublin to America. Rosie is lost without him. Then, just as she is
about to join Alex in Boston, she gets life-changing news – news that
will keep her at home in Ireland.

Their magical connection remains but can their friendship survive the
years and miles – as well as new relationships? And always at the back of
Rosie's mind is whether they were meant to be more than just good
friends all along. Misunderstandings, circumstances and sheer bad luck
have kept them apart – until now. But will they gamble everything –
including their friendship – on true love? And what twists and surprises
does fate have in store for them this time …?

'A heart-warming, completely absorbing tale of love and friendship'
Company

'A winner' *Glamour*

www.cecelia-ahern.com

978-0-00-726082-9 • £7.99

Save 10%

when you buy direct from
HarperCollins – call 08707 871724.

Free postage and packing
in the UK only.

IF YOU COULD
SEE ME NOW

**What if love was right there in front of you
– you just couldn't see it?**

Elizabeth Egan is too busy for friends. As a reluctant mother to
her sister Saoirse's young son Luke and with her own business to run,
every precious moment is made to count.

But with Saoirse crashing in and out of their lives, leaving them both
reeling, Luke and Elizabeth are desperately in need of some magic.

Enter Ivan. Wild, spontaneous and always looking for adventure,
Ivan changes Elizabeth in ways she could never have imagined.
With her newly open eyes and heart, Elizabeth sees what
she's been missing all along.

As for Ivan, he thought he was there to help Luke, not Elizabeth
– or himself …

'Captivating' *Irish Independent*

'Enchanting and unexpected' *You*

www.cecelia-ahern.com

978-0-00-726081-2 • £6.99

Save 10%

when you buy direct from
HarperCollins – call 08707 871724.

Free postage and packing
in the UK only.

A PLACE CALLED HERE

Anything is possible with Cecelia Ahern

Ever since the day her classmate Jenny-May Butler vanished, Sandy Shortt has been haunted by what happens when something – or someone – disappears. Finding has become her goal.

Jack Ruttle is desperate to find his younger brother Donal who vanished into thin air a year ago. So when he spots an ad for Sandy's missing persons agency, he's certain that she will answer his prayers and find his missing brother.

But then Sandy disappears too, stumbling upon a place that is a world away from the one she has only ever known. Now all she wants, more than anything, is to find her way home.

'Brilliant …beautifully bittersweet' *Heat*

'There's more than a touch of fairytale about Cecelia Ahern's novels' *Glamour*

www.cecelia-ahern.com

978-0-00-719891-7 • £6.99

Save 10%

when you buy direct from HarperCollins – call 08707 871724.

Free postage and packing in the UK only.